A TREACHEROUS MOTION

MAGIC OF DUST AND MOVEMENT
BOOK ONE

DEBORAH GRACE WHITE

LUMINANT PUBLICATIONS

For Tallie
May your joyful heart always know what it is to be loved
unconditionally

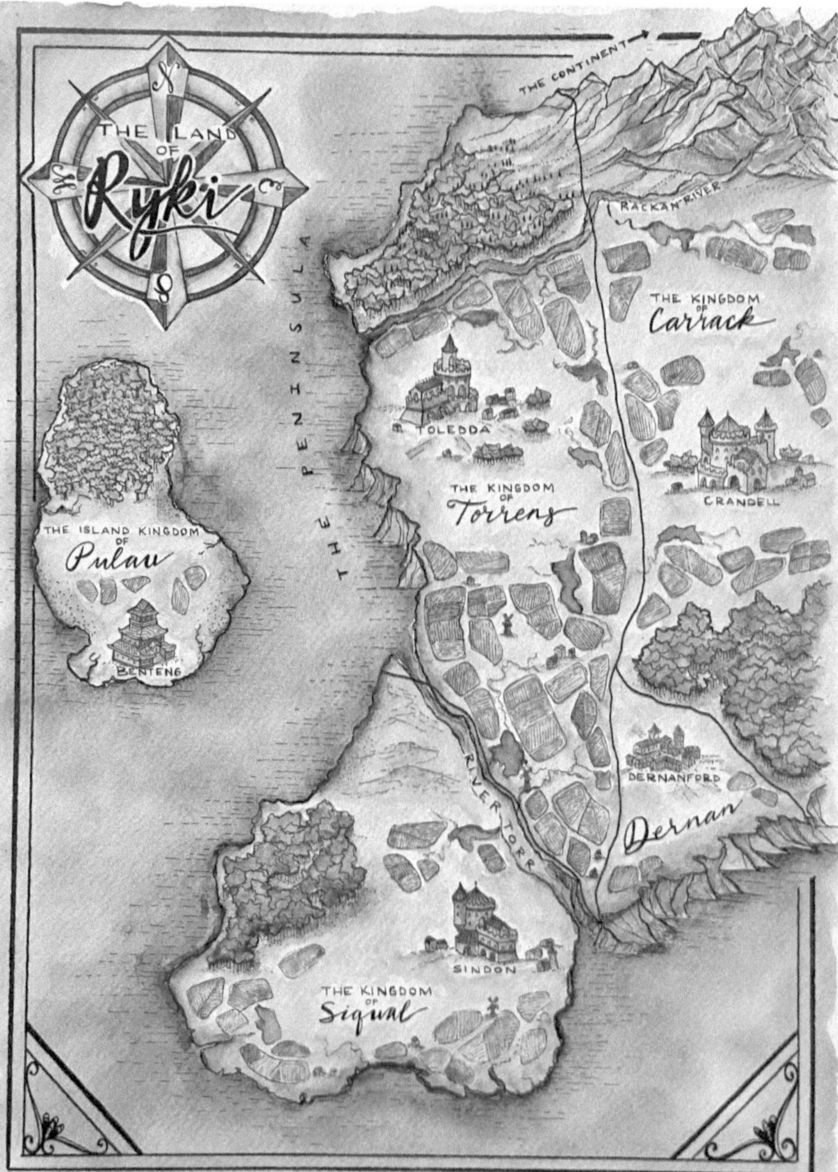

THE LAND
OF
Ryki
THE CONTINENT
THE PENINSULA
RACKAN RIVER
THE KINGDOM OF Carrack
TOLEDDA
THE KINGDOM OF Torrens
CRANDELL
THE ISLAND KINGDOM OF Pulau
BENTENG
RIVER TORR
DERNANFORD
Dernan
SINDON
THE KINGDOM OF Siqual

PROLOGUE

Theo

"Come on." Theodore shook his brother impatiently. "Wake up, Xavier, it's time."

The older boy groaned, rolling over and tugging his covers with him.

"Xavier." Theo's whisper was more a hiss, and he flicked his brother's ear hard enough to elicit a protest.

Xavier rocketed up, making a grab at Theo's wrist. But Theo was faster. His brother had fooled him with that trick too many times in former years.

"Xavier, it's almost the hour of the solstice! We have to go now."

The older prince's eyes flew wide, awareness fully returning as he threw off his blanket and slipped his feet into boots. "Why didn't you say so to start with? How did I fall asleep?"

"You fell asleep because you stayed up half the night last night flirting with the viscount's daughter," Theodore said disdainfully.

"Oh, her." Xavier yawned as he pulled on the overcoat he'd left by his bed. Theodore was already swathed in his. "Her laugh sounds like metal scraping against rock."

"Why did you flirt like that if you don't even like her?" Theo demanded, unable to keep the distaste from his voice as he remembered how he'd caught Xavier actually kissing their host's daughter—while she giggled foolishly—in the manor's garden. He couldn't see the appeal in the pastime, himself.

Xavier just laughed, ruffling Theo's hair in a condescending manner. "Because Father can't stand it, that's why. Plus, there's not much else for a prince to do, is there? I guess it's more than a twelve-year-old can understand, but you'll get there one day, little brother."

Theo grumbled to himself, irked by the airs his brother was putting on, as if he was an adult instead of being only two years older than Theo himself. But it wasn't worth arguing about. If they didn't hurry, they'd miss the hour of the solstice, and it would all be for nothing. His heart hammered in his chest as he slid the window up and climbed carefully onto the grass below. They had to succeed. He *had* to get that carbuncle favor.

"It's such a stroke of luck, isn't it?" he said excitedly, as the pair of them crept through the manor's garden. The air was cold, but there was no snow here at the southern tip of the Peninsula, not even in the dead of winter. Even the biting wind from the ocean couldn't cool his excitement. "Father never lets us all accompany him on these trips. The fact that he said yes the one time he's traveling over the solstice is so lucky, it's almost like we've got the carbuncle favor already."

"Don't count your anzu chicks before they show their powers," Xavier warned him. "I agree it's good luck that we're at the southern coast just at the right time, but it doesn't guarantee anything. The creatures are highly sought after for a reason. Sightings are rare."

Theo shook his head stubbornly. "We're going to find one. I can feel it. Good luck is just around the corner."

They were almost at the stables, and he dropped his voice,

the two of them slipping into the building as silently as shadows. There was no one there but a solitary stable boy, fast asleep on a mound of hay. He was no doubt supposed to be keeping watch.

Theo's eyes lit up as he caught sight of the beautiful bay stallion sleeping peacefully in one of the stalls.

"There he is," he whispered. "He's a beauty, isn't he?"

"You're still on about that horse?" Xavier's voice was also a murmur as they moved down the moonlit aisle of the stable.

Theo nodded. "If we find a carbuncle, and get the favor, that's what I'm going to use it for," he said fervently. "The good luck should be enough for me to convince Father to buy it from the viscount."

"That's what you'll use your luck for?" Xavier sounded incredulous. "For some horse?"

"It's not just some horse," Theo contradicted. "It's the most beautiful specimen I've ever seen." He stroked the stallion's nose, watching eagerly as the creature emerged from sleep and accepted the sugar cube he was offering it. "I'm going to ride it to the shore."

"Suit yourself." Xavier was already easing out the next horse over. "Father will have your hide if he finds out you rode it after he expressly forbade it, but I'm not about to try to talk you out of angering him."

Theo puffed out his chest as he saddled the stallion as quietly as he could. He was proud of how well he could manage the process, even on such a big horse.

"He won't forbid it if he sees how well I can handle myself. I want this horse, Xavier," Theo confided. "I want it more than I've ever wanted anything in my life."

His task complete, he led the horse out alongside his brother. Once they were clear of the stables, they used a low brick wall to help them mount their rides. Only then did he risk speaking again.

"Don't you think he'd be impressed if he saw how cleanly I can get up into the saddle?"

Xavier snorted. "If your heart's desire is to prove yourself to Father, you'd best give up before you begin. He's not likely to be impressed by anything either of us does. Nothing's ever good enough for him, trust me."

Theo said nothing. He was determined to prove his brother wrong, but he knew that saying so would just earn him more cutting words from Xavier. He didn't really understand the tension that had recently arisen between his brother and his father, but it had become all-consuming for the crown prince. Defying the king seemed to be all Xavier thought about.

"Stop!"

The squeak made both brothers freeze, a groan escaping Xavier as a small figure catapulted out from behind the garden wall to block their path. Miriam's eight-year-old frame looked frail and tiny in the moonlight, her hands on her hips as she glared up at her two brothers.

"You swore you'd wake me, Xavier. You lied."

"Xavier," Theo grumbled. "Why did you promise her that?"

"Obviously I didn't mean it," Xavier muttered. "She figured out we were up to something, and I had to say something to get her off my back, otherwise she would have told on us."

"And I still will," the miniature princess said shrilly. "Unless you take me with you like you promised. "I want a carbuncle favor, too."

"Miriam, you can't come," Theo told her. "The cliffs are dangerous, and you're too little."

Predictably, she bristled. "If you're not too little, I'm not too little, Theo. And Xavier *promised*."

Theo threw a look of frustration at his brother. He didn't

want his little sister tagging along, but he didn't like Xavier's cavalier attitude about lying to her, either. If the other prince had said she could come, he felt bound to honor that promise. Heaven knew Xavier wasn't likely to. Besides which, he did have sympathy for her position. It was hard to be always missing out. Of course she would want her chance to find an elusive carbuncle, and try to attain one of the lucky favors the magical creatures dropped. And since the winter solstice was the only time they emerged, this was her only chance, just the same as them.

"Come on, then," he sighed, sliding down from the bay stallion and leading it back to the brick wall. "You can ride with me, my horse can easily carry us both."

He ignored Xavier's noise of protest, and instead focused on helping his sister scramble into the saddle of the large mount.

"Thanks, Theo," Miriam said breathlessly. "Is this really your horse?"

"No," Xavier informed her flatly.

Theo ignored him as he hoisted himself up in front of his sister. "It's going to be. Once I get a carbuncle favor and convince Father to buy it for me." He settled into position. "Now hold on tight around my waist, Miriam," he said grandly. "This horse is really much too big for you, you don't want to fall off."

"A horse is a good idea, Theo," Miriam said excitedly, as she complied so forcefully she squeezed the air from his lungs. "If I get a carbuncle favor, I'm going to use it to convince Mother to let me make friends with the village girls. Those girls have so much more fun than all the courtiers' daughters."

Xavier snorted as the two princes urged their horses forward through the moonlit garden. "Good luck with that, Mim."

She tossed her brown curls defiantly. "That's my exact plan. I know I need good luck to convince her."

"No need to mock her idea," Theo told Xavier. "What will you use the favor for, anyway?"

"Never you mind," Xavier said, his voice thick with something Theo couldn't decipher. "But something better than a horse, that much you can be sure of."

They'd left the manor's garden now, and they all fell silent as they navigated the deserted road toward the coast. The nearest section of cliffs was no more than fifteen minutes' ride away, and the sound of the waves grew steadily clearer. Theo felt his excitement rise, and he leaned down to stroke the horse's neck.

"We'll be friends for life, you'll see," he told the creature. "You'll like the royal stables at the castle. As many oats and carrots as you can imagine."

The horse gave a soft huff, prancing a little at the attention. Theo had to tighten his grip so as not to lose hold of the reins, and Miriam let out a squeak as he felt her slip a little behind him.

"Careful," Xavier told him, frowning over at the trio. "That horse is too big for you, Theo, and too spirited. "Don't manhandle the bit like that, you'll wreck his mouth."

"I'm not manhandling anything," Theo said, hoping the darkness hid his flush. The horse was strong, but he refused to admit that he was having trouble controlling it. "And he's not too spirited, he's the perfect amount of spirited."

Xavier just shrugged, urging his own horse onward. "We're almost there," he said. "Remember, the carbuncles look like small dogs, but they don't move like small dogs. If you see one, you can't let it out of your sight for a second, or you'll never find it again."

Theo felt Miriam nod against his back, where she'd laid her

head to help her hang on better. "They move like they have wings, like dragonflies skimming over water," she added helpfully. "I read about it in the manor's library today."

"And if you catch the moonlight glinting on their foreheads, that's when you know they're dropping a favor," Theo said, bouncing a little in the saddle.

Miriam giggled. "Do they really drop them like...you know... droppings?"

"That's the tale." Xavier loosened enough to grin at her. "So if you find one, you'd best give it to me, Mim. You won't want to touch animal droppings."

Theo couldn't see his sister, but judging by the sound she made and Xavier's resulting laugh, he would guess that she'd stuck out her tongue at him.

"Shh," he told them both. "The cliff is just ahead, and I think I hear voices."

"Blast." Xavier scowled. "Looks like we're not the only ones out hunting carbuncles tonight. I should have expected this."

They pulled up in the shadow of a yew tree, squinting into the darkness. The sound of the waves on the stone far below was loud now. The cliffs looked treacherous in the dark, but it wasn't deterring the half dozen figures Theo could see moving slowly along the jagged rocks, no doubt as determined as they were to see the magical carbuncles manifest themselves.

"They're all that way." Theo pointed to where the cliffs stretched away to their right. "Let's go the other way, and have a section of cliffs to ourselves."

"Unless they know something we don't, and they've all gone that way because that's where the carbuncles nest," Xavier frowned. After a moment's thought, he dismounted and tied his borrowed horse's bridle to the yew tree. "I think I'll sneak out past them."

"You really think they won't notice three children joining the search?" Theo asked impatiently.

"That's why you two will wait here," said Xavier. "If I find more than one favor, I'll share."

Miriam gave an indignant protest with which Theo was in full agreement. But Xavier didn't stay to hear it.

"Forget him," Theo scowled. "We'll go the other way, where it's more deserted. We're just as likely to find a carbuncle as him."

"More," Miriam agreed with spirit. "Because we're small and sneaky."

Theo laughed as he nudged his horse along the cliff top in the opposite direction from where Xavier had disappeared. "Only when we need to be."

His little sister sighed. "I feel like I do need to be sneaky any time I want something. No one ever just says yes to what I want."

"I said yes to you coming with me tonight," Theo pointed out.

She brightened. "That's true. You're the best brother, Theo. You're much more fun than Xavier."

"I wish." Theo glowered over his shoulder toward his absent brother. "Xavier has way more fun than I do."

"Yes, Xavier has more fun," Miriam said practically. "But you *are* more fun. Because you don't always leave me out of it. If it was up to Xavier, I'd be back in my bed right now."

"Which is where you should be, to be fair." Theo couldn't help reminding her of his superior age, just a little.

But he didn't really mind having Miriam with him. The quest for the carbuncles was sure to be more fun with a companion than alone, and he should have known that Xavier would ditch him at the first opportunity.

He steered the horse slowly along the lip of the cliff, his eyes searching the darkness of the jagged stones below.

"Don't go too close to the edge," Miriam squeaked.

"I know what I'm doing," Theo told her, irritated at the distraction. "Just look out for something shiny, like moonlight on smooth shells."

She fell silent, and the two of them scoured the cliff face carefully. Minutes ticked by tortuously as they rode up and down the small stretch of accessible cliff. Several times, Theo thought he saw a glint, only to realize it was just the moon's rays catching on some of the small white flowers that sometimes grew out of patches of soil among the cliffs.

But then, just as Miriam was starting to grumble about being cold, he saw something different.

"What's that?" he breathed, pointing. "Between those rocks, you see?"

"I think it's more flowers." Miriam's words were punctuated by a yawn.

Theo shook his head. "I don't think so. It looks like a huge shell, mostly hidden away in the cliff." He pulled the horse to a stop, sliding down from its back on the land side. "Stay here, Mim."

She didn't protest, just clutched the saddle with her small hands, looking weary. Theo climbed carefully down the cliff face, making for the point where he'd thought he saw a shell amongst the rocks. The climb was harder than it looked from above, and his heart was in his throat. The drop below him was sheer—if he fell to his death in the hunt for a carbuncle favor, it would be ironic. Certainly not a case of good luck.

When he reached the opening in the cave, there was no sign of anything. But he was sure something had been there. He turned, disappointed, and froze, one hand clutching the stone of the cliff as he balanced precariously.

There, before his eyes, fully exposed on the cliff in front of him, was a large shell in the act of slowly opening. As he watched, too stunned to even make a sound, the shell peeled all the way back, revealing a small, stocky dog. Except for the shell still receding impossibly into a point on its forehead, the creature looked for all the world like a normal canine. Theo kept his eyes fixed on it until the shell was all gone, except for a smooth patch sticking out of the creature's forehead. That was what he needed to watch. If it caught the moonlight, it meant the creature had released a favor.

Suddenly, the carbuncle zipped past him, moving in an impossible fashion that startled him so much, he almost lost his balance. His gaze remained stuck on the creature, which was further away now, but still within easy sight. Moving slowly and carefully, Theo started to follow it, not wanting to scare it, but eager to keep it within his vision. Excitement pooled in his stomach as the shell on its forehead began to glow.

"THEO!"

The scream ripped through the night, and the carbuncle fled. By the time it disappeared into the closest patch of cliff, the shell was almost all the way around it again. Theo barely caught sight of an object glowing on the rocks where it had been before he whipped his head up to where his sister was waiting.

His heart leaped into his throat at the sight of Miriam clinging desperately to the saddle as the horse plunged and shied. It must have been spooked by the carbuncle's movement, and Theo had been too focused on the smaller creature to notice. The horse was terrifyingly close to the cliff's edge, and its eight-year-old rider had no idea how to control it. He should never have left her mounted by herself.

"Hold on!" he called to his sister.

Turning his back regretfully on the favor the carbuncle had left, he started climbing frantically up the cliff face. His palms were sweating, and he slipped alarmingly as he grabbed for new holds.

Just don't look down, he told himself.

He forced himself up over the final lip of the cliff just as another scream from Miriam, this one wordless, preceded a cracking sound. Theo threw himself toward the horse as the poor creature bucked, trying to throw off the burden that seemed to be confusing it.

He wasn't quick enough. With a scream, Miriam was thrown from the horse's back, just moments before the stallion's front hooves came crashing down right on the edge of the cliff.

A second splintering crack rang out as the section of cliff gave way. Theo watched in heart-stopping horror as the beautiful horse plunged downward, disappearing over the cliff with a whinny of terror. Time was suspended for a moment as it fell, then a sickening thud met his ears.

Theo could hardly take it in, but he forced himself to push the thought aside as he spun, searching frantically for his sister.

"Miriam?"

A broken sob was all the reply he got, and he threw himself forward, a fresh wave of fear battering him as he caught sight of Miriam. It was so much worse than the broken limb or other injury he'd feared. When the horse threw her, she hadn't fallen clear on the solid side—she'd been tossed toward the cliff's edge. Somehow, she'd managed to grab hold of jutting stone half a yard down, but her position was precarious. Already she looked like she was barely holding on.

"Miriam!" he shouted, throwing himself onto his belly and reaching for her. But she was too far away.

"Don't let me fall, Theo," Miriam sobbed. "I don't want to die." With the words, one of her hands slipped a little.

Terror pounded through Theo's chest, making it hard to think. He cast his eyes around for something to help him, but there was nothing.

"I won't let you fall," he promised his sister, the enormity of having her life in his hands threatening to crush him. "Just hold on."

"I can't," she wailed, tears running down her face.

Theo scrambled up onto his knees, his mind swirling chaotically. If only he had a craftsman on hand—someone skilled in the manipulation of magic would surely be able to rescue Miriam. He waved his hand through the air in a frantic motion, but it was no use. He could feel the Dust he'd generated—the invisible magic stirred up by his movements—but identifying it was the extent of his training in magic craft. Even if he'd had a way to generate a substantial enough volume of magic, he wouldn't have had the skill to harness it to something useful.

I should have defied Father and studied the craft when my tutor said I had an aptitude.

The thought flashed through his mind, but he banished it quickly. Defying his parents was exactly what had led to his current, disastrous situation.

Suddenly he remembered all the people they'd seen further along the cliff. He raised his voice as loud as he could manage, screaming into the night.

"HELP! WE NEED HELP! XAVIER! SOMEONE!"

An answering cry, faint but sharp, reached his ears.

"HELP!" he screamed again. "MY SISTER HAS FALLEN!"

The sounds of other people increased, and the pressure around Theo's heart eased slightly. He cast his eyes around again, and this time spotted a long branch. He snatched it up, throwing himself back over the edge and extending it out.

"Can you reach it?" he asked Miriam. "Don't give up, Mim, help is coming!"

She tried to reach for the branch, but it just made her slip further, and fear hammered Theo once again. A moment later, a man thundered up beside him, rope coiled around his arm.

"Who's fallen?" he asked sharply, peering over the edge. He let out a sharp whistle. "Is that horse…"

"I think the horse is dead," Theo said thickly. "It's my sister who needs help. Do you have any skill in magic?"

He heard the man's intake of breath as he caught sight of the diminutive figure on the cliffs.

"Hold on, lass," the man said. "I'm coming."

He cast a look at Theo as, working swiftly, he tied the rope around a tree close to the cliff's edge, then looped it around his middle.

"No, lad, I've no skill in magic, but I don't need it to help your sister. Stand back now."

The next thing Theo knew, the stranger was walking himself backward down the cliff. A small crowd had gathered by now, more people abandoning the carbuncle hunt to see what was going on.

Xavier was nowhere to be seen.

When the man reached Miriam, he scooped her into one arm, the muscles of the other straining as he started to walk back up the cliff. Several of the onlookers rushed to the other end of the rope, hauling on it carefully to help the ascent. Within moments, the stranger had reached the top, safely depositing the trembling princess onto the grass beside her brother.

"Miriam, are you all right?" Theo knelt next to her, squeezing her shoulder as the enormity of what had just happened started to hit him.

She nodded, hiccuping. "That was so scary, Theo."

"I know." He looked around, searching the darkness for Xavier. There was still no sign of him.

"What do we do now?" Miriam asked. "How will we get home without the horse?"

The horse. A sick feeling settled in Theo's stomach as he remembered the sight of the poor creature's body sprawled on the rocks below. Miriam must have seen his face, because she let out another hiccup.

"I'm sorry, Theo."

He shook his head mutely. This wasn't her fault. It was his. He was the one who'd killed the horse. That beautiful stallion. He'd been so sure he could find a carbuncle favor and get the horse for himself. And instead...

The sick feeling threatened to choke him, and he pushed himself to his feet.

"Come on. We need to find Xavier."

Any hope of escaping inconspicuously died as he realized that one of the people hovering around was the head groom of the viscount who was hosting the royal family. Theo saw the recognition that flashed into his eyes, and he knew they were lost.

Sure enough, by the time Xavier appeared several minutes later, the group was in an uproar at the realization that the unaccompanied children were the prince and princess. The trip back to the manor was a nightmarish blur, Miriam crying most of the way and Xavier more frustrated than alarmed.

Theo's next moment of sharp awareness came when he found himself standing before his father, Xavier at his side. The queen was with Miriam, who was being examined by a physician for any injury from her ordeal, and the king had sent everyone else away. It was just the three of them, and the expression on his father's face was possibly the worst thing Theo had ever seen.

"I barely know where to begin." The king's voice was calm, and it was more terrifying than shouting would have been. "You stole horses? Theodore, I didn't expect this from you."

Theo shook his head frantically. "No, Father, I wasn't stealing. The viscount said I could ride it. He said—"

"I know what he said, Theodore," King Madoc cut in. "He said you could ride it around the manor, during the day. And then I told you that you weren't to do even that."

"I meant to bring it back." Theo's voice came out a whisper.

"But you didn't, did you?" his father said harshly. "You killed it. I'll have to pay the viscount for its purchase now, but it's a shameful waste, Theodore. It was a fine creature."

Tears pricked at Theo's eyes, and he fought valiantly to stop them from falling. He couldn't let his father see him cry—he knew he was too old for such behavior.

"I have never been more disappointed in my life," the king went on, his eyes passing between his sons. "In both of you. You disobeyed me, you took something that wasn't yours, and you endangered your sister's life. Miriam was almost killed."

"We didn't want Miriam to come," Xavier said hotly. Theo couldn't imagine where his brother found such spirit in the terrible moment. "I said she was too young."

"Whereas you are old enough to know better," their father said with a snap. "You are my heir, Xavier. You cannot conduct yourself in this way. I've had enough of your defiance and your anger. You will learn to behave in accordance with the responsibilities of your station."

"Why should I behave with responsibility if you refuse to give me any responsibility?" Xavier demanded, still unchastened. "You can't have it both ways, Father."

"You will not speak to me like that." The king's anger was burning hotter by the moment, and Theo wanted nothing more than to slink away and hide. "Time and again you show yourself unworthy of responsibility. You almost got your sister killed tonight. And Theodore also could have been seriously injured."

"Xavier isn't responsible for me," Theo said quickly. "It wasn't his fault that I was out there."

"Of course it wasn't," Xavier said. "And Miriam is fine, Father. You accuse *me* of being dramatic."

The king swelled visibly, and Theo shook his head at his brother. Xavier hadn't been there to see it, but Theo was painfully aware that there was no exaggeration. Miriam was lucky to be alive.

He was lucky that Miriam was alive. If she'd fallen, he would never have forgiven himself. Even as it was, he didn't know if he'd be able to.

"Father, I'm sorry," he whispered miserably. "I never meant anyone to get hurt. I just wanted—"

"Just wanted what?" the king shot back at him. "A carbuncle favor? You live a life of privilege and luxury, Theodore. What could you possibly need good luck for?"

Theo swallowed. There was no way he was going to tell his father his plans for the favor. He could see now how foolish and irresponsible his desire had been.

A knock at the door heralded the entrance of a messenger.

"Forgive the interruption, Your Majesty, but the queen has requested your presence."

"Is the princess well?" King Madoc asked tensely.

"Yes, Your Majesty," the messenger assured him. "She's sleeping."

"Wait here. We are not finished." With those words to his sons, the king swept from the room, leaving Xavier and Theo in uncomfortable silence.

"I wish we'd never left our beds," Theo said hollowly.

"If only Miriam had kept sleeping, we would have been

fine," Xavier said impatiently. "I never even caught a glimpse of a carbuncle."

"I did," Theo said, his voice expressionless. "I saw one drop a favor."

"Really?" Xavier stared at him. "Did you get it?"

Theo shook his head. "That was when the horse…" He swallowed, struggling once again to keep tears at bay. He didn't want his brother to see him cry any more than his father.

"I am sorry about the horse," Xavier said unexpectedly. "It was a beautiful stallion."

"So am I," Theo said. "But what happened to Miriam is much worse."

Xavier hesitated. "Was she really in so much danger?"

"She almost died," Theo whispered. "She would have, if someone else hadn't come running when I called. I've never been so scared in my life."

Xavier fidgeted, clearly uncomfortable with the information. For a moment, Theo thought he would relent, and acknowledge at last the recklessness of their venture. But the next moment, a scowl descended on his face. He was apparently choosing a different way to handle what he was feeling.

"She shouldn't have been there in the first place. Like I said." Xavier flung across the room.

"Where are you going?" Theo protested. "Father said to stay."

"I'm not waiting around for another scolding," Xavier said.

The next moment he was gone, leaving Theo shivering next to the unlit fireplace. He debated fleeing himself, but he didn't want to be like Xavier, refusing to admit when he'd done the wrong thing. He'd never admired his brother less.

It was only a couple of minutes before the door opened and the king re-entered. A cloud descended on his brow when he realized that only one of his sons was present.

"Where's your brother?"

Theo didn't answer. He didn't know what to say.

After a painful moment, the king let out a breath. "I'll deal with him later." He strode into the room, surprising Theo by gesturing him into a chair, then pulling one forward himself.

Theo sank down, realizing only once he was off his feet just how much his legs were trembling.

"Your sister is fine," King Madoc said, his voice still curt but not as angry. "She's had a scare, but there appears to be no physical injury."

Theo nodded, a lump in his throat.

"You were very foolish tonight, Theodore," the king said. "Do you understand that?"

"Yes, sir." Theo forced himself to look his father in the eye.

The king nodded slowly. "Do you agree with your brother? That you bear no responsibility for Miriam's near-disaster?"

Theo shook his head frantically. "I'm not denying responsibility. It was my fault. Xavier didn't want to let her come, but I felt sorry for her, because she didn't want to miss out. And Xavier told us to stay by the tree, but we wanted to search too, and—"

"You misunderstand if you believe I'm trying to shift responsibility from Xavier," the king said dryly. He sighed. "Xavier is young, but he will learn. As will you. Your position gives you a great deal of responsibility, whether you want to claim it or not. Your decisions affect the wellbeing of many, not just yourself. Just like tonight your actions endangered Miriam's life. And ended the life of that horse, incidentally."

"Yes, Father." Theo swallowed. "I accept that."

"Good man." The king gave another nod. "You are not my heir, Theo, but that doesn't mean you can afford to take your position lightly. You, too, will have great influence all your life, not just Xavier." He frowned. "If your brother is not inclined to take his responsibilities seriously, you must do so doubly. I know you will learn from tonight's disaster."

"Yes, Father," Theo repeated obediently. "I will."

"A prince cannot afford to think just about what he wants," the king pressed. "He must think about what's good for his kingdom. Otherwise those under his care will suffer. Do you understand?"

"Yes, Father," Theo said yet again.

The memory of the horse falling flashed before his eyes, followed by a horrible image—his sister's brown eyes, wide with fear as she dangled from the cliff. That had happened because he'd chased what he wanted, selfishly and childishly. He would never make that mistake again.

"I won't disobey you again, Father," Theo said, straightening his back.

"I trust you won't," the king said soberly. "You should return to your bed, Theodore."

Theo went, his mind churning and his heart heavy. He'd never coveted his brother's position as heir. He hadn't wanted the pressure. But that had been another example of his selfishness. Just because he wasn't Siqual's future king didn't mean he could escape the duties of being a prince.

Determination coursed through him, the sense of purpose pushing back the guilt a tiny bit. His father had said it himself—if Xavier wasn't going to take responsibility, Theo would need to. He wasn't going to let his own desires get in the way of what the kingdom needed, and he would do all he could to prevent Xavier's desires from doing so as well.

He couldn't let anyone else pay the price for his failure to act as a prince should. Starting that very moment, he would be what Siqual deserved, even if he was the only one willing to do it.

TEN YEARS LATER

ONE

Elowen

"It does look unstable."

Elowen squinted up at the moss-covered walls of the watchtower, a remnant from centuries past, when the Peninsula had been at war with the kingdoms of the continent.

"I suspect Father will order it pulled down."

"You're probably right," agreed Sophia amicably.

Her friend's agreement came as no surprise to Elowen. Sophia was the most good-natured creature alive. Elowen sometimes wished her friend had more independence of mind —for Sophia's own sake—but no one could accuse her of being unpleasant company.

"If you ask for my opinion, I think His Majesty would be wasting resources to pull it down."

The second voice was less welcome as Sophia's brother inserted himself into the conversation. Elowen had to stop herself from reminding Bertrand that no one *had* asked his opinion.

"Why do you say that?" she said instead, mustering the

politeness expected of a princess speaking to the son of her father's most influential duke.

The viscount shrugged. "It will come down by itself, sooner or later."

"No doubt." It was difficult to keep the incredulity from her voice. "On top of the livestock that graze in this area, or even the children from the local village whom we saw playing around the base of the tower when we rode up."

"They shouldn't be playing here," Bertrand said dismissively. He eyed his sister. "Speaking of people who shouldn't be here...Sophia, how did you end up on the prince's escort today? Princess Elowen is one thing, but you shouldn't be riding out of the city with a troop of guards. It's not seemly."

"I was invited, Bertrand." Sophia frowned at her brother, although she spoke without much heat. "Elowen wanted me to come."

"Of course I did," said Elowen firmly. "Sophia and I rarely get the chance for a decent ride, the opportunity was too good to pass up."

"Say no more." Bertrand swept an elegant bow, his narrow face split by a grin as he straightened. "You know, *dearest princess*, that I would never want to stand in the way of your enjoyment." He took in her disapproving expression, his smile only growing as he added, "Even if you may not always know your best interests. You can do better than Sophia for a companion in your adventures, you know." He sent her a wink.

"We'll have to agree to disagree," she said stonily.

He considered her face with an indulgent air that set her back up.

"Tell me the truth, Princess, is this outing a last snatch at freedom? Doesn't your dashing foreign prince arrive tomorrow?"

He said the words with a hint of disdain, and Elowen felt a

flush rise to her cheeks. To her annoyance, Bertrand had clearly noticed it. He looked much too pleased with himself as he went on.

"No, I've got that wrong, haven't I?" he asked lazily. "Crown Prince Xavier is supposed to be the dashing one. Rumor says Prince Theodore is the stiff, dull brother. Let's hope that for once, rumor is wrong, and he lives up to the high standards we Torrenese expect for our princess."

With a final smirk that stopped just short of a wink, he sauntered away.

Elowen waited until he'd rounded the tower before letting out an irritated huff. She wasn't in a hurry to comment on his mocking words about her upcoming betrothal, but his disparagement of his sister she couldn't let pass.

"Do better for a companion? As if I wouldn't prefer your company a hundred times over his."

Sophia smiled at her indignant tone. "Don't mind Bertrand's jokes. He's too charming for his own good sometimes, but I know you love us in spite of it."

Elowen hardly knew what to say to her friend. She understood the impulse to defend her brother, but did Sophia really think that Bertrand's manner was charming?

"I love *you*, Sophia," she settled on. "I tolerate Bertrand."

"Oh no, that's not true." Sophia turned to her in distress. "You know it's not." Her eyes strayed in the direction her brother had gone, her forehead pinched in concern. "He walked around very close to the tower, didn't he? Do you really think it's unstable enough to just collapse by itself?"

Sophia looked around, her eyes falling at once on a slight, sandy-haired young man who'd just moved forward from where he was hovering beside their horses.

"Do you want me to check that Lord Bertrand is all right, Lady Sophia?" the man asked respectfully.

"Yes please, Simeon."

Sophia looked relieved, and Elowen understood why. Simeon was reliable—he would see that no harm came to the over-confident young viscount. He'd been a quietly consistent presence beside his employer for years. Elowen was surprised Bertrand had gone off without him—he usually kept the servant close at hand, for ready access to his magical capabilities. Simeon was unusually skilled at the craft of magic.

The two girls watched him go, Elowen half wishing Sophia would see sense when it came to her brother, and half regretting her words. She shouldn't speak so critically of the son of a duke, no matter how accurate her complaints were. She just wished that both Bertrand and Sophia would take the hint that she didn't find his charm at all charming.

"I'm also surprised you were allowed to come," Sophia commented. "With the Siqualian delegation arriving tomorrow."

"I didn't ask permission," Elowen admitted. "Well, I did from Patrick." Her eyes strayed to her brother, sitting astride his horse and talking to the castle's head builder next to the crumbling tower. He looked every bit the confident crown prince. "He just assumed I'd cleared it with Mother and Father, and I didn't correct him."

Sophia's laugh was a little pained. "I wish I had your courage, Elowen."

Elowen just shrugged, not in the mood to celebrate the minuscule win against the constant restrictions of her life. Small skirmishes like this one mattered little when she was about to surrender the whole battle and enter a bloodless marriage.

"Let's ask Patrick what he's going to do about the tower," she said, walking forward with her friend beside her.

There was no need to ask, however. As they drew close, she could hear her brother giving instructions to the builder.

"Yes, it will have to be pulled down, the local masons were right. And we shouldn't delay. I'll initiate the process immediately for formal royal approval to dismantle a historic building. It's a shame, but there are other sites that can serve as a monument to our victory in the war against the continent."

Elowen glanced idly up at the watchtower, then froze.

"Patrick! Look!"

Her brother followed her gaze, rapping out a command as he also saw the top layers of stone wobbling visibly.

"Clear the area!" He looked at his sister. "Elowen, move back. It looks like it's going to fall the other way, but we should still be cautious."

It was Sophia he should have been worried about. Her face had gone pale, and she jumped forward before Elowen realized what she was about.

"Sophia, stay here!" She darted after her friend, intending to pull her back.

"Bertrand and Simeon went around there!" Sophia said, eluding Elowen's grip. "They'll be crushed!"

Elowen heard her brother's sharp cry behind her, but she couldn't just let her friend run beneath a collapsing building. She tried once more to grab at Sophia's arm.

She'd just seized her when an angry rumbling sound made them both freeze. There wasn't time to do anything but look up at the huge slabs of deteriorated stone now falling toward them.

Elowen closed her eyes, wishing her ears weren't full of shocked screams in her final moments, but nothing struck her. Crashing and cracking sounded all around them, but when her eyes flew open, she and Sophia were untouched. Her friend's gasp drew Elowen's eyes upward, to see several large stone blocks hovering impossibly above their heads.

"Simeon." As Sophia murmured the name, Elowen understood.

Her eyes searched the area for the servant, even as she tugged the still-frozen Sophia out from under the boulders. As soon as they were clear, the stones crashed to the ground.

A stumbling motion revealed the source of their rescue, as Simeon appeared from alongside the partially collapsed building and leaned on an upended boulder for support.

Sophia made as if to run toward him, but then Bertrand appeared at his servant's side, and she checked herself.

In moments, they were swarmed by members of the royal guard, who all but dragged both girls further from the tower, back to where the prince was surrounded by a small human barrier of his own guards.

Bertrand and Simeon followed, the latter's movements labored.

"You saved our lives," Elowen said as soon as they were close enough to hear. Her knees were belatedly shaking as she realized how close she'd been to disaster. "I can't thank you enough."

"No thanks necessary, Princess." The satisfied words came from Bertrand. "I was concerned about something like this happening. It's a very good thing that I thought to bring my craftsman along. When I realized the upper level was falling, I sent him around immediately to clear the area."

"Your foresight is to your credit," Patrick said, inclining his head toward Bertrand. He'd dismounted and moved to his sister's side. "It's very fortunate you came, Bertrand."

Elowen's noise of protest was lost amid the general chaos. She saw a flash of something go over Simeon's face, but the next moment it was gone, his usual respectful expression restored. His attention seemed focused on the still-quivering Sophia, and he started when the prince spoke to him.

"You did well also, young man. You should be commended."

Patrick's hand was on Elowen's shoulder now, but she shrugged it off. Her brother's light praise of Simeon's heroics only irked her. The injustice of any credit at all going to Bertrand was galling. As was the swift look of annoyance that Bertrand directed at Simeon, as if he resented even the prince's moderated praise of the servant.

"Thank you, Your Highness." Simeon bowed low, his body straightening more slowly than was natural. Elowen felt a surge of sympathy for him.

"You must be exhausted," she said, turning to one of the guards. "Assist Simeon to somewhere he can sit."

The guard did so, but Patrick frowned as he watched. "We can't linger, Elowen. We can't be certain the danger has passed, and to be on the safe side, we should ride back to the capital immediately."

"Just give him a minute," she insisted. "It must have taken a lot of magic to stop those stones mid-air like that. You don't want him to pass out during the ride, do you?"

The prince didn't look happy, but he didn't protest. He'd received no more official training in magic craft than Elowen had, but he knew she was right, because they'd both been taught the basics. All movement stirred up the invisible magic that was known as Dust, and theoretically, anyone could learn to harness it and craft it into useful enchantments. Most people had basic comprehension of how to use the tiny amounts of Dust which were stirred up by the movements of their own bodies and which were therefore automatically harnessed to them should they choose to take hold of them.

To be able to do anything significant with that magic, not to mention to harness Dust generated by other sources of movement as Simeon had just done, required not only a natural aptitude, but years of dedicated training. It wasn't a part of royal education in Torrens. Elowen knew it wasn't considered dignified for members of the court to study any trade, magic included, but she had always regretted the policy, more even than her family imagined. At the thought of her secret, her eyes flicked to Sophia, but her friend wasn't looking at her.

One aspect of magical theory that Patrick knew as well as Elowen did was that the act of harnessing magic drained the human body of energy like no other activity under the sun. And the cost increased relative to the scope of the enchantment. Proper practice was for a craftsman to use half the magic seized from the relevant movement to pour back into his own body as energy. That energy couldn't be stored, but it could be used to fuel whatever activity the craftsman directed the magic to do— or rather, directed the remaining half of the magic to do. This practice avoided over-exertion which could lead to serious damage and in extreme cases even death.

Looking at Simeon's face, which had gone so pale that the faint sprinkling of freckles on his nose had become prominent, Elowen wondered if he'd cut a corner in how much magic he repurposed as energy for himself. It was surprising, because she knew he was skilled in the craft, and given the source of magic used had presumably been the motion of the falling stone, there should have been plenty of magic at his disposal. The chunks of masonry had been enormous, and their movement had been rapid.

And yet, he looked like he was about to pass out.

Patrick had ordered the group to remount, ready for departure, but Elowen ignored the instruction. Side-stepping the guards still protectively flanking her, she approached the servant, Sophia by her side.

"Thank you," Elowen told Simeon earnestly, speaking

quickly. She likely didn't have long before she would be chivvied onto her horse whether she liked it or not. "You saved my life, and Sophia's, and I'm incredibly grateful."

"You needn't thank me, Your Highness," he told her, his head bent deferentially and his form sagging a little. "I'm honored to be of service to you."

She disregarded these expected niceties. "Are you well, Simeon? You seem to have been hit particularly hard by that enchantment."

"I...Yes, I'm well, Your Highness."

But Elowen had caught the moment of hesitation, and she frowned. Simeon's brow was furrowed, the worried expression unfamiliar to her.

"What's on your mind?" she pressed him. "Please speak freely."

"It's probably nothing, Your Highness," he said.

"But...?" she prompted.

His eyes drifted over his shoulder, back toward the tower. "Something felt strange about the magic generated by the tower's collapse. It didn't respond as I expected, which is why my energy is more depleted."

"Strange how?"

The question had been on the tip of Elowen's tongue, but she wasn't the one who uttered it. Patrick had appeared unnoticed behind her, and his expression was keen as it rested on the servant.

Simeon straightened, his tone becoming even more respectful as he addressed the prince.

"I'm not entirely sure, Your Highness."

"Just do your best to explain what you experienced. You needn't try to have all the answers." Knowing him as she did, Elowen could tell that Patrick was making an effort to be reassuring. He still sounded stern.

Simeon nodded slowly. "Yes, Your Highness. I only meant that there was a lot of movement. But there wasn't a lot of magic. At least...not a lot available to me."

"What do you mean, not a lot available to you?" Patrick's voice was sharper now, and Elowen looked between him and the servant in confusion. Why was her brother so tense?

"I sensed a relatively small amount of magic." Simeon smiled deferentially as he explained himself. "But perhaps I overestimate my abilities of assessment."

"Perhaps so," Patrick said thoughtfully. "Were you formally trained in magic craft by the Craftsmen's Guild?"

Simeon shook his head. "No, Your Highness. I was trained by a tutor, by the generosity of His Grace."

Sophia shifted slightly beside Elowen at the words, but she made no comment.

"Ah, I see."

Patrick's tone seemed to dismiss the subject. Elowen had the impression that her brother had decided that Simeon's inferior training explained any problems he'd had with the magic he harnessed. She didn't believe it though, given how consistently she'd seen Simeon manipulate magic with ease. Usually for Bertrand's benefit.

The viscount had pushed his way through the guards, and he chose that moment to insert himself into the conversation.

"Are you still making a fuss, Simeon? Surely we're ready to depart by now."

"I'm ready to travel, My Lord," Simeon said. "I apologize for inconveniencing the group."

"Not at all." Patrick waved a magnanimous hand. "You've acquitted yourself well, young man."

The epithet was comical to Elowen. If Simeon was younger than Patrick, it would only be by a couple of years. But Patrick was like that. He never exploited his position for his own gain, but he always seemed to converse with others from the height of his status. Sometimes she wondered if it made him feel lonely.

"If you need more time to recover, a guard can stay behind with you," Patrick added.

"Thank you, Your Highness, but I'm well," Simeon insisted.

"I'll see to my servant, Prince Patrick," Bertrand told the prince reassuringly. "You needn't concern yourself with the details." He sent a reproving look at Simeon. "There's no need for you to keep addressing the prince, Simeon, try to behave with decorum."

Elowen was well used to the imperious way Bertrand treated his servant, and she didn't let it distract her from studying Simeon himself as she remounted her horse.

"Do you think Simeon is all right?" she asked Sophia quietly.

"No, I don't." Her friend's reply was immediate. "I've never seen him so affected by harnessing magic."

Elowen looked around, making sure no one was watching her as she rhythmically slapped the reins against her saddle in a gentle but persistent motion. Ochre, well used to her, ignored the movement, but Elowen's senses immediately caught the Dust it was stirring up. Harnessing it, she sent it toward where Simeon was mounting his own horse. Under her clandestine direction, the magic caused the stirrup to rise helpfully as soon as Simeon's weight shifted onto it. The young servant's movements were smoother as he moved into the saddle, and he cast a furtive look around. When his eyes caught on Elowen's, his face relaxed into the smallest of smiles. Elowen wasn't sure if it was gratitude or professional pride, but either way, it lasted only a moment before his expression returned to a neutral one.

"Be careful," Sophia murmured, as always nervous of getting into trouble. She'd pulled her horse alongside Elowen's.

"Don't you think he deserves a little help and consideration after saving our lives?" Elowen demanded, also speaking in an under-voice.

"Of course I do." Sophia sounded unhappy, and Elowen didn't push the point.

As they left the watchtower behind, Elowen glanced back. The damage was considerable—more of the tower had collapsed than she'd realized during those terrifying moments of chaos. The top third of it was gone, the base surrounded now by rubble.

How had that much falling stone not created enough magic for a skilled craftsman like Simeon?

She could only be grateful Simeon had found a way to work with what he had access to. She and Sophia were lucky to be alive—although at the same time, she couldn't help thinking that it was very unlucky that the tower had chosen the moment of their visit to fall, after being reported as unstable and potentially dangerous weeks before.

To Elowen's annoyance, Bertrand drew his horse alongside hers as the group began the ride back to the capital. For most of the two-hour journey, she endured his comments about Sophia's and her near miss—loaded with the implication that they should have left the whole expedition to the men—and his sly and borderline mocking comments about her upcoming betrothal.

It was a great relief when they reached the capital and he finally peeled away. Elowen was surprised to find the queen waiting for them the moment they entered the castle's courtyard. She'd known she was dancing on the line of earning a reprimand by going with Patrick without asking her parents, but she hadn't thought her parents would actually be concerned. She'd hoped they wouldn't even notice, aware that they were spending much of the day in final preparatory meetings for the Siqualian delegation's arrival.

Elowen wasn't included in those meetings. It wasn't necessary for her to contribute diplomatically to alliance negotiations with the Siqualians. She wasn't expected to offer anything.

Anything other than her hand in marriage and therefore her entire life.

"Elowen, where have you been?" Queen Lisbeth's eyes widened as she took in her daughter's state. "And what have you been doing? You're covered head to toe in dust!"

Elowen glanced down and realized her mother was right. Her gown was coated in traces of the watchtower's gray stones.

"Do you tell me you were unaware that Elowen accompanied me?" Patrick asked, his brows drawn together as he cast his sister a disapproving look. "Mother, I apologize. I mistakenly assumed you'd given your consent for her to—"

"I was fine," Elowen interrupted him impatiently, as she slid from her horse. "I was with you, Patrick, it was hardly dangerous or improper."

He raised an eyebrow at her. "You are quick to forget that you were almost crushed to death by falling stone two hours ago."

"What?" The queen looked aghast, her eyes flying back over Elowen's form.

"I'm all right, Mother," Elowen told her quickly. "The tower partially collapsed, and I was closer to it than I ought to have been, but I didn't suffer any harm, truly."

"Thanks to the timely intervention of a servant of Bertrand's," Patrick interjected.

Elowen glanced around, looking for Simeon. He'd dismounted too far away to hear their conversation, and as she watched, Bertrand approached him, issuing instructions she couldn't hear.

"Good gracious." The queen put a hand to her forehead, her manner distracted. Putting that same hand gracefully but insistently on her daughter's shoulder, she steered her into the castle. "He should be rewarded, of course, and we will speak more of this later, but for the moment—"

"By *he*, I hope you mean Simeon," Elowen cut her off.

"Who?" The queen looked lost.

"Simeon," Elowen repeated. She glanced behind her, but Simeon, Bertrand, and Sophia were all gone. "The servant. Bertrand did nothing deserving a reward."

"It's natural for the actions of a servant to be a credit to his master," Patrick informed her. "It's appropriate for us to express our thanks to the young man's employer—in this case, the duke—and it's for him to appropriately reward the servant in question."

Elowen gave him an incredulous look. "Who'll reward him? Have you *met* Bertrand?"

"Elowen, this is no time to be gossiping about servants in the entranceway," the queen scolded her. "You must get to your room and change at once!"

"I'll be glad to," said Elowen. "But why the hurry, Mother?"

"If you'll refrain from interrupting me, I'll tell you," her mother said crisply. "We received a scout half an hour ago from Prince Theodore's party. They've made unexpectedly good time on their journey and will be with us today. We expect them within the hour."

"Within the hour?" Elowen froze. "But Mother, the prince isn't supposed to arrive until tomorrow!"

"I'm well aware of that," the queen said. "You picked a poor time to slip off for a dangerous adventure, Elowen. Now up to your room and change!"

"But what about the matter we discussed?" Elowen asked, fighting a feeling of panic. She was supposed to have one more night to collect herself. "You and Father were going to give me an answer at dinner."

"Never mind that." The queen made a stately version of a shooing motion. "Make yourself presentable, and meet us in the blue audience room. As quickly as you can, child!"

"But—"

Elowen's protest was lost as a host of maids appeared, ushering her toward her rooms. She barely had the chance to catch her breath as they stripped her, scrubbed her, and dressed her in one of her finest gowns. Her hair, free of dust and restored to its usual pale blond silkiness, was brushed to within an inch of its life and styled elaborately on her head.

She wasn't blind to the effect. She emerged looking beautiful and graceful, but she couldn't take pleasure in it. Her thoughts were too snarled up as she tried in vain to adjust to the prince's imminent arrival. She'd allowed herself to think of her impending betrothal as a problem for the future for far too long. Now, suddenly, she was out of time and out of options. It was as though she could feel her freedom slipping through her fingers like the thin silk of the wrap draped becomingly over her shoulders.

Prince Theodore was almost there. Prince Theodore, a total stranger, would be her betrothed in a matter of days.

She was about to see the face of the man she would wake beside for the rest of her life.

The whole idea was impossible to grasp. What would he be like? She remembered Bertrand's mocking words.

Rumor says Prince Theodore is the stiff, dull brother.

She'd heard the same rumors, of course. Since whispers of the betrothal had spread, every courtier and servant alike had been eager to repeat to her any information they'd ever heard about Prince Theodore, however garbled it might be.

But all rumors came from somewhere. What if Prince Theodore was as cold and aloof as people said? Worse, what if he was cruel? A thrill of fear went through her at the thought. Her parents wouldn't wish to marry her to someone cruel, but he could easily hide it until the marriage was complete. Then she would be living in Siqual, away from her family and all her friends.

Even if he stopped short of intentional cruelty, there were other ways she might suffer. What if she attempted warmth, and he met it with disdain? What if he made light of their vows and humiliated her with unfaithfulness? Perhaps he wouldn't do so openly, out of respect for their alliance, but even privately it would crush her.

What if, whispered a voice, *he's none of those things?* Elowen had dreamed of romance the same as the next girl, in spite of always knowing she was unlikely to be free to pursue it. Somewhere under the apprehension was a hint of excitement, an optimistic daydream that Prince Theodore might be the opposite of her fears. Maybe he *was* the dashing prince, in spite of Bertrand's snide words. Maybe he would be warm and charming, with a kind smile and eyes only for her.

Elowen sighed, banishing the thought. No sense in raising her hopes only to have them disappointed. She would be wiser to assume that she was saying goodbye to dreams of romance forever.

She met her own eyes in the mirror, steeling herself. She didn't want to say goodbye to romance. She may have only minutes left, but at least that was something. She had to convince her parents to give her back a tiny measure of control, little though they might understand her reasons for it.

"Am I done?" she asked the closest maid impatiently. "I wish to join my parents."

"Of course, Your Highness." The maid's eyes shone with excitement. "You'll be eager to meet the Siqualian prince, I'm sure." She lowered her voice. "Rumors say that he's handsome, Your Highness. Tall, and dark-haired, and mysterious."

Elowen almost snorted at the last word. It was the polite way of saying stiff, she supposed. "Mysterious only because we know so little of him," she said aloud. "As for handsome, well...I suppose we'll find out soon enough."

She swept from the room, followed by a posse of attendants. When she reached the blue audience room, she dismissed them all. She could tell from the air of poised expectation that the Siqualian group hadn't arrived yet. She still had time.

"Father, Mother." She burst into the room, her skirts swirling around her.

"Elowen." Her mother's tense posture relaxed as she quickly studied her daughter's form. "Much better. You look lovely, child."

Elowen dismissed the compliment with a wave of her hand.

"Yes, the maids outdid themselves." Her eyes pinned her father, who was in conversation with Sophia's father and another man she vaguely recognized.

"Have you thought more about what I asked?" she prompted.

"Elowen." Her mother spoke reprovingly. "Don't interrupt your father's conversation, what will the duke and the guild master think?"

"It's all right, Lisbeth." The king raised a hand to the man whose name Elowen didn't know, directing the next words to him. "I understand your concern, and investigation into the situation will continue." He looked at the duke. "Do you have anything to add, Your Grace?"

The Duke of Nirocha inclined his head to the king, then turned to the guild master.

"Only my assurance that I am committed to discovering the cause, as His Majesty has requested me to do," he said.

"Thank you, Your Grace." The guild master didn't sound reassured. He wrung his hands, looking stressed. "But Your Majesty, I must tell you that I believe the situation requires urgent attention. If the Dust continues to move unpredictably, there could be a great many implications for all the city's inhabitants."

"I understand," the king repeated, a note of finality in his voice. "I have placed the matter in the duke's capable hands, and if you make a time with His Grace, I'm sure he will hear all relevant information you can give him. But I cannot discuss it further at present."

The man at last accepted his dismissal, bowing to both the king and the duke before allowing the king's steward to usher him from the room.

"I will begin my own inquiries," the Duke of Nirocha said quietly to the king. He bowed to Elowen and her mother. "Your Majesty, Your Highness."

Elowen watched him stride toward the door, momentarily distracted from her purpose.

"What was that about? I recognized that other man. Isn't he the head of the Craftsmen's Guild? Is something strange happening with the magic in the city?"

Did Patrick know about whatever it was? Was that why he'd been so tense about Simeon's account at the watchtower? If so, the issue wasn't confined to the city.

"Never mind, my dear," the king said peaceably. "You have more important matters to focus on."

Elowen frowned, a familiar frustration gripping her at always being kept in the dark over anything important. But then memory returned, and she realized her father was right.

"Yes, I do," she agreed. "I'm here for your answer to my question, Father, and I need it now, not at dinner."

"Elowen." There was a warning note in her mother's voice.

"I know, Mother, but we're out of time for subtlety," Elowen said.

Her mother wasn't appeased. "You don't seem to understand how much is at stake for our kingdom, Elowen. This alliance is important. Do you forget how recently we were on the brink of war with Carrack, the strongest military power on the Peninsula? And they weren't the only ones withdrawing from diplomatic relationship with us. Now that Carrack has an alliance of sorts with Siqual and Dernan, we cannot afford to remain isolated."

"I know, Mother," Elowen said. "But they all know now that we weren't behind the violence and unrest they were experiencing."

The king shook his head with a sigh. "It's not that simple, Elowen. Suspicion settles deeply within a kingdom. Simple facts are often not enough to remove it. Your mother is right. This alliance with Siqual will bring security to our kingdom. Carrack will no longer be a threat."

"So you must be cooperative, Elowen," the queen added. "You will, won't you?"

"Of course I will," Elowen said, a little hurt. "When have I ever failed to do my duty, Mother?"

The queen's face softened. "Never, of course. You're a good girl, Elowen. And I know you'll do our kingdom proud in this alliance. But you must admit that I have cause to remind you of your duty, with all this talk of yours about conditions."

"Condition, request, I don't care what you call it," said

Elowen. "I just want to know whether you've decided to grant it." Her eyes were back on her father, their expression pleading as they returned to the main point of the conversation. "I'm going to be completely cooperative with the alliance, I swear. I just want this one concession."

The king studied his only daughter. "This is truly important to you, Elowen?"

"Very important," she assured him.

He nodded slowly as he thought it over. "Well, I don't see any harm in granting the request, Lisbeth."

Relief flooded Elowen, her future suddenly feeling much more bearable. She didn't let her mother's noise of disapproval worry her. The queen might sometimes be impatient with her husband's overly soft heart toward his children, but she would never actually stand against the king.

"I don't see the necessity at all," Queen Lisbeth said half-heartedly.

"And I don't see the harm," the king repeated. "It's not as though I'm in a great hurry to send the child away, Lisbeth."

"She's not a child. She's eighteen, and certainly old enough to be forming a marriage of alliance." But there was no conviction in the queen's protest. She'd already resigned herself to the decision.

Elowen had won. And no victory had ever tasted sweeter to her. She could face Prince Theodore with equilibrium now.

A very good thing, too, given that the door to the audience room swung open at that moment to reveal the castle's steward.

He bowed to his sovereigns. "The prince's delegation is approaching the castle, Your Majesties."

Elowen smoothed her gown and took a deep breath. She'd gotten her promise not a moment too soon. It was time to meet her future.

CHAPTER

TWO

Theo

Theo looked up at the castle towering ahead. It was a beautiful building, he noted with approval. Solid but elegant. The capital through which they'd just traveled seemed well-maintained and prosperous, and everything about the castle proclaimed strength, from the broad moat to the battlements above. His eyes lingered on a tall, narrow tower of a type he hadn't seen before, curious as to its purpose.

He didn't think Siqual would have reason to regret the planned alliance with Torrens. It was time to put the tension of the past few years to rest and move forward.

As for whether he'd have reason to regret the alliance...well, he didn't let himself consider that question, because there was little point.

He directed his horse across the drawbridge behind the escort of the Torrenese guards who'd accompanied them through the city. The courtyard within the castle gates was large and busy, although all activity paused as Theo dismounted and handed his horse off to a groom. Within minutes, he was being led up the castle steps and into a large, open entranceway.

He paused, allowing his eyes to adjust to the lower light. It had been hot under the late afternoon sun, and the cool of the castle was a welcome change. A group was waiting for him, the four members of the Torrenese royal family unmistakable at its front.

Curiosity flared within Theo at the knowledge that he was, for the first time, in the same room as his future wife. But politeness kept his gaze fixed calmly on the king and queen as they greeted him.

"Your Majesties." He executed a quick bow. "Thank you for your welcome. I'm delighted to be your guest."

"I trust your journey was smooth," Queen Lisbeth said graciously. Her smile was very regal. "We know it was at least efficient."

Theo inclined his head. "I must apologize for the inconvenience of my early arrival."

"Not at all," King Ronan said. "It's our gain to welcome you sooner. Allow me to introduce to you my son and heir, Patrick."

Theo greeted the prince, his mind still fighting with the constant pull on his gaze that was the princess on the queen's other side. Crown Prince Patrick was tall and upright, his features stern beneath his ash-blond hair. Nothing like Siqual's crown prince, Theo reflected, sparing a rueful thought for his often-outrageous older brother.

"And of course, my daughter, Elowen."

At last, Theo allowed his eyes to follow their desired course. He turned to greet the princess, a little shocked by how much he struggled to keep his expression steady as his gaze fell on her face.

"Princess." He took her offered hand, bowing over it before returning his eyes to her face. "It's a pleasure to meet you at last."

He kept his voice even and formal, as was appropriate. But his thoughts were much more animated.

Princess Elowen was beautiful. Stunningly beautiful. She was, he acknowledged frankly in the privacy of his mind, the most beautiful woman he'd ever seen. Her features were delicate and her frame willowy, but she didn't project fragility. Her bearing was confident, and her eyes—a clear blue—were sharp with intelligence. Pale, silky hair was piled atop her head in elegant braids, and her gown was fit for the royalty she was.

Warm satisfaction flooded Theo, and he scolded himself for caring so much about something so superficial. He hadn't thought Princess Elowen's appearance mattered to him, but his own reaction proved him wrong.

He didn't show that he was starstruck, of course. There was the honor of Siqual to be upheld, and he maintained a calm front.

"I'm pleased to meet you as well," Princess Elowen said calmly. "I hope you'll feel at home here."

Impossible not to wonder about her thoughts. Was she pleasantly surprised, like him? Or disappointed with what she saw? He suddenly realized he was still holding her hand, and lowered it at once.

"The arrangements are all made for the betrothal celebrations to begin in two days' time," Queen Lisbeth said. "I regret that your family are unable to attend."

"As do they," Theo said politely. "But they'll come for the wedding, so they won't have long to wait."

"We can discuss a date for the wedding at a later time," interjected King Ronan. "In the meantime, I'm sure you'll wish for the chance to change from travel before dinner."

Theo looked from the queen to the king. "Yes," he said carefully. "That would be welcome."

There was something strange about the king's dismissal of

his mention of the impending wedding, but he didn't know his host well enough to assess what it was. Surely the Torrenese weren't going to pull out of the agreement?

He exercised his iron self-control to stop his eyes from straying back to the princess as a servant led him toward his rooms. He was disappointed with himself for losing his head over her beauty.

As he changed his clothes in preparation for dinner, Theo's mind was on the king's strange manner regarding the wedding date. He knew he hadn't imagined it. A lifetime of learning to suppress his own reactions had made him good at reading those of others.

When he emerged from his room a short time later, a servant was waiting to show him to the dining hall. They made their way down a wide and pleasant corridor, lined with portraits of austere-looking individuals in the fashions of bygone times.

Theo felt a tiny surge of disappointment, swiftly pushed down, when the servant ushered him into a large and elaborately presented dining hall. Not that there was anything wrong with the space—the enormous wooden table, polished until it gleamed like marble—was imposing, and the spread laid out upon it even more so. Elegant crystal chandeliers bathed the room in soft light, and two large fireplaces kept the chill of the early evening at bay.

No, his disappointment was at the number of people in the room. Some thirty people stood as he entered—it was a court event, then, not the private meal with the royal family that he'd hoped for. He should have guessed as much. He knew from his training with a cultural advisor before he left Siqual how elaborate Torrenese royal betrothal ceremonies were. He'd caught a glimpse of the preparations just outside the city as he'd approached. Most of the court would gather for it, and much of the city's population would crowd in to watch what they could.

It wasn't the form he would choose for his betrothal, but he'd been thoroughly prepared, and understood his role in it all. He was to carry Princess Elowen off to Siqual once they were married, after all. It wasn't so much to ask that before she embraced the ways of his own kingdom for the rest of her life, he submit to the traditions of hers in the betrothal process.

The king and queen were absent from the dining hall, but their places were easily located, the king's at the head of the long table, and the queen's to his left. Prince Patrick occupied the seat to his absent father's right hand. Theo's eyes scanned the rest of the group, pausing on the golden-haired figure seated beside the queen's empty chair. He was heartened by the vacant seat on Elowen's other side. At least he would be able to talk to her.

There was another empty seat on Prince Patrick's other side, but as Theo had hoped, the servant directed him to sit beside the princess. He strode down the room, perfectly composed as he felt the gaze of many pairs of eyes.

"It seems rumor didn't lie on this occasion, Princess. Stiff *was* the word, wasn't it?"

By no flicker of his expression did Theo betray that he'd heard the carrying whisper from the young man seated on the other side of the empty chair beside Prince Patrick. But Princess Elowen wasn't similarly successful in hiding her reaction. Color flooded her cheeks, and Theo's heart sank.

He reached his chair, and with a rustle of fabrics, the other guests resumed their seats as well. There was no time for greetings, however, because a moment later, they were all rising again as King Ronan and Queen Lisbeth were announced. Another middle-aged man in an immaculately tailored jacket walked alongside the king. Watching the trio, Theo saw at a glance that this was someone important, who enjoyed the confidence of the monarchs.

The man was introduced as the Duke of Nirocha, supporting Theo's assessment. By the time the necessary formalities were complete, and the servants began ladling soup into everyone's bowls, Princess Elowen's flush from the earlier whisper had long subsided. But she still seemed hesitant to meet Theo's eye.

Theo felt his frustration rise. This wasn't the beginning he wanted with his future wife. He wanted her to like him. He wanted to make a good impression.

It doesn't matter what I want. The rebuke came swiftly to his mind. It wasn't his desires that mattered, but his duty, and duty required him to show a strong and confident front. It was Siqual's honor on the line, so he would ignore both the insult from the young nobleman, and the implication that Theo's betrothed had discussed him—evidently negatively—with another man.

What had he expected, after all? He knew his reputation for being stiff and uninteresting. It would be childish to let it trouble him. The opinions of idle gossipers didn't matter. He knew the truth—that unemotional steadiness was better for a kingdom than volatile charm.

Marriage alliances with powerful neighbors were also good for kingdoms, so there he was. His eyes strayed to Princess Elowen, his thoughts wandering for a moment as he took in the graceful line of her neck where she bent her head toward her mother, listening to a quiet comment from the queen.

Unemotional steadiness, Theo reminded himself, looking away before she caught him staring. His eyes fell instead on the young man seated across from the princess, the one who'd made the snide comment. The duke had been placed between him and the prince, and Theo realized that the duke's narrow face bore a strong resemblance to the younger man.

Theo was surprised to find the stranger watching him unashamedly, the hint of a challenge in his eyes. Theo held his gaze, in no hurry to break the silent exchange.

"Prince Theodore, allow me to introduce you to both the Duke of Nirocha and his son, Lord Bertrand, Viscount of Linner," Prince Patrick interjected helpfully.

The duke said all the appropriate things before the king claimed his attention from Prince Patrick's other side.

"I've been eager to meet you, Your Highness." There was a satisfied glint in the young viscount's eye that sent a frisson of irritation over Theo. "My family is honored to add our welcome to that of Their Majesties."

It was an irreproachable speech as far as the words went. But Theo was no fool, and he could read more than was said in plain words. If the mocking aside hadn't already done so, the tone of the viscount's welcome would certainly have marked him an enemy.

"Thank you for your welcome, Lord Bertrand," he said mildly. "I look forward to better making your acquaintance."

He meant it. He may not be staying long in Toledda, but he didn't intend to waste that time. He wanted to learn as much as he could about his future father-in-law's court—the unfriendly as well as the benign.

"Prince Theodore."

A much more pleasant voice brought Theo's attention to the princess beside him. Princess Elowen had an air of determination, and he got the sense she was eager to prevent further discussion between Theo and Lord Bertrand. That suspicion did nothing to decrease Theo's dislike of the man.

"I'd also like to introduce you to Lady Sophia." Elowen indicated the young woman seated beside Lord Bertrand, with a riot of dark curls tastefully arranged on her head. "She's Lord Bertrand's sister, and my dearest friend."

"It's my pleasure to meet you, Lady Sophia," Theo said, trying to insert more warmth into his words this time.

He doubted either Lady Sophia or Princess Elowen could hear it. Friendliness to strangers didn't come naturally to him at the best of times—*stiff* as he was—and he wasn't thrilled to know that the viscount's family was so closely intertwined with the princess. But good manners prompted him to engage the other young woman in polite conversation for a few minutes. It wasn't her fault that her brother showed signs of being combative, after all. Her demeanor certainly held no veiled hostility. She gave a general impression of sweet timidity, her dark eyes kind but her expression uncertain as she responded to Theo's conversation, her gaze flicking repeatedly to her brother.

She was wasting her effort. To all appearances, Lord Bertrand was paying no attention to his sister's conversation with the prince. He was leaning forward on one casual elbow, his eyes fixed on Princess Elowen as he took advantage of Theo's distraction to draw her into conversation.

When Theo looked over to find the nobleman's eyes resting on him, a slight smirk on his face, he felt nothing but disdain. Did this fool think Theo was going to compete with him? He was betrothed to Princess Elowen, he had no need to prove anything to anyone.

"Are you sure you're well enough for all this fuss, Princess?" the viscount said. "I thought perhaps you would be recovering from your ordeal. No one would blame you for being discomposed by a near-death experience."

Theo turned his head, captured in spite of himself. Princess Elowen flushed again under his scrutiny, her expression making him think she would have preferred him not to hear about whatever ordeal Lord Bertrand had referenced.

"Lord Bertrand exaggerates, Prince Theodore," she said with a light smile. "I suffered a mishap earlier today, but I'm neither injured nor discomposed."

"No exaggeration is required," Lord Bertrand contradicted her. "My dear princess, you threw yourself under a falling building."

"I did no such thing." The princess looked increasingly irritated. The brazenness of the viscount in smiling fondly on her annoyance made Theo's heart sink further. How close was their relationship that Lord Bertrand teased her so openly? She drew a deep breath, turning to Theo again. "I came too close to a collapsing building, but not by design. Naturally I didn't wish to be crushed."

"Naturally," Theo agreed, his tone reassuring. "I'm glad you're unharmed."

"Of course you didn't wish to be crushed," the viscount said, as if Theo hadn't spoken. He leaned closer, lowering his voice conspiratorially. "Only a fool would listen to the idle gossip of the servants who are claiming you hoped for injury so as to avoid...unpleasant responsibilities."

With the last word, his eyes flicked to Theo, who felt himself stiffening.

"Bertrand." The pained murmur came from Lady Sophia, but her brother didn't seem much chastened.

Before Theo had decided how to respond to the startlingly bold attack, the duke pulled his attention from his conversation with the king to look at his son. He said nothing, but under his slight frown, Lord Bertrand leaned back in his chair, his words ceasing as he idly lifted his wine glass.

Prince Patrick had also become aware of their conversation. His eyes darted over Princess Elowen's strained demeanor and

Theo's stiff silence, and a small crease appeared between his brows.

"Forgive my distraction," he said lightly. "What are we speaking of?"

"Lord Bertrand was telling me of the princess's unfortunate accident earlier today," Theo said blandly.

A brief flash of annoyance crossed Prince Patrick's face, suggesting he also would have preferred the incident not to be mentioned.

"Fortunately no one was harmed," the prince said tightly. "The building had just been condemned, but we were clearly too slow in acting on its deterioration."

"I'm simply glad I happened to be present to intervene on the princess's behalf," Lord Bertrand said, inclining his head in apparent deference to Princess Elowen.

"Indeed, Princess," interjected the duke. "As regrettable as the incident was, I was very pleased to hear our family was able to assist in your protection as well as Sophia's."

His eyes flicked to his daughter, a hint of anxiety visible. Theo concluded that the young noblewoman had also been placed in danger.

Princess Elowen's face gave little away. "Thank you, Your Grace," she said. "It was indeed fortunate that your servant was there, and able to use his considerable skill in magic craft to protect Sophia and myself." She glanced at the servants lining the wall behind the table, frowning slightly. "Where is Simeon, incidentally?"

Theo followed her gaze, but none of the servants seemed to catch her attention.

"I'm not sure." Lord Bertrand didn't bother looking around.

"What do you mean, you're not sure?" Lady Sophia frowned at her brother, showing the first sign of animation Theo had seen from her.

Lord Bertrand shrugged. "He disappeared after we returned from the watchtower, and when I called for him to accompany me to dinner tonight, he was nowhere to be found."

Theo didn't miss the look that passed between Princess Elowen and her friend, neither woman looking pleased with this information. Who exactly was this Simeon?

"Irregular behavior, to be certain," said Prince Patrick with the air of one wishing to close the conversation. "But I daresay he can be forgiven the need to rest after his exertions today."

"He wouldn't go to rest without alerting you," Lady Sophia interjected, apparently not ready to let the matter drop.

Lord Bertrand just shrugged again, but the young man to Lady Sophia's other side leaned forward.

"Are you talking about your manservant, Bertrand? He left Toledda."

"What do you mean?" Lady Sophia demanded.

"I saw him riding out the northern gate when I was arriving a couple of hours ago," the newcomer said. "He was hard to miss, because he was covered in ash, or something. Very disheveled, he looked."

"That would be the stone dust from the tower collapse." Princess Elowen sounded startled.

"The northern gate?" The duke's tone was sharp. "He returned home without seeking leave?"

Lord Bertrand's demeanor was no longer languid, the frown across his brow identical to his father's. "That goes beyond the line," he agreed. "Especially after he's just received leave to visit his family up in their forest village."

Theo remained silent, taking note of the varying expressions on the faces around him. There was more to this situation than met the eye, but he didn't yet have the understanding to decipher it.

The conversation petered out as the servants cleared an

enormous platter of pheasant from in front of him and replaced it with an array of fruit and sweet tarts, and a stone pitcher of hot, sweet tea.

"Prince Theodore." The queen drew his attention, her smile warm as she watched him select a sugar-dusted pastry. "As you know, the betrothal celebrations don't begin until the day after tomorrow. Since we have the pleasure of your company earlier than expected, I hope you'll take the time to enjoy Toledda. Perhaps Elowen can take you to the floating gardens tomorrow."

"I would be glad to," the princess said, smiling tentatively at him. "They're beautiful—a small marsh was discovered during construction of the city, and instead of filling it in, someone had the happy thought of enhancing it and turning it into a beautiful, water-based garden. We have all kinds of unusual flowers, even floating lilies imported from Pulau."

She became more animated as she spoke, her smile infectious by the time she mentioned the island kingdom to the west of Torrens.

Theo returned it. "I look forward to learning more of these gardens tomorrow."

He thought he caught a small movement from Lord Bertrand, but when he glanced over, the nobleman remained silent, his posture relaxed.

Lady Sophia, however, cleared her throat. "The gardens are so beautiful, aren't they? I haven't been in an age. I wonder if..." Her voice trailed off, its tone uncomfortable, and Princess Elowen came to her rescue.

"We would be delighted for you to join us, of course, Sophia."

Theo inclined his head, trying to hide his disappointment. He'd hoped for the chance for private speech with Princess Elowen, but that was unlikely with her friend in tow.

"I wouldn't wish to intrude," Lady Sophia said hesitantly.

"You're never an intrusion," Princess Elowen assured her.

"Perhaps we could make a group expedition," Lady Sophia said. She glanced at Prince Patrick. "Your Highness, do you intend to join the outing?"

"Certainly, if Elowen wishes to host a gathering, I'll be glad to join," the prince said politely, his true feelings hard for even Theo to read under all that diplomacy.

"Sounds like a fun morning." Lord Bertrand's cheerful interjection was no less irksome for being predictable. "I look forward to it."

"Excellent." Queen Lisbeth, at least, seemed pleased. "The arrangements will be made." She lifted the delicate porcelain cup into which her tea had been poured, then set it down without drinking any. The gesture was subtle, but a servant behind her immediately shifted. Inconspicuously, the woman pulled out a small wooden ball attached to a string, that she lowered and lifted in rapid succession by some means Theo couldn't identify.

Theo's senses—untrained and not particularly sharpened —picked up the faint stirring of Dust. After a moment, steam rose once more from the cup of tea, and the queen raised it to her lips in a graceful movement.

Theo returned his gaze to his food, ashamed of the tiny pang of jealousy that went through him. Absurd—irresponsible, even—for a prince to be envious of a serving woman. It was fascinating, though, to see this evidence that magic was used more freely in Torrenese daily life than he was used to.

When the king rose soon after, the rest of them did as well.

"I apologize, Prince Theodore," King Ronan said amicably. "But I have matters requiring my attention." His sweeping gesture encompassed the whole table. "Please feel free to continue to enjoy yourselves."

He directed a nod to Prince Patrick, who fell into step with his father as they crossed the room, the king's steward materializing when they reached the doorway.

Conversation bubbled up again, but it was no more than ten minutes before the queen also stood. She bid the company good evening, sweeping her daughter from the room with her, and thus removing any interest Theo had in lingering. He could tell at a glance that Lord Bertrand had every intention of continuing to needle him, so he excused himself and left the dining hall as well. It was early to retire, but he was weary enough from his journey that he would have no difficulty falling asleep.

His last thought as he drifted was of the princess, her eyes straying back to him for the briefest of moments as her mother ushered her from the dining hall.

Elowen

Elowen was the first to arrive for the projected outing to the floating gardens. The appointed courtyard was empty when she came to a stop by the central fountain, a servant hurrying on to alert the stables that she was ready for her horse.

Elowen drew her riding gloves between her hands in a rhythmic motion, her eyes unseeing as they stared at the tinkling water of the fountain. She hadn't slept well, and her thoughts were distracted. But her awareness still latched on to the water's steady flow, and she felt the stirring in her mind that told her she'd identified the magic being created by the water's movement.

She didn't attempt to take hold of it, and not just because it wouldn't do to reveal her secrets in a public place. It would have been pointless given, as with all sources of perpetual movement within the castle walls, the Dust produced by this fountain was protected by a magical barrier. One couldn't have magic leaking freely throughout the castle grounds for any passerby to take hold of, no matter how small the trickle produced by the fountain might be.

But magic craft was a sore spot she didn't need to dwell on right now. She had plenty of other grievances clamoring for her attention, such as the unintended group outing. She hadn't minded Sophia joining them. In fact, a cowardly part of her had welcomed the insulating presence of her friend. But that was because Sophia was good at melting into the background when necessary. Bertrand was another matter entirely.

A scowl crossed Elowen's face at the thought of the viscount. She was miserably conscious that the dinner hadn't gone as well as she would have liked, and she laid the blame at his feet. Bertrand had always been irksome, but she'd never seen him as brazen as he'd been the night before. She would never have dreamed he would be so insulting to the foreign prince's face. What could he possibly hope to achieve by embarrassing her and insulting Prince Theodore?

Prince Theodore.

Her thoughts turned yet again to the Siqualian prince. She wished she'd had more success figuring him out. But she supposed there would be time enough for that. They had the rest of their lives, after all.

The thought didn't excite her, but at least it didn't fill her with dread. He hadn't shown much warmth—all right, he hadn't shown *any* warmth. She wished he'd given some indication of admiring her. She was used to overblown compliments, weary of them even, but still, the absence of admiration had been notable. It was probably vain of her to think it, but she'd been dressed to her very best, and she hadn't been able to detect even a flicker of appreciation in his gaze when he laid eyes on her.

She was being foolish. He'd been in no way unkind, and at least *he* was pleasant to look at it. She pictured in her mind his dark hair, straight nose, and slightly pointed chin. His appeal wasn't primarily because of his features, she decided. It was in his bearing—his stride, his unruffled posture, his steady gaze. He wore his confidence like a well-fitted coat, and it was attractive.

If only he wasn't so...she winced to echo Bertrand in her mind, but...stiff.

"It's strange to see an empty fountain."

Elowen started at the voice, spinning around to see Prince Theodore himself behind her. He was dressed in a thick, embroidered coat of a deep blue, the garment perfectly fitted to his muscular form, with dark breeches and tall riding boots. One of his guards had accompanied him, but the man slid discreetly past, following her servant toward the stables.

Left alone with the prince, Elowen smoothed her skirts self-consciously, feeling as discomposed as if he'd been able to read her thoughts about him.

"Good morning, Princess Elowen." The prince smiled, the expression friendly, but in a cautious way. His eyes didn't crinkle at the corners.

"Good morning," she said. "And please, call me Elowen."

He studied her for a moment, then nodded, his smile marginally more relaxed. "Thank you. Feel free to call me Theo."

Theo. She felt a flicker of surprise.

Apparently he could read it, because his smile turned slightly rueful. "Even stiff princes have nicknames, you know," he informed her. "Theo is what my friends and siblings call me. My parents, too, but only if they're particularly pleased with me."

Elowen fought back the color rushing to her cheeks. His use of the word *stiff* was an uncomfortable reminder of her embarrassment from the night before, but at the same time, it made her like him more. He'd surprised her for the second time—she hadn't expected him to make a light joke of the gossip about him.

"That sounds pleasant," she informed him. "I don't think the thought of giving me a nickname has ever crossed Patrick's mind."

Prince Theodore—Theo—tilted his head slightly to one side, his expression searching. "You and your brother aren't close?"

"No, I didn't mean—" Elowen stumbled over her words, alarmed that she'd cast her family, and thus the kingdom, in a poor light. "Patrick and I are very amicable. We don't. I mean, we've never—"

"It's all right," Theo cut her off, his tone gentle but still managing to remain light. "I didn't mean to make you uncomfortable, and you have no need to explain anything to me."

Elowen drew a deep breath, deciding to take the opening. "Actually," she said, "I do wish to explain something to you. I'm afraid the wrong impression was given last night. The incident with the watchtower yesterday was nothing but an inconvenient accident, and the timing was purely...coincidental."

"Of course it was coincidental." Theo raised an eyebrow. "What else would it be?"

"Well, nothing else, of course." Elowen fidgeted uncomfortably, starting to wish she'd never brought it up. "I just...Lord Bertrand spoke out of turn at dinner, and I didn't want you to..."

Her voice trailed off as the stiff politeness returned to Theo's face.

"To get the wrong impression?" he finished for her. "Not at all."

Elowen felt herself deflate. She could see she'd made it worse. She should have left it alone. Why must Bertrand be such an interfering nuisance? She bit back the urge to keep trying to explain herself, wise enough to know she would just embroil herself further.

"What...what did you mean about the fountain?" she asked instead.

"The fountain?" He was politely bemused.

"When you first arrived, you said it was empty," she explained, glancing at the still-tinkling water. "It doesn't look empty to me."

"Oh, that." Theo relaxed a little. "At the palace at home in Sindon, all of our fountains are infested with anzu birds."

She stared at him, amusement trickling in to leaven her embarrassment. "Infested?"

He smiled, although his eyes still didn't crinkle. "Inhabited would be a politer term, wouldn't it? They're much admired—and they know it—but personally, I find them a nuisance."

"Why?" she demanded, fascinated.

She'd never seen an anzu bird, as they were primarily found in Siqual, but she'd seen pictures. They were a bit bigger than cats, but only their heads resembled that creature. The rest of their bodies bore the shape of birds. They were creatures of magic, naturally—no mundane animal would boast such an illogical configuration of form.

"You know how all anzu birds spout either fire or water?" said Theo, answering her question with another.

Elowen nodded. "So I've read."

"Well, they make quite a show of it," Theo explained. "The castle ones, at least. They've become very tame, and they expect an audience. It can be tedious, because if people don't stop to admire them when the fancy takes them to put on a display, they get cranky and make a fuss."

"What kind of a fuss?" Elowen asked, trying and failing to

picture Theo breaking his purposeful stride through his own castle to politely applaud a display by a conceited anzu bird.

"Generally they set things on fire," he said matter-of-factly. "It's a terrible inconvenience."

Elowen stared at him. "Why are they allowed to keep living in the castle, then?"

"We've become used to them, I suppose." Theo shrugged. "They're beloved—most people seem to enjoy their displays. Besides, if we tried to remove them, I imagine there would be a great deal more setting things on fire."

"Goodness." Elowen didn't quite know what to say. All she could think of was her private thoughts earlier, wishing that Theo had shown some admiration for her the night before, when she'd been all dressed up to impress him. Had she been preening, like the anzu birds he described? Would he find *her* tedious if he knew her thoughts?

"Elowen." Theo's voice had turned more serious, and Elowen's eyes flew up to his. "I came early in the hope of some private speech."

"So did I," she said quickly, and she thought he looked pleased.

"It's a little awkward, isn't it?" His voice was the softest she'd heard it. "There's inevitably a lot of pressure on our meeting."

Her smile was rueful. "Yes. I suppose there is."

"I don't know how to avoid that," he said frankly. "But I hope you won't let it trouble you. We'll be married in a matter of weeks, and—"

"Hold on." Elowen raised a hand to stop the flow of calmly confident words. "Who says it will be within a few weeks? The wedding date isn't set yet."

Theo frowned. "I understood that was merely a practical matter, with arrangements waiting for my arrival. I anticipated that the date of the wedding would be set as soon as the betrothal ceremony is complete."

Elowen lowered her eyes, her courage failing her under his scrutiny.

"I haven't heard talk of a specific date."

"Elowen." She felt compelled to look up again. "Be plain with me, please." Theo's eyes searched hers, and even with the edge of hardness that had entered them, it was an immersive sensation. "Is Torrens reconsidering the alliance?"

"No," she said quickly, swallowing. "I swear we're not. The practical details are yet to be finalized, but we remain committed to our alliance, as agreed."

He frowned, his expression giving her the impression that he was trying to read her thoughts. Of course he was confused. He was no fool, he must be able to tell she wasn't being entirely open.

"Princess…and Your Highness."

Elowen barely held in a sigh at the drawling new voice, as her least favorite viscount appeared behind Theo. The drop in respect from the tone of the first title to the second was marked.

"Lord Bertrand," she said tightly, giving the viscount a nod.

Sophia was only a step behind him, and Elowen greeted her friend with much more pleasure. At least until she got a good look at Sophia's face and saw the concern lurking there. Abandoning Theo and Bertrand, who were eyeing each other coolly, she went to her friend, dropping her voice.

"Are you all right?"

"I'm fine," Sophia said unconvincingly. She saw Elowen's disbelieving expression, and bit her lip. "I didn't sleep very well. I know it's foolish, but…I had dreams of being crushed under falling stone."

Elowen made a sympathetic noise in her throat. Poor

Sophia. They'd been friends all their lives, and Sophia had always been the less confident of the two, but as she neared adulthood, her timidity had increased startlingly. Elowen didn't like to see it. But she didn't comment, instead turning to practical matters.

"By the way, Sophia," her voice was very low, "you've probably guessed as much, but I won't be able to meet as normal this afternoon, because of Prince Theodore's visit."

"Yes, I assumed that," Sophia said. "It doesn't matter anyway, because Simeon really does appear to have left the capital. I couldn't find him anywhere."

"Without asking leave of your brother?" Elowen demanded. "That's very unlike him."

Sophia cast an unhappy look at her brother, then shrugged.

"Whatever the reason, he's not available for our...weekly ride."

There was no time for more. Patrick had just arrived, along with a few other younger members of the court who'd evidently been invited after Elowen retired from dinner the night before. A number of grooms were also waiting on the far side of the courtyard, each holding a mount, Elowen's own mare among them. Her heart lifted at the sight of Ochre. She preferred being on horseback when she was with a group of courtiers. It provided a natural and much appreciated barrier from the overeager ones among her peers.

Speaking of whom...

"Princess Elowen." One of the gathered men, the younger son of an earl, approached her with a spring in his step. "I'm honored to be included today."

Elowen barely managed to keep her smile neutral. As if she'd been the one to invite him.

"I look forward to competing in your honor at the betrothal

celebrations," the man went on, his eyes shining as they swept over her features. "I hope to prove myself worthy in your eyes, even if..." His voice trailed off, and he glanced darkly at Theo.

Elowen wanted to groan. Why must her parents insist on upholding the traditional betrothal tournament, when the event hadn't been meaningful in at least three generations? The whole week was bound to be full of mortifying conversations like this one.

"I'm sure you'll acquit yourself well, My Lord," she said, her tone polite but firm as she edged toward Ochre, gripping the saddle like an anchor. To her chagrin, she saw that Theo was studying the nobleman with a contemplative air. When his eyes slid smoothly to her face, she looked away.

She was about to mount Ochre when Bertrand materialized at her side, not waiting for any sign from her before grasping her waist and boosting her up toward the saddle.

"I don't need assistance," she told him sharply, her eyes flicking back to Theo. Once again, he was observing the exchange in expressionless silence.

"My mistake, Princess," said Bertrand, his good humor undimmed by her displeasure. She would never understand his idea of charm. The viscount sprang lightly onto his own horse, addressing the group at large.

"What a perfect day it is for our outing. Did I mention that you're all expected back at my family's city dwelling for a luncheon after we've visited the gardens?" His eyes slid to Theo. "Not that I mean to unduly claim your time, Your Highness. Of course I will understand if your diplomatic duties prevent you from joining us."

Elowen drew in a breath at the thinly veiled rudeness. Theo regarded Bertrand in cool silence, wisely not responding to his words at all.

"What is Bertrand doing?" The muttered aside came from Sophia, and Elowen was heartened to hear her friend recognizing her brother's poor behavior for once. When she turned to respond, however, Sophia was urging her horse forward, apparently not eager to discuss it.

The remaining members of the party mounted quickly, everyone eager to reach the floating gardens. Elowen couldn't claim much excitement about the outing anymore. She'd pictured a quiet ride with Theo, and a chance to get a sense of the man she was to marry, not a spectacle for the courtiers. She knew how it would be, with the girls giggling over her every interaction with Theo, and the men vying to pull her attention away from him.

The group had barely ridden through the castle gate, however, when Patrick was hailed by a man Elowen recognized as a member of his guard. They all drew to a stop as Patrick steered his horse, an enormous stallion, back to where the man waited at attention.

Elowen urged her horse toward her brother, catching only the end of the report.

"—imminent, according to the reports. The duke has already left the capital, and he desired me to carry a message to Lord Bertrand. His Majesty is unable to attend to the matter himself, but has requested that you do so, Your Highness."

"Certainly, I will," Patrick said. "I'll leave immediately." He dismissed the man with a nod.

"Leave for where, Patrick?" Elowen asked.

"It's nothing to concern you, Elowen," he said. "You enjoy your ride with Prince Theodore—please give him my apologies for not joining you after all. I imagine I'll be back by evening."

"No." Elowen's voice was firm as she reached out, grabbing the stallion's bridle at an awkward angle. "You and Father are keeping something from me, and I want to know what's going on, Patrick."

"Don't be dramatic, Elowen," he said, removing her hand. "Nothing drastic is going on. A dam is on the point of bursting its bounds, which would have significant effects for the surrounding farms. I'm going to visit the site and try to avert the disaster."

She raised her eyebrows incredulously. "They need *your* expertise on the structural reinforcement of a dam? What are they expecting you to do that local stonemasons can't? Will you wedge your crown into the crack?"

Patrick just shook his head at her, as if her question was frivolous. But Elowen was serious. She could sense something wasn't right. And her indignation only increased when Patrick pulled his horse alongside Bertrand and murmured something inaudible. Bertrand's eyes widened, then he nodded, guiding his horse around as well.

"I regret the necessity of missing our time together, Princess," he said, a glint in his eyes as they passed from Elowen to Theo. "I'll have to content myself with the anticipation of taking part in the celebrations in your honor tomorrow."

Whatever his words, he didn't look as regretful as she would have expected. He looked tense, his focus clearly on whatever Patrick had just told him.

"My apologies, everyone," Bertrand called to the group. "But Sophia will still be delighted to host you all for the promised luncheon."

A glance at Sophia showed that she wasn't delighted so much as considerably distressed. Elowen had sympathy for her friend, even if she thought Sophia's reaction overblown. She may not like attention, but Sophia was an intelligent, socially adept young woman, perfectly capable of hosting a luncheon for her peers.

The two men prompted their steeds forward, Patrick's small retinue of guards flanking them as they moved northward around the castle wall.

"Is all well?"

Theo had come up alongside Elowen, but she didn't immediately answer him. She was still frustrated and, in all honesty, a little humiliated. Not to mention suspicious.

"Princess Elowen?"

Theo's prompt decided her. She turned her head, eyeing the prince speculatively.

"I gave you leave to drop the title, if you recall." She tapped her fingers on the saddle in front of her. "I confess that I've lost enthusiasm for visiting the floating gardens. Would you instead be interested to see more of our kingdom, outside Toledda?"

Theo raised an eyebrow, sensing that she was up to something. "I was privileged to do so extensively on my ride through Torrens on the way to the capital."

"Ah, but you didn't see anything north of here, did you?" she said innocently.

Theo's eyes traveled northward, along the route taken by Patrick and Bertrand. "No, I didn't." His expression was hard to read—she had no idea what he was thinking of her machinations. But for the moment at least, he was going along with them.

"We should rectify that." Elowen turned her horse again, raising her voice and addressing the rest of the group. "I'm very sorry, everyone, but something has come up to detain both my brother and myself. Please continue to the gardens without us, and enjoy the beautiful day."

There were a few disappointed murmurs, and a number of the young men in the group looked crestfallen. With an internal wince, Elowen saw Theo's eyes resting unerringly on each of her most tiresome admirers in turn. He didn't appear to miss much, which made her uneasy. But on the whole, the group seemed inclined to take her advice. For the girls at least, it would be more enjoyable in her absence. She knew a number of them were eagerly anticipating her marriage and departure so that the more eligible of her suitors might turn their attention to lesser targets.

They were welcome to every one of them, as far as she was concerned.

"Come on, Sophia," Elowen said determinedly. "You're coming with me."

"But...the luncheon," Sophia protested half-heartedly.

"That's Bertrand's mess, and I see no reason for us to clean it up for him," Elowen said.

"If you say so." Sophia sounded doubtful. "Where are we going?"

"Northward," said Elowen, steering her mount after the others. "Come on, Ochre." She caught the uneasy glances her guards exchanged as they followed her. "We're going after the boys. Apparently a dam is about to burst, and Patrick wants to get there in time to stop it, somehow."

"Bertrand won't like it," Sophia said, biting her lip.

"Bertrand doesn't have to like it," said Elowen with spirit. "My movements are no concern of his." She shot a self-conscious glance at Theo, who'd kept pace on his own mount, but had remained silent.

Sophia gave her a confused look. "I meant he won't like *me* following him."

"Oh," said Elowen. "Well...Patrick won't like me doing it, either, but even princes have to deal with disappointment." She cast a semi-defiant look at Theo. "I suppose you have an opinion on it all."

"An opinion on whether princes have to deal with disappointment?" he asked dryly.

"No." She lowered her gaze, an uncomfortable prickling going over her. "I suspect I'd rather not know your answer to that question." Making her voice more natural, she raised her head again. "I meant an opinion about our change in activity."

For a moment, she thought Theo looked confused, but his face was so hard to read, she couldn't be sure.

"If you're asking whether I'm going to attempt to dictate your actions, the answer is no." To her surprise, he sounded faintly amused, but his gaze was perfectly serious as he once again subjected her to that scrutiny that made her want to fidget. "You seem to think more is going on than what's been said."

Elowen shrugged, urging her horse faster as the road northward widened. "A tower collapse yesterday, and a dam failure today...it might be coincidence." *But if it wasn't*, she added silently, *Patrick wouldn't tell me.*

"But you don't think it is coincidence." Theo's words weren't a question. He looked very thoughtful, then he gave her a nod. "Well, I know nothing of the situation, so I'll defer to your judgment. If some kind of misfortune is plaguing the region, I'm certainly not averse to discovering what's happening."

Elowen felt her cheeks grow pink. He hadn't dismissed her with polite reassurances not to worry, like Patrick had. And when he'd said he would defer to her judgment, she could detect no hint of mocking, as Bertrand would surely have injected into any such declaration. He didn't know her at all, and already he took her more seriously than those closest to her.

She was fast losing track of how many times he'd surprised her that morning.

They still hadn't caught the others by the time they passed through the gates of the city. The guards on duty took note of

Elowen—she could feel their eyes following her—but with the visiting prince by her side and both her own pair of guards and Theo's solitary guard behind her, they didn't challenge her. Patrick would be none too pleased when she caught up to him, but she didn't think he'd actually compel her to go back. Not in front of Theo.

FOUR

Theo

Theo's spirits lifted when they cleared the city. Any desire to visit the celebrated floating gardens had evaporated the moment the viscount had weaseled his way onto the outing. Giving his horse its head on an open road was infinitely preferable. Elowen seemed more relaxed as well. She had a good seat, her willowy form in perfect harmony with the bronze-colored mare she was riding.

He found himself stealing looks at her as her hair started to come loose from its bindings, streaming in a golden wave behind her. He was startled by a sudden desire to reach over and run his fingers through it.

Enough, he told himself sternly. He needed to get hold of himself. He thought he'd grown beyond frivolous desires, but they seemed to be flitting through him with alarming frequency since he'd met Elowen. He needed to act like the prince and representative of Siqual that he was, not like some minor noble vying for the princess's favor.

"There they are."

Elowen's call drew Theo's attention to the road far ahead. He could see the small party that consisted of the prince, the viscount, and four guards. They didn't seem to have noticed their pursuers, and as Theo watched, they followed the road under the shelter of a copse of trees in the distance.

"I wish we had time to stop," Elowen said brightly. "But this isn't the time for a hunt."

Her friend laughed. "I suppose not."

"A hunt?" Theo asked, mesmerized by how Elowen's increasingly casual air changed her countenance. She was even prettier when relaxed, if that were possible.

The smile she sent him was only a little self-conscious. "This is the route to Sophia's family estate, which I visited a number of times as a child. This region is known for wolpertingers and we used to hunt for them in all the wooded areas along the way. Drove our minders mad."

She sent a cheeky look toward her two guards, whom Theo noticed had an air of long-suffering. His own guard, an easygoing middle-aged man who'd been with Theo for years, met Theo's eyes with a twinkle that seemed to say, *take the opening.*

Theo shot him a wry look, not eager to receive romantic advice from his attendants. Although he supposed Paulson should know, given he'd been happily married for some thirty years.

"Did you ever find any?" Theo asked Elowen a short time later, as they passed beneath the first branches of the copse.

She shook her head. "I don't think so. We thought we caught a glimpse once, but I have a feeling it was just an ordinary squirrel."

"What do you think, Paulson?" Theo asked his guard. "Do you sense any movement from wolpertingers among these trees?"

"I don't, Your Highness."

"Are you a craftsman as well as a guard?" Elowen asked

curiously, immediately grasping the implication of Theo's question.

Wolpertingers weren't a source of fascination solely for their unusual shape, with the form of a squirrel, the wings of a woodland bird, and surprisingly large antlers. They were also known for the excessive and disproportionate volume of magic generated by their movements. It was why they were protected, and it was illegal to breed, farm, or hunt them. Difficult as they were to spot, someone with a good sense of magic should be able to feel the movements of nearby wolpertingers.

"I've recently begun the study, Your Highness," Paulson told the princess with a respectful smile. "It's most fascinating, but I'm far from an expert in the field."

"My sister's recent experiences have highlighted to my family the value of having guards who are trained in the manipulation of magic," Theo explained.

Elowen nodded as she murmured reassuringly to her horse, which had shied from a low-hanging branch.

"We heard about the attack on Princess Miriam. I'm relieved she was unharmed."

"As am I."

The words came out a little terse. Theo hated reliving the moment his sister had been saved from death from a speeding arrow only by the swift reaction of her magically trained body-guard. It had certainly been no act of his that had averted disaster. For a moment, his memory swirled, the peaceful copse turning into the chaotic scene beneath the trees the day of the attack. When the memory started to follow its usual course and morph into a horrifying image of his sister's child-like face, white with terror as she dangled from a cliff in the moonlight, Theo pulled himself back to reality with an iron hand. Mim was home and safe, and no one—at least no humans—had died from his failures on either occasion.

Wallowing in memories that scared him would only distract him from his duties, and make it more likely he would harm others with his mistakes.

"I'm just relieved everyone stopped thinking Torrens was somehow behind the incident," Elowen went on, thankfully not noticing his abstraction. "We would never wish your sister harm. I met her once, did you know? During the years when she was studying at an academy in Toledda." She smiled at him. "I was jealous that she got to return to the academy at the end of the dull, royal luncheon in her honor, whereas I had to go back to my stuffy tutor."

Theo returned the smile sympathetically. "I know Miriam counts herself fortunate to have had the opportunity to study at an academy."

"I heard they were even allowed to study magic craft," Elowen added. She sighed. "It wasn't ever part of my approved education."

"Nor mine," Theo said regretfully. "But even without the aid of magic, I still occasionally see wolpertingers in the forest in the west of Siqual. It's riddled with them. I'll organize an official search for you."

She smiled shyly at him. "I would like that."

Theo felt bolstered as they rode through the rest of the copse. Things were going better with his intended bride in this relative privacy. They'd lost some ground under the trees, and they had to ride hard once they left the copse to bring Prince Patrick's group back in view.

They'd reached a town, and it had required them to slow down, allowing the second party to gain ground. They'd almost caught up when the prince's group cleared the town. One of Elowen's guards had ridden ahead, and he hailed the prince just as he was about to increase his pace again.

The look on Prince Patrick's face as they drew level told

Theo that his presence was saving Elowen from a scold, at the very least.

Theo felt a flash of sympathy for the princess. He knew that Miriam was sometimes frustrated with his caution on her behalf, and the greater restrictions she faced compared to her brothers. But he had no doubt she knew he cared about her. There was no such warmth in Prince Patrick's eyes. Theo couldn't imagine ever looking at his sister the way the other prince looked at Elowen.

"This is certainly a surprise, Elowen." The prince's voice was forbidding, although he injected a note of respect as he added, "Prince Theodore."

"Don't let us slow your progress," Theo said. "I understand there's some urgency to your errand."

"There is," Prince Patrick agreed. "And I find myself now in the difficult circumstance of being unable both to safely escort my sister back to the capital and pursue my original task efficiently."

"Surely there's no need to escort anyone back to Toledda," Theo said mildly. "We will ride onward with you, of course. The princess wished to inspect the damaged dam with you, and I was glad to offer her my company."

"My, what an indulgent husband you'll be, Your Highness." There was no mistaking the derision in Lord Bertrand's voice, or the anger in his eyes as he looked at Lady Sophia. Elowen wasn't the only one who would be taken to task by her brother later. Theo's only response to Bertrand's mocking words was his frostiest look, which didn't dismay the viscount.

Prince Patrick shot a fleeting look of annoyance at Lord Bertrand before responding to Theo's words. "Certainly, if you wish it, Your Highness." He inclined his head with a hint of stiffness.

His manner convinced Theo that he hadn't wanted the

visiting prince to witness whatever situation they were about to reach. It made Theo all the more determined to understand what was going on within the allied kingdom.

The group started into motion again, crossing a small river by means of a stone bridge. Theo's eyes fell on a mill a short distance downriver. The large wooden wheel was churning powerfully, the water falling from it in a steady cascade.

"You'll see a few mills like that in this area," Prince Patrick told him, noticing him watching the wheel. "But this isn't our primary wheat region. The wealth of this region comes from ore mined from further west," he pointed, "and from vast orchards. Both the ore and the fruit are some of Torrens's primary exports."

"Those, and princesses," Elowen murmured, the addition so quiet Theo barely caught it. He glanced over at her, but her eyes were straight ahead, and her expression steady.

Theo cleared his throat, politely thanking Prince Patrick for the information and refraining from pointing out that he was already well versed in the kingdom's imports and exports. He noticed that Lord Bertrand was throwing him a disgruntled look, not seeming happy about the conversation, and the next moment, Prince Patrick had pulled ahead to join the viscount. Theo threw one more glance back at the mill.

"It might not be the biggest wheat region, but there are still a lot of wheat farms in this area," Elowen commented, following his gaze. "And they produce a fine quality of flour." She nodded toward the man sitting alongside the mill, his posture tense and his eyes focused on the movement of the wooden wheel. "They use the Dust already being generated by the mill's movement to further treat the flour. That's how they get it so fine."

"So that man is a craftsman, then?" Theo asked, interested enough to slow his horse for a better look.

She nodded. "I believe some mills employ more experienced craftsmen who can even use the mill's magic to remove imperfections and pests from the wheat before it's processed. It's a well-developed system, but I don't know all the details."

"It's an excellent notion," Theo said. "I've heard of craftsmen being employed to harness the magic of mills in Siqual, but I believe they only increase the volume of wheat that can be processed, rather than further refining the product."

They needed to hurry now to catch the others, but he lingered for one more moment, watching as another man came out of the building, slapping his fellow on the back. Theo could see the posture of the first man relax as, with a nod, he retreated into the mill.

Theo understood the necessity for frequent changes in shift. He'd learned enough theory of magic craft to know that the magic produced by movement couldn't be stored. It had to be harnessed and used as it was created, or it was simply reabsorbed into the environment. A sophisticated craftsman could mold it into an enchantment that might have an extended effect, but they couldn't store it as raw power to be molded later. It would take great concentration and endurance for a craftsman to continuously mold power for any length of time, hence the need for regular shift changes. And any time the mill didn't have a craftsman on duty, the Dust stirred up by the wheel's movement would simply drift back into the landscape. It was impressive that the business had been able to employ two craftsmen.

The group was soon moving with a sense of urgency that told Theo they were nearing their destination. Sure enough, as the road wound around the base of a small group of hills, a body of water came into view. Prince Patrick spurred his horse off the main road and along a smaller track that ran around the water's edge.

A sharp intake of breath sounded from Lady Sophia's direction. "That's the dam that's in peril?"

"What is it, Sophia?" Elowen asked.

The noblewoman looked troubled. "It's the biggest dam in our region. It services a dozen farms, and it provides drinking water for a number of towns." She nodded toward a hamlet visible between the folds of some low hills in the distance, on the other side of the dam. "That one, for example."

Theo could see what she meant. Irrigation channels spread out from the dam in multiple directions, sunlight glinting off the lines of water.

"Not to mention that town would be flooded if the dam were to break," he said.

"You're right." Elowen sounded distressed. "We have to stop it somehow."

She pushed her horse forward, trying to catch up with her brother once again, and Theo kept pace with her. They found the prince conversing with a burly man who was practically sweating with stress.

"I don't understand it, Your Highness. The damage to the foundation is extensive. I've no idea what would cause it. We've had no floods or tremors or anything like that. It was discovered only this morning, and we've been working hard to try to repair it, but the pressure coming against it is too strong. I'm not confident we can prevent a burst."

"We must prevent a burst," Prince Patrick said. "The results would be catastrophic for the region."

"I understand, Your Highness." The man mopped his brow. "If we had some magic craftsmen, it might help, but we don't have an official guild house in the area. We've requested some craftsmen from the capital, but we're still waiting. His Grace arrived a short time ago, and he's leading an evacuation effort for that hamlet there, in case we can't prevent disaster."

"Simeon," Lady Sophia said suddenly. "He might be able to help. Didn't he return home yesterday evening, Bertrand?"

"I think you exaggerate his abilities, Sophia." Bertrand's tone was incredulous. "He's one servant, he wouldn't be able to hold a dam together on his own."

"He could help," she insisted. "We should find him."

"I thought of Simeon, My Lady," the local man said. "He's well known around here, often helps out with little magical tasks. But I thought he was in the capital with Your Lordship." He looked inquiringly at Bertrand.

"He was yesterday, but no one seems to know where he is now," Bertrand said in irritation. "It's no matter, I'm sure it wouldn't make a difference. What we need to do is shore up the barrier. Show me where it's weakened."

The man led them down the sloping side of a hill, toward the base of the dam. Theo followed with a twinge of misgiving, his eyes fixed on the golden head in front of him. If the dam was so close to giving out, any of them who weren't actively helping with the restoration effort would be wise to keep some distance from it.

"Father!" Lady Sophia's cry made everyone look up.

The Duke of Nirocha was approaching at a smart trot from the other side of the retaining wall, his expression sober. The two groups had almost met in the middle of the plain when a cry went up from the rim of the dam above.

Theo's eyes darted up to see two men sprinting along the stone barrier in opposite directions, each desperate to clear the area before the whole structure collapsed.

"She's done for!" one of them bellowed. "Everyone back!"

Elowen

Cries of dismay went up on all sides, and for a brief moment, Elowen froze in panic. Then a firm hand took hold of the reins, and a voice spoke steadily into her ear.

"Come, Elowen."

She responded at once, pressing her knees into Ochre's side to encourage the mare in the direction Theo was guiding them. She was barely aware of where they were going, but she felt a strange sense of relief and security in the midst of the panic. Then she heard a cracking sound behind her, and her alarm returned. She looked wildly around, relieved to see Patrick also riding hard to get clear of the dam. Her heart seized, however, when she saw that Sophia was struggling to get control of her horse. It was borrowed from the royal stables, not her own mount, and it was clearly panicking.

"Sophia!" she called.

Theo's head whipped around, his eyes serious as he made a warning sound. "I'll help her, Elowen, you keep moving."

She felt she should protest, but some part of her recognized that he was more likely to have success, so she just gave a curt nod.

"You can manage?" he pressed.

"I'm fine!" she cried, as another crack rent the air, followed by the sound of rushing water. A small fissure had appeared near the top of the dam. It wasn't in total collapse yet, but it would be at any moment. "And please don't drown!" she called foolishly after Theo's retreating back.

She urged Ochre forward, her attention divided as she tried to watch Theo's progress. He reached Sophia in moments, his calm and steady hand bringing the horse swiftly under control. Elowen breathed a sigh of relief as she saw the two of them swing around in a canter that rapidly became a gallop. Elowen slowed to wait for them. She was fairly certain she was clear of the danger now.

"I've got you, Princess, never fear."

Elowen turned her head, irritation rising in her at the hint of a smirk on Bertrand's face as he seized her reins in a superfluous imitation of Theo's earlier action.

"You don't have me, and you don't need to," she told him crisply, pulling the reins free of his grip. "I'm in no need of assistance."

The words had barely left her mouth when an echoing boom sounded across the area. Elowen instinctively ducked, her hand trembling as she ran it over Ochre's flank. "It's all right, girl," she told the horse soothingly.

Her first thought was that the horse seemed calmer than she was, given the terror rising in her as she watched a wall of water burst from the shattered dam, alarmingly close behind the still-galloping Theo and Sophia.

But a moment later, Ochre gave a sudden, violent start, a whinny of alarm escaping her. Before Elowen knew what was happening, the mare had plunged forward. Ochre had never bolted with Elowen before, and it was all she could do to keep her seat. The horse was clearly in a blind panic, because she wasn't galloping away from the danger, instead bolting alongside the out-of-control torrent of water now engulfing the small plain.

Elowen could hear the screams and cries behind her, but she tuned them out, focusing on getting her steed under control.

"It's all right, Ochre," she called to the horse, pulling firmly and steadily on the reins as she clung on desperately with her knees. "We're all right. Trust me, girl, we can get clear of this."

Her heart was hammering in her chest as Ochre stumbled, the horse's hooves dancing right on the edge of what was becoming a furious river. But Ochre recovered her footing, and Elowen thought the animal was starting to respond when another horse suddenly crashed into Ochre's side, almost crushing Elowen's leg.

"I'm here, Princess!"

Bertrand's shout was extremely unwelcome—Elowen could have screamed with frustration as Ochre was sent back into a panic. Bertrand was thundering alongside her, the terrain doubly dangerous now two horses were galloping down such a narrow space so close to the churning water.

"What are you doing?" she yelled, as a hand seized her arm and started tugging her roughly off her horse. It was hard enough to keep her seat without Bertrand trying to drag her out of it.

"I'll pull you onto my horse!" he called.

He gave another violent tug, which caused Elowen to slide down Ochre's flank, making the horse lurch wildly to the side. Elowen barely managed to stay on, and fear gripped her as Ochre floundered, up to her shins in swirling, sucking water.

She heard Bertrand let out a curse, and dimly saw that a

huge boulder ahead had forced him to peel away and ride around it, further from the water.

Good riddance.

Ochre was valiantly trying to keep her feet, but the horse was moments from being truly swept into the torrent, and Elowen would go with her. There was no way to safely dismount the horse, even if she'd wanted to.

Then, somehow, another hand appeared, grasping Ochre's reins. In the chaos of the torrent, Theo still radiated the same calm as he had before the dam burst. His horse, obedient to his iron hand, was thundering along at the outer edge of the water, past its ankles in the flood. Relief flooded Elowen for a moment, before it was replaced by dread as she braced to once again be hauled from the relative security of her seat.

But Theo didn't seize her arm. He kept his hand on Ochre's reins, maintaining his own seat with incredible grace considering his precarious position. By small degrees, he angled them away from the water, and within moments, Elowen went from the edge of disaster to clear ground, Ochre already starting to slow her frantic pace.

She drew in gasping breaths, her heart showing no sign of slowing to match the horse's gait. Theo said nothing, keeping hold of Ochre's reins as they cantered in a wide arc, giving the horse time for its panic to subside. When at last they slowed and stopped, a long way from where they'd started, he still didn't release the reins.

"Are you all right?" His voice was low and urgent, and Elowen realized he was breathing as hard as she was.

"Yes," she said, the word not coming out steady. "Thanks to you."

Their eyes met, then, abruptly, Theo released the reins, his hand shifting to cover hers instead. It engulfed her smaller hand completely, and she felt her fingers trembling under his firm touch.

"You're all right," he said, a tremor in his voice. "I won't let you fall."

"Fall?"

She blinked, confused by his words and feeling dazed as the enormity of events caught up with her. Two disasters in as many days. And she'd been idiotic enough to get herself embroiled in both of them. Her eyes passed over the devastation the flood had left in its wake, hardly able to take it in.

The sound of thundering hooves met her ears, and the next moment Bertrand came into view, his face red and angry.

"What were you thinking?" he spat at the prince. "Why didn't you get her off the horse to safety?"

"Your attempt to pull her off the horse almost got her killed." If Bertrand's voice was fiery, Theo's was ice.

"And you almost killed Ochre as well," Elowen said indignantly, remembering how the horse had been thrown off course further into the flood when Bertrand had tugged her half down its flank.

"You made a dangerous situation infinitely more so," Theo agreed. "There was no need for any loss of life."

A sneer marred Bertrand's face. "You would risk the princess's life to save a horse? Are you witless?"

Anger rose in Elowen, but before she could voice it, they were engulfed by the rest of their group. Theo's horse pranced away from hers, the absence of the prince's hand leaving her own cold. His guard, the man he'd called Paulson, was gripping the prince's shoulder, searching him for injury as her own and Patrick's guards surrounded Elowen.

They were both shepherded back toward the road that had brought them to the dam, although they had to go a long way around in order to avoid the flood. Elowen looked in vain for

Theo—he seemed always to be blocked from her view by a myriad of overprotective riders. Sophia was among them, her face white and her eyes anxious as she stayed close to Elowen.

"I'm fine, Sophia," Elowen assured her. Her eyes widened as she remembered something. "The town!" She twisted in her saddle, but she didn't have a good view of the hamlet, which must have been hit hard by the flood.

"It was evacuated in time," Sophia told her softly, rubbing her hands along her arms in an anxious gesture. "Simeon told me. The homes will have been destroyed, but no one died."

"Simeon?" Elowen repeated, bewildered.

Sophia nodded. "He appeared just after the dam burst. I don't know where he came from. He didn't give me a straight answer."

"Did you say Simeon?" Bertrand pulled up beside his sister, his brow still stormy from his argument. "He's decided to reappear, has he?"

"He's helping the displaced townsfolk," Sophia told him shortly. "Someone told him that we'd come, so after the dam burst, he came to check that we were all right. He was...he was worried." Her voice was unsteady by the end, but Bertrand gave no sign of noticing her distress.

"No doubt," he said darkly. "Worried about the repercussions of his desertion, most likely. I'll deal with him later." He ran a hand through his hair, casting agitated eyes over the destruction that would have such serious repercussions for his family's holdings.

Elowen turned away, not wanting to deal with Bertrand. The initial shock of her second near miss had worn off, and her mind was also full of all the awful implications of the dam's failure. The region would be hit hard in a number of ways. The displaced residents of the hamlet in the dam's direct path were only the beginning.

The immediate aftermath of the flood was chaos, but in spite of the seriousness of the situation, Elowen knew they couldn't stay to help the recovery effort. She was unsurprised when Patrick gave the order to his guards to prepare to return to Toledda.

"I feel bad to leave them in this state," Elowen said.

He gave her a look that made her wince internally. "As do I. And if you weren't present, Elowen, I would likely be able to stay and assist. But I need to see you safely back to the capital as soon as possible. I haven't forgotten that your betrothal celebrations start in the morning, even if you have."

"Believe me, I haven't," she said, her own voice a little crisp.

"If we're returning, we should leave promptly." Bertrand inserted himself into the conversation, as usual.

"You're coming back with us?" Elowen demanded, momentarily forgetting in her surprise that she'd decided to ignore him. Her eyes passed from him to his father, who was deep in conversation with a small knot of men from the hamlet. "But this is part of your father's lands. I thought for certain you would be needed here."

"You would think so, but my father has insisted that Sophia and I return to the capital," he said.

His voice was curt, in the way she usually heard him direct toward his sister. Seeming to remember to whom he was speaking, he took a breath. When he spoke again, it was with a return of his usual, unwelcome attempt at charm.

"Not even such dire circumstances as this would keep me from your betrothal celebrations, Princess." His eyes flicked toward Theo, his expression disdainful. "Some of us are willing to give due priority to you, rather than to every man and beast that crosses our path."

The prince, who had dismounted and was standing nearby in conversation with his guard, gave no sign of having heard him. But Elowen had already learned to recognize that it was not a reliable indication. Theo was very capable of keeping his reaction to rudeness inside.

Losing patience with the viscount, Elowen walked Ochre away from him. Maybe she should have more sympathy for him, given how closely he was connected with the crisis, but it was hard to find any. Her movements were jerky as she ran a hand over Ochre's neck, but she stilled when Theo appeared at her knee.

"Bertrand is wrong," she said abruptly, not waiting for him to speak. "I'm grateful to you for saving my horse as well as me."

Theo gave a tight nod. "Horses don't deserve to die for humans' stupidity."

She flushed. "You're right. It was stupid of me to end up in the path of danger for the second time in—"

"No." The word came out so harshly, Elowen instinctively recoiled. Theo seemed to see it, because he tried to soften his tone. "You misunderstand," he said, still more gruff than gentle. "It's not your stupidity I was referring to. The incident wasn't your fault at all."

She still couldn't quite meet his eyes, fiddling with the horn of Ochre's saddle. "That's generous of you, after my shameful inability to control my own horse. I don't understand what made her bolt like that, but I'm disappointed in myself." She dared to sneak a look at him. "A feeling we all have to deal with, I suppose."

Something sparked in his eyes at her words, and a frown creased his brow.

"Elowen, you said something before about princes and disappointment. I hope you didn't misunderstand me to be saying I was disappointed with my current situation."

"Disappointed with your current situation? That's not very chivalrous, Your Highness."

Bertrand's voice carried gratingly across the group as he pulled his horse alongside Elowen's. She could have screamed at him. Why wouldn't he just go away?

Theo also seemed to have reached a limit with the impertinent viscount, his voice once again icy.

"I believe this conversation is private."

"Then let me speak more privately." Bertrand, looming over the foreign prince from his mounted position, dropped his own voice. "If anyone has cause to be disappointed, it's Princess Elowen. Those of us who know her realize how far you are from what she needs." He sent a pitying look at Elowen. "Not quite a mysterious stranger with a broken heart only you can mend, or a romantic adventurer who writes odes to your sparkling eyes, is he? I don't recall dull and stern being on your list of desirable virtues in a man."

Elowen's breath caught in her throat, heat rushing all the way up her face. She was horrified not just because of Bertrand's open hostility, but because she recognized his words. Foolish as they sounded, those were true examples of girlish daydreams she'd entertained—giggled over and built imaginary lives around, in her younger years. She'd certainly never mentioned anything of that nature to Bertrand, of course. But she and Sophia had whispered about such dreams. The sense of betrayal by her friend cut deepest of all.

Perhaps not, actually. Theo's expression cut even deeper, his lip curling in an expression that was undeniably derisive. He had the good manners not to say his thoughts aloud, however, contenting himself with a curt retort to Bertrand.

"Imagine my distress to learn that I don't live up to your expectations, Lord Bertrand."

With the words, he turned away, leaving Elowen more miserable and mortified than she'd ever been in her life.

"Princess," Bertrand started, no hint of apology in his indulgent tone.

"Do not speak to me," Elowen said, barely able to look at him. "How dare you? I have nothing to say to you."

Furiously, she pulled on Ochre's reins, plunging blindly toward the road after the first few members of the party, who'd already departed.

The ride home was a nightmare. For once, Bertrand took the hint and stayed away, and she rode alone. She avoided Theo out of mortification, Patrick out of habit, and Sophia out of hurt. And yet, she couldn't seem to stop herself from watching Theo, noticing every change in his posture, and imagining each one to be fueled by scornful thoughts about her foolishness.

Her observation of him was the only reason she noted the mill when they passed it again. She was momentarily distracted from her misery by the intent way Theo studied the structure. Following his gaze, she realized why it had caught his attention. The river must not have been connected to the dam, because it continued to flow unchanged, and the wooden wheel still turned. But the man on duty beside it was no longer in a posture of strained focus as if manipulating magic. In fact, both of the men they'd previously seen were standing by the river, looking lost and confused as they examined the structure and peered into the water.

Elowen didn't know the details, but she wasn't blind. Something wasn't right with the magic, just as Simeon had said near the watchtower the day before. Just as the head of the Craftsmen's Guild had said to her father.

Her memory felt its way uncertainly back over the chaos of the flood. She'd been too distracted by Ochre's panic to recognize it in the moment, but she realized in retrospect that something had been conspicuously missing. She'd told the truth when she said to Theo that learning to sense magic had never been part of her approved education. But she'd had other education that her family knew nothing about. She was by no means an expert, but she had enough awareness to be able to recognize the presence of Dust when it was released by significant movement.

The dam's collapse had been the biggest source of movement she'd ever witnessed. And she couldn't find in her memory any rush of magic, any notable movement of Dust through the environment.

Something was definitely wrong.

She felt a thrill of fear as another layer of discomfort was added to the turmoil of her mind. Whatever it was, she had a feeling it was only going to get worse.

SIX

Theo

Theo stood before the looking glass in his room, waiting without much patience as a servant adjusted the stiff collar of his jacket. He'd never been enthusiastic about the betrothal celebrations, and they felt doubly ridiculous after the events of the previous day. Anyone with sense would prefer to focus on the catastrophic effects of the dam failure. Instead, they were all forced to stay in the capital and take part in a competition that was purely symbolic, and frankly a waste of everyone's time.

Princess Elowen's betrothal had already been decided—her parents had committed their daughter and their kingdom to the alliance. Why did he have to pretend to compete for it?

In his reflection, he saw his scowl darken. Even without the tournament, the over-confident viscount seemed determined to provoke Theo into competing for Elowen's attention and favor.

He would find himself disappointed in that endeavor. Theo had no intention of making either himself or Siqual ridiculous in order to prove something to an imbecile like Lord Bertrand.

"Your Highness." He turned to see Paulson sliding into the suite, looking alert as always.

"Paulson, good." Theo dismissed the servant with a wave of his hand, giving the guard his full attention. "Thank you for coming so promptly. I'm expected momentarily, but I first wanted to speak with you about the dam."

Paulson nodded. "Yes, Your Highness. There wasn't much chance yesterday, was there?"

Theo grunted at the hinted reference to the chaos that had engulfed the castle on their return the evening before. He shifted away from the mirror, gesturing for Paulson to precede him into the receiving room of his suite as he smoothed out the cuffs of his jacket.

He felt a twinge of guilt at the memory of the look on the monarchs' faces when they learned that for the second day in a row, their only daughter had slipped from the city without their knowledge, and then nearly lost her life in a freak accident.

It was almost too astonishing a coincidence to be credible, he reflected. One unlucky accident, yes. But two, and in such quick succession?

The thought rubbed uncomfortably at his mind, but it made no difference to his guilt. Whether or not the incidents were truly unrelated, he shouldn't have gone along with Elowen's plan when she clearly wasn't supposed to leave the capital.

Her face flashed before his sight, blue eyes wide and terrified but posture determined as her hair tangled around her neck and her horse plunged wildly on the edge of a dangerous torrent.

Theo strode beside Paulson, trying to clear his thoughts as curtly as he cleared his throat.

"What can you tell me about the breach at the dam?" he

asked. "What did you sense, magically speaking? Something was off, am I right?"

"You are, Your Highness," Paulson acknowledged. "I couldn't figure out what I was feeling at all. The magic was acting strangely."

"How so?"

"The water that burst from the dam generated a huge amount of movement." Paulson paused, then added dryly, "As we all saw. I should have felt a corresponding torrent of Dust."

"You didn't feel any Dust stirring up?" Theo demanded.

Paulson shook his head. "No, I felt magic being released. It was just nowhere near the volume I would have expected from such a dramatic movement. The Dust should have been all tangled up with the water, weaving through every current, but it felt like no more than a steady rain. That's barely a fraction of what such a violent movement should have caused." He bowed his head. "That's why I was unable to use magic to assist in the crisis with Her Highness, for which I'm deeply sorry."

Theo waved him off. "You have no need to apologize, Paulson, it wasn't you who endangered Princess Elowen."

Irritation spiked through him as he remembered Lord Bertrand's heavy-handed and foolish behavior. It had been clear to him from the outset that Elowen had an excellent seat on her horse, and he'd seen that she was handling the mare's panic skillfully. He had no doubt that if not for the viscount's interference, she would have been able to get herself and her horse to safety without assistance. If the idea hadn't been absurd, he would have suspected Lord Bertrand of spooking her horse on purpose to give himself an excuse to rescue her.

But he was becoming distracted from the point.

"Do you think someone else harnessed the magic?" he asked. "Perhaps more than one person? There were plenty of onlookers."

"I don't think so, Your Highness," Paulson replied. "No individual would be capable of taking hold of that volume of magic at once, let alone wrestling it into an enchantment. And doing so in a group would require planning and coordination, which I think unlikely in this instance. And even if I'm wrong, and some people did harness the magic, that shouldn't have prevented me from sensing it. The opposite, in fact. I would have sensed it being released by the movement of the water, and then also sensed the second release when it was manipulated into an enchantment."

"Yes, of course." Theo ran a hand absently along his jaw.

They said no more, Paulson falling respectfully behind as Theo increased his pace. It would be the height of rudeness to be late for the breakfast that would formally mark the beginning of the betrothal celebrations.

The impending ceremony didn't occupy his mind as he walked, however. He was too troubled by the previous day's events.

His thoughts flew to the servant Elowen had mentioned. Simeon. Elowen had said something about him having considerable skill in magic craft. And apparently he'd been present when the dam burst. Maybe he'd felt something Paulson hadn't. It would be worth finding out. He was starting to suspect that King Ronan was keeping some information from him, and he wanted to know what Siqual was getting itself into with this alliance. It might prove challenging, however, to question a servant of Lord Bertrand's family without creating even more ill will than already existed.

Thoughts of Lord Bertrand sent Theo's mind back to the viscount's pathetic and humiliating display after the flood. He'd been trying not to dwell on it—he knew he shouldn't give the viscount what he wanted by letting his words discomfit him—but it was hard to banish the bitter taste on his tongue whenever he thought about it. The fact that he didn't live up to Elowen's ideals for her husband was simply an unfortunate reality of impersonal, political marriages. The fact that she'd apparently spent her youth confiding in Lord Bertrand as to what she wanted in a man was harder to swallow, for some reason. Was the viscount's overconfident, smug manner some attempt to imitate one of her daydreams? It did her imagination no credit, if so.

If she hoped he would play the role of lovelorn poet, or wayward rogue ready to be reformed by her ministrations, she would be disappointed.

Xavier would probably be a more acceptable suitor to her. The thought flashed across Theo's mind, surprising him with the sharpness of the pain it left in its wake.

He banished the topic from his mind as he strode into the large, formal dining hall. Everyone else around him might behave foolishly if they chose. He knew his duty. He was there to complete a marriage alliance for the benefit of his kingdom, and he would do so while upholding Siqual's dignity.

The commencement breakfast wasn't being held in the dining hall he'd previously eaten in. This new room was three times the size, and it appeared that the whole court had gathered for the affair. Checking just through the doorway, Theo noticed a series of wooden cranks lining one wall, each attached to a mill-like wheel. Most of them were being operated by servants, and as Theo watched, he saw that as the servants turned the cranks, what appeared to be wooden balls were falling in a constantly cycling cascade within each wheel. There was no mistaking the look of intense focus on the servants' faces. They were manipulating magic.

Theo glanced back, to where Paulson had entered behind him.

"Do you think the purpose of those mills is simply to produce Dust?" he asked his guard quietly.

Paulson nodded, his gaze fascinated as he took in the line of miniature mills. "Definitely, Your Highness. I can sense the manipulated magic."

The magic wasn't visible, of course, but Theo's eyes followed an imaginary stream toward the tables, noting the sparkling silverware and the steam rising from uncovered platters of food.

"I see they've lined the wheels with wool on the inside to muffle the sound," Paulson commented. "It would also absorb some of the Dust, so they'd produce more magic without it, but the noise would likely be too great an inconvenience." He gave his head a small shake. "It's a shame magic can't be stored for later use. Think how convenient it would be. The servants could prepare magic in the servants' hall overnight and have it ready to go in the morning."

"Yes, I suppose so," Theo agreed absently, scanning the room for a sign of Elowen. She wasn't present. "Although if we had that capacity, menial tasks wouldn't be its most likely use. The potential power that could be accumulated that way would require careful regulation to make sure it didn't become a dangerous weapon in the hands of the unscrupulous. What do you think they're using this magic for?"

"It seems to be multiple things, Your Highness. I notice that it's warm in here, but there are no fires. Also, there seems to be a light layer of magic sweeping constantly over the food, the way someone might fan away flies. And I sense some moving through the guests. Possibly some kind of security check. My captain will be very interested in an account, for use in training us craftsmen-guards."

"Well," said Theo, "once the alliance is formalized, no doubt we can benefit from these innovations as well."

"Yes, Your Highness." Paulson inclined his head respectfully before moving to join the other on-duty guards along one wall.

Theo had just reached his seat when the royal family entered. His eyes flew immediately to Elowen, and although her eyes were cast down, he could tell from the way her cheeks reddened that he'd almost caught her in the act of watching him. He'd once again been given a seat next to her, but he doubted it would do him much good. The awkwardness between them after the previous day was tangible.

"Good morning, Elowen," he said, his voice determinedly even and pleasant. "Today is a big day for us all, I take it."

"I suppose so." She didn't meet his eye.

To their mutual relief, the exchange ended as a member of the court welcomed the guests and announced that he had been given the role of master of events for the tournament. The applause following mention of the tournament was particularly riotous from the young people, Theo noted. Everywhere he looked, he saw excited faces, although a handful of the more lined ones looked somber and anxious. Clearly not everyone had forgotten about the burst dam and its likely impacts.

"Given we haven't held a betrothal tournament for over twenty years, we will all need a reminder of the format," the nobleman continued. "The tournament will last six days and will include the following events: archery, jousting, the maze, hand-to-hand without weapons, and, the main event, weapons combat. All members of His Majesty's court and visiting members from the courts of our allies will have the opportunity to pit their skill against their fellows."

A cheer went up from a group of young men seated on the other side of the room. The master of events smiled indulgently before continuing.

"And for his common subjects, His Majesty will host running races, lumber-felling, hay baling, pig races, and of course the craftsmen's competition to showcase the magical abilities of our kingdom."

Theo tilted his head to the side, interested. If the craftsmen's competition was part of the commoners' events, clearly Torrens was no more inclined than Siqual to encourage nobles to pursue magic craft.

Movement brought his glance down the table, to where a young nobleman was trying to catch Elowen's eye, his chest puffed out in what Theo took to be a silent declaration of his intent to fight for her favor. His posture was familiar from all the times Theo had seen similar attempts to impress his sister Miriam. Theo wasn't sure whether to be irritated or amused as the young nobleman finally succeeded in getting Elowen's attention and crossed an arm over his heart. Amusement won as the clumsy gesture resulted in his elbow knocking a goblet of ale. As the cup teetered on the edge of the table, Theo braced for a fall. But the unbalanced moment stretched out impossibly, long enough for the knight to realize and to hastily snatch the cup to safety.

Theo's eyes moved to the servant standing closest, working a hand crank and concentrating hard on that stretch of table. Just how many everyday tasks were being enhanced by Dust in King Ronan's castle?

"After which," the master of events was continuing, "the tournament's crowning event will be the victor's feast." The answering cheer was even louder than the last, probably because those with no interest in actually competing could still get behind the prospect of a castle-funded feast. As he waited for the noise to die down, the master of events bent into a half bow in Theo and Elowen's direction. "At which we will celebrate the princess's betrothal."

Theo inclined his head in recognition of the gesture, although he noted that his name hadn't actually been mentioned. It would probably ruin the image, however artificial, of a tournament to win the princess's hand. Theo's eyes strayed to Elowen's face, noting that she looked uncomfortable. Unease trickled over him. She'd assured him Torrens was committed to the alliance. So why didn't it feel that way?

Once everyone had been invited to eat, the nobleman in charge of the tournament moved discreetly to Theo's side.

"Your Highness," he said, after tediously formal introductions, "are there any questions you wish to ask regarding your role in the tournament?"

Theo fought to keep his tone pleasant instead of rueful. "I believe I understand," he said. "I'm invited to compete in any of the events I choose, to whatever level I can...honorably perform."

"That's right, Your Highness." The man dipped his head in approval. "And when you are ready to do so, you can withdraw with all honor so as to let the court enjoy their tournament."

"I wouldn't wish to outshine anyone," Theo said with a touch of humor that he doubted the other man could hear. He supposed that if the tournament was important for the sake of tradition, they needed some way to avoid the embarrassment of the politically chosen suitor being bested by someone—potentially everyone—else.

"Very gracious of you, Your Highness," the master of events said without a hint of irony. "It is customary for the princess's intended to compete in the first round of at least the archery and the weapons combat. Rest assured you will be judiciously matched in these events."

Meaning he would be pitted against someone fairly useless whom he could easily best. It was a small blow to his pride, but he would live.

The master of events took his leave, and Theo turned in time to see Elowen's lip curl slightly. He raised an eyebrow.

"You disapprove?"

Elowen lifted a porridge-laden spoon to her mouth. "I didn't say that."

"You think I should be required to compete in all of the events through to the end?" Theo pressed.

"No, of course not."

The answer was unconvincing, and Theo turned to more fully face her.

"Perhaps you would prefer to be bound to abide by the tournament's true result?" he said, a sharp edge to his voice. "Or would it bring you pleasure to have your betrothed proved unworthy by his challengers?"

"No," said Elowen, her irritation clear in the lift of her chin and the arch of her neck. "I think the whole charade should be dispensed with. It hasn't been used as an actual decider for generations. I can't comprehend why it's still considered a necessary attachment to the betrothal of a princess."

"Well, I can't help you with making sense of your own kingdom's traditions." Seeing the thin line of Elowen's lips, Theo reined in his annoyance. He didn't want to argue with her. He wanted to be kind. And it wasn't kind to forget how awkward all this must be for the princess. "But if it makes you feel better," he said, his voice more amicable, "Siqual has plenty of traditions that don't hold up to much intelligent scrutiny. We still like to follow them, out of sentiment, I suppose."

"I wouldn't have suspected you of being prone to sentiment," Elowen said, clearly still irked with him.

Maybe not, Theo thought, fighting his own annoyance. But good manners would have to be sufficient in place of the emotional volatility she apparently expected from him.

"I understand your feelings," he said with cool politeness. "I also am not excited about the idea of having to engage in a meaningless competition for your hand when the matter is already settled."

Elowen said nothing, but judging by the stiffness of her posture, she wasn't softened by his words. Abandoning the attempt to say the right thing, Theo turned his focus to more important matters.

"Did I understand the master of events correctly that at the end of this tournament, our betrothal will be formally sealed?"

"That's correct," Elowen said.

Finally, a straight answer. "And is that when our wedding date will be set?"

Elowen didn't reply, too focused on drinking the cold juice a servant had just poured into her chalice. When she was finished, she rose, addressing Theo as if he hadn't spoken.

"Excuse me. I have preparations to make before the first event."

She swept from the room, leaving Theo to watch her retreat with a frown creasing his forehead. What wasn't she telling him?

Prince Patrick appeared before he could get too lost in his thoughts, inviting Theo to accompany him to the tournament field. The area that had been prepared was just outside the city wall, at the point closest to the castle and the noblemen's district that surrounded it. In no more than ten minutes, the two princes had left the city and were approaching a small city of large tents interspersed between marked fields and training yards. On the far side of the fields, Theo could just catch a glimpse of a staggering number of hay bales collected for a purpose he didn't yet know.

He noticed as he walked, responding politely to Prince Patrick's somewhat tedious conversation, that Dust swirled faintly around them at all times. A glance to the side showed that at least one of the prince's guards was surreptitiously swinging a pendulum with a leather thong attached to it, and wore a look of intense concentration. Theo had thought his kingdom progressive with the employment of a magically trained bodyguard for his sister, Princess Miriam. But perhaps he'd been wrong. Was the use of magically trained guards in Torrens inspired by the recent attack on Miriam, or had Siqual been further behind than they realized?

There were a number of temporary stands erected for spectators at different points of the vast tournament fields. Judging by the crowd beginning to gather in the nearest one, the first event—a foot race for commoners—would be held on the circular dirt track that had been cleared just within the festival area.

"The first day is mainly commoner events," Prince Patrick was explaining with the serious air that seemed habitual for him. "They require less organization. But all the court events are now open for registration, so most of the court will be here today, signing up for their chosen events."

He inclined his head, and Theo followed the direction to see two notaries sitting behind a large table. The king's steward hovered watchfully behind them, and a line of men dressed in the garb of noblemen was forming on the table's other side. The younger ones were jostling and laughing together, elated with all the excitement.

"The notaries will check their lineage documentation," Prince Patrick explained. "But naturally your entitlement to compete has already been approved by my father directly, so please enlist at your convenience."

"Thank you," Theo said. "I'll do so as soon as I've reviewed the schedule of events."

Prince Patrick dipped punctiliously into a half bow, then took his leave. Theo watched him go with private relief. He saw no malice in the other prince, but he was thankful that Elowen wasn't as solemn. Honestly, the Torrenese people had some gall to gossip about Theo's stiffness given the manner of their own crown prince. He felt a flash of sadness at the thought of Elowen's words about her brother, both for her sake and Patrick's. Much as Theo had learned from a young age that it was best not to let emotion enter into any part of his duty, at least he could be natural with his siblings in private. He would be ashamed to show as little warmth to Miriam as Elowen received from her brother. And as for Xavier...well, Theo usually wanted to push him off a galloping horse, but somehow that didn't make him any less fond of the infuriating heir to their father's throne.

Paulson shadowed him as he moved through the crowd, but he had no need of the guard's magic craft to clear his path. Space opened all around him as he moved, many of the eyes on him showing as much suspicion as curiosity. Theo wasn't surprised. It would be unrealistic to think that the proposed alliance between Torrens and Siqual would wipe away all the tension of the previous period, when all the other kingdoms of the Peninsula had suspected Torrens of involvement in the spate of unexplained attacks within their borders.

Theo took his time exploring the tournament fields, only returning to examine the lists of events once the foot races had started and the crowd around the tables had dissipated. As he approached, he saw two figures standing off to the side behind the table, and increased his pace. The king was unmistakable both from his bearing and the presence of his guards. No one hindered Theo as he also moved behind the tables, and he was able to catch the end of the conversation between the king and a man Theo now recognized as the Duke of Nirocha.

"That sounds promising, Your Grace," King Ronan was saying. "Continue that line of inquiry. I want the highest priority given to this investigation."

"Of course, Your Majesty." The duke bent his upper body. "I'm equally eager for answers."

"I can imagine," the king said. "I regret the impact this dam failure will have on your holdings."

"Indeed, Your Majesty." The duke's voice was heavy.

"As devastating as it is for the farmland, it's fortunate that the mining and orchard regions weren't affected. I trust that with judicious management, the export income will help bolster the losses from the farms."

There was a slight pause before the duke replied. "Indeed, Your Majesty."

The words were the same as before, but the tone was more guarded, something in the duke's voice causing Theo to surreptitiously search his face. There was nothing to see. His scrutiny drew the other man's attention, however, and a moment later the king turned and noticed his presence as well.

"Prince Theodore," King Ronan said pleasantly. "Have you had opportunity to explore the tournament?"

"Yes, Your Majesty," Theo said. "I was about to add my name for the main events."

"Excellent," the king said. He looked between the prince and the duke. "You've met our royal guest, I believe, Your Grace?"

"I've had that honor." The duke bowed again, his manner pleasant now, if still a little solemn. "I regret that I was prevented from much conversation with you at the welcome dinner, Your Highness, and that events on my land have detained me since."

"Not at all, Your Grace, naturally you have other matters on your mind. Please accept my sympathy for the recent disaster, and be assured of my assistance if there's any way in which I can help."

"You're very gracious, Your Highness," the duke said, with

another bow. His natural and courteous manner made Theo wonder how his son could have failed so dismally to learn from his father. The duke turned to the king, bowing again. "With your permission, Your Majesty..."

"Yes, you should continue your inquiries immediately," King Ronan agreed, dismissing the duke with a nod.

King Ronan's court manners were also impeccable, but Theo could nevertheless see the concern on the older man's brow as he watched the duke leave. Deciding to be frank, he turned to his future father-in-law.

"Were you discussing the dam rupture?" he asked.

The king gave the smallest of sighs as he nodded. "We were."

"And the strange behavior of the magic when it happened?" Theo pressed boldly.

The king's gaze traveled quickly to Theo's face.

Theo smiled apologetically. "My guard sensed something amiss at the time, Your Majesty. And even I could observe that the magical current at the mill on the river wasn't behaving the same on our return as on our outward journey. If we noticed, I couldn't imagine you were unaware."

"I am aware," King Ronan said soberly. "But of what exactly, no one seems to know. Some concerns have been raised before now by our Craftsmen's Guild. The duke is undertaking an investigation at my instruction."

"He must feel a particular interest, given the impact of this disaster on his holdings."

The king shook his head. "His appointment to the task is unrelated to that. The duchy of Nirocha has been a steady and loyal subject of the crown for as long as there's been one, and there's no one I'd trust more to get to the bottom of this than the duke. Already he's pursuing some hopeful lines of inquiry."

"That's excellent news, Your Majesty," Theo said. "I would

love to be of service in the investigation. Naturally, as your ally, Siqual wishes to provide whatever support we can in ensuring the safety and prosperity of your lands."

"I am grateful," King Ronan said. Whatever his words, he didn't look excited about the idea of the foreign prince involving himself in the investigation.

"There's another matter, Your Majesty," Theo said, sensing it was time to change the topic. "It seems the information I received regarding wedding plans prior to my arrival may not have been accurate. I'd thought perhaps the wedding date would be set at the conclusion of the tournament, but Princess Elowen seemed reluctant to confirm that when I asked her."

"Don't worry yourself with those details, Prince Theodore," the king said in a paternal fashion. "Just enjoy the tournament, and all the celebrations in your honor. The wedding will come around quickly enough, we can discuss all those details after the tournament is complete."

Theo frowned, unsatisfied. The king had dodged the question as neatly as his daughter had done. But why? The king was already moving smoothly away, however, so there was nothing for Theo to do but continue on his errand to sign up for his chosen events.

He'd just finished submitting his name for the archery, the maze race, and the weapons combat, when a musical voice hailed him.

"You've signed up for one more than is required of you. Industrious."

Theo turned to see Elowen watching him.

"It seems you'll have the dubious pleasure of watching me compete for your hand after all, Princess."

She said nothing for a long moment, her face hard to read as she studied his. "Why the extra event?" she asked at last.

Theo shrugged. "I thought I'd try the maze race as well. It

sounds interesting—the description promises problem-solving challenges beyond simply navigating the maze. It seems a fitting test, since for someone in our position, problem-solving abilities are often more useful than physical strength."

She considered his words, and he felt impatient with himself for wondering if she was impressed by his sense. Why was he trying to impress her? They were already betrothed, by promise if not formally. He had no need to win her approval.

"I notice you didn't sign up for the jousting," Elowen said. "I had the impression you enjoyed horseback riding, and you certainly have an excellent seat."

"Thank you." Theo bowed, a hint of irony in the formal gesture. "I've always loved horses, it's true. Honestly, that's what puts me off jousting. I've seen too many horses injured in what seems to me a pointless event. Not that I mean any offense," he added.

Again Elowen said nothing, and again her eyes studied him with a clarity of sight that threatened his steady front. She seemed to be trying to measure him with her gaze and, if he was any judge, struggling to do it to her satisfaction.

Theo didn't know what to feel about that.

SEVEN

Elowen

E lowen settled back into her seat in the special section of the stands dedicated for her use. The public luncheon to mark the first day of the tournament was over, and the afternoon events were about to begin. She watched the archers in the first group lining up, each sporting a beautifully carved wooden bow likely worth more than most of the morning's competitors made in a year. She fully expected the court competitions to be tedious compared to the fun and chaos of the commoners' events. The pig races she was especially looking forward to.

Her eyes found Theo in the line, his figure upright and calm, showing no hint of either nerves or excitement, unlike many of his fellows. She noticed that a lot of the other competitors appeared to be young and a little awed.

"Do you know if His Highness is skilled in archery?"

Elowen took a moment before responding, hating the coldness that crept over her. She'd arranged ahead of time for her friend to accompany her, afraid of being a spectacle all alone in her box whenever her family members had other duties. But after the events at the dam, she wasn't deriving much comfort from Sophia's presence.

"I don't," she said. "But I suppose we're about to find out."

Her eyes glazed over as the first archer took aim at the target, her interest not captured by the near-stranger who was the son of some minor noble. She wasn't sure what to make of Theo. He was so cool and inexpressive most of the time. But when she'd been in danger in that flood, she'd seen real warmth and emotion, in spite of how calm he'd remained.

And she'd certainly seen emotion when Bertrand had so successfully humiliated her in front of Theo. Better not to dwell on that.

Was his cold manner a mask, covering a warm heart in some misguided attempt to protect his pride? No, she shouldn't assume him to be anything more than what he showed himself to be. If he was trying to present a stoic, unemotional front, surely he wouldn't admit to refraining from the jousting out of sympathy for the horses. She was no stranger to the type of bravado the younger members of her father's court sometimes assumed in their attempts to impress her. And it couldn't be further removed from the calm, unashamed way Theo had owned to an attitude of gentleness and protectiveness toward animals. Was he warm but acting stiff? Cold but acting gentle? Depressing new thought—warm toward only horses, just not her?

She was back where she started, unable to figure him out.

"He's next," Sophia commented, pulling Elowen from her thoughts.

Her eyes followed Theo as he stepped up and took his mark. She was too far away for a good view, but she could imagine the muscles in his arms straining as he pulled back the bowstring.

Thud.

His arrow found its mark, near the center of the bullseye.

Elowen clapped politely along with the crowd. He'd clearly been trained in archery, as he seemed to have good form, but she didn't see any sign of elite skill. To be fair, he didn't need it in this round. Even with the target so close, many of the others missed it altogether, or only reached the outer ring.

"I think he'll win this round," Sophia said, her voice encouraging.

"Probably," Elowen agreed. She could feel her friend looking at her uncertainly, and she hurried on. "How are things back at your family's estate? Your parents must be distressed."

"We're all distressed," Sophia said heavily, and she certainly looked it. Her eyes roamed over the crowd, aimless and anxious. "Many families are suffering, and it will get worse before it gets better. We won't be able to resolve everyone's situation."

"The crown will help," Elowen said quickly.

"I know." Sophia's smile was grateful. "It's just...well, we're all feeling the tension."

She didn't seem eager to elaborate, and Elowen's forehead creased in a frown. But before she could press for answers, Sophia redirected the conversation.

"Not many made it through to the next target," she commented. "I think Prince Theo will be shooting again soon."

"Yes." Elowen saw that she was right. Theo was behind only one other archer, flexing his bow experimentally as he waited for his turn on the longer target.

"How are you feeling about all of..." Sophia waved her hand vaguely toward Theo. "That?"

Elowen shrugged. "Fine."

She could feel her friend's confusion at the non-answer.

"Do you have much of a sense of what he's like? He's not very expressive, is he?"

"It's too soon for me to know him well enough to comment on what he's like," Elowen said.

"But do you like him?" Sophia pressed. "So far, I mean?"

Elowen shrugged. "That's a meaningless question, isn't it?"

"I don't think it's meaningless whether you like your future husband," Sophia said, with a flash of spirit. "You really don't feel like you know anything about him?"

"I know that all he wants to talk about is setting the wedding date," Elowen said shortly, irritation flaring in her again regarding the stilted conversation over breakfast.

"So…" Sophia spoke carefully, wary of her friend's bad mood. "So you're *not* glad that he's eager to marry you?"

"It has nothing to do with him being eager to marry me," Elowen said. "He just wants to be done with all the fuss and go home."

"And you…don't want that?" Sophia asked.

Annoyed with her own chaotic emotions, Elowen turned to face her friend. "To be blunt, Sophia, I don't want to talk to you about matters of the heart. I'm not sure I can trust that what I say won't make it back to your brother."

Sophia's eyes widened in shock, guilt flashing momentarily across her face before confusion replaced it.

"What…what do you mean?"

"Yesterday," Elowen said tartly, "Bertrand threw in my face a very specific account of some of the sillier daydreams we used to joke about when we were younger. I'd half forgotten the wild stories we used to construct, about the romantic men who would one day sweep us off our feet. But he was kind enough to remind me in detail, and he did it in front of Prince Theodore. It was mortifying."

"Elowen, I'm so sorry."

Sophia sounded genuinely tearful, but Elowen couldn't

bring herself to look at her friend this time. She was still stiff with the tension of finally getting the reproach off her chest.

"I...I should never have repeated any of that to Bertrand, I know," Sophia tried again. "But he asked me about your ideal man, and..."

She trailed off, so Elowen finished the sentence, her tone bitter and a little scathing.

"And no one ever says no to Bertrand."

"It's not like that," Sophia insisted. "He asked because he cares about you, and...and he's worried that you won't be happy in Siqual, truly."

Elowen just shook her head, in no mood for her friend's willful blindness when it came to her brother.

"I wanted to help him," Sophia insisted. "He's my brother, and I—"

"Never mind," Elowen cut her off. "I'd rather not discuss it further."

They sat in painful silence for several minutes, while Theo performed very creditably in the second round of archery. A number of the other competitors looked around after each shot, to see if the princess for whom the tournament was being held was watching, and if she approved of their performance. She greeted these silent tributes with a wave or a smile.

Theo didn't look around at her once.

After his third attempt, Elowen was sure he was going to come out in first place. But of course he waited on the field with the rest of those competing, waiting for the remaining challengers to take their last shots.

On the other side of the large field, another group was simultaneously undertaking the same archery event. The winners of that event would face the winners of Theo's event in the following round on a different day. Elowen tried not to watch the other group, Bertrand's lithe figure too infuriating even from a distance. They were finishing up a little ahead of Theo's group, and she could see the archers filing from the field.

Refusing to let the meddling viscount poison her friendships as well as her courtship, she averted her eyes and forced a cheerful tone for Sophia.

"Come on," she said. "It's almost done, let's get down from the stands before the stampede starts."

Sophia obediently followed her, the two of them picking their way down the makeshift steps.

"Archery is all very well," Elowen commented, "but not nearly as interesting as magic. I'm looking forward to watching the craftsmen's competition."

"Yes." Sophia's voice was faint and unhappy. "So am I."

"Do you know if Simeon plans to compete?" Elowen asked.

"No, I'm sure he won't," Sophia said, shaking her head.

"That's a shame, I think he'd have a real chance." They'd reached the grass, and Elowen glanced around to make sure no one could hear as she lowered her voice. "How do you think we'd do? Did you know that unlike the court events, the commoners' events allow women to enter? Imagine if you and I competed. I'm not saying we'd be amazing, but we might get through the first round."

"But we're not commoners," Sophia said, alarmed.

"True," Elowen acknowledged, still forcing a falsely pleasant voice. "Maybe we should instead use magic in the court events, to secretly help our favorites win."

"Elowen, please don't."

Sophia's anxiety made Elowen turn and properly look at her for the first time since she'd scolded her.

"Sophia, I'm obviously joking. What's going on with you? I know you've never been a big risk-taker, but when did you become *this* fearful about getting in trouble?"

Sophia twisted her hands in her skirt, her expression troubled. "I think I've been careless in the past," she confessed. "I'm realizing much later in life than I should have that when I make mistakes, it impacts others as well as myself."

"What do you mean?" Elowen demanded, sure her friend was speaking of something specific. She took Sophia's arm and drew her down onto an empty stretch of bench on the bottom row of the stands, thoughts of leaving before the crowd forgotten.

It was evident that Sophia didn't want to answer, and a moment later her face lit in recognition as she looked over Elowen's shoulder.

Elowen turned, finding no pleasure at the sight of the young man striding toward them. Bertrand might be unknowingly rescuing his sister from a conversation she didn't want to have, but he was never a welcome addition as far as Elowen was concerned. Instead of sitting next to his sister, he placed himself on the empty bench beside Elowen.

"Do I dare to hope that you beautiful ladies watched my performance in the archery with bated breath?"

"No," said Elowen petulantly. "I was watching His Highness, actually."

"Were you?" Bertrand's carefully raised eyebrow perfectly expressed his contempt. And how did your fair prince perform?"

"Naturally, he won," said Elowen.

Her words seemed to amuse rather than discourage Bertrand. He laid his arm along the next level of the stands, which served as a backrest for their bench. Elowen inched forward discreetly, not eager to feel his arm against her shoulders. He was sitting much too close.

"Did he indeed?" Bertrand's gaze was faintly malicious as it slid from Elowen's face to the field in front of them.

With a jolt, Elowen realized that Theo was coming off the

field. She suddenly understood that Bertrand's approach, and his overly familiar manner, were strategically planned for the moment when Theo would walk past. The prince's eyes fell on the three of them, and while he didn't do anything as unguarded as frown—after all, that would require emotion—Elowen saw the way his brow set as he took in Bertrand's proximity.

Trying desperately to soften the image, she hailed Theo, so that politeness forced him to stop and join them. He came to a halt just in front of her, his bow still held in his hand.

"You did well," Elowen said brightly. "Congratulations on your win."

"Thank you."

Theo's voice was deep, and he held the bow slung across his shoulder in a posture that made him look much less scholarly than usual. Elowen was reminded vividly of the strength of his hand when he'd guided Ochre out of the flood and saved her life.

"Yes, I was just hearing how well you did in the novice cohort, Your Highness." Bertrand's voice cut across Elowen's thoughts, the nobleman still maddeningly relaxed as he leaned back against the stands. Brazenly, he reached forward and twanged Theo's bowstring. "Not a bad weapon," he commented. "It almost looks Torrenese-made."

"You are mistaken," Theo said, his voice cool and his eyes disdainful.

"On multiple counts," Elowen interjected in annoyance. "There's no novice cohort, everyone was spread evenly across the groups. I saw some of the men in your group unable to get their arrow halfway to the target."

"I thought you said you weren't watching my group," Bertrand said, a lazy smile on his face.

Coloring, Elowen turned away, avoiding Theo's eyes.

Bertrand had no call to be so self-satisfied. Lounging back, idle hands empty, he was cast very much in the shade by Theo's imposing presence, with his upright posture and his impressive bow.

"Such a shame that we don't get to learn archery, isn't it, Sophia?" she said, directing her words to the only safe member of the party. "It looks much more fun than jousting or swordplay."

"If you're interested to learn, Princess," Bertrand interjected, "we employ a private archery instructor. You'd be welcome to join me in my lessons at any time."

A hot retort burned on Elowen's tongue, but Sophia intervened first.

"Don't be foolish, Bertrand," the other girl said with surprising sternness. "I'm sure Elowen would have no need to look outside the castle if she wished for archery instruction." She stood. "We're dining with our parents tonight, remember? We should be going."

Bertrand stood as well, although he showed no sign of being chastened by his sister's rebuke. With a lingering glance between Elowen and Theo, he strolled away, leaving awkwardness in his wake, as seemed to be his new skill.

Elowen rose to her feet, folding her hands in her skirts in an attempt to appear natural. Theo didn't break the silence, and she forced herself to look up into his face. He was watching her thoughtfully, maybe even searchingly. If he wanted to get to know her, she wished he would say so, would ask her something that might give shape to all the unformed questions in her own mind.

Her eyes moved cautiously over him, noting the thin sheen of sweat on his forehead from the sun, and the absence of his usual formal attire. He was in breeches and a loose shirt—still of excellent quality—and he looked...different. His grip on the bow was confident, and his muscles stood out where he'd rolled up the sleeves of his shirt to allow for better movement during the archery. He would almost be dashing, if not for the politely disapproving expression on his face.

"I apologize for Lord Bertrand's rudeness," Elowen blurted out. "I don't know what's come over him the last few days."

Theo cleared his throat. "Perhaps some prejudice remains from the tensions of the past. Now we know that Torrens was never behind the misfortunes that befell the other kingdoms of the Peninsula, I can appreciate that it must have been a cause of resentment for many in Torrens that the kingdom was unfairly suspected of targeting its neighbors."

"Perhaps," Elowen said, but she knew the subdued reply wouldn't fool him. They were both smart enough to tell that Bertrand's antagonism was personal. "I know the viscount's behavior is over the line. Even Sophia intervened, and it's very unusual for her to reprimand her brother in front of other people."

She paused, contemplating the rare behavior. Perhaps she should have been kinder when Sophia tried to apologize. Clearly her friend was wrestling with something she hadn't shared.

"At any rate," she went on, "the family is unswervingly loyal to my father. Lord Bertrand doesn't mean any harm. Everyone knows that our alliance will be to the great benefit of Torrens, and he has no reason to wish harm to his kingdoms' interests." Seeing that Theo didn't look particularly softened by this assurance, she added, "I will try to speak to him about his behavior, however."

Theo's answer was swifter this time. "You will of course do what you think is best, Elowen. But if I have a say, I would prefer you not to discuss me with Lord Bertrand, or any other man."

With a stiff bow, he excused himself, leaving Elowen more deflated than ever. As she watched him walk away, the bow and the lithe muscles of his forearms drawing more interest than usual from the various passersby, she felt a pang. She couldn't help remembering her foolish daydreams about her betrothed turning out to be romantic and smitten with her, and she was horrified to feel angry tears threatening. She blinked them back, determined not to outwardly show the anger she felt with herself for indulging even for a moment in such absurdity. Not to mention her frustration with herself and Theo—and frankly Bertrand, as well—for how poorly things were going so far.

She longed to retreat to her rooms, but she knew she was expected to be present when her father closed the tournament's first day with an official address. At the appointed time, she made her way to his side, plastering on a smile as she waved at the crowd. Some of the more eager among the young noblemen put fists over their hearts in response to this sign from her, their eyes shining with the type of romantic fervor she doubted Theo was capable of feeling. At least he didn't embarrass her with overblown attention like some of the young noblemen were in the habit of doing.

When her father had finished his address, he offered her his arm, and they descended the raised stands together, moving slowly through the tournament field amidst a loose ring of his usual guards.

"How did you find the first day of the tournament?" he asked her.

"It was fine, Father," she said. "The people seemed to enjoy themselves."

"Did you enjoy yourself?" His gaze was too piercing. "I saw you speaking with Prince Theodore after the archery. He acquitted himself well, don't you think?"

"He did," she agreed. "Which is fortunate since it saves us all embarrassment."

He frowned for a moment over her tone before continuing. "Elowen, Prince Theodore asked me again about setting the wedding date. I get the sense he's doubting our commitment to the alliance, and we can't have that. Don't you think it would set his mind at ease—perhaps remove some tension from your own mind—to have a definite wedding date?"

"I can't speak to what would set his mind at ease," Elowen replied frankly. "But my own resolve is unchanged." Feeling herself on firm ground, she squeezed his arm. "If there's one thing I know you to be, Father, it's a man of your word, and you promised me, remember?"

"I know I did," he said calmly. "But I wish I understood the reasons behind your request."

"Ah," Elowen said lightly, "who can understand the mind of a flighty young woman?"

Her father gave her an affectionate smile as he laid a hand over hers where it rested on his arm, returning the pressure. "You may sometimes err in judgment, my dear, but I wouldn't accuse you of being flighty."

They were halfway across the tournament area, and the king released her arm, moving forward to meet his approaching head guard. A happy chaos surrounded Elowen as the day's events were packed up and preparations began for the following day. She wandered through the crowd, trailed by a guard of her own, and stopped to survey the lists now posted to a temporary wall.

There were many familiar names in the court lists, Theo's prominent among the three events he signed up for. In the commoner's events, however, Elowen saw very few names she knew. As Sophia had predicted, Simeon's name was absent from the craftsmen's competition. The commoners' lists weren't closed yet, but Sophia had seemed very certain he wouldn't compete.

Turning away from the wall, her eyes fell on just the man she'd been thinking of. Simeon himself was passing not far away, carrying the absent Bertrand's bow and quiver out of the tournament area. His eyes flicked to her and then away, and she was sure she caught a hint of disappointment in his frame. Had he hoped to see her accompanied by her friend, as she so often was?

With an uncomfortable pang, Elowen wondered if the servant was mixed up in whatever had Sophia so distressed. She'd known for a long time that there was something unspoken there, but she'd kept out of it. Had her forbearance been too passive? If Sophia nursed a hidden fondness for a man she could never be with, who was himself too gentle to ever discourage her impossible daydreams, would she remain stuck in unhappiness forever?

Gathering her courage, Elowen approached Simeon, who stopped respectfully as soon as he realized she wanted to speak with him. He bent in a bow, no sign in his deferential bearing of how casual they'd grown to be with one another in their now-abandoned magic lessons.

"Simeon," she greeted him. "I don't see your name on the list for the craftsmen's competition. Sophia mentioned that you didn't intend to participate."

"No, Your Highness," Simeon agreed, dipping his head again.

"In fact, just the thought of the competitions seemed to distress her," Elowen pressed, watching his face carefully. "Many things seem to make her anxious at the moment."

A flicker of something crossed the servant's face, but it was quickly suppressed.

"I love my friend," Elowen went on, her voice gentle. "But

sometimes it pains me to see how timid she's become." She cleared her throat, trying to strike the right balance between sounding casual in case her guard was listening but also making it clear to Simeon that she was in earnest. "It's natural for her to perhaps be drawn to others of a similarly yielding temperament, but I doubt it would serve her well to be surrounded by others with an equal lack of resolution."

Simeon gave her a quick look, his eyes sharper than she was used to. He said nothing, but she knew he understood that she was crossing a new line and making specific reference to him. Whether he fully took her meaning, and if so how he felt about it, she couldn't be sure. He said nothing at all in response, merely bowing respectfully and moving away.

Elowen watched him go, feeling no more at peace than she had before. Neither she nor her friend were on promising paths when it came to matters of the heart.

EIGHT

Theo

Theo rose early on the second day of the tournament. It wasn't that he was eager to resume the competition. But the discomfort of his mind was hard to shake, and he thought some training in the castle's practice yard might clear his head. He checked his steps as he approached the training yard, his eyes drawn to a small enclosure adjacent to it. He'd only ever seen the enclosure empty before, but now it housed a beautiful young roan with a reddish mane and tail. The horse was prancing nervously, letting out angry snorts from time to time. Curious, Theo approached the railing, wishing he had a cube of sugar in his pocket.

"I wouldn't get too close, Your Highness," said an approaching guard. He was hefting a small bale of hay in his arms. "They're having trouble breaking that one. He's dangerous, doesn't trust people."

He tossed the hay into the enclosure from a safe distance, the bale almost hitting the horse.

Theo frowned at the guard's retreating back. Obviously the horse wasn't going to trust people if he was treated like a wild, terrifying animal. Theo paused at the railing, taking the opportunity while the horse was distracted by investigating the bale of hay to speak soothingly to it. He couldn't tell if the horse was listening to him, but it didn't snort or shy away from his voice.

When Theo entered the training yard, it was immediately obvious that he wasn't the only one to have the idea of warming up before breakfast. Many members of the court were staying in the castle for the duration of the tournament, and half of them seemed to be at the yard. Curious eyes followed Theo, but at least it wasn't difficult to find partners with so many men ready to spar.

The hour he spent engaging in casual bouts also helped him size up the competition he would face in the upcoming events featuring weapons combat. There were some excellent fighters amongst King Ronan's court, as well as many aspiring ones whom he'd have no difficulty beating.

Theo felt secret satisfaction at the obvious surprise of some of the spectators in the training yard when he bested one of the more capable fighters. He might have a reputation for being stiff and responsible, more likely to focus on trade negotiations than military matters, but he was a prince of Siqual, after all. He'd been trained by the best swordsmen his kingdom had to offer, and he'd always held his own against his brother and any other challengers. He would have enjoyed pursuing the skill more if other matters hadn't taken priority out of necessity. For much of his life he'd shouldered many of the duties of crown prince in addition to his own responsibilities. Xavier, the actual heir, was no less capable than Theo, but much less inclined to be reliable in performing his duties.

In any event, while Theo was not a match for the most skilled of King Ronan's court, he anticipated being able to beat enough opponents in the weapons combat event to maintain an honorable reputation before he withdrew as instructed.

The maze event was another matter entirely, and he had

no idea how to prepare for that. Given he had another round of archery in the morning, and the maze event was to take place that afternoon, he wouldn't have the opportunity anyway.

When the breakfast hour was near, he moved into the enclosed part of the training yard used for toweling off and re-donning more formal wear. The atmosphere was much more relaxed than Theo had yet experienced from the Torrenese court, and he enjoyed it. Somehow sparring together removed barriers in a way no social event ever would. No one looked up when he entered the space, and he went about his preparations amid the comings and goings of several others.

He was maybe too inconspicuous, because as he was toweling his sweaty face, a pair of others entered, his name on their lips. He paused, not in a hurry to uncover his face or turn around and cause them embarrassment by his presence.

"...to Prince Theodore?" one was saying.

"Of course I've noticed," scoffed the other. "Bertrand hasn't exactly been subtle with his disrespect toward the visiting prince, I don't think there's anyone who's not aware."

Theo grimaced. Of course Lord Bertrand's vendetta against him would ignite gossip. It was inevitable.

"It's no surprise that he's sour, he's been boasting of the princess like a sure thing for years," the first man replied. "But word is the duke isn't happy he's showing it so openly. My manservant's brother works for Bertrand, and he told me that he overheard the duke scolding him for his rudeness. Apparently Lady Sophia went running to their father. Probably knew Bertrand would never listen to her."

The other man made a noise of derision in his throat. "She was right about that."

"My servant said the duke told Bertrand that he hoped to see *more of both honor and common sense* from his son."

They both laughed, enjoying the thought of the absent Bertrand's chagrin. Apparently they were no great friends of his.

"I wish the duke success in his hopes, but I wouldn't place a wager on them," one of them said indulgently. "The viscount has never learned the talent of not getting what he wants. He's not likely to start now."

Theo remained still, waiting until the men had left before moving away from the wall he'd been facing. His thoughts explored every aspect of what he'd overheard, trying and failing to ignore his anger over the viscount's supposed claims on the princess.

Elowen had said that Lord Bertrand meant no harm and wouldn't wish to damage his kingdom by threatening the alliance. Did she really believe that? Because it seemed obvious to Theo that the viscount had a very specific reason to wish harm, not to the kingdom, but to Theo. But his actions remained absurd. Theo had seen the proof of the position of trust and influence held by the duke. However indulged Lord Bertrand might have been, he was still a grown man. It was hard to understand how he could let petty personal jealousy sabotage such an advantageous alliance for his kingdom. And yet that was what he appeared to be trying to do. He was clearly determined to draw Theo into jealous competition, and that was something Theo absolutely refused to enter into.

His path forward was clear. He would be even more circumspect and detached. The honor of his kingdom was at stake, and Siqual would not be the subject of jest at the hands of a man like the viscount.

The second round of the archery proceeded similarly to the first. The competition was a little more authentic, but Theo was still able to successfully progress alongside the top contenders. He'd expected to face the group Lord Bertrand had been part of the day before, but the winners from that round had apparently already completed their second round against others from a third group. Once his session was finished, he watched the other group for a while, and became convinced of what he'd already suspected.

Elowen was wrong. The groups were not evenly spread. Theo had been placed with all the least competent archers, so as to allow him to look impressive up until he chose to withdraw. It stung his pride, but he chose not to dwell on it. Whatever the viscount had said, he didn't appear to be matched against elite archers, either. In fact, the man after Lord Bertrand missed the target altogether. Surprising, given Theo was sure he'd seen him at the training yard, hitting the target every time.

A third group were also undertaking their round, some of them very impressive. Theo could see after a few minutes that he was outmatched by many of them, which was no surprise. He was a competent archer at best. Turning away from the ongoing competition, Theo made his way to the nobleman who'd been appointed master of events.

The man nodded approvingly when Theo announced his intention to bow out of the archery. It was probably the only way the rest of the competitors would feel free to compete naturally, but he didn't say as much.

When he strode off the field, he felt eyes on him, and looked up to see Elowen watching him from the stands. He expected her to look away when his eyes found her, but she didn't. He was gripped by a sudden impulse to make a sign, like he'd seen others do when she watched them, a hand fisted across the heart. He dismissed the idea quickly, wondering what had come over him. Hadn't he just promised himself he would keep himself and his kingdom above any petty competitions for favor?

His resolve was galvanized when he belatedly saw who was next to Elowen. Once again Lord Bertrand had been faster than

Theo in reaching the stands and had placed himself alongside the princess. Theo was too far away to hear whether the viscount was minding his father's rebuke, but by the twist of the other man's face, he doubted it. Theo strode past, annoyed with the flare of jealousy he felt, and uninterested in joining them. His memory threw before his eyes a flash of blonde hair as it whipped in the wind while he and Elowen rode out of the city, followed by an image of striking blue eyes, brimful of emotion as she looked up at him after he steered her from the flood.

Theo tried to push sentiment away. Maybe he'd been as guilty of romanticizing their situation as any daydream Elowen might have had. That version of the princess seemed out of reach, perhaps not even real. And the polite distance between them now shouldn't bother him so much. That was weakness on his part. He had no need for impatience. They would have a lifetime to get to know one another.

The afternoon brought the much-anticipated maze race. At the appointed time, Theo made his way to the huge space at the very back of the tournament fields. Since he'd last seen it, many hands had been hard at work rearranging the hay bales. Walls of hay rose in front of him, above the height of his head, and judging by the hugely elevated stands that ringed the area, the maze stretched for a reasonable distance. Spectators on the stands would likely catch only glimpses of whatever was happening within. Theo took his place beside the other challengers, impressed as he considered the walls of hay. The scope of the task was enormous—Theo suspected magic had been involved to arrange it in such a short time.

His eyes moved to the stands, drawn at once to a splash of pure gold on the highest level. Elowen was accompanied by her brother in a roped off section of stands, and she looked as fascinated by the hay maze as Theo was. His heart jolted ever so slightly, even though it was absurd to feel nerves over her watching him. At least Lord Bertrand wasn't with her this time.

The master of events stepped with a flourish onto a raised dais in front of the hay maze. He looked pleased with himself as he explained the rules of the event, and Theo suspected he'd been the mastermind. The buzz of curious excitement that pervaded the crowd suggested this was a new event. Theo listened as the nobleman explained that it was a timed event, with contestants completing the course separately, one after another, competing for the fastest time.

"The maze will test our brave competitors on much more than their sense of direction," he said at the end of his explanation. "While many of our events at this tournament test strength and skill with weapons, this challenge also requires strength and quickness of mind. Contestants must display their ability to detect and face danger, to solve problems quickly, to employ strategic thinking, and to prove their strength of character."

That seemed like a lot for one medium-sized hay bale maze, but Theo clapped politely along with the riotous cheers from the spectators. He was halfway down the line of contestants, but the order must have been determined by rank, as he was called forward first.

With a beaming smile and a low bow, the master of events waved him toward the entrance to the maze. Theo had just stepped up to it when a loud blast sounded from a bugler nearby. His time had begun.

Curbing the instinct to sprint into the maze, Theo paused to examine a wooden box placed on a stand right next to the entrance. Written on a paper next to the box, in the flowing script of a royal scribe, were the words, *"To aid in your quest."* A second glance showed that what he'd taken to be intricate carvings on the box were actually joining lines between different pieces of wood.

He'd seen items like this before. It was a puzzle box, cunningly designed so that only the right sequence of movements would open it. He and Xavier had been given one each by a nobleman from the island kingdom of Pulau on a rare diplomatic visit. They'd spent hours figuring them out, and then spent too many afternoons tormenting their tutor by hiding essential items inside.

The box in front of Theo was larger than the ones he'd seen before, but it was clearly a similar concept. He picked up the box, coming to a stop in front of the stand. Impatient murmurs grew in the crowd as he twisted it around, testing one section, then prodding another. He could hear some muted jeers from his fellow contestants as one minute stretched into two. He ignored them beyond angling his body to block their view so as not to give any advantage.

It took maybe three minutes before he found the secret, and the box came apart in his hands. He heard an admiring whistle from a squire nearby, and a flash of boyish triumph swept over him as he scooped up the contents of the box. These were a fresh apple and a few gold coins. Pocketing them, Theo turned and moved into the maze. It proceeded around a corner without offering him options, presumably so the other contestants couldn't see which turn he would take. The hay rose up around him, obscuring most of the stands, although he could still see the pennants that rose, fluttering, from the spectators' boxes. He avoided touching the walls, not eager to be itchy and dusty for the rest of the day.

When he reached the first fork, he chose a direction at random, proceeding down it for only a few paces before he paused. Straining his ears and trying to block out the noise of the crowd, he heard it again. A rumbling growl, like a tiger but too high in pitch. The hair stood up on the back of his neck in an instinctive response. From the descriptions he'd heard, it sounded like the distinctive growl of the pantherine, the winged snow leopards found only in the mountain range in the north of Carrack, right at the point where the Peninsula ended and the continent began. Legend was that the Dust created by the movement of the reclusive creatures' wings emerged already formed into enchantments that a person of even the most rudimentary skill could simply harness.

Legend also had it that they were swift and vicious, swooping on their prey from above before their presence was detected. Very few had seen one and lived to tell of it.

It seemed unlikely to Theo that the Torrenese had managed to catch one and bring it here for the tournament, but he'd prefer not to find out. Perhaps rushing headlong in to investigate was what the master of events had meant by showing his "ability to detect and face danger", but it seemed foolish to Theo when there was an alternate, growl-free route to explore. Retracing his steps, he proceeded the other way. He moved quickly through the maze, encouraging him to think he'd chosen well. A couple of times he met a dead end and had to backtrack, but never very far.

He estimated he was halfway across the expanse of the maze when he turned a corner and found himself faced with a small swamp. It was quite ingenious, really, how contained it was while still clearly deep and boggy, and emitting a smell that would be familiar to anyone who lived near swampland. Stretched over the surface of the swamp were a series of small wooden platforms, in various shapes. They were rigged up to a clever pulley system, and Theo discovered that by manipulating the ropes that lay on his side of the swamp, he could shift them. He pulled one close to the edge and stepped onto it, only to quickly jump back as it listed wildly. He looked carefully over the platforms again, and suddenly understood. He was supposed to fit the shapes together to form a path, and once in position, they would stabilize each other enough for him to cross.

He let go of the rope, resisting the temptation to start pulling them into place at once. Instead he studied all the shapes, trying to fit them together in his mind. If he'd had paper and a quill pen, he would have sketched them out, but as it was, the best he could do was scratch a few shapes into the dirt. It took several minutes to solve the puzzle and several more to maneuver the platforms into position, but at last he had his path. It held steady for him as he crossed quickly over, wrinkling his nose at the smell issuing from the bog with a burping sound.

Soon after the swamp, he once again heard an animal sound, although this one wasn't a growl. It was the angry whinny of a horse, and Theo instinctively hurried toward it rather than away. When he rounded a corner of hay bales, he was confronted with the sight of the beautiful roan he'd seen that morning, tied to a stake on a lead that was far too short for its size. Scowling disapprovingly, Theo moved toward it, only to pause when it shied and reared.

He would need to be careful. It was no flying leopard, but those hooves could do plenty of damage if the horse decided he was a threat. Theo once again wished he had a cube of sugar in his pocket, then suddenly remembered the items from the puzzle box.

"I doubt you want the gold, do you?" he said to the horse, a smile in his voice as he tried to speak soothingly. "But an apple might be just right."

He moved forward slowly, offering the apple in his outstretched hand while continuing to speak kindly to the nervous creature. Behind it, he could see the path twisting on, and was sure it was the route he needed to take. It was tempting to rush past the horse and take his chances, but he forced himself to instead take the time needed to soothe it, for its own sake as well as for the competition. He would have liked to untie it, but he knew that was overstepping, so he contented himself with waiting until the horse was calm enough to take the apple from his hand.

"You're not so wild, really, are you?" Theo said, smiling as he ran a hand down the horse's flank. "Just wild enough, hm?"

His movements still slow and predictable, Theo slid past the horse, calmly explaining his intentions as he moved. He stayed at the head end, continuing to talk gently until he was fully clear. He knew time was slipping quickly away, but he hovered one more moment.

"I'm sorry about this ordeal, my friend," he told the horse frankly. "I hope you'll at least get plenty of apples out of it."

The horse gave no reply, and Theo hurried on through the maze. He'd barely rounded the next corner when he became aware of something strange. Everything had gone very still, and Theo thought for a moment that the spectators had stopped making noise altogether. He paused, straining his ears and wondering what dramatic incident outside the maze had silenced a whole crowd. But once he focused on it, he realized that the hum of the crowd was still there. Following some instinct, he reached out instead with his under-developed magic sense.

Something definitely seemed off. He waved his hand in front of his face, focusing on the movement. Even with all his concentration bent to the task, he could sense no Dust being stirred up by the motion. The air felt empty without it, everything off balance and wrong. Uneasy, Theo looked around him, wondering if it was part of the competition. But then, as he started cautiously back into motion, the sensation of Dust returned to the air with a whoosh that was almost audible. Once again, his mind faintly sensed the comforting cushion of magic that followed on every movement of his body, and the air no longer felt empty.

Unnerved, Theo hurried through the hay corridor more quickly now, eager to be done with the challenge. He reached another fork, and glancing to the left he felt his heart thud erratically as something small flashed through his vision. Surely they could no more have gotten a carbuncle into the maze than a pantherine. But he'd seen the flash of light hitting the forehead of the small canine.

Any reference to carbuncles always engulfed Theo in a wave of discomfort so potent it turned his stomach. But the sighting felt especially eerie after whatever had just happened with the magic. Turning resolutely away, he took the other path. He wouldn't get distracted from his purpose.

A moment later, he wondered if he'd chosen the wrong way when he found his route blocked by three burly men holding clubs. Theo came to a standstill, eyeing their threatening posture. Surely they wouldn't actually be allowed to beat the visiting prince with their clubs. But judging by the size of them, they wouldn't have to do more than defend in order to stop him proceeding.

"Good afternoon, gentlemen," Theo said pleasantly.

The only reply was three menacing growls. So diplomacy wasn't the solution here. Was he supposed to fight his way through? He could try, but the idea was absurd. Why would he, an unarmed solitary traveler, rush a trio of hulking strangers with clubs? He shifted his weight from one foot to the other, and caught a faint clinking sound.

Of course! The puzzle box had given him more than just an apple. He pulled out the gold, and the group in front of him relaxed visibly at the sight of the three coins.

"I'll give you one each in exchange for safe passage," Theo said curtly.

They held their hands out, and as soon as Theo handed over the gold, they melted to the sides, allowing him through. Theo strode past them, waiting until they were out of sight before resuming his jog. Two more twists, one more fork requiring investigation to identify a dead end, and he emerged into an open space that could only be the center of the maze.

In the middle of the space was a small wooden room. There was a door on the side closest to Theo, with a prominent brass handle. It was hard for him to get a good look, however, because in front of it stood another three men. These ones were different from the burly club-wielders, however. Each was different from the others, as well.

The first man had an ax over his shoulder, but he didn't wield it threateningly. His garb declared him as a woodcutter. The second wore the uniform of a member of the Torrenese Craftsmen's Guild. A skilled magic manipulator, presumably. At the third, Theo did a double take, surprised to see the castle steward in such a place. But a second look showed that this man wasn't the steward, although he had been dressed to look just like the well-known figure, down to the styling of his hair.

"Congratulations on reaching the center of the maze, Your Highness," the imitation steward said. "You have one final challenge before your task is complete. You must get inside the locked room. You may ask one of us to assist you, and you are allowed to ask each one of us three yes or no questions before making your decision. But once you have requested help from one, you may not receive it from any others. Do you understand your options?"

"I understand," Theo said calmly.

He studied each of the three men in turn, then the door. The woodcutter's axe would be able to get through it, certainly. But the door looked thick, and hacking it open enough to allow a man to pass through would likely take longer than most people would assume. The craftsman could no doubt get him through using magic if he was willing to do so. Although if Theo went that way, he would be wise to use his questions to confirm that the man was actually a skilled craftsman, not just dressed in imitation of one.

His eyes returned to the steward lookalike, and he noticed a thick chain around the man's neck that he hadn't seen at first. It disappeared below his tunic, obscuring whatever was pulling it taut. A glance back at the door showed a keyhole below the handle. Theo felt a smile grow on his face.

"I have a question for you," he informed the third man. "May I see what's on the end of your chain?"

The steward's smile matched his as he answered. "Yes, you may." He drew out the chain to reveal a small brass key.

"Does that key open the door into this room?" Theo asked, gesturing in front of him.

"Yes, it does."

"And my final question," Theo said, "are you willing to unlock the door for me if I ask you to?"

"Yes, Your Highness, I am willing." The man was beaming at him, apparently pleased with Theo's quickness.

"I choose you to assist me, sir, if you please," Theo said.

CHAPTER
NINE

Theo

The man stepped forward and unlocked the door, gesturing respectfully for Theo to enter. He did so with swift steps, to find that nothing was inside but for a large bell on a pole. Theo rang it vigorously, and immediately heard an answering blast from the bugler outside the maze. He had finished the task, and his completion time would be recorded. The sound was quickly dwarfed by the cheers of the spectators, and Theo couldn't resist a grin as the three men applauded him politely.

The craftsman moved forward, swinging his robe around him in a sweeping motion that generated enough Dust for Theo's dull senses to recognize. The next moment, a ladder emerged from a pile of hay nearby, leaning itself up against the side of the maze without aid from any visible hand.

Theo climbed the ladder and emerged onto the top of the nearest hay wall. The crowd roared with excitement, and he waved a hand to acknowledge their praise. His eyes were drawn at once to the splash of gold that signified Elowen. From his new position, he could see her more clearly. As he walked along the hay wall to get out of the maze, his eyes kept drifting to her.

She was applauding enthusiastically, her face flushed with excitement, and her features all the more attractive as a result. In fact, she was absolutely stunning in a deep purple gown, with her hair twisted into a golden crown around her head, and her eyes as bright as bluebells. Their eyes met, and although he again fought back the urge to make a sign with his fist over his heart, he found himself grinning. It may have been his imagination given the distance, but her answering smile seemed shy, although not in the aloof way of their first meeting.

She was glad he'd performed well in the maze event, that much was clear. A sense of common feeling swelled within Theo, buoying him up as he jumped from one hay wall to another on his way out. Archery and weapons combat were the standard fare of tournaments, and they were well enough in their way...but that event had been *fun*.

As Theo passed along the top of the maze, he saw various flurries of activity within, as the challenges were reset for the next competitor. When he reached the front of the maze, he was congratulated by the master of events, then released. Thankfully no one expected him to stand around waiting while all the other contestants took their turns. Theo noticed Elowen still watching him, and made his way toward the stands where she was sitting. She moved forward to lean over the front of her roped off section of stands as he took the steps two at a time.

"That's an ingenious event for a tournament," he said, by way of greeting.

"I'm dying to hear details of what was inside," Elowen said, her eyes eager. "We couldn't see much from up here. I definitely caught a horse's head rearing up at one point!"

"You'll have to wait until the event is completed to interrogate Prince Theodore for details," Prince Patrick said, his tone the closest to indulgent Theo had ever heard it. "He's bound to secrecy until all contestants have attempted it, remember?"

"Yes, I suppose that makes sense," Elowen sighed. "Was it exciting, though?"

"It was well-designed to be challenging and intriguing," Theo said. He smiled at Elowen. "Thank you for coming and cheering me on."

"Of course," she said lightly. "I have to cheer for my champion, it's an integral part of tournament tradition."

A smile flitted across Theo's face at her falsely innocent expression. Her champion? Was she trying to flirt with him?

Was he liking it?

He wasn't sure which discovery surprised him more, but he was happy to accept Prince Patrick's invitation to sit with them as the next competitor started his run through the maze. He quickly learned that it wasn't nearly as entertaining being a spectator as it was a competitor. The time dragged on, with nothing much to indicate the contestant's progress.

"There were a number of separate challenges within the maze," he commented. "They should ring a gong each time a contestant completes a challenge. It might help the crowd remain invested."

He glanced around at the stands, from which spectators were already starting to trickle out as they lost interest.

"That's a good thought," Prince Patrick said gravely. "I'll pass it on to the master of events."

"Lighten up, Patrick," Elowen said with the hint of a laugh. "You sound like you're acknowledging advice on a serious state matter. It's a tournament, it's supposed to be fun."

Theo raised an eyebrow at her, although a smile played on his lips. He'd rarely seen her so bubbly and happy—it was irresistible.

"You've certainly changed your tune on the tournament."

"Oh, well..." Elowen shrugged. "I still think it's silly, but I have to be here, so I may as well enjoy it. I saw someone selling roasted chestnuts and candied almonds earlier. I must find them when this event is done."

"The tournament isn't silly, Elowen," Prince Patrick said disapprovingly. "It's an important tradition to our people."

"Come on, Patrick," she said. "Are you really going to tell me you *wouldn't* rather be discussing a serious state matter?"

Privately, Theo thought that the tightness on Prince Patrick's face suggested that Elowen had hit a nerve. It must chafe him to be stuck at the tournament when the country was dealing with irregular magic and a region devastated by flooding.

"Mother and Father have committed me to a marriage of alliance," Elowen went on. "There's really no point in pretending to have a tournament for my hand."

"Elowen." There was a warning note to the prince's voice, and his eyes flicked to Theo.

"No need to choose your words carefully on my account," Theo said pleasantly. "I'm intimately familiar with the details of the marriage alliance, after all, and I don't have any problem describing things just as they are."

"Thus displaying a surprising amount of common sense for a prince," Elowen said approvingly. She shot a provocative look at her brother, but he just sighed.

Theo turned away to hide his smile. He was enjoying seeing Elowen's more playful side. It made him want to find more ways to bring it out, but that desire wasn't very consistent with his resolve to be circumspect for the honor of Siqual.

It took several hours for all of the contestants to complete the maze, and the royal group had abandoned their part of the stands long before then. Prince Patrick had been the first to rise, inviting Theo to walk with him as he inspected the field for the weapons combat. Perhaps he assumed, incorrectly, that Theo would prefer that activity over Elowen's continued light chatter. But politeness required Theo to accept, and once he parted from Elowen, their paths didn't cross again for the rest of the afternoon.

The sun was setting and it was almost time to return to the castle for yet another dinner banquet when Theo was chased down and called to return to the maze for the official completion of the event.

He felt a pang of disappointment to see no sign of Elowen in the stands or on the field. She'd likely returned to the castle to ready herself for the meal. Whatever the reason, she didn't witness Theo being pronounced the clear winner. No one had come within ten minutes of matching his time, and he felt a private flush of pride.

"His Highness performed in each challenge with near perfection," the master of events was saying enthusiastically. "He was not too proud to accept help freely offered, and displayed quickness of wit both in cleverly solving the puzzle box, and in making judicious use of the favors found within. Once inside the maze, he didn't try to use brute strength when he could negotiate his way out of trouble, and he was adept at avoiding both danger and distraction."

Here he nodded to a nearby squire, who grinned as he held up the small dog Theo had caught a glimpse of in the maze, a small mirror still attached to its forehead by means of an unobtrusive strap. The dog panted happily, its manner so far from the mystical movements of a true carbuncle that Theo chuckled along with the crowd as he thought of how he'd momentarily believed it to be a creature of magic.

"His Highness displayed speed, strength, strategy, and diplomacy. He is most deserving of his position as winner of our maze event."

Theo accepted the ribbon offered to him, waving calmly at the cheering crowd. Unlike with the archery, there hadn't really been a way to pit him against lesser opponents in this event, and his authentically skillful performance seemed to have won him some goodwill among the Torrenese populace. That was worth much more than the ribbon in his hand.

Aware of the late hour, he moved quickly through the emptying tournament fields, eager to reach the castle. When he passed the sign-up table, however, a snatch of overheard conversation caused him to slow his steps.

"So you felt it, too, during the maze event?"

"Of course I felt it, I don't think there's a craftsman in Toledda who missed it. I've never felt the Dust do anything like that. It was like it was blocked up in a dam then suddenly burst out again."

Theo frowned, remembering what he'd felt while completing the maze run. He glanced surreptitiously over to see that the two men speaking were hovering next to the list for the craftsmen's event. One wore the uniform of a guild-employed craftsman.

"It's got me worried," confided the first man. "I suppose if you knew about the Dust disturbance, you've already heard about the accident it caused at the mill on the edge of town?" His companion shook his head, and he continued. "A craftsman was using magic to help hold himself up in a good position for his work, and the Dust in the air suddenly disappeared, so he fell. He's lucky to have no more than a broken leg."

The second man gave a low whistle. "The guild won't be happy about yet another incident. That's five this week in the capital alone, and word is it's even worse in some parts of the country."

Theo frowned thoughtfully. Five incidents that week? Clearly he wasn't being kept in the loop, a fact that didn't really surprise him. Begrudgingly, he felt some sympathy for Prince Patrick's stiffness earlier in response to Elowen's teasing. Theo also wished he wasn't stuck taking part in a meaningless competition rather than assisting with the investigation into the strange movement of the magic in Torrens.

As he watched, a third man approached the pair.

"Simeon!" one of them greeted the newcomer. "Where have you been all day, lad? I haven't seen you around the tournament fields."

"No, I missed today's events, unfortunately," the servant said lightly. "I had other duties. But I wanted to sign up before they closed the lists for the day."

"You've decided to compete?" The man in the guild uniform looked pleased. "I'm glad of it. What's changed your mind?"

Simeon's smile was disarming. "Your persuasions, of course."

The man chuckled as he added Simeon's name to the list already pinned to the wall. "I doubt it, somehow."

Simeon looked on the point of leaving, and Theo realized it was the best chance he'd likely get to ask the servant about the dam burst. He moved forward, causing all three men to fall silent and bow respectfully.

"Simeon, isn't it?" Theo greeted the younger man.

Simeon acknowledged it with another bow as his companions packed up their papers and melted away, not eager to be caught in conversation with the foreign prince.

"I've been hoping to speak with you," Theo said. "I understand you're a skilled craftsman, is that right?"

"I'm flattered by the description, Your Highness," Simeon said. "I have some training in the craft, yes."

"And you were present when the dam burst on the Duke of Sirocha's holdings?" Theo pressed.

This time Simeon hesitated, a wary look coming over his face.

"I was there, and I'm sure I saw you," Theo said mildly.

"Yes, Your Highness," said Simeon, his eyes respectfully averted. "I was nearby, although I didn't personally see the dam burst."

"Did you feel anything strange about the Dust released by the water's movement when the dam failed?"

Again Simeon took a moment to answer. "Strange, Your Highness?"

Theo curbed his impatience, knowing that severity wouldn't make the servant more inclined to speak freely.

"Did you feel the Dust released by the dam?"

"I did, Your Highness."

Theo searched his face. "And did it feel normal to you?"

The servant cleared his throat. "I'm not qualified to speak as to what's considered normal, especially at such an unusual event. It's the only dam failure I've ever been present for, so I have no basis for comparison."

Theo tried a different approach. "You seem uncomfortable, Simeon. Perhaps you've already been asked to report on the matter by His Majesty or His Grace, and are reluctant to betray whatever trust they have in you. Commendable, if so."

"No, Your Highness, no one has asked me not to speak about it," Simeon said quickly. "That is, I simply have nothing of value to tell."

"I see." Theo was less convinced of that than ever, Simeon's manner and tone putting all his senses on alert.

But there seemed little point in pressing further. With a word of parting, he moved away, rounding the curved edge of a nearby tent before it occurred to him to ask about whether Simeon had felt the disturbance during his maze run. Perhaps the other man would find it harder to be guarded when he'd had much less time to decide on his story.

Theo had made it halfway back around the tent when a new voice brought him to a stop, still out of sight of the servant.

"Simeon." Apparently Elowen hadn't returned to the castle yet after all. "You've signed up for the craftsmen's competition." Judging by her tone, the information had come as a great surprise to the princess.

"Yes, Princess Elowen."

Still hidden from sight, Theo raised an eyebrow at the boldness of the servant's tone in responding to the princess. It was a far cry from the overly deferential manner he'd just shown Theo. He was even more stunned when Simeon continued.

"I'm not timid, Your Highness. Don't be concerned," he went on quickly. "I carry no presumptions. But whatever my restraints, I'm not a weak or hesitant man. Perhaps my temperament seems yielding to you, but I don't believe I have a lack of resolution."

It was clearly a reference to an earlier conversation, and Theo felt discomfort prickle over him. What exactly was the servant speaking of? What made him so brazen as to address the princess in that challenging way?

"I see," Elowen said, her voice quieter now. "I don't know what to say, Simeon, except to ask you to forgive my assumptions. And, of course, to wish you well in the competition."

The voices fell quiet, and a moment later, Theo chanced a look around the tent. Elowen was strolling away toward the castle, and Simeon had a faint smile on his face, the expression one of private, gentle satisfaction.

Jealousy flared in Theo, hot and foolish and distracting. It made him angry. He felt ashamed of his weakness, first threatened by a fool like Lord Bertrand, now by a servant? He had to quell this childish jealousy. He remembered how refreshing he'd found Elowen's light and playful manner that afternoon, because it was so unusual. But the way she'd spoken to Simeon just now had been so natural. He would almost have said they'd spoken with the ease of friendship, which made no sense given their relative stations. He was embarrassed by how much he wanted her to speak to him in that comfortable way, instead of with the cautious politeness he usually received.

The realization of how much he wanted her approval made him recoil, the sensation close to fear. *You can't pursue what you want*, he reminded himself. *That will lead to disaster for more than just you. It's not about your desires, but your duty.*

But he couldn't seem to hold on to the assurance when he remembered the elation he'd felt when he saw Elowen cheering him on. He needed to be careful or he'd be in danger of caring too much about both the tournament and his emotions.

Elowen

Having enjoyed the maze event so much, Elowen was disappointed to learn that she'd missed the declaration of the results. Doubly so when she heard that, unsurprisingly, Theo had won it easily. Her disappointment wasn't softened by sitting next to him at dinner, thanks to his inexplicable return to the polite but aloof manner she found so disheartening.

The following day had no court events scheduled for the morning, and Elowen's mother had her under strict instructions to at last take Theo to the floating gardens. This time, she was careful not to invite Sophia or anyone else who might turn the event into a group affair, which Bertrand would do all he could to dominate.

She half regretted it, however, when she found herself riding out with a quiet, solemn Theo after breakfast.

"Did you sleep well?" she asked, wincing as the meaningless chatter left her lips.

"Yes, thank you." Theo didn't seem to be paying much attention, his eyes on the water tower they were riding past. "What's the function of that tower?" he asked suddenly.

Elowen followed his eyes up the narrow structure topped with a wider stone chamber. "It's a water tower," she said. "Water is drawn up gradually from wells underneath by use of magic, and stored up high. Then, if there's ever a need for a sudden release of a lot of Dust, we can drop the water in a torrent, back down the tower, with skilled craftsmen on hand to manipulate the ensuing magic."

"Clever," Theo commented. "Useful for the defense of the city in the event of an attack, I imagine."

"Precisely," Elowen said. "We used to only have two. The one you're looking at was built recently, when there were constant whispers that the other kingdoms on the Peninsula were preparing to go to war against us."

Theo fell silent, perhaps hearing the edge of accusation hidden under her mild tone. Elowen forced herself to speak more cheerfully, mindful of the presence of the guards behind them. But it felt artificial, and she was sure she wasn't the only one relieved when they reached the floating gardens.

It was a lovely, peaceful spot, and her spirits lifted as she caught the scent of jasmine and lilac. In spite of the fine weather, the normally popular gardens were deserted, likely thanks to the commoners' events taking place at the tournament field.

They pulled their horses up, looking out over the marsh-turned-water-garden and admiring the artful way the plants grew along, into, and sometimes out of, the water. The section where they'd stopped was ringed with flat stones, a willow drooping its branches into the water not far away. Large lily pads floated lazily on the surface of the water, dragonflies skimming past them. Ochre shifted her weight, and in response, a frog jumped off a lily pad and disappeared into the greenish depths with a soft plop.

"It's beautiful," Theo said, his deep voice sending a foolish little shiver over Elowen's skin. What would it take for him to speak of her with that resonant approval? "I see why you like it here."

"Yes," she said, trying to swallow her illogical nerves.

Her eyes moved to the far bank, where an area of firm turf rose from a marshy section of pond. Jasmine bushes grew in profusion around the base of a tulip poplar tree. She could smell the sweet, familiar scent from where they stood.

"My father used to bring me here when I was a child," she told Theo. "When he'd been especially busy, or away from the capital on state affairs, he would always say he owed me a trip to the gardens to make up for it." She smiled softly for a moment, until she realized Theo was watching her, and self-consciously smoothed her features.

"He's an indulgent father, I think," Theo said quietly.

Elowen felt her brows crease. "He's firm when he needs to be."

"I didn't mean it as a criticism," Theo assured her. "If I sounded somber, it was only because I was thinking how difficult it must be for him to send his only daughter to another kingdom."

Elowen said nothing, but Theo didn't seem perturbed by her silence. He lifted an arm to point at a patch of swamp that was roped off.

"It looks like someone's been digging there. I suspect they used some of the material to create the swamp I saw in the hay maze. Perhaps they were able to enhance it using magic."

"Are your parents...indulgent?" Elowen asked abruptly.

The day before, she would have been interested to hear about what he'd found inside the maze, but she was more irked than she should be by the cool manner he'd regained since then. She wanted to draw him out. Childish maybe, but...she wanted to get a reaction.

Theo seemed surprised by her question, but he considered it seriously before answering.

"No, I wouldn't describe them that way. They're honorable and fair, however, and I certainly wouldn't call them unkind."

"But they're not warm," Elowen finished for him. He hadn't said it, but he didn't need to. The information wasn't exactly a surprise. "And do you take after them?" she asked boldly. "Rumor is that your brother doesn't, especially. And when I met your sister, she seemed warm enough, if a little shy."

"Miriam isn't shy," Theo said. "Just careful in unknown company."

"You didn't answer my question," Elowen pointed out.

He let out a breath that was a little too long. "How can I? How can I hope to assess my own manner objectively? I believe I'm considered both responsible and unemotional, as my father is."

"Like Patrick, too," Elowen said, determined to draw him into something more than this cool formality. "Appropriate for a future king, I suppose, but I thought a younger prince would be allowed to have more fun."

Theo smiled, but the expression startled Elowen. There was a bitter twist to it that she'd never before seen on his face.

"As a princess is?" he challenged, and Elowen deflated.

He was right. She knew better than to think that either Theo's time or his responsibilities were up to him. But surely his manner was his own affair.

"You know the answer to that, I suppose, having a sister yourself. You were quick to defend Princess Miriam from being called shy. I think you have warmth for her if for no one else."

"I hope I have warmth for all my family," Theo said shortly, apparently not enjoying the conversation. He relaxed slightly as he continued, however. "Miriam and I have always been friends as well as brother and sister. I do care about her, a great deal.

She wished she could come with me, to meet you properly and experience the tournament. She'll pester me for every detail when I return to Sindon. Many of her questions I doubt I'll be able to answer."

He cast a sidelong look over Elowen's form, and she straightened the folds of her dress self-consciously.

"Is something amiss?"

"Not at all," Theo said. "I'm just trying to commit one gown to memory so I can try to satisfy her. Thick, golden brocade with a matching scarf."

Elowen laughed. "That's a poor description of my favorite riding gown," she informed him. "And I suspect Princess Miriam will be more interested in what I wear to a gala than an everyday garment like this."

He smiled faintly. "I'm sure you're right. I won't pretend to understand these things."

Elowen eyed him thoughtfully. "Your sister had a political marriage tentatively arranged before ours was ever discussed, didn't she? She had an eleventh-hour escape from hers. Do you wish for the same?"

"Of course not." Theo sounded startled, and the look on his face as his eyes flew to Elowen's almost looked like penitence.

Elowen lowered her gaze quickly, unable to meet his eyes. The softness she'd seen there made her feel suddenly unmoored, unsure of her footing. She waited, half ashamed of her secret hope that he would say something flattering, or even vaguely positive about her and their proposed marriage.

It was a hope destined to be disappointed. Perhaps she'd imagined the change in Theo's manner, because as the silence stretched on, she felt his suspicion grow. When he finally broke the silence, his tone was stiff.

"I hate to repeat the same question, but Elowen...do I need

to be concerned about the commitment of your kingdom to our alliance?"

"I have no answer for you but the same one," she said coolly. "We're fully committed, as ever. Why must you even ask?"

"Because you wouldn't meet my eye after asking if I wished to be released from our engagement," he said disbelievingly. "What else was I to conclude but that *you* wished for release?"

Elowen had no answer for him. She could hardly tell him the mortifying truth, which was that her purpose had been to elicit compliments from him. She'd never felt more childish. She at least appreciated Theo's forbearance in not listing his other reason for doubt, namely the fact that he still hadn't received a straight answer about a wedding date.

"That's not the case," she said at last, her voice small.

Not eager to discuss it further, she urged her horse into a walk, and Theo kept pace with his own mount. They meandered through the floating gardens in a silence that couldn't be called companionable.

"Congratulations on your victory in the maze run," Elowen said at last. "You won it convincingly, I understand." The polite, impersonal way Theo inclined his head in acknowledgment of the compliment irked her, and she couldn't resist adding, "Perhaps it almost makes you wish the tournament was real, for the satisfaction."

"Hardly," said Theo coolly. "I would have been very reluctant to enter into a marriage of alliance that required me to perform like a dancing animal in order to secure it."

"How unfortunate for you that my kingdom's traditions are so damaging to your pride," Elowen shot back with a snap. "But I thought any reluctance you or I felt had no relevance to this betrothal."

Theo gave her a sideways look. "I've offended you," he said. "I apologize."

"I'd rather you didn't apologize than do so without meaning it," retorted Elowen.

"Who says I don't mean it?" Theo demanded.

Elowen made an incredulous noise. "Everything in your manner."

There was a moment of silence. "I can acknowledge that I'm not skilled in pleasant manners," Theo said, surprising her with the honesty. "But I didn't intend to offend you, and my apology was sincere. What you said is perfectly reasonable—our opinions didn't factor into our betrothal, and I can understand your frustration over that."

Elowen was silent for a moment, softened by his straight speaking.

"It's not that I resent our betrothal," she said slowly. "But I wish I knew you better. I feel that I'm learning daily what you don't like, but I wish I knew what you *do* like."

"In a woman?" Theo seemed so taken aback that Elowen had to hold in a laugh. It seemed he would have no idea how to answer that particular question, and as his betrothed, she wasn't sure whether that was depressing or heartening.

"No," she said, still trying to curb her smile. "I meant in general. Your interests, your preferences."

"My apologies." Theo paused, collecting himself. "I enjoy reading. Riding, as we are now."

She waited, but he said no more.

"That's all?" she demanded, exasperated. "Don't you want to get to know each other? Do you have no interest in deepening the connection between us?"

She knew she was speaking more frankly than a proper, decorous princess should, and perhaps that was why his voice was a little stiff when he replied.

"Of course I do. But we'll have ample time to get to know one another."

Elowen wasn't at all satisfied by that answer, and she turned away to hide her irritation. He was so sure of her, and although her sense acknowledged he had reason, her heart didn't appreciate his emotionless confidence.

She came to a stop near the water's edge, dismounting smoothly and handing off her horse to one of her guards. Moving on foot, and aware of Theo following at a stately pace, she strolled over an arching footbridge that spanned this section of garden.

Elowen paused at the far end of the bridge, leaning over the railing to look down into the water. She was delighted to see a small cluster of tadpoles darting through the shallows, and she moved around the side of the railing, disregarding her gown and kneeling down at the edge of the water. She noticed Theo coming down the bridge behind her, and a foolish, fleeting thought flashed through her head as she tried to imagine his reaction if she were to push him in. She put a hand to her mouth to keep back an almost hysterical giggle that suddenly threatened to emerge. The image defied imagination.

Elowen reached out over the water, trying to get hold of a beautiful water lily of a shockingly bright pink. She was so close, but she couldn't quite reach it. Her arm simply wasn't long enough.

She was gripped with an absurd defiance, suddenly unwilling to accept her limitations. She narrowed her eyes, focusing on the movement of a large fish wending its way through the water, and trying to recall her training on accessing Dust stirred by animals. Waving her scarf around would be a simpler means of harnessing magic, but it would be too conspicuous. Elated, she felt the moment the steady trickle of magic entered a deeper layer of her awareness, and she focused her mind on shaping it into a movement enchantment. It was a simple process—the magic had come from movement through the water, and she didn't have to change its shape to direct it to do the same for a different object. The lily pad on which the pink flower floated inched nearer to her outstretched fingers. Encouraged, Elowen persisted with her efforts, needing only another moment before the lily pad had slid smoothly within her reach.

She snatched up the flower, standing up and turning around in triumph with it clutched in her hand. She was met with the sight of Theo, much closer than she'd realized, watching her with an expression that was uncomfortably piercing.

"It's a nymphaea," she said, clearing her throat in an attempt at nonchalance. "They're imported from Pulau, and they're my favorite. The color is so striking, don't you think?"

"I'm less struck by the color than by your casual use of magic craft," Theo said bluntly.

Elowen flushed, pulling the flower back toward her. "I don't know what you mean."

Theo frowned, and he went up in her estimation when he lowered his voice with a glance at her guards.

"Was I not supposed to see that? Did you really think I wouldn't notice?"

She sighed. "Yes, to be honest, that's exactly what I thought. Didn't you say you weren't encouraged to study magic?"

"I did," he said promptly. "And you said the same."

"Yes." Elowen looked down at her hands, fidgeting with the flower. "I...I have studied magic," she said in a rush of honesty. "But it wasn't with my tutor."

"Who did you study with?" he asked, clearly confused. When she hesitated, he prompted her again. "Elowen?"

"It was Simeon who taught me," Elowen confessed. "You've met him. He's a servant in the household of the Duke of Nirocha, and he's very skilled in magic craft."

One of Theo's straight eyebrows flew up at her words, and when he spoke, something in his tone made her uneasy.

"I see."

"I suppose you'll disapprove," Elowen said, a defiant flush on her cheeks. "I know that in Siqual, as in Torrens, magic isn't considered a proper pursuit for ladies of high birth."

"Or men of high birth, either," Theo confirmed. "I'm astonished this young man, Simeon, was willing to risk his position to teach you clandestinely."

"So was I, to be frank," Elowen said. "I have no idea how she convinced him. But she was confident he'd agree."

Theo's brow was furrowed. "She?"

"Oh, Sophia," Elowen said quickly. "Didn't I say? She's the duke's daughter, and it was her idea. Simeon taught us together, in weekly sessions over the last year or so. I'm by no means proficient, but I feel I've made excellent progress."

Theo considered her thoughtfully, his manner altered by this new information for reasons she didn't yet grasp.

"I don't disapprove of your desire to learn to manipulate Dust," he told her. "I see the sense in it. In fact, I was jealous of my sister when she was allowed to study magic at her academy here in Torrens. I believe the academy was unusual in that regard."

"Yes," said Elowen with a sigh. "I begged to be allowed to go to that academy, but my parents were adamant I be educated at the castle." She snuck a look at him. "It's strange to think your sister and I may have been friends if I'd been allowed to attend. So it's true, then, that in Siqual, magic isn't generally studied by members of the court?"

"Not beyond a rudimentary level of understanding," Theo

confirmed. "In fact, magic in general isn't used much in my castle. I've noticed it in use much more here. In my family, we're taught that while it can be useful, we should take care not to become reliant on it, and that it ought not to be wasted on trivial matters like our comfort, but used for purposes that will benefit the whole kingdom."

"I can see how that's a noble perspective," Elowen commented. "But we see it a little differently. Certainly the study of magic is a craft and isn't considered a proper use of time for upper classes, as in your kingdom. But I was never taught any reluctance to use it for everyday purposes. We just do so through our servants. I was taught that as a princess, it's appropriate that I let others serve me in that way, and focus my energies on my own role. Such as it is." The last phrase was added in a murmur, and she thought she caught a sympathetic hint in Theo's answering smile.

"A cultural difference, I suppose," he said. "I had understood from Miriam that magic was used much more commonly at her academy, but I thought it was perhaps a quirk of that institution rather than Torrens in general. Do you think it risks making people lazy?"

It was Elowen's turn to smile. "Perhaps. But when we're speaking of people whose every need is met by servants, I think that risk exists with or without magic."

"An excellent point."

Theo's lips tugged up in one corner in a smile that brought a hint of warmth to Elowen's cheeks. She liked how his features were softened when he was surprised into a genuine smile. She liked even more knowing that she was the one who'd drawn it out.

"Are you going to tell my father?" she asked him, an entreaty in her eyes. "I don't wish to get either Sophia or

Simeon in trouble. Or myself, for that matter," she added with a rueful smile.

Theo looked surprised. "You can trust my confidence," he assured her. "Naturally I respect your father and defer to his authority as king while I'm in Torrens. But on personal matters, I don't answer to him now any more than I will once we're married."

Elowen brightened. "Does that mean I might be allowed to further study magic when we're married and I live in Siqual?"

A hint of Theo's smile was back. "I certainly wouldn't object."

Warmth rushed over Elowen as, for the first time, she felt genuine excitement about her future in Siqual with Theo. Impulsively, she laid her hand on his arm.

"Thank you."

Theo's muscles tightened under her touch, and for a moment, he held her gaze in charged silence. His eyes refused to release her, their scrutiny nothing like the perceptive but bloodless assessment she was used to from him. She'd never suspected so much intensity was hiding under his usual control.

Then he stepped back, and the moment was gone. She dropped her arm to her side as the contact was broken, struggling to understand the abruptness of the shift in Theo's mood.

"I should return to the castle," Theo said gruffly. "I need to prepare for this afternoon's event."

"Yes," said Elowen, breathless from some combination of their charged moment and her subsequent embarrassment. "Of course, it's the first round of the weapons combat, isn't it?"

Theo acknowledged it, already turning away to cross back over the bridge. Elowen followed him, deflated when he mounted his horse at once instead of offering to help her. They rode back to the castle in silence, and parted ways as soon as they entered the courtyard.

Elowen completed her own preparations in confused distraction. What exactly had she done wrong to turn him from the warmer Theo she'd been so fascinated by to the polite prince of before?

If it wasn't so wildly inconsistent with what she knew of him, she would have suspected Theo of trying to lure her by blowing hot and cold, as she'd seen some of the more skillful flirts in her father's court do with such success. Not that his manner could be called hot even at its warmest. In any event, Theo's changing moods didn't repel her. If anything, they just increased her desperation to understand him, and she found herself impatient to get to the tournament field.

There was no opportunity for private speech with Theo during the weapons event, but Elowen didn't mind. She had enough to occupy her in watching him from the royal family's section of the stands. She could hardly take her eyes off him as he performed much better than she'd expected. He was skilled and confident with a sword, and she felt her lips curl in a smile of girlish satisfaction as she watched him best his first opponent within minutes. Cheering for one's champion was part of a princess's duty, after all. And it was pleasant, especially if you didn't actually get to choose your champion, to discover that he was worth cheering for.

She was relieved not to see Bertrand competing in that round, or even watching from the stands. His absence was a welcome relief. She was vaguely aware of the favorites for this event, and she didn't see any of those in Theo's opponents. But he capably beat every man he fought, his movements graceful and fluid in a way he rarely was in social interactions. Confusion leaked in to complicate Elowen's satisfaction as she watched his performance.

She felt like she was living a strange dual existence. In face-to-face interactions with Theo, she was constantly frustrated by his coldness, the gulf between them seeming uncrossable. And yet, at the same time, she was more and more fixated on him, watching him from afar with growing fascination. As he emerged the winner of his pool in the first round, she was reminded of how she'd been on the edge of her seat following his efforts in the maze run.

With each passing day, she learned more of the man she was to marry. He was intelligent, physically strong, had a powerful sense of honor, and wasn't too proud to show care for vulnerable creatures like her horse. If he was to be believed, he was even inclined to give her license as her husband to pursue magic in defiance of tradition.

There was just one fairly significant problem.

He was completely uninterested in *her*. Any time they seemed to get closer, he would pull back. The more she tried to draw him out, the colder and stiffer he became. She wanted him to chase her, at least a little. But instead it felt like she was chasing him. And even though they were betrothed for all intents and purposes, she still couldn't seem to get his interest.

She suddenly understood her flare of emotion at the floating gardens, when she'd been unable to reach the nymphaea. It was the same with Theo, she realized. He was so close, and sometimes she felt she was almost there. But try as she might, she couldn't quite reach him. Just as her arm, while perfectly functional, wasn't long enough to get to that flower, it seemed she simply didn't possess the ability to captivate her future husband.

And she didn't think she'd ever be able to accept that.

CHAPTER
ELEVEN

Theo

The day after Elowen took him to the floating gardens was a rest day for the court. A few commoner's events were still being held, but most noble-born competitors were taking the day to recover their strength after the first round of the weapons combat. Theo decided not to visit the training yard this time. Perhaps he'd be wise to prepare for the next round, but he didn't have the heart for it.

His thoughts were on Elowen, and they were too murky for him to understand. His mind kept dwelling on her confiding manner when she'd trusted him not to betray her secrets. It had been a good feeling. But then his memory would fly to the sensation of her touch when she'd grabbed his arm, and he found himself shying away in thought just as he had in reality. It was a painful memory, exposing his weakness. The rush of longing that had gone over him had shocked him. A bare touch of her hand, and he'd wanted to pull her into his arms and compel those expressive eyes to look up into his face again. He'd lived by rigid control for so many years. What was it about Elowen that threatened to fracture it every time he let himself soften even a little?

Most unsettling of all, under his disappointment in himself were other sensations. A part of him didn't care that he'd showed weakness, instead reveling in the memory of her touch. That was the selfish part, he knew, and it could never be the guiding voice for a prince bound by duty to his kingdom.

There was no denying that his selfish emotions, however tightly bound, were growing increasingly eager for the marriage he'd committed to. And he was fortunate, because marrying Elowen would serve his kingdom. But losing control of himself to emotion, and therefore allowing himself to be drawn into petty jealousies and childish competitions, wouldn't serve Siqual. It would dishonor it in front of their Torrenese allies.

Pulling away instead of indulging his desires at the floating gardens had been the responsible course. So why did he still feel so conflicted?

Elowen's behavior since that moment hadn't done anything to lift his spirits. He'd seen how closely she watched his fights in the afternoon. In fact, he wished he could deny how much he'd been motivated to win every match by the desire to impress her. More evidence of him letting his emotions distract him, and pointless as well. She hadn't shown any sign of being impressed. In fact, not only had she failed to approach him after the match, she'd barely spoken to him at dinner beyond what politeness required. It seemed he'd been the only one to feel a moment of connection at the floating gardens.

Theo had no delusions about himself. He'd known he was considered stiff long before Lord Bertrand had so snidely said it in front of him. He'd never expected to have much success in wooing a woman. He wasn't Xavier, he reflected dryly, with women falling all over him every time he smiled. But he had an arranged marriage, and the woman in question was already fully committed to him, by her own words as well as their kingdoms' agreement. How was he still failing so dismally? He'd tried to show her by his actions that he was dependable and committed, and that he would always behave with honor. He supposed she was disappointed that he wasn't like any of the daydreams Lord Bertrand had described. The thought did nothing to improve his mood, and his strides were jerky and unsettled as he made his way to breakfast.

Just inside the door to the dining hall, he was greeted by King Ronan, who was deep in conversation with the duke. The king's greeting suggested he would have preferred Theo to keep moving, but instead Theo joined the pair.

"Good morning, Your Grace," he greeted the duke, inclining his head politely. "Is there any update on the issue with the magic?"

The duke bowed, his tone respectful but his words careful as he looked to the king for guidance.

"Good morning, Your Highness, and thank you for your interest. Rest assured that all possible resources have been put into the investigation."

"Yes, your efforts have been commendable," King Ronan said. He inclined his head to Theo. "His Grace has been thorough and strategic, as he is known for. In fact, many innovations in the capital—especially those involving magic craft—are thanks to his generosity with his time and resources."

"I've admired some of those innovations myself," Theo commented. "I hope in time perhaps you'll be so gracious as to share your insights with Siqual as well."

The duke's expression was a little more forced as he bowed again. Theo suspected he was eager to return to his task. Theo shifted slightly back, allowing the men to continue the conversation he'd interrupted. Privately, he wrestled with the question of whether to report what he'd felt in the maze the day before. He was hesitant because Elowen's words at the floating garden told him that, like his own parents, King Ronan would be unlikely to commend him for the focus he'd given to his magical sense. He was even afraid the king would think he'd been trying to use it to cheat in the maze event.

Discomfort trickled through him as he remembered what Elowen had told him about her clandestine magical studies. She had been too generous in assuming his disapproval had related to the magic. In reality it had a much pettier cause, and he hadn't wanted her to know the flicker of jealousy he'd felt at the thought of her shared secret with the servant Simeon. He hadn't criticized that aspect, knowing that doing so would reveal his childish jealousy. And the knowledge that Elowen's friend had been not only part of these lessons but their orchestrator certainly softened the information.

Theo's attention returned to the pair in front of him, dismayed to realize he'd once again let his emotions distract him. The duke was speaking of his plans to leave after breakfast and travel northwest of the capital.

"I beg your pardon for the interruption, but what's to the northwest?" Theo asked, determined not to be kept out of the matter.

The king's eyes flicked to him. "A forested region," he said. "His Grace is following a trail, and he intends to investigate reports of a suspicious landslide."

"A landslide?" Theo repeated, thoughtfully. "I would be grateful to be included in the expedition, Your Grace. I have no commitments at the tournament today."

The duke hesitated. "You're very generous, Your Highness, but I wouldn't wish to pull you from the safety of the castle."

"I believe our roads are as safe as any on the Peninsula," the king said mildly. "If Prince Theodore wishes to accompany you, I don't object."

The duke bowed, accepting the polite command without further argument. "We will prepare to leave after breakfast," he told Theo.

"Leave for where?"

Elowen's voice made them all turn, to see the queen and princess entering the room behind them.

"Prince Theodore is going to accompany the duke on an investigative trip northwest of the capital today," King Ronan informed his daughter.

Elowen's gaze was shrewd as it passed between her father and Theo. "I'd like to go as well."

"Absolutely not," the queen interjected quickly.

"Why not?" asked Elowen.

"The tournament, for one reason." The queen's brow was creased in a warning.

Elowen blinked. "But ten minutes ago, I asked if I needed to go to the commoners' competition today, and you said that I don't have to."

Queen Lisbeth didn't look impressed to have this information shared. "I said so in the belief that you needed rest after the three days of the tournament so far."

"Oh, I don't need rest," Elowen said cheerfully. "A good gallop on Ochre will be more restful for my spirits than lying on a settee somewhere."

"It's an excellent idea, Elowen," said the king. "A chance for you and Prince Theodore to come to better understanding of one another."

There was something very specific in the look he gave his daughter, but Theo couldn't read it. Judging by the hint of defiance that crossed Elowen's immaculate features, she could.

"Surely it's not wise," the queen protested. "Have you forgotten what happened last time Elowen joined such a venture?"

"I have not," the king assented. "But this is different, Lisbeth. The landslide has already happened, this is an investigation after the fact. Not to mention, on this occasion it's not as far from the capital, and naturally she will take a full complement of guards."

His words were so decisive, the queen had no choice but to be satisfied. Theo didn't object to Elowen's inclusion, but he did wonder what the king hoped would be achieved by his orchestrations. Was Elowen supposed to distract him from paying close attention to the investigation? That thought seemed unfair to King Ronan.

"If a party is being formed, perhaps my own children would wish to join," the duke said.

"I believe, Your Grace, that Lord Bertrand is occupied for the day in training for tomorrow's competition," Elowen cut in smoothly. "But I would be delighted to ask Sophia if she'd like to join us."

Theo noted that neither the duke nor the king seemed pleased with this answer, although neither said so. For his part, he wasn't sure whether to be glad that Elowen seemed to be trying to exclude Lord Bertrand or concerned that she knew his training schedule. Picturing the sea of sweaty, mostly shirtless men to be found at the training yard each day, he hoped that Elowen hadn't been watching on.

With the prospect of getting out of the city, each member of the group ate their breakfast quickly, and it wasn't long before they were ready to depart. Elowen had found Lady Sophia as she'd promised, and the two of them rode side by side behind Theo and the duke.

Theo tried at first to find out more about the progress of the investigation, but in the absence of the king, the duke was even less inclined to give him information. Once they'd cleared the city, the duke increased his pace to speak to a member of the

Craftsmen's Guild who'd accompanied them, and Theo drifted back toward Elowen and Lady Sophia. The loose ring of guards shifted seamlessly to accommodate the change, Paulson falling in with their formation.

The group rode for a couple of hours before crossing a river by means of a wide, stone bridge. On the far side of the river, the road plunged immediately into a forest large enough that Theo hadn't been able to see either end as they approached.

"No time for a wolpertinger hunt today," Elowen said lightly, as their horses carried them beneath the arching branches that now formed a roof over the road.

"No," Lady Sophia agreed. Theo had never seen much liveliness from her, but during the ride she'd been especially subdued. There hadn't been much light chatter between the two young women.

"I've never been to this area before," Elowen said. "Isn't this the region Simeon's family comes from?"

Theo's eyes flicked over to them at the name, noting the quick, conscious look Lady Sophia shot in his direction.

"Yes, it is," the noblewoman confirmed. "At least, his mother's family. His father's family have lived and worked on our estate for several generations."

"And didn't he just visit his family recently?" Elowen pressed.

Lady Sophia cleared her throat, once again glancing at Theo before she spoke.

"Yes, I think so. That sounds right."

Elowen's brow crinkled as she studied her friend, but she didn't push further.

They rode for less than an hour through the trees before emerging into a large, cleared area. They were met by a collection of scattered stone cottages nestled below a wooded slope of surprising height. It would have been a picturesque scene if not for the enormous section of slope that had fallen sharply away and the signs of several ruined houses under the debris at the base. There was rubble and dirt everywhere, and branches stuck out of the mud at strange angles, bearing testament to the trees that had been ripped out by the motion of the landslide.

Everyone had fallen silent at the confronting sight, dismounting in silence as the village head approached. The duke took the opportunity to address his daughter, his voice stern.

"Sophia, you and the princess are to keep well back. Stay with the guards, all right?"

"Yes, Father, we will," Lady Sophia said earnestly.

Theo handed his horse over to Paulson, following the duke with only a swift glance back at the women. Elowen looked disappointed but resigned. Given the events of the dam rupture, not to mention the tower collapse right before he arrived in Toledda, Theo was relieved she was being cautious.

He, on the other hand, intended to be right among the action. He shadowed the duke closely as he spoke to the village head, and heard several similar accounts of what had occurred. The incident was bizarre, given the mild weather they'd been having and the absence of any known cause of the landslide, but there wasn't anything beyond that to support the view that the event was suspicious.

Until the village head took them around the far side of the destroyed area, and introduced them to one of the men working to clear it.

"You've heard the basics of what happened," the village head said. "But Ralph is the one who was closest, and he reckons he saw something none of the rest of us did."

His interest caught, Theo strode alongside the duke to meet

this Ralph. He was a muscled man in middle age, with graying hair and work-roughened hands.

"Yer Grace, Yer Highness," Ralph said, bowing briefly to them both after the village head had explained the purpose of their visit. "I doubt I can help much, but I'm happy to answer any questions. Only I'd prefer not to leave the fellers to continue without me too long, since I'm directing operations."

"We won't keep you long," the duke said. "Apparently you were close at hand when the landslide occurred?"

"Aye, that's right," Ralph said. "Not a blessed thing I could do to stop it, though."

"Of course not," the duke said reassuringly. "Are you familiar with Dust? Magic, I mean?"

Ralph looked bemused. "I know what it is, if that's what yer asking. But I don't know how to manipulate it. Never learned. Never learned much beyond my father's trade, actually. My family've been woodcutters long as anyone can remember."

"So there's no one in this village proficient enough in magic to tell if anything was different at the time of the landslide?" Theo pressed.

The man shrugged. "Don't reckon so, Yer Highness."

"And what time did it happen?" Theo asked.

Ralph scratched his chin, considering. "I'd had cause to stop home at lunchtime that day, and was just leaving the village again. I reckon about half past one."

Theo said nothing, but he was silently calculating. It was a similar time to when he'd felt something strange in the maze run. A chill went over him. There wasn't enough evidence to draw a clear connection between the two events, and he found himself hoping it was only his imagination bringing them together. He didn't like to think how significant a magical event would be required for something happening out here to affect the movement of Dust in the capital.

"We were told you saw something no one else did," the duke prompted Ralph.

"Aye, Yer Grace." He nodded. "I saw a young feller running away just after the landslide."

"Someone you recognized?" the duke asked.

Ralph shook his head. "His face was covered with a scarf, so I can't be sure. But I know all the lads in the village, and I don't reckon he was one of ours. Mebbe that's why, but it seemed odd to me, the way he was running away."

"Wasn't everyone running away?" the duke asked.

"Yes, but from the base of the hill," Ralph clarified. "This feller was at the top. Mebbe he was just scared of sliding down the hill along with all the mud and rock and trees, or mebbe he had something to do with it. Who knows?"

"What else can you tell us about him?" the duke asked, his eyes sharp with interest. "His clothes, any details you can remember."

"I didn't get that good a look," Ralph admitted. "All I could see was the purple scarf over his face. And he was cradling something in his arms. Couldn't tell what, but it must've been valuable, because he didn't drop it when he was running."

Theo looked from Ralph to the duke, to see a small frown creasing the older man's forehead. He seemed to be deep in thought over Ralph's tale. It certainly gave them something to look into.

They were subjected to accounts from many more people, some of whom hadn't even been present, but were still eager to share their speculations. Nothing more of interest was added. They were well and truly ready to leave by the time the guild member completed his inspection of the site. The whole process had taken longer than hoped, and they were unlikely now to make it back to the capital in time for the dinner hour.

Thanking the village head for his hospitality, they rode out of the clearing, eager to be on the road.

"What's your conclusion?" the duke asked the guild member as they passed beneath the trees once again.

"I examined the source of the landslide. While it's possible it was caused by magic, there's no great evidence of that," the guild member said, frowning. "But the magic in the area feels strange, even now."

"Strange how?"

"Well, I used Dust generated by the movement of the trees to fuel some simple enchantments. And while it worked as normal, the Dust didn't settle like I expected once my enchantments were complete. The branches were still moving, but the magic issuing from them was unsettled and uneasy, as if my minimal access had exhausted it."

Theo frowned, shooting a look at Paulson, who happened to be riding very close by. The guard looked somber, his expression when he met Theo's eye seeming to give confirmation of the guild member's words.

The duke relapsed into thoughtful silence when the report was finished, and Theo didn't try to press him for his conclusions. He fell back, riding alongside Paulson for a while, although they shared no words, only a troubled silence. After a time, the road through the trees widened enough to allow several people to ride side by side. Paulson moved to join the guards' new formation, and Theo found himself alongside Elowen, Lady Sophia on the princess's other side. He'd heard nothing of their conversation, so was caught by surprise at Lady Sophia's words to the princess.

"Simeon told me once that there are sometimes carbuncles in the cliffs on the other side of this forest."

Theo stiffened, engulfed by the same rush of emotions—

none of them pleasant—that he always felt when carbuncles were mentioned.

"It's such a shame it's not the solstice," Elowen said brightly. "Or we could have gone hunting." She looked over at Theo, those piercing blue eyes too perceptive for his current state. "What do you think, Theo?"

"I have no interest in the creatures," he said curtly.

One of Elowen's perfectly sloping eyebrows rose, but it was Lady Sophia who responded, surprising them both by speaking up.

"I do. I would give a great deal for a carbuncle favor."

Theo eyed the noblewoman's wistful expression.

"You would be likely to regret it if you found one," he told her. "Whatever you hope it would magically give you, you'd be better off working to achieve it by honest, non-magical means."

"No doubt you're right," Lady Sophia said, her polite tone forced and unhappy.

"Wise words," Elowen said, although her tone contradicted the compliment. She was nettled by his chastisement of her friend, apparently. "But some of us try the best we know how and still fail to achieve our desires through non-magical means, don't we?"

Theo said nothing, his thoughts circling uncomfortably around his various recent failures.

"There really isn't anything you want favor for?" Elowen was needling him now. "Maybe a carbuncle favor would let you magically set the wedding date you're so determined to lock down."

Theo felt his jaw set. "If I can't get what I need without magical favor, perhaps I don't deserve it."

"Perhaps." Elowen sounded miffed, but he also thought he detected a flush on her cheeks. Did she regret her blunt words? Or just his cold answer?

Theo pulled his horse away, keeping his distance for the rest of the ride.

As expected, dinner was over by the time they reached Toledda. Tired and saddle-sore, the three younger members of the group ate a late dinner together in a small dining parlor in the castle, the duke having gone on to his city manor. The spread was still excellent, and they mostly ate in appreciative silence.

Theo therefore had plenty of time to regret his part in the uncomfortable moment on the road, and he decided to stay with Elowen until she'd said goodbye to her friend, in hopes of a private moment to apologize.

He should have known better. The three of them had just finished eating and were emerging back into the castle's large entranceway when an unwelcome addition strolled up to the group.

"My dear, foolish Princess!" Lord Bertrand's eyes were over-bright as they rested on Elowen's face. "What did I hear about you riding all over the country without me to keep you out of mischief?" He didn't give her time to respond before directing his attention at Theo, his expression indulgent. "Of course, you had your dashing prince at hand, so no doubt all was well."

Elowen, not looking pleased, seemed on the point of responding, but Lord Bertrand wasn't finished. His gaze was cool as it rested finally on his sister.

"I'm burning with curiosity to hear the extreme circum-stances that prevented you from informing me about the expe-dition, Sophia."

"Sophia had no reason to raise the matter with you," Elowen said. "You weren't invited."

"Because Elowen thought you were training today," Lady Sophia added quickly.

Elowen sent her friend a swift frown at the amendment, but Lord Bertrand didn't seem to see it. He waved an airy hand.

"I only trained for an hour or so. No one at the tournament gives me enough competition to require serious training."

Theo raised an eyebrow. It was a bold declaration given some of the sword work he'd seen from others in the training yard. He was aware that he had been placed in a pool of less skilled swordsmen to make sure he emerged looking capable, but he knew there were other groups with much stiffer competition.

"Perhaps you were misinformed about my activities," Lord Bertrand told his sister. "But taking Simeon along with you without clearing it with me was too far, Sophia."

Lady Sophia stared at him. "What do you mean? Simeon didn't come with us. Why did you think he had?"

Surprise flashed across Lord Bertrand's face, followed by irritation. "I've been unable to find him all day."

Lady Sophia looked concerned, but she said nothing. Theo saw the way Elowen looked to her friend, as if hoping for a moment of silent communication, but Lady Sophia avoided her eye. Something clearly wasn't right between them, and Simeon seemed to have something to do with it.

"I was just heading home, Bertrand," Lady Sophia said. "We can walk together."

"I've just come from there," said her brother. "I thought I'd see if the princess would like to take a walk with me in the castle gardens."

"Actually, it's been a long day, and I'm ready to retire," Elowen said. She stepped back, as if to take her leave, but was hailed by another young member of King Ronan's court. The man bustled over, clearly full of news.

"Your Highness!" He bowed deeply to Elowen then, as an

afterthought, more stiffly to Theo. "I didn't see you at the tournament today. I hope you're well?"

"Did you go to watch the commoners' pig racing, Erik?" Lord Bertrand said, lazy derision in his voice.

"Yes, I did, and it was very entertaining," the other young man said, unashamed. "At least until the news came in, then everyone was too busy talking about that to pay much attention to the pigs."

"What news?" Elowen demanded.

He turned to her. "There was a huge forest fire not far to the south of here. No one knows how it started, and they're calling it suspicious. It was enormous, it's destroyed a whole section of the forest."

"How terrible!" Elowen said. "Was anyone killed?"

"They don't know yet. It's not a very populated area of forest, but there were a few houses destroyed. They're trying to ascertain whether everyone got out in time."

A friend of the newcomer called him from across the entranceway, and he quickly bowed before hurrying away.

"Another disaster?" Theo's eyes met Elowen's, his own frown reflected on her face. "The tower collapse, the dam failure, the landslide, now a fire." He lowered his voice. "Have you noticed that all of these disasters are of a type that could generate significant magic?"

"Are you an investigator, Your Highness?" Lord Bertrand sounded amused. "A forest fire surely doesn't fit that description."

"If you mean it wouldn't generate a lot of magic, it could, actually," Lady Sophia interjected. "The fire isn't tangible enough for its movement to stir up Dust, but the smoke is. A huge forest fire would no doubt create a vast plume of smoke, which moves constantly and swiftly."

They all looked at her in surprise, Lord Bertrand's eyebrow

rising toward his hairline. "You seem to know a great deal about the matter, Sophia."

She just shrugged, her cheeks pink but a hint of defiance in her posture. Her gaze wandered over the entranceway, and her color deepened as she caught sight of an approaching figure. Following her eyes, Theo saw Simeon coming in, looking weary and dusty as if from travel, his gaze searching the space. When he saw their group, he moved quickly toward them.

"Simeon!" Lord Bertrand scowled at him. "Finally."

"Apologies, My Lord, I heard you were looking for me," the servant said, bobbing his head.

"Yes, all day."

Something flitted across Simeon's face at the terse words, but Theo didn't know him well enough to read it.

"You seem unconcerned with leaving me to manage without magic during a particularly challenging time," Lord Bertrand chastised. "You must think beyond your own convenience, Simeon."

Lady Sophia made a protesting noise, and Elowen looked openly angry. It didn't surprise Theo to learn that the young viscount saw his servant's skill in magic as an extension of his own capabilities, his to claim by right. He remembered King Ronan's words about the duke's family being generous with time and resources in contributing to magical innovations in the capital. He wondered how much of it had been single-handedly completed by Simeon, to the sole credit of his employers.

The young servant said nothing in response to the viscount's rebuke, but as Theo studied him, he saw a hardness in his expression that Simeon seemed to be trying to hide. There was defiance in his eyes. The thought flashed through Theo's mind that he was looking at a man on the edge of something, and it made him uneasy.

"Lord Bertrand, Lady Sophia." Another man, this one in the uniform of a servant, came toward them. "Have you seen—Simeon!" He cut himself off as he caught sight of the servant. "There you are."

"Yes, were you looking for me?" Simeon's voice was quiet and pleasant, the hardness held at bay.

"You dropped this in the courtyard just now," the servant said, holding out an item of clothing.

"Careless of you," Bertrand said casually.

Simeon stared down at the garment, his expression wary. After a moment, he accepted it from his fellow with a murmured word of thanks.

As the item changed hands, Theo realized that it was a scarf. A purple scarf. He stiffened, remembering the words of the man at the site of the landslide. His eyes searched Simeon's face, noting that the servant looked uncomfortable and eager to be gone. Surreptitiously studying the rest of the group, Theo saw that Bertrand looked unconcerned, and Elowen barely seemed to have noticed the exchange.

Did the garment not trigger her memory of the forester's story? Then it hit Theo—neither of the girls had heard the account. He and the duke had been followed around the site by many from their party—guards, servants of the duke, assistants to the member of the Craftsmen's Guild. But the princess and her friend had been told to stay well back from the site of the disaster. So mention of a purple scarf would mean nothing to them.

And yet...his eyes traveled last to Lady Sophia, and he realized that she looked even more uneasy than Simeon as her eyes lingered on the scarf. Where exactly had she been standing? Had she heard after all?

Theo frowned as he remembered the young noblewoman confirming that Simeon had recently visited family in that area.

How recently? And now, after he'd apparently been absent from his master all day, a suspicious fire had broken out not too far from the capital. Hadn't he also been with them when the tower collapsed, almost crushing Elowen and Lady Sophia? Theo distinctly remembered hearing his intervention praised. It was the first he'd heard of the servant, the first day he'd arrived in Toledda. And Simeon had showed up after the dam burst, too.

Unease and suspicion swirled through Theo. The worst of it was that Elowen wouldn't want to hear his thoughts. She had some kind of attachment to the servant. The familiar and hated spark of jealousy tried to light inside him again, and he fought back against it, trying not to let it color his judgment. Impossible to tell if it had done so.

He was relieved when the uncomfortable silence was broken by Lord Bertrand, regretfully saying that he'd best see his sister and servant home after all. Theo had never been more glad to see the back of anyone.

Elowen started to move toward the royal wing, but Theo stepped after her.

"Wait, Elowen."

She turned, looking up at him with a questioning, almost hopeful expression. Theo swallowed, wishing all he wanted to say was an attempted apology as he'd earlier intended.

"How well do you really know Simeon?" he asked, his voice gruff with the discomfort of the question.

Elowen's smooth brows drew together. "What do you mean by that?" There was an accusatory note in her voice.

"Only...how well do you trust his intentions?"

"His intentions?" She was moving rapidly toward haughty offense. "He's never shown any sign of improper behavior toward me."

"No." Aware he was bungling it, Theo shifted forward,

laying a hand on her arm to stop her as she half angled herself away. "I don't mean that."

Elowen stilled at once, swallowing visibly as her eyes flicked to his hand on her arm then up to his face.

"Then what do you mean?"

Speaking low, Theo laid out his suspicions, searching Elowen's face as confusion was replaced by disbelief then alarm.

He thought she would refute his words, but she was silent for a long moment after he finished speaking.

"Why are you telling me this?" she asked at last.

Theo let his arm drop at last, rocking back and frowning at the question. "Because...because I thought it might be important for you to know all this. And I thought you might be able to help me understand it."

"Really?" Her expression softened. "I appreciate you giving me your trust, Theo, I really do. But you're wrong about this. There's no way Simeon would be involved in anything like these disasters."

Her words were confident, but he saw the unease in her eyes. His information had unsettled her. He wanted to press her for more, but for one thing, they still stood in the bustling entranceway, and for another, she really did look tired after the day.

"I understand," he said, inclining his head in acknowledgment. "Hopefully the truth about all these incidents will come to light in the investigation."

"Yes," she agreed faintly. "I'll see you tomorrow."

He watched her go, her movements graceful even in her weariness. Her hair had come partially loose over the course of the day's ride, and the effect was very appealing. He wondered fleetingly how it would be if he could follow her, if they were retiring to the same room, if they were truly allowed to speak privately, to be just Theo and Elowen away from the eyes of the court and the expectations of their positions.

But that wasn't the case. And even though both Elowen and her father had assured him that the alliance was secure, he was sure they weren't telling him everything. And he couldn't shake the suspicion that the problems with the magic, the series of disasters, and the unconfirmed wedding date were all connected. And this Simeon was mixed up in it in some form or another, that much was clear.

Theo strode from the entranceway, finding his quarry just outside the royal stables.

"Paulson." He beckoned his guard to him, and the man hurried forward.

"Is all well, Your Highness? I was just checking our horses were properly cared for, and all seems in order."

"Paulson, I have a job for you." Theo spoke quietly and quickly, scanning the area to make sure no one could hear them. "The Torrenese royal guards have immediate security well in hand here. I want you to leave the capital and make some inquiries."

"I don't like to leave you, Your Highness." Paulson sounded uneasy.

"I trust it won't be for long," Theo said. "None of the locations in question are too far away." Still speaking at a murmur, he gave his instructions. "Be back as soon as you can," he said, dismissing Paulson with a nod.

Theo's mind was on the following day as he returned to the castle. He wasn't needed at the tournament until the afternoon. In the morning, he would avail himself of the castle's library for all the information he could learn about a specific aspect of magic craft.

CHAPTER

TWELVE

Elowen

Elowen slept poorly the night after the trip to the forest. The expedition hadn't afforded much chance for her to spend real time with Theo, and the interaction they had managed hadn't been entirely pleasant. She still stung a little over his frostiness when they'd talked about carbuncle favors. Certainly she wasn't suddenly ready to oblige her father, as he'd hinted at when orchestrating for her to accompany Theo on the trip.

But her irritation melted away when she remembered what Theo had said to her after dinner. It had floored her that he'd chosen to share his concerns with her and ask for her opinion. It was more than Patrick had ever done. Even her father, *indulgent* though he might be, wasn't in the habit of including her in any conversations about matters affecting the kingdom.

That wasn't the only reason the interaction took her mind off the uncertain state of her heart, however. Theo's words made her too uneasy regarding Simeon for her to think about much else. Surely he would have no hand in whatever was happening. But some of what Theo said had been uncomfortably hard to explain away.

Elowen opted to have breakfast brought to her rooms, too tired for court drama so early in the day. She'd been foolish to imagine it would be a peaceful alternative, however, since the maid who delivered it stayed to tend to Elowen's fire and lay out her clothes, chattering all the while. She was full of excitement over the announcement the queen had just made to the servants, that there was to be a smaller feast and ball that night, in addition to the victory feast everyone was expecting at the end of the tournament.

"I hadn't been told that," Elowen said, startled. "Why is Mother adding another ball?"

"Apparently Their Majesties just received word of some foreign dignitaries who'll be passing through Torrens, and they insisted that the party break their journey in Toledda, so they can be properly hosted."

"Who are the dignitaries?" Elowen demanded.

"I'm sure I don't know, Your Highness," the maid said. "Someone important, no doubt."

She was clearly much more interested in the ball than the visitors, and understandably so. The castle staff were usually encouraged to enjoy the food remaining after feasts, and Elowen knew the maids were always excited to see the court ladies in their finery.

For her part, she just felt exhausted. More formalities, more eyes on her. She wondered fleetingly if Theo would dance with her. He would probably be obliged to, given his status and their position. She doubted he would get much enjoyment from it. He didn't seem the type.

Deflated, she finished her food quickly, turning her mind to more immediate matters. She needed to speak to Simeon and set her doubts to rest. She knew she couldn't ask after his whereabouts without raising eyebrows, and reluctantly concluded that her best option was to ask the chatty maid to discover where Bertrand might be. He almost always kept Simeon close by.

The maid received her mission with a look Elowen knew well, and she realized with a sinking heart that a garbled version of the request would no doubt make its way around the servants' hall. She just hoped that Theo wouldn't hear of it and get the wrong idea. He was always particularly frosty when Bertrand was around, and honestly she didn't blame him. The viscount was an absolute nuisance.

The servant came back with a regretful posture.

"I wasn't able to find out where he is, Your Highness. But someone said they saw his manservant, Simeon, making his way toward the armory, so I could try to find him and ask if he knows."

"I can ask him," Elowen said lightly. "I could do with a walk."

As soon as the maid was out of sight, she hurried forward, eager to catch Simeon before he left the general area described. With any luck, he was retrieving something of Bertrand's, ready for the tournament events that afternoon, meaning he probably wasn't currently accompanying the viscount.

She was almost to the armory, having just passed the library door, when good fortune found her. Simeon appeared around a corner ahead, his arms full of Bertrand's chainmail.

"Simeon." Elowen looked around to see that the corridor was currently deserted. She slowed to a stop as Simeon bowed.

"Your Highness. Can I be of service?"

Elowen didn't answer at once, her eyes searching his face. He looked tired, and older than he used to, she realized. He'd never been fully relaxed in her presence, but when she and Sophia took lessons from him, he'd been lighter, happier. He'd laughed when their attempts at magic manipulation led to strange results, and been warm in his praise of their progress.

Now he was on edge every time she saw him, and there was a careful, almost wary edge to his respectful demeanor toward her.

"I wonder, Simeon, if I can be of service to you, actually," she said at last, speaking with studied lightness. "Are you...are you in some kind of trouble?"

"Trouble, Your Highness?" he repeated blandly. "I hope not."

Her brow creased as she studied his face. "Simeon, where were you yesterday?"

"I was—" His response had come quickly, but he cut himself off. "My duties kept me out of the capital much of the day."

"Duties?" she repeated, raising an eyebrow. "What duties could have kept you when neither Bertrand nor Sophia knew where you were?"

His lips were pressed into a line. It was clear he wasn't going to answer.

"I'm your friend, Simeon," she said earnestly. "At least, I'd like to be. If something is troubling you, let me help you."

"I have no troubles that you can help with, Your Highness," he said firmly. "And it wouldn't be appropriate for me to ask even if I did."

"Simeon, that scarf you dropped..." She trailed off, at a loss for how to ask him her questions in a way that wouldn't make him close off further.

"What of it, Your Highness?" Simeon asked, when she didn't continue.

"It's yours?"

"Of course."

"Are you...are you sure? You're not just being...agreeable?"

"I know you think I'm weak, Your Highness," Simeon said, the line of his jaw setting harder. "And maybe I am, in some ways. But I have a mind of my own, and the things I do, I do for reasons of my own. I don't feel the need to explain them to you. I know that I'm strong enough to fight for what matters."

"I…I'm sure you are," stammered Elowen, taken aback by the fire in his response. She studied his defiant face for a long moment before deciding to be bold. "Is this about Sophia, Simeon?"

A flicker crossed his face, but he mastered it, his jaw clenching briefly before he spoke.

"With respect, Your Highness, it wouldn't be the actions of a friend to carry tales to her. Better she stay out of it."

"Stay out of what, Simeon?" Elowen asked sharply. "I want to help you, if I can. I…" She faltered, choosing her words with care. "I know you have some reason to feel frustration, maybe even resentment. But please…" Daringly, she reached out a hand and gave his arm what she hoped was a reassuring squeeze. "Please don't do anything drastic, not without at least letting me try to help you first. You've been a true friend to me with your training, and I owe you this much, Simeon."

For a moment, Elowen saw longing enter his eyes, and she felt sure he was wrestling with a desire to unburden himself. Then his gaze moved past her shoulder, and he stepped quickly back. Giving her a respectful bow, he turned and walked away.

Elowen frowned after him for a moment before turning to see what had startled him. With a sinking heart, she saw Theo's familiar figure striding past, his face turned away but his form even stiffer than usual. She had no idea why he'd been in the library, but that was clearly where he'd just emerged from. He wasn't close enough to have heard their conversation, but he'd no doubt seen them. He'd been surprisingly supportive about her secret magic lessons, but that didn't mean he would approve of a personal friendship between her and a servant. She wished that if he objected, he would stop and say so, instead of being silently disapproving and absent.

Disheartened, Elowen made her way back through the castle, looking for her parents. They were nowhere to be found, so she had to content herself with informing Patrick of her plan to go to the duke's town residence in search of Sophia. She and her friend were supposed to attend the afternoon's events together, and Elowen didn't feel like being alone with her thoughts until then.

Patrick approved her outing with a paternal air that irked her, but she didn't waste energy on her brother's heavy-handed ways. It was a short ride to the duke's residence, made slightly longer by the slow pace made necessary by the quartet of guards Patrick had insisted on sending with her. When she arrived, she rode into the courtyard of the smart town manor at a trot, eager to dismount and get inside.

"No need to announce me," she said in an imploring voice to the house maid whom she encountered just inside the door. "I'm just here to collect Lady Sophia, we'll leave for the tournament fields at once."

The girl gave her an indulgent smile, sympathetic to the cause of avoiding the formality that would inevitably attend a princess's visit to the home of a duke and duchess. With a grateful smile, Elowen hurried toward the wing of the manor where the family's private rooms were located. She knew the house well, and knew that Sophia would probably be in the parlor they used when not entertaining. If she was unlucky, Bertrand might be with her, but the duchess was on the country estate, helping with the aftermath of the dam failure, and the duke was very unlikely to be relaxing with his family at this time of the day.

She'd almost reached the parlor when this confidence was shattered by the sound of a raised voice. Elowen's steps faltered, discomfort washing over her. She should have let the maid announce her. She'd never heard the duke so angry, and she knew he wouldn't wish a member of the royal family to witness it.

"You will not argue with me, Bertrand, your behavior has been ridiculous and ill-mannered. Your open hostility to Prince Theodore is the subject of gossip in every circle of the castle household. You are bringing shame to me and your mother."

Elowen flinched at the sharp words, even as she cheered internally to know that someone was doing what she couldn't, and reprimanding Bertrand for the trouble he was causing in her life.

"Your notions are archaic." Bertrand's answering voice shocked Elowen with its snide unconcern. "You must be the only one in our court who thinks there's any shame in treating a Siqualian however we might wish. You know as well as I do what filth they are."

Elowen put a hand to her mouth, stifling the gasp that had almost escaped. She knew many in Torrens still held some resentment against Siqual and Carrack, but it shocked her to hear it acknowledged so openly and forcefully. Besides which, she could hardly believe the lack of respect Bertrand showed his father. He didn't seem to care at all about the stinging rebuke the older man had given him.

"Your words are as dangerous as they are foolish," the duke snapped back now. "You are clearly too young and hotheaded to understand these matters. What do you hope to achieve by publicly alienating the Siqualian prince? No good can come of that."

"We'll have to disagree on that matter," Bertrand said, his unconcerned tone sounding arrogant even without the benefit of his expression. "I know exactly what I'm doing, and I won't fail to achieve what I want."

"And what exactly are you doing?" The duke's voice was more dangerous now, and Elowen found herself edging backward. "A straight answer, Bertrand."

"I don't think you'd like it if I obeyed that instruction."

Bertrand still spoke dismissively, and there was a moment of painful silence. Elowen thought the duke would surely force his son to answer, so the change in topic surprised her.

"Clearly you shouldn't attend tonight's event," the duke said crisply. "If you can't be trusted to conduct yourself with the dignity due your position, you cannot expect to enjoy the benefits."

Bertrand began a hot retort, but Elowen didn't stay to hear it. A door opening somewhere nearby made her jump, and she scurried back toward the manor's front door, afraid of being caught eavesdropping. She was just hesitating inside the door, unsure what to do, when footsteps brought her gaze up to the corridor she'd just fled down.

Sophia appeared, her steps heavy for such a slight frame, and her eyes a little red. She started when she saw Elowen, who tried to make her smile natural.

"Sophia. There you are."

"Elowen! I'm sorry if you've been waiting, I didn't know you were here."

"No, I dropped by unannounced, quite rudely," Elowen said lightly.

"Never mind that. Did you come to tell me about the ball tonight? We've already heard."

"No," said Elowen, tongue-tied as the comment reminded her of the conversation she'd just overheard. "But I'm sure it will be an...exciting event."

Unlike her own, Sophia's manner was becoming more natural, and she looked almost hopeful as she asked, "Did you come because you want to leave for the tournament fields now?"

"Yes, let's go," Elowen said emphatically.

Sophia was quick to agree, and soon the pair of them were leaving the manor. When they reached the tournament fields, they sent their horses back with a groom, strolling into the bustling area on foot. They had plenty of time before the second round of the weapons combat began, and they spent it wandering between the stalls that had popped up around the fields, buying fruit skewered on sticks, and sticky pastries to enjoy as they explored.

"This is the only time in my entire life I will ever be allowed to eat while walking," Elowen said through a mouthful of sweet, jam-filled pastry. "Or in public. I need to make the most of it."

"Don't hold back on my account," Sophia laughed. For a moment Elowen caught sight of the friend who'd been her companion through years of escapades. Then the cloud descended again, and Elowen's heart ached.

"What's wrong, Sophia?" she asked abruptly. "And don't say *nothing*, because you're not yourself. You haven't been for weeks and weeks."

Sophia's eyes darted around anxiously, the little shake of her head seeming unconscious. "I...I don't think I can explain it."

"Is it because your father and brother are fighting?" Elowen suggested.

Sophia's eyes were startled as they flew to her friend's face.

Elowen shrugged. "I overheard them arguing when I went to collect you just now. They both sounded...agitated."

Embarrassment flashed over Sophia's face, then, with a sigh of surrender, she let her shoulders slump. "They have been fighting a lot lately, and I hate it."

"But that's not what's been causing you so much distress," Elowen prodded gently.

Sophia said nothing, but the truth of Elowen's words was clear on her face.

"Sophia, is it because Simeon is in some kind of trouble?"

Sophia couldn't stifle her quick intake of breath. Elowen was sure she was onto something, and she stopped walking, turning to face her friend.

"Sophia, talk to me."

Sophia bit her lip, her eyes troubled as they finally met Elowen's.

"I can't talk to you, because he won't talk to me. I think something's seriously wrong, but he won't acknowledge it. He barely speaks to me anymore. And he's...different."

"Different how?" Elowen pressed.

"Well..." Sophia's eyes drifted over the nearby jousting field, glazed and unseeing. "He always used to be so gentle, you know how he is."

Elowen nodded. "One of the most patient and forbearing people I know."

"But now every time I see him, he seems tense and almost... angry," Sophia said. "I've never seen him like that before." She hesitated, guilt crossing her face. "Bertrand has been giving him a hard time. Simeon's always been so respectful to Bertrand, as he should be," she added hurriedly. "But more recently, sometimes I see something on his face. Like he's..."

Her voice faded, but Elowen finished the thought in her mind. *Like he's reached his limit.*

"I have this fear," Sophia went on, her voice constricted. "That Simeon is going to do something rash. Something he can't take back."

Elowen had no words of comfort for her friend. She was feeling her own trickle of fear that maybe Simeon already had done something he couldn't take back. Theo's words came back to her, as well as the altered manner she'd noticed herself in Simeon.

Surely Simeon wouldn't, *couldn't* cause these accidents. He was skilled in magic craft, yes, but he'd never use it for destruction. The dam failure especially had hurt his own region, the duke's region, sorely. And the tower had almost fallen on Sophia, whom she knew he'd never want to hurt.

But Sophia hadn't been near it when it started to collapse, had she? Only Bertrand had been. Discomfort swirled within Elowen. If anyone had reason to be tempted to hurt Bertrand, to hurt the interests of the duke and by extension his son, wasn't it Simeon?

No. Simeon wasn't like that. Elowen tried to shake the thought from her mind, but both girls were subdued as they watched the next round of the weapons combat from the stands.

There were two pools of fighters, competing in fields side by side, and Elowen's seat was right in the middle, where she could watch both.

Theo was in the one on the left, and she watched rapt as he progressed. He was really very good. She was impressed. His general manner was more that of a scholar or diplomat than a fighter. She wouldn't have guessed he had such wiry strength hidden beneath his somber demeanor.

Much as she admired his sword work, she gradually realized as she watched the two fields simultaneously that he wasn't being matched against the best fighters. He was facing new opponents, but the two top favorites from the previous round of that group seemed to have dropped out altogether. It was surprising. Elowen hadn't watched their whole round, but she didn't think anyone in it would have defeated either of them.

Sophia's attention was less focused on Theo, and she kept commenting on the progress of her brother in the field on the right. Elowen didn't feel much interest in Bertrand's prowess with a sword, but she listened as graciously as she could to Sophia's celebration of his victories. They were barely able to stay until the end of the round, the last-minute gala requiring them to retire early to prepare. But they saw the listings, and that both Theo and Bertrand were in the top five of their groups and would progress to the final round.

Elowen dressed for the feast with her thoughts far away. She hoped nothing too tedious would be expected of her with the visiting dignitaries. Between the mess that was her betrothal and whatever was happening with Simeon, she had enough on her mind. Her mother had selected her gown for her, which a maid had laid over her bed. It was a full-skirted gown of a dusky pink silk, and the lacing at the back took her maid fifteen full minutes to complete to her satisfaction. Elowen's hair took much longer, and she sat patiently as two assistants intricately braided it, then wrapped it in a complex crown around her head.

The result was good, she acknowledged to herself, as she studied the effect in her looking glass. The bodice of the dress was snug, its long lace sleeves tailored perfectly to her arms, and the expansive skirts swished pleasingly as she turned this way and that.

Surely Theo had to admire the effect. She tried to tell herself it was vanity to worry about that, but the question persisted.

She'd been summoned to attend the banquet hall early, to meet the visitors before the guests were invited to arrive, and she dutifully made her way through the castle as the sun was starting to set. When she entered the room, it was to find no visitors, but her family and Theo all gathered. Theo's eyes flew to her at once, and she tried to keep her expression steady.

That was admiration. He'd tried to hide it—*why* had he tried to hide it?—but she knew it too well to mistake it. A flush of pleasure buoyed her up as she sailed across the room, and she greeted her family more warmly than usual.

"Who are these important guests?" she asked lightly. "Some stuffy old earl, or an opinionated diplomat?"

"Elowen," Patrick said with a frown. "The prince and princess will be here any minute, watch your words."

"Prince and princess?" she repeated, looking to her mother.

Queen Lisbeth nodded. "Crown Prince Cassius and his wife, Princess Flora, have just returned from a visit to Pulau. They informed us of their desire to cross Torrens on their way back to Carrack, so naturally we invited them to break their journey here."

THIRTEEN

Elowen

"Prince Cassius and his wife?" Elowen's eyes lit up. She doubted the pair were eager to be forced into a formal gala halfway through an arduous journey, but selfishly, she was excited. She was very curious to meet them. "The famous, scandalous pair," she said, grinning at her mother.

"There's nothing scandalous about the heir to the Carrackian throne and his lawful wife," the queen said sternly.

"Well, not now," Elowen conceded. "But I remember plenty of whispers when she was serving as his bodyguard. It was quite a sensation, even here in Torrens."

"It was a sensation in Siqual as well," Theo interjected. "Although in our case it was largely outrage that the Carrackians had stolen away my sister's bodyguard to protect their prince."

Elowen stepped toward him eagerly. "Of course, you know Princess Flora well, don't you?"

"Fairly well," he confirmed. "She and my sister have been close since they attended the academy together." He inclined his body in a half-bow toward the king and queen. "Here in Toledda."

"Yes, we're very proud that Her Highness was educated here in our capital," Queen Lisbeth said with a regal smile.

Elowen made a scoffing noise that drew a veiled scowl from her mother. "I assume you mean Princess Miriam, because I don't recall anyone being proud of Princess Flora studying here back when we'd never heard of her."

"Elowen." There wasn't much heat in her father's rebuke, but Elowen raised a hand in surrender. She turned to Theo. "You must be looking forward to seeing your friend again."

The opening door made them all turn to see their visitors being ushered into the room by the king's steward. They'd obviously changed since their arrival, but Elowen could see the weariness of the road on both their faces. They hid it politely, however, as they greeted their hosts with gracious manners.

"It was very kind of you to invite us to stay, Your Majesty," Princess Flora said to Elowen's mother. "Our suite is beautifully appointed."

"We're delighted to receive you back in our city," the queen said, the emphasis on the word *back* not very subtle. Elowen's eyes flew to Theo, and they both turned away quickly, hiding their smiles.

The shared moment was quickly replaced by self-consciousness for Elowen, when she looked up to see Princess Flora watching them with interest. As her husband greeted the king and queen, the princess turned to Theo.

"Theo, I'm so glad to see you!" She took the hand he offered, smiling warmly. "How's Miriam?"

"She was well when I left Sindon," he said. "She misses you."

"I miss her as well," Flora said. She sent a meaningful look toward Elowen. "Are you going to introduce me to your betrothed?"

"Elowen, Flora," Theo said with a smile. "I'm sure you two will get along."

"I hope so, since I've seated them together." Queen Lisbeth's interruption was their cue to move toward the banquet hall, where the other guests would be starting to gather.

Prince Cassius politely offered Elowen his arm, but he was too engrossed in a conversation with Patrick to actually speak with her. She surveyed him surreptitiously. His hair, a lighter brown than Theo's, was longer than was the fashion in Torrens, but it wasn't unruly. In fact, everything about him was ordered and powerful. His arm was muscled under her hand as he led her into the banquet hall, and the line of his jaw was straight and a little severe. The story she'd heard of his romance with his now wife had been dramatic and exciting, but she would never have guessed from his demeanor that he was capable of that kind of passion. Maybe looks could be deceiving, even in stiff princes.

She resisted the urge to let her eyes follow the direction of her wistful thoughts, but her focus still shifted to Theo, walking behind her with Princess Flora. The princess obviously didn't realize that Elowen wasn't immersed in the conversation between her brother and Prince Cassius, because she spoke with the humorous ease of believing her words private.

"Oh dear, Theo. It's a bit of a problem, isn't it?"

"What's that?" Theo's deep voice rumbled at a lower volume than his companion's, but Elowen had become attuned to it and had no difficulty hearing.

"Your princess. She's gorgeous. Possibly the most stunning woman I've ever seen."

There was a moment of silence, in which Elowen's cheeks felt warm.

"I've noticed." The calm response from Theo fanned the

warmth into a raging inferno. He had? "Why is that a problem?"

"Well, she's too captivating, isn't she? We need someone lively and enchanting like that for Xavier, but I always pictured you with a staid, serious girl, who wouldn't mind not being swept off her feet in a whirlwind of romance."

The words were spoken in a jesting tone, but the pause that followed them was painful, and when he finally replied, Theo's voice was stiff.

"Well, unhappily for both her and Xavier—and you also, it seems—she's not betrothed to Xavier. She's betrothed to me."

A strange sensation went over Elowen at the rumbling words. She should probably be offended by the possessive edge to his voice. But she wasn't.

"Theo, I've offended you." Princess Flora's voice was instantly contrite. "Truly, I was only trying to tease. Of course you and your bride will do very well together. And I wouldn't wish Xavier on her for a moment. We both know that as much fun as he is, the woman he marries will have all our sympathy."

Elowen couldn't catch the words of Theo's reply, but his tone had relaxed in response to the humor in Princess Flora's voice.

They'd entered the banquet hall, and for several minutes they were all consumed by the bustle of the king's welcome and everyone taking their seats. When everything settled, Elowen found herself seated beside Princess Flora, as her mother had promised. Theo's place was on her other side, but he hadn't taken it yet, standing for a moment in conversation with Patrick.

"I'm so glad to get the chance to meet you, Princess Elowen," Princess Flora said.

"You as well," said Elowen. "And please, no need for the title."

"Likewise," Flora said, sounding relieved.

Elowen looked her over surreptitiously. She was pretty, but in a more everyday way than she'd expected, after hearing her story. Her hair was a similar color to her husband's, a little too straight to be fashionable. And while her face had a softness to it that made Elowen instantly warm to her, she held herself with a watchful, capable posture that couldn't have been more different from the manners adopted by the women in the Torrenese court.

"I don't claim the level of friendship with Prince Theo I'm so lucky to enjoy with Princess Miriam," Flora went on. "But I have a very high opinion of him, and will be so glad to see him happy in marriage."

"Let's hope you will see that," Elowen said lightly.

"I'm sure I will." There was something more than politeness in Flora's words, and Elowen found herself more invested in the stranger's verdict than she should be. "He likes you," Flora added. "Very much."

"Did he confide in you so quickly?" Elowen laughed, wishing her cheeks weren't so quick to get warm.

Flora's smile was a little too knowing. "No, I don't think Theo is in the habit of confiding in anyone. But I used to be a guard, you know. I'm good at noticing the little ways people give their intentions and opinions away. It's part of the role."

She nodded toward where Theo and Patrick were speaking, and Elowen followed her gaze.

"See how he's angled toward you? His eyes are on your brother, but his feet are pointing toward you. He's aware of you, every moment. If you needed him, or I suspect even wanted him, he's unconsciously placed himself in a position to instantly respond."

"That's quite a conclusion from the direction of his feet,"

Elowen said, although under her casual words she was fascinated.

"There are other things," Flora said comfortably. "As we walked in, his eyes were on you more often than anything else." She grinned. "He even scanned the room as we entered with a look I saw many times when guarding Princess Miriam. An ever so slight hint of jealousy as he assesses any competition." Her expression became pained. "Poor Mim is probably still putting up with it from every eligible nobleman in her court, since she remains unmarried. Thanks to my unplanned interference," she added as an afterthought.

"Your story sounded very exciting," Elowen said, her mind half on the other girl's revelations. Was she right about Theo? Did Elowen dare ask her whether she also had some insightful answer for why he was so reluctant to show the attachment he apparently felt?

"It was certainly an adventure," Flora said. "I confess I'm glad it's over and everything's settled, though. I still have too many guard-like instincts to enjoy danger, especially danger coming after Cassius."

Her eyes drifted to where her husband had just joined Theo and Patrick, her expression somehow both softer and more fierce than before. Elowen felt a prickle of jealousy, not over Prince Cassius, but over the intimacy of the understanding between the couple. Her eyes drifted to Theo, and she stilled when she found his gaze on her as well. Her heart beat a little faster as he abruptly broke off his conversation with Patrick and strode to his seat at her side.

"My apologies, Elowen," he said, in his deep, steady voice. "I'm a poor dinner companion so far."

She just smiled. "You did very well in your event this afternoon," she said. "Congratulations on progressing to the next round."

"I'm sorry we won't be able to stay to watch the rest of the tournament," Flora cut in. "It sounds fascinating. But we really do have to leave first thing. We're not even going to be able to join the dancing tonight."

"Very understandable," Elowen said kindly. "You're midway through an exhausting journey, a solid sleep and clear weather for travel is what you most need."

"Nonsense," Theo said unsympathetically. "As a former guard, you should be able to survive on very little sleep."

"Chivalrous of you," Flora said. "You may recall, Your Highness, I'm not a guard anymore."

Theo's answering smile was so relaxed, Elowen would almost have called it a grin. "True, you've certainly risen in the world. Do you outrank me now that you're a crown princess, and I'm merely a lowly second-born prince?"

"Naturally," said Cassius calmly. "As a royal of Carrack, Flora outranks most of her peers."

Elowen was a little shocked, until Theo's chuckle told her that Cassius had been joining in the banter. She still had a way to go in learning the hidden humor of these solemn princes, it seemed.

"Watch yourself, Prince Cassius," Theo retorted. "You wouldn't wish to offend an ally." He dipped his head toward Elowen, a barely visible twinkle in his eye. "Especially when that ally is on the brink of strengthening its ties with the fair kingdom of Torrens, which can rival even Carrack in power and prosperity."

"Oh dear, you've slighted Carrack's honor," sighed Flora. "Now we'll never hear the end of Cassius singing the praises of his homeland."

Elowen laughed, barely able to pull her eyes from Theo. She was mesmerized by the relaxed side of him the visitors had brought out.

"To save us from that fate," Theo was saying, "how about you instead tell us about your trip to Pulau?"

"It was interesting," Prince Cassius said, becoming serious at once. "The islanders are very different culturally, and we were there far too short a time to really understand their ways. But they were open to discussions about the security of the region, which is encouraging." His broad brow creased slightly. "We got the sense that they were keeping their cards close, though. I would feel easier if we had a better strategy for strengthening bonds between Pulau and the rest of the Peninsula."

Theo's expression was thoughtful, and Elowen wondered what was on his mind.

"You seem very concerned about the security of the Peninsula, Cassius," Theo said at last.

Prince Cassius's response was prompt. "I have grave concerns. I fear that if we can't unify, we may see an end to the peace we've enjoyed since the first war with the continent. They're no longer content to keep distance and pretend we're not here."

"You sound very certain of that," Elowen said, alarmed.

"I am, Your Highness." Prince Cassius looked her in the eye, his expression serious, with no sign that he resented her inserting herself into the conversation. "Something is definitely amiss on the continent. We know for certain they were behind the recent trouble that our kingdom only just headed off. But unfortunately, we don't have any concrete evidence that we can do much with."

He exchanged a frustrated look with his wife.

"Besides which," Flora added, "we obviously don't want to level accusations that would lead to war when war is exactly what we want to avoid. But we're sure that at least one kingdom from the continent, and possibly an alliance of them, has aggressive intentions toward the Peninsula."

"We've communicated these suspicions to all our neighbors," Prince Cassius added. "Whether they believe them on the limited proof we can offer is out of our control. All we can do is try to shore up relations within the Peninsula." He nodded gravely to Theo. "I applaud you doing the same."

"Very romantic, my dearest and most charming prince," Flora said in exasperation.

Prince Cassius looked confused for a moment, then his eyes flicked to Elowen and she saw understanding drop.

"My apologies, Your Highness, I didn't mean to refer to you as merely a tool for political purposes."

Elowen shook her head, surprised by the softness in his tone, even the hint of humor. It wasn't what she would have expected from the reportedly proud prince. It must be Flora's influence.

"I don't take offense, Prince Cassius," she assured him.

"To be fair, if you're offended by the implication, so should Theo be," Flora pointed out.

Theo grinned. "Not at all. If one sibling had to be sacrificed on the altar of political marriage, I'm glad I could save Miriam from the fate of being exiled to Carrack."

Flora and Prince Cassius both laughed.

"I only hope Miriam sees it that way," Flora said. "I still sometimes feel guilty for unintentionally stealing such a catch from my closest friend."

"I haven't seen much evidence of guilt," Prince Cassius said dryly.

Elowen had been silent through this exchange, fiddling with her soup spoon. She looked up just as Theo's eyes drifted to her. He took in her withdrawn demeanor, and seemed to suddenly realize what he'd said.

"Elowen, what I said just now—I'm sorry if I seemed to be… that is, I was joking, I didn't actually mean to suggest I was being sacrificed by—"

"It's all right." There was a laugh in Elowen's voice as she took pity on him and cut him off. She'd never heard him stumble over his words like that before. It was endearing. "I think on balance I prefer the idea of being the fearsome beast receiving the sacrifice rather than the hapless maiden being thrown to the monster."

Flora and her husband both laughed again, but while Theo smiled, he had a very shrewd look in his eye as he searched her face. Elowen's cheeks reddened under his scrutiny. How much did he really see of her? More than she gave him credit for, probably.

She found herself wishing it could be this way more often. The effect of these other royals, friends of his, was so different from his manner around her court, so many of whom were suspicious or resentful of him. It was no wonder he was on his guard all the time, watching his back. Elowen was surprised to realize she was almost longing for when they would go to Siqual, where maybe he would be natural and relaxed like this all the time, instead of so clearly out of his territory.

"So can you explain to me, Elowen," Flora said with the air of one turning the subject, "if the tournament isn't finished yet, why was I told we'll be toasting the victors tonight?"

"Some of the events are finished," Elowen told her. "And we'll toast those victors tonight—Lord Devin for the archery, for example, and Lord Bertrand for the jousting."

She saw how Flora's eyes flicked quickly between her and Theo as she said that second name, apparently using her guard training to pick up something in their body language that they would both no doubt prefer her not to see.

Theo's eyes shifted, Flora's quickly following their trajectory. Elowen reluctantly did the same, to see Bertrand himself, seated some distance down the table. He was watching the four royals, and although he did seem to be trying to hide his resentment for once, he wasn't succeeding. She felt a sinking disappointment that apparently the duke hadn't followed through with forbidding his son to attend. Or perhaps he had, and Bertrand had ignored him. Although Sophia sat near Bertrand, Elowen saw no sign of the duke. The possibility that Bertrand was there in defiance of his father was unsettling.

"And, of course," she pulled her focus back to the conversation with an effort, "we'll toast our own Theo for his victory in the maze run." She smiled at him before continuing her explanation. "But the real winner, the event everyone cares most about, is the weapons combat. That has one more round tomorrow morning, then a few commoners' events in the afternoon, and the tournament will be finished."

She chuckled. "Truthfully, we don't usually have a feast like this while the tournament is still underway. The real reason, which I shouldn't tell you, is to impress our royal visitors."

"Very gratifying." Flora spoke with good humor, but she didn't quite manage to stifle a yawn with the words.

Prince Cassius obviously saw it, too, because he jumped in. "I hope no one will be offended if we withdraw after the meal, given our exhaustion from our journey."

"No, of course, we all understand," Elowen assured them.

She felt regretful, however, when the couple retired soon after. Patrick approached Theo, and she saw his manner return steadily to its usual, more aloof state. Finished with her food, she rose from her seat and wandered toward Sophia, who stood alone by a table laden with enormous punch bowls.

"Enjoying the meal so far?" Sophia asked her.

"Sure," said Elowen, pouring herself some punch. "It's... lavish."

Sophia said nothing, looking as distracted as Elowen felt.

Elowen's eyes found Theo across the room, being introduced by Patrick to someone whose name she couldn't remember but who was no doubt important. She ran back over every detail she'd ever heard about Prince Cassius and Flora's story. Some parts she didn't envy them, such as the danger Flora had mentioned. But it certainly made an arranged marriage to a husband who was sure of you before you'd even met feel flat by comparison.

"I'm not foolish to want romance," she declared suddenly.

"What?" Sophia jumped a little, startled by the miniature outburst.

Elowen moderated her tone. "Is it really so ridiculous to want to be pursued by a man? A good man, I mean. A man whom you actually really *want* to..." She trailed off with a sigh. "What am I talking about? Of course it's ridiculous."

"It's not," Sophia said softly. "What daydream is more appealing than a good man being willing to overcome all obstacles to make you his?"

Elowen looked at her friend, no longer sure which man they were speaking of. But she didn't pursue the topic, because the musicians were starting up, and Theo was making his way across the room to claim her for the first dance.

FOURTEEN

Elowen

Feeling illogically as though Theo had heard her complaint, Elowen took his hand without meeting his eyes.

"Do you enjoy dancing?" Theo asked her, as they took up their positions.

"Often," she told him. She looked carefully up into his face. "It depends on the partner, of course."

He held her gaze for so long, her heart started to speed up. When he spoke, his words caught her by surprise.

"You look beautiful tonight, Elowen." Theo's voice was a deep rumble. "I don't believe I told you that when I greeted you this evening."

Or ever. The words were on the tip of her tongue, but she held them in.

"Thank you," she managed.

She should be elated by his compliment, but her emotions were too tangled. Was he saying it because Flora had basically prompted him? Did he really admire her as the other princess claimed? Or were his own words about sacrifice, however humorously spoken, closer to the truth?

Elowen moved smoothly through the dance, her eyes focused determinedly away from her partner. She recognized the troupe of musicians. They were one of her family's favorites for castle events. They boasted a musician-craftsman among their number, a fiddle player who used the motion of his bow to embellish the performance with sparkling flashes that danced throughout the ballroom periodically, like miniature indoor fireworks.

One burst over the head of a nearby couple, causing the woman to give a cry of delight.

"That's a pretty trick," Theo commented.

"Yes." Elowen watched as a sparkling shower zoomed over their heads and dissipated.

"Is everything all right?" Theo asked her after a prolonged silence.

"Yes, I'm sorry," she said quickly. "I...was lost in thought."

Theo pulled her close as the dance required, and her thoughts became even harder to gather as she found herself a mere couple of inches from the firmness of his chest, and felt an unyielding arm circle its way around her waist. What was wrong with her? How could she both delight secretly in his strength and confidence, and also be irked that he was *too* confident of her?

"What's troubling you?" Theo tried again, as he spun her out away from him. Extremely familiar with the dance, Elowen performed the step with graceful ease. She drew in a relieved breath as the distance loosened her mind a little, allowing her to cast around for an acceptable answer other than her convoluted thoughts about him.

"I'm concerned about Simeon, after what you told me. Sophia's concerned too, but I don't think she's telling me everything."

"I see."

Theo's distant tone of voice told her at once that her choice of excuse was a mistake. She suddenly remembered the moment outside the library, and she waited for him to express his displeasure. But he said nothing, just continued the dance in cool silence. Elowen was annoyed with herself for her clumsiness, but more annoyed with him. Why didn't he just talk to her?

"I was also thinking about the fact that you didn't ask me to dance," she added crisply.

"What?" Theo seemed confused. "We're dancing right now."

"But you didn't actually ask me," Elowen said. "You just walked up and...claimed me."

Theo pulled her back in, his raised eyebrow uncomfortably close now. "I assumed it was settled. Did I misunderstand the etiquette? Were you supposed to open the dancing with someone other than the prince to whom you're betrothed?"

"No, your etiquette is impeccable," she said, her tone dampening.

"I don't understand your meaning," Theo said, his own voice terse now. "Was I wrong to assume we're supposed to dance together?"

"It's not the dancing but the assuming that's the issue," Elowen said.

Theo searched her eyes. "Why are you angry with me, Elowen?"

"I'm not," she protested. "You're angry with me. But you're too proper to admit it." He tried to contradict, but she cut him off. "I know you saw me talking to Simeon earlier, and I know you're not happy about it. If it bothers you, why don't you say so?"

Theo's brow lowered in a frown. "Is that your aim, Elowen?

To provoke a reaction from me? Because I'm not interested in childish games.'"

"I absolutely was not trying to provoke a reaction from you," she said, outraged.

"Is that why you brought it up just now and specifically sought my reaction?" he demanded dryly.

Elowen was struggling to keep a scowl from her face. "I want you to be honest about whatever your reaction is, that doesn't mean I acted for the purpose of getting a reaction from you. Is it so unreasonable to want to know what you want?"

"I'm a prince of Siqual," he said dismissively. "I want my kingdom to thrive."

"An empty answer," Elowen said contemptuously.

"It's not empty to me." Theo's grip on her was tighter now than the dance required. "It's everything."

"No, it's not, it's meaningless platitude," Elowen contradicted. "I'm royal as well, don't expect me to be impressed by empty speeches. I want to know what *you* want." Her frustration was rising, stripping away her better sense along with it. She was sick of being proper and compliant. "Don't you care at all? Am I just a stranger to you, joined by a contract and nothing more?"

"Don't ask me what I want." A strange intensity had entered Theo's voice now. "I'm not allowed to want anything."

His grip was even stronger, and when the dance required him to pull her in, he tugged her more flush against him than necessary. His eyes burned into hers in a way that made it hard to breathe properly. She'd seen it in the tournament, but for the first time she *felt* the strength hidden beneath his stiff exterior, a strength that was barely contained as he fought visibly for control. What had come over him? She'd never seen him show such emotion, and it was intoxicating.

"What does that mean, you're not allowed to want anything?" Elowen asked, breathless.

Theo ignored her question, his mind on a track of its own.

"You ask what I want?" His eyes flicked down her face before he wrenched them back up. "I want to know why our wedding date isn't set. What's the delay no one will tell me about?"

Thrown, Elowen felt her face heat. She hadn't expected an attack in that direction, and she would have stumbled in her steps if Theo's hands hadn't held her so steady. Still in the grip of his strange new intensity, she found herself blurting out the truth before she could think it through.

"Me," she said. "I'm the delay."

"What does that mean?" Theo demanded.

"I promised my parents I would cooperate with the alliance," she said. "And I meant it. But they made me a promise as well—that it would be for me to set the date of the wedding, and they wouldn't push me to do it before I'm ready."

"Why?" Theo demanded. "If you're committed to the marriage, what's the point of that promise?"

"The fact that you don't understand is exactly the point," Elowen said with spirit. "You're too sure of me, Theo. Usually a man has to try at least a little to secure himself a wife."

"Am I not trying hard enough for you?" he demanded, jaw clenched. "Competing in your hollow tournament, dealing with open disrespect and derision from your court, keeping quiet about your clandestine habits with servants."

Anger and mortification mingled freely in Elowen as she drew in a sharp breath. Some part of her was glad that Theo was at least showing emotion, but it was all so difficult in such a public place.

"Evidently you truly were upset from the start that the

tournament isn't real," he went on. "You felt the need to create your own competition."

"It's not like that," Elowen protested, but the song was ending, and the dropping music required them to stop the conversation abruptly.

"Thank you for the dance." Theo bowed stiffly and retreated before she could get a word in, the musicians not even finished winding down.

Elowen watched him go, her fists balled into her skirts. Stubborn, infuriating icicle, with his unwavering stride and his closed-off heart. She had too much dignity to run after him, but her feelings demanded release. Feeling reckless, she used the cover of the few couples still completing the dance to execute one graceful, solitary spin. Her full skirts fanned around her, providing plenty of movement to work with. She snatched up the magic, shaping it even as she walked with apparent unconcern toward the punch table. Without any further movement, she threw the sloppy enchantment in Theo's direction, causing the decorative carpet he was passing over to pull up slightly under his feet.

The stately prince stumbled, and Elowen felt a stab of triumph. Not so perfect and impenetrable after all. Theo slowed his pace, glancing around. His eyes narrowed in suspicion as he found her watching him defiantly, and she didn't try to hide her silent challenge.

Her moment of satisfaction was short-lived, however. The sight of the storm raging on his face stripped away any sense of victory. She'd been glad he was showing emotion, but she hadn't meant to inflict on him the turmoil she saw there. If only he would open up to her.

Distracted, Elowen failed to see Bertrand's approach until it was too late to refuse him the next dance without open rudeness. Inside, she was festering with frustration as she followed him onto the dance floor, her thoughts on Theo on the far side of the room, with very little attention to spare for her partner.

Maybe Bertrand sensed it, because his manner as he led her into position was more aggressive than usual. No doubt he was annoyed about having been supplanted, given he was used to being the highest-ranking unmarried man in the room, and unchallenged in his right to open the dancing with the princess.

"Your steps aren't as light as usual tonight, Princess," he said shortly, as Elowen moved correctly but not very gracefully through the opening motions of the dance.

She didn't reply. It was a different type of dance, one which had them cycling through many different partners and didn't allow for much private speech. Bertrand's irritation was evident every time she swirled away from him, but to Elowen, it was a relief. Her eyes kept drifting to Theo, who wasn't taking part in the dance. He was brooding by a refreshments table, looking anywhere but at her.

The dance felt interminable, but finally the instruments slowed.

"Thank you," she said coolly to Bertrand.

"You look tired," Bertrand said. "I imagine you'll want refreshments."

"I—yes, all right, a drink would be welcome," Elowen said, hoping he would go to get it and leave her in peace.

Instead, he kept hold of her arm as he steered her across the room.

"An excellent innovation of Her Majesty's," he said pleasantly. "Having a refreshments table with cool drinks in the garden. When so many young ladies get overheated from dancing, a chance to cool down out of the heat of the ballroom is perfect."

As he spoke, he moved steadily toward the far end of the

room, where a few floor-to-ceiling windows showed glimpses of the gardens beyond, illuminated by softly glowing lanterns. The two outside windows had glass doors in their lower sections.

"Drinks in the garden?" Elowen repeated, bewildered. "We've never done that before. I don't think that's the case."

"Of course it is," Bertrand said smoothly, opening one of the glass doors and ushering her outside. "Come and see for yourself."

Elowen glanced back, but she couldn't see Theo anymore. She couldn't really see anyone of note, her view blocked by the many couples still crowding the dancing space.

Her skirts swished their way through the narrow door, and she took a few paces onto the stone platform beyond, frowning around it. The area was empty of either ball-goers or tables, the smooth stone giving way to shallow steps down into an open garden.

"As I said." She turned to Bertrand, who'd appeared at her side. "No refreshments."

He laughed, putting a guiding hand on the small of her back. Elowen stepped away in annoyance, retreating down a few steps to get out of his reach.

"Of course not, Princess," Bertrand said. "It was just an excuse to get you alone."

A rush of anger went over Elowen. "You're over the line, Bertrand," she said hotly.

The infuriating viscount laughed again, his tone still indulgent. "No need for the act, Princess. I heard what you said to Sophia earlier, about wanting to be pursued."

There was a glint in his eye that Elowen didn't like, and her heart gave an uncomfortable lurch. She cast a surreptitious look around, realizing that he'd been strategic in every movement. Without her realizing it, he'd herded her down the steps in a direction that meant they were no longer in clear view of the window into the ballroom. She knew there were guards posted at the outside entrances to the garden, but none were positioned just outside the ballroom. Had anyone noticed her going outside?

Bertrand advanced down the steps toward her, and she took another step back. She was a princess, used to living under the care of guards, protected by her rank from impertinence. Never in her life had she been in a situation like this. She didn't know what to do other than the instinct that told her to tread warily.

"I don't like whatever game you're playing, Bertrand," she said carefully. "I'm going to return to the ballroom now."

"I see clearly now," Bertrand went on, ignoring her words completely, "that I've been too gentle, too forbearing."

Gentle and forbearing? Is that how he saw himself? Elowen could only stare at him in stupefaction.

"I should have taken charge from the start," Bertrand said, his eyes overly bright. "Then you wouldn't be tangled in this mess with the Siqualian ice sculpture."

Those words drove away some of whatever was causing Elowen's mind to freeze, and she drew herself up with a haughty gesture.

"My betrothal is none of your affair, Lord Bertrand," she said coldly.

She moved forward with purpose, intending to brush past him. As highly charged as her instincts were, she was still completely shocked at Bertrand's sudden movement. She could hardly comprehend what was happening as he shifted smoothly, but the next moment she found herself pinned to the wall.

"In fact, it's exactly my affair," he breathed into her shocked face. "And I intend to make it even more so. The Siqualian will never pursue you like you need. I know what you really want is mastery, and clearly it's past time for me to take control of the situation."

Elowen's heart was in her throat, fear paralyzing her mind as it tried to assess her options. Should she scream, and make a scene? By every standard she'd ever been taught, it was unthinkable conduct from her. But his grip was too strong to just break away from. Could she generate movement and use Dust to get free of him? She was scared of the consequences, and she couldn't recall any of her lessons with her mind in this state. All of this passed through her thoughts in the blink of an eye, before she fell back on what she'd always been taught. Diplomacy.

"Bertrand," she tried, hoping desperately he'd be reasonable. His flushed face and the triumph in his eyes that told her he was enjoying her consternation weren't promising. "I—"

Her placating words were cut off as a figure loomed into sight on the steps above them. Bertrand whipped around, hot with anger, but the only emotion flooding Elowen at sight of Theo was relief. If Theo was here, she was safe. She had never, *could* never, feel in danger from him.

The realization rushed over her, stilling her fears completely and filling her with gratitude that her parents had chosen an alliance with Siqual over the perfectly likely alternative of arranging a marriage between her and the son of their most influential duke. The thought of marrying Bertrand, never appealing, was now absolutely repulsive.

As for Theo...there was no comparison. No matter how icy or aloof he might be, he would never push himself on her, never hurt her, never try to control her. And more immediately, he wouldn't let Bertrand touch her.

"You're interrupting, Your Highness," Bertrand said through

gritted teeth, his fingers flexing as though itching to reach for his sword.

"Evidently."

If Bertrand's anger was fiery, Theo's was solid ice. For a long moment, the two men stood chest to chest, neither backing down. Theo seemed to have left the door to the ballroom open, because the sound of another song striking up reached Elowen's ears where she still hovered against the wall. Bertrand seemed to hear it, too, because he abruptly stepped back, then, with one angry glance in Elowen's direction, strode around the corner and out of sight.

As soon as he was gone, Elowen turned to her rescuer.

"Thank you." Her voice was breathless and her eyes full of her emotions as she looked up into Theo's face.

He didn't even meet her eye. He gestured toward the ballroom and, in a frosty and painfully polite voice, he said, "Perhaps we should return to the gala."

Crestfallen and clinging to what dignity she could muster, Elowen moved forward. Her limbs were shaking in an echo of the fear she'd felt before Theo arrived, and she folded her hands in her skirts to hide the tremors. For a moment, she hoped that Theo was just being circumspect in returning to a populated area before speaking to her, but as soon as they entered the ballroom, he strode away, leaving her to move alone across the room in a numb haze.

"Elowen?"

Elowen turned stupidly to see Sophia approaching, her kind features crinkled in concern.

"What's going on? Where have you been? I've been looking for you."

Elowen just shook her head, unable to bring herself to talk about it. If it had been anyone but Bertrand, she would have confided in her friend immediately. But she was horribly afraid

Sophia would try to justify her brother's behavior, and she couldn't bear that.

"I...I think Theo is upset with me," was all she managed.

Sophia made a sympathetic noise, steering her toward an upholstered bench placed along one wall.

"Elowen...is the betrothal really so set?"

Elowen stared at her friend, stunned. "Of course it is. What do you mean?"

"Wouldn't you prefer to marry within Torrens?" Sophia pressed.

"Marry *who* within Torrens?" Elowen asked stupidly.

"Well..." Sophia gave a laugh that was more pained than humorous. "Bertrand, of course."

"Of course?" The words were ripped from Elowen, revulsion washing over her at the thought. "What do you mean, of course? Sophia, why are you always trying to push me toward Bertrand?"

"Because I want you as a sister," Sophia said. "And..." She swallowed, then said in a rush, "And because I don't want to marry Patrick."

"What are you talking about?" Elowen demanded, glad to feel her mind emerging from the fog somewhat.

Sophia twisted her hands together in her lap, not meeting her friend's eye. "I'm not supposed to say this, but my parents have been urging us to make one of those matches happen for as long as I can remember. I always thought it would be you and Bertrand, so I never worried too much. But then this betrothal alliance changed everything."

Elowen sat in stunned silence for a moment, fighting a feeling of betrayal. But why should she feel surprised? Of course the duke and duchess would wish for one of their children to marry into the royal family. And Sophia had never seemed to understand about Bertrand. She probably really did hope for Elowen as a sister.

"As far as Bertrand and I are concerned, the betrothal alliance changed nothing," she told her friend firmly. "There was never any thought of my marrying him, and if he believes we were somehow intended for one another before the alliance was proposed, he's out of his mind." Her voice hardened. "If your parents covet a crown, you'll have to marry Patrick."

"It's not like that," Sophia protested, her face pale. "Please don't be angry, Elowen. My parents meant no harm, they just..." She trailed off, and when she spoke again, her voice was more determined. "And please don't be offended, but I don't want to marry Patrick."

"My sweet Sophia, of course I'm not offended," Elowen said in incredulous impatience. "But surely I can expect the same consideration when I tell you that I have no desire at all to marry Bertrand."

Sophia made a noise in her throat. "I know you find his manner of teasing tiresome at times, but he would settle down once he was sure of you," she assured Elowen. "Don't you think you'd be happy as his wife, staying here in Torrens?"

"No, I don't." The words came out with too much force. "I think I'd be miserable!" She studied her friend's earnest face. "Sophia, I'm sorry to speak bluntly and cause you pain, but I don't know how else to make you understand. Bertrand is not a good man."

"How can you say—"

Elowen cut off the protest she was sure came from pure force of habit. "You see the way he treats Simeon."

Distress crossed Sophia's face. "Yes," she said softly. "And I hate it. I can acknowledge Bertrand has a blind spot when it comes to Simeon. I think he's a little jealous, because he was never allowed to study magic. But—"

"No, Sophia." Elowen cut her friend off again. "It's you who have a blind spot when it comes to Bertrand. The way he treats Simeon is perfectly in keeping with everything else he does."

Elowen's emotions were threatening to ride her once again, the relief of finally saying all these things to her friend vying with the near-hysteria that threatened to rise whenever she remembered the way Bertrand had pinned her against the wall.

"That's not fair, Elowen," Sophia said. "He's always been so attentive to you, his preference for you has always been made clear."

"Yes," Elowen agreed, frustrated at the overwhelmed tears stinging the corners of her eyes. "And my repeated attempts to show that I don't welcome his attention have made no difference. That's not honorable behavior, Sophia."

"Elowen, I—you don't understand—the thing is, Bertrand..." Sophia's weak words trailed off as Elowen rose.

"I don't feel well," she said, not caring that her words were abrupt. "I'm going to retire to bed." Not looking back at her friend, and avoiding both searching the room for Theo and her mother's attempts to catch her attention, Elowen strode from the room.

FIFTEEN

Theo

Theo had intended to rise early the next morning to see Flora and Cassius off on their journey. But when dawn came, he couldn't face it. They wouldn't be sorry for an inconspicuous departure, and he was in no state to be seen after one of the least restful nights he'd ever passed. Every time he'd closed his eyes to sleep, his vision had been filled with the sight of Lord Bertrand leaning in toward Elowen, their posture intimate, and her calm demeanor suggesting it wasn't the first time.

First her clandestine moment with Simeon outside the library, then an attempt to steal a kiss with Lord Bertrand at the ball?

No. Theo took hold of his thoughts, sternly pulling them back into line. That kind of sordid speculation was beneath him. Maybe he'd get momentary satisfaction from telling himself that Elowen was lacking in virtue, but that didn't make it true. They weren't strangers anymore. He'd come to know a lot about her since his arrival in Toledda, and the more he'd discovered, the more convinced he'd become of her intelligence and character.

In other words, the harder he'd fallen, an unhelpfully emotional voice tried to correct him, but he pushed it aside. That wasn't the point. The point was that the idea of Elowen being loose was contrary to all he knew of her and of her circumstances. And he despised the kind of man who thought all women unfaithful and untrustworthy simply because the one he wanted wasn't pleased by him. He fought down a pang at the fresh reminder of how little he apparently pleased Elowen, trying to focus on the issue at hand.

Since he couldn't believe she was brazenly engaging in real dalliances, the only explanation he could find was that she was trying to provoke him into competing for her, as she'd basically admitted she'd intended from the start.

Was that much better?

Theo was tempted to avoid breakfast, but he told himself sternly that he owed it to his kingdom and his honor to face his enemies head on, even if the enemy in question felt suspiciously like heartbreak. Would it please Elowen to know how much her campaign was affecting him? It didn't seem like a good kind of satisfaction to give, if so.

There was a buzz in the castle as Theo strode toward the royal family's dining hall. It was the final day of the tournament, and the stands were sure to be packed to capacity.

Theo had theoretically made it through to the final round of the weapons combat, but he didn't feel much sense of achievement. He knew he hadn't faced any of the best fighters yet. He should withdraw, he'd known it for some time.

It was all so pointless, all just politics. He'd seen how highly skilled fighters had withdrawn rather than facing certain high-ranking opponents, Lord Bertrand among them, curse him.

Theo had been struggling to decide on the best time to drop out as he was expected to do. Before the event actually started, he'd planned to drop out fairly early to avoid embarrassment for everyone given he couldn't match the impressive swordplay he'd seen from some of the young noblemen. Then, after he'd watched people dropping out and realized the results were never going to be accurate, it had made him even more motivated to drop out, because he didn't want to win any fight he thought his opponent had lost on purpose.

But watching Lord Bertrand rise through the ranks, often through forfeiture rather than actual skill, had tested that resolve. And so he was still in. He needed to rectify that before the finals started. He had to stop letting his personal anger toward Lord Bertrand affect the betrothal tournament.

The jealousy he felt was weakness enough, but the worst of it was that it wasn't the main thing. It was agony to think that Elowen didn't want him, that she preferred Lord Bertrand's attention. The viscount was so pathetic to Theo that any preference for him on Elowen's part should have made Theo think less of the princess. But it didn't. It just filled him with pain at his own inability to win her favor. Just the thought of how much he wanted her affection sent fear spiraling through him, potent and paralyzing and a weakness he couldn't afford.

Theo had almost reached the dining hall when he suddenly remembered something he'd been told the night before. All competitors in the final round had been invited to breakfast with the royal family before the last event began. He slowed his steps, unsure if he could handle sharing a meal with Lord Bertrand in his current mood.

It was too late to avoid encountering him, however. The viscount's voice reached Theo's ears as he rounded the final corner. The scene before him caused Theo to draw back, watching through narrow eyes as Lord Bertrand grabbed his servant by the arm.

Simeon. The one who was somehow mixed up in the chaos

with the magic, and somehow had Elowen on his side such that she wouldn't believe him capable of anything questionable.

"How dare you?" Lord Bertrand was saying in an angry hiss that carried much further than he seemed to realize. "How dare you go behind my back to sign up for the event? I saw you, Simeon. I *heard* you. Reading out the rules of the event, as cool as if you were an emperor. You are nothing without my family, Simeon, we are the only reason you're standing in a royal castle right now. How dare you throw our generosity in my face?"

Simeon's face was blank, too blank. Whatever he was holding in, it was strong enough that he knew he could never take it back if he let it out. Theo was debating whether to intervene when soft footsteps sounded behind him. He turned to see Elowen hurry into sight, her expression tense as she also took in the scene just outside the dining hall.

But there wasn't much more to see. Lord Bertrand seemed to have come to his senses regarding his surroundings, and was compelling his servant to move toward the castle's entrance. Theo let some of the tension drain out of him, turning his attention to Elowen.

She looked like she'd slept as much as he had. Her hair wasn't as tightly pinned as usual, her eyes were a little red, and her lips were pale.

She remained the most beautiful woman he'd ever set eyes on.

Heart heavy, he broke the silence between them. "What a charming display before breakfast."

Elowen jumped, her eyes widening as they found him. "Theo. I'm sorry, I didn't see you."

"Do you know what that was about?" Theo asked her.

She nodded, biting her lip in concern. The movement drew his eyes.

"The maids were gossiping about it, that's why I hurried

here. Lord Bertrand is apparently very angry with Simeon because he forbade Simeon to sign up for the craftsmen's competition, but he did it anyway. Lord Bertrand just found out."

"Why would he not want his servant to compete?" Theo asked. "And why did Simeon defy him?"

Elowen winced. "For the second one, I think I goaded him into it, although it wasn't my intention. As for why Lord Bertrand wouldn't want him competing, well." She shrugged, the motion like flicking off an irksome fly. "He doesn't like Simeon drawing attention to himself or his extraordinary skill. That makes it harder for everyone to forget that Bertrand deserves none of the credit he always claims for it."

Theo raised an eyebrow at her tone. There was something especially bitter in it, which seemed quite the turnaround from the night before.

"Why was he so angry about Simeon reading out the rules of the competition?"

"Was he?" Elowen's voice was a murmur now. "I wondered...that must be what Sophia meant." After a moment, she realized he was waiting expectantly, and hastened to explain. "Sophia told me she knew she could convince Simeon to teach us magic because he owed her. I think she taught him to read, without Bertrand knowing."

"I thought Simeon had been educated at the duke's expense," Theo said, lost.

Elowen's lip curled in contempt. "Yes, that's what everyone thinks. But Bertrand took charge of coordinating that education, and he specifically wanted to keep Simeon from becoming literate. I imagine he knew it would open opportunities for Simeon that might tempt him out of the family's employ and therefore out of Bertrand's reach."

Theo hadn't thought his opinion of Lord Bertrand could

sink further, but he'd been wrong. What a short-sighted, self-centered fool. And yet he was more acceptable to Elowen than he was?

"You don't have high standards, do you?" The words slipped out before he could moderate himself.

"What?" Elowen looked cautiously up at him.

"I know now that you're willing to be pleased," Theo said, his voice curt as he tried to keep his emotions at bay. "I suppose I can only regret that I'm so unappealing."

Confusion crossed her face, but he didn't wait to hear what response she would find. He strode into the dining hall, seating himself beside Prince Patrick—a companion guaranteed not to raise any emotions—and making short work of his breakfast. Elowen sat far enough down the table that speech was impossible, but he could feel her eyes on him throughout the meal.

When he rose, so did she, following him from the room. She said nothing to him, and at first he thought she meant to go her own way, but after he'd traversed a couple of corridors and found himself in a quieter part of the castle, he realized she was still behind him.

He turned to face her, much more in control of himself now, and wishing he hadn't let his tongue run away with him before.

"Did you wish to speak with me?" he asked calmly.

"Yes." But her eyes remained on her feet, and it was a long moment before she went on, her manner embarrassed. "I was confused by what you said before breakfast. I think I understand...that is, I think you misunderstood what you witnessed last night."

She cast a quick, uneasy look around the deserted corridor before taking a breath and forcing herself to look up at him.

"I wasn't on the terrace with Lord Bertrand willingly. He tricked me into going outside, and when I tried to leave, he physically restrained me. It didn't occur to me at the time that you didn't understand that, I thought you were angry with me for allowing it to happen. But on reflection, I realized that it may not have been obvious from my demeanor that I..." She trailed off, swallowing before continuing. "Forgive me, it's humiliating to confess...that I was frightened of him in that moment. I was relieved when you arrived. Relieved and grateful."

Frissons of shock were running over Theo, intensifying with every word she spoke. His hand reached out toward her, but he forced it to drop before it reached her.

"Elowen, is this true?" He searched her eyes. He didn't need an answer—he could read it on her face. It was clear that the confession had cost her some embarrassment. She would never have fabricated it. "Are you all right?"

"I'm fine. Thanks to your intervention." Her voice was very small.

There was a long silence during which Theo's earlier conviction that he was more in control now mocked him. He'd never been less in control, but he didn't intend for Elowen to see that.

"All I can say then," his voice came out choked, "is that I apologize sincerely for my assumption last night. And my manner toward you."

She was looking at her slippers again, and he gave in to the impulse this time, letting his hand make it all the way to her chin. Her skin was soft as his fingers gently tilted her face up.

"I mean it, Elowen," he said, his voice rough with all he was keeping in. "I truly am sorry."

She seemed to have no words, but her eyes were so expressive she didn't need them. Theo let his hand drop, moving past her with tense strides.

"Wait." Elowen's voice made him turn. "Where are you going?"

"To have a conversation with Lord Bertrand," he said, struggling to keep his voice even as he said the man's name.

Elowen hesitated, as if wondering whether to try to stop him, but he was already striding down the corridor. He walked blindly for several minutes before he was calm enough to ask a guard where Lord Bertrand could be found. After a few inquiries, he was told that the viscount was at the training yard, in preparation for the day's event.

Theo directed his steps that way, his strides increasing. He'd been angry enough at Lord Bertrand over his clandestine moment with Elowen even when he'd thought Elowen had been using the viscount to make a point. The knowledge that the man had instead been forcing himself on Elowen had fire racing through Theo's veins.

He was going to kill Bertrand.

His fury wasn't confined to the viscount, either. He deserved a beating of his own for his coldness to Elowen the night before. How could he have assumed so much from her demeanor, without even giving her a chance to explain? How many other times had he made a similar mistake, assuming from Bertrand's boldness and her self-conscious reaction that they had some kind of history? Had all those instances been nothing more than unwanted imposing on Bertrand's part? So many interactions took on new meaning, each one fueling Theo's anger. He'd thought Bertrand a buffoon, but it seemed the viscount had skillfully manipulated both Elowen and him.

He swept into the training yard without breaking stride, ignoring all the pairs sparring as they got ready for the day's event.

Bertrand wasn't difficult to spot. He was standing on the far side of the yard, in conversation with another young nobleman. Judging by their gear, they'd just finished a bout.

Theo retained enough sense to go around the edge of the

training yard rather than charging right through it, so he had ample time to hear their conversation as he approached.

"Well, I'd say you'd best win the weapons competition today, Bertrand, because it's clear you're not going to win the other one," the nobleman was saying with a grin.

Bertrand scoffed. "If you're talking about the princess, I'm not worried."

"You should be," the other man said. "General opinion is that she rarely takes her eyes off him. The ladies all say she's besotted."

"Hardly." Bertrand's tone was contemptuous. "*Prince* Theodore is too stiff and polite, he'll never satisfy the princess." He gave an unpleasant laugh. "If they'd sent Xavier, maybe I'd be worried, but not this ice statue. What women want is mastery, and he's too polite. I have the princess right where I want her."

Theo had heard enough. He was still in a stiff brocade tunic, but that could be rectified. His strides almost a run now, he started yanking one arm from its sleeve, his hand already balled into a fist.

"Whoa, there, Your Highness." He collided solidly with a torso that hadn't been in his path a moment before.

"Get out of my way, Paulson," he growled.

"And if I obey, what are you going to do, Your Highness?" the guard asked.

"I'm going to kill Bertrand," Theo told him, perfectly calmly.

"I think I'd best not obey, then," Paulson said in a mild tone, still blocking Theo's path with surprising strength. "I never thought I'd see you overreact to an insult to your ego, Your Highness, if I'm not too bold to say it."

"The insult to me is nothing," Theo said impatiently. "That

contemptible rodent accosted Elowen last night, and now he speaks of her like she's his possession."

Paulson made a noise of disgust in his throat, but he stood firm. "Best not to do something you'll regret, Your Highness. Your time would be better spent hearing my report."

That pulled Theo up. Breathing hard, most of his mind still roaring at him to pound Bertrand's face into the dust, he looked at his guard properly for the first time.

"You're back."

"Yes, Your Highness. And I have a report for you."

"Good. You can give it to me after I make him regret ever letting the princess's name pass his lips in public."

But when Theo looked up, he saw that Bertrand was leaving, presumably for the tournament. Short of chasing him from the training yard with fists raised, Theo couldn't confront him right now.

With great effort, he contained his anger and curtly demanded Paulson's report. He listened with a sinking heart as his guard laid out everything he'd learned. This wasn't going to be pretty.

"Leave it with me," he told his guard. "But be ready to report to King Ronan when I call on you."

"Yes, Your Highness." The guard looked him over with a critical eye. "Are you well? Have you been safe in my absence?"

"Yes, I'm fine," Theo said impatiently. "I was never in any danger in the first place." At least not physical danger.

Still coursing with frustrated energy, Theo left for the tournament. All thought of dropping out was gone. It was clear that if he did so, Bertrand would win, because no one was going to challenge him.

No one but Theo, obviously. He may not be able to beat every member of the court, but he could beat Bertrand.

He felt the eyes of the master of events on him when he

entered the tournament field, and knew the nobleman expected him to withdraw. Well, he'd be disappointed. Theo's gaze found Elowen in the stands, her hands clasped over her heart in a tense gesture he didn't think she was aware of. But her posture relaxed when she caught sight of him, and that buoyed Theo up more than any training session could have.

She'd called him her champion once, and that was what he intended to be. If it was in his power, he would never let any man make her feel fear again. Feeling reckless and giving in to impulse, he raised his right fist and laid it over his heart. He thought he caught surprise on her face as he turned away.

Theo's first two fights were swift and decisive. The prospect of facing Bertrand was the best motivation he could ask for, and his sword work had never had more force or precision. He watched critically from the sidelines as Bertrand won the second of his fights as well. The man he was facing was one of the best Theo had seen in the training yard. His disappointment at having to throw the match was visible on his face, but Bertrand either couldn't or wouldn't see it. His cocky sneer as he saw Theo watching him acknowledge his victory made Theo wish there wasn't a scheduled break before their fight.

At least Theo could be sure Bertrand wouldn't throw their bout. It would be much more satisfying to annihilate him with the knowledge that it had been a genuine match.

Theo was tempted to approach Elowen during the break, but he decided he should keep his mind clear. The memory of her pale face and expressive eyes when she'd confessed to being afraid was already wreaking enough havoc on his mind. Better not to have a close view of those speaking eyes.

When he emerged from the tent ready for his final fight, however, he was confronted with exactly that. The stands were packed with spectators, but the princess wasn't among them. She and the rest of the royal family occupied a small raised dais right next to the narrow strip where Theo and Bertrand were to fight. Had she been so inclined, she could have leaned over the railing and touched them while they listened to the master of events introduce the final round of weapons combat.

Theo and Bertrand paced away from the center as instructed, turning to face one another as they waited for the bugle blast that would signify the start of the fight. They each wore light chainmail because it was required by the tournament rules, but Theo would have preferred the agility that came with only his training clothes. He spun his sword in his hand as the seconds stretched out, neither he nor Bertrand having opted to use a shield.

Bertrand's face was derisive and arrogant, clearly confident of a win. Theo's face showed nothing. The blind fury of the morning was gone, replaced with a calm determination that would likely serve him better. He was going to punish Bertrand for his treatment of Elowen. He was going to do it in front of everyone whose opinion Bertrand cared about. And it was all a sanctioned, civilized activity.

Really, it was quite a windfall.

SIXTEEN

Theo

The bugle blast sent both men churning into motion. They didn't take time to test the waters or size each other up. Both had been doing that from the sidelines through each round of the tournament, and both were eager for blood. Their weapons clashed together with a vicious clang that ran through the silent, watchful stands.

Bertrand drew back and lunged again, their weapons crossing as Theo held him off, faces close enough to see the sweat starting to bead on each forehead.

"You're out of your depth, Siqualian," Bertrand said nastily. "You should have withdrawn when you could still do it with your honor intact."

Theo ignored him. It wasn't his own honor he was fighting for. Even the slight to his kingdom had no impact on him now. It was all for Elowen, nothing else mattered in that moment. Making the most of Bertrand's distraction, he feinted toward his open flank, then whipped his weapon around ferociously the moment Bertrand parried.

The viscount barely managed to block the fresh attack in time, and Theo saw surprise and anger flit across his face.

"You're mistaken, My Lord, if you think you're fighting an ice statue."

Theo's calm words made Bertrand hesitate, thrown off at the possibility that Theo had heard him in the training yard. Theo once again took advantage of the moment and drove his blade forward. He scored a hit on Bertrand's mail-clad side, and the point was loudly acknowledged by the master of events.

The two contestants drew back, taking the offered water and wiping their foreheads. Then the bugle sounded again, and they began to circle. Bertrand seemed furious that Theo had scored a hit, and he fought with dogged determination until he managed to sneak one under Theo's guard as well. Both were in a strong position, but neither had come close to what would be considered a killing blow, which would automatically end the fight.

The third clash of their weapons was faster and less precise. Both were tiring, and both were angry. In fact, Theo hadn't seen any fight in the whole tournament with half the emotion this one had. Neither of them was burly, their physiques and strength levels well matched, but Theo was sure he had greater skill. Bertrand's confidence was unrivaled, and no doubt he'd won many more matches in his life than Theo. But the difference was that Theo had never had an opponent surrender out of deference to his rank. He'd grown up facing—and losing to— fighters more skilled than he was, and as a result he'd never stopped improving. He suspected Bertrand, while possessing some natural aptitude, had plateaued long ago.

As the bout continued, Bertrand's increasing struggles to get close seemed to support Theo's conclusion. It was also becoming clear that he had the advantage over Bertrand when it came to endurance. He was sure of the outcome long before the bout ended, drawing it out as he played with his opponent, enjoying the rising anger in Bertrand's face. The viscount became increasingly desperate, his hacking movements no longer designed to tap. Theo could see in his eyes that Bertrand was losing control of himself, and would run Theo through in earnest if opportunity offered. The murmuring from the crowd suggested others were noticing it, too.

Theo wasn't worried. He had full control of the bout now, and since he was starting to tire himself, he decided it was time to bring it to an end. They were close to the railing but some distance from the royal family's seats when he performed another feint, letting Bertrand think he had an opening.

A stifled cry from behind him told him that Elowen had also fallen for his maneuver, but she wouldn't be long in suspense. As soon as Bertrand took the bait, Theo's foot shot out. He hooked it around Bertrand's ankle, tripping him up. He'd barely hit the ground when the flat of Theo's blade was laid against his throat.

The bugle blasted, and the master of events delightedly announced the end of the match. The crowd in the stands was cheering, but Theo ignored them all. Leaning down so that his face loomed over the viscount's, he spoke, his voice clear and vibrating with veiled passion.

"Stay away from my affianced wife. You have mastery over nothing, and if you try to touch her again, you'll feel my blade."

He could see pure hatred on Bertrand's face, but he didn't care. He lifted his blade, stepping back but not taking his eyes off the snake on the ground before him. Movement to one side drew his gaze away, however, and he stilled as he saw Elowen standing right on the other side of the railing. Had she been concerned enough to run close when she believed him about to be bested?

Their eyes locked for a poignant moment, her lips parted slightly and her eyes wide with some emotion Theo didn't know how to read. It was clear she'd heard what he said to

Bertrand. Then Prince Patrick appeared at Elowen's side, reaching out a hand to congratulate Theo on his win, and the moment was broken.

Theo turned to calmly acknowledge the crowd's applause, doing the traditional lap around the combat strip before returning to stand before the royal family's box.

A section of fence had been removed, and a small platform set up to allow Elowen to move forward. A squire ran forward with a wooden step, and Theo mounted to the platform to join the princess.

"Congratulations to our champion," Elowen said, her voice clear and carrying. "It's my honor to present you with your reward."

Under cover of the crowd's cheers, she asked Theo in a voice that wasn't quite natural, "Do you remember the traditional options?"

"I think I recall something from my Torrenese etiquette training," he said. "But why don't you remind me?"

She gave him an exasperated look, but he just smiled at her.

With a sigh, she said, "Very well. Traditionally the victor receives from the princess his choice between a favor he can keep," she held up a handkerchief embroidered with her initials, "or one he can treasure only in memory." Theo raised his eyebrows expectantly and, looking even more exasperated, she said, "A kiss."

"Surely I should choose the kiss," Theo said gravely. "Don't you think so?"

Elowen didn't answer, casting a self-conscious look around at the eager crowd.

"Come, Elowen," Theo said, each word hanging in the air between them. "I know you didn't get to choose the champion of this fight, but even princesses have to live with disappointment."

Elowen flushed, seeming confused and wrong-footed as she again snuck a surreptitious look at their audience.

"It seems my right to claim it," Theo went on. "I won the competition, didn't I? Haven't I at last earned it?"

Something flashed in her eyes, and Theo knew she understood as well as he did that they weren't speaking merely of a victory kiss.

"No." Elowen surprised him with the strength of her retort. "You haven't *earned* it. What's it to me if you can best Bertrand?"

Theo considered her for a long and thoughtful moment, noting that this time, she held his gaze with her chin lifted. A slow trickle of comprehension worked its way through his mind. Maybe it had never been about him competing against other men, but about him earning her heart. And no sensible woman would lose her heart over an arbitrary feat of arms. Her comment during dinner the night before came back to him, about preferring to be the monster rather than the maiden, and another flash of insight followed it. Her condition, which he'd chosen to see as petty and manipulative, hadn't been intended to make a fool out of him. It had been a desperate attempt to gain some control over her own life.

He reached out, the back of his finger brushing featherlight against her jaw for the briefest of moments.

"I think," he said, his voice deep and somber, "that I will choose the favor I can keep."

He lowered his hand with deliberate care, holding it out for the handkerchief.

Elowen stared into his eyes, clearly taken aback by his change in direction. Taken aback and, if he wasn't mistaken, not entirely pleased. Smiling a little to himself at the chaos that was the human heart, Theo raised his eyebrows in a silent request.

Remembering herself, Elowen hastened to place the handkerchief into his hand. Theo turned and raised his fist to the sky, the white fabric fluttering merrily in the breeze. The crowd roared its approval, delighted by the spectacle. Elowen might not be won by prowess with a sword, but it certainly seemed to have warmed the crowd to Theo.

King Ronan moved forward, adding his congratulations to his daughter's. Bertrand was nowhere to be seen, but Theo didn't spare him more than a passing thought. The viscount had been sufficiently humiliated. As the group moved down from the dais, however, Theo caught sight of Paulson standing at the edge of the field, and he sobered.

"Your Majesty," he said quietly to King Ronan. "I need to speak to you about the duke's investigation."

"The investigation?" the king repeated, surprised. "Now?"

"Yes, it shouldn't wait," Theo said. "I fear that you haven't been given all the information, sir."

The king studied him thoughtfully. "Very well. I'll call the duke to—"

"Actually, Your Majesty," Theo cut him off, "it may be best to hear it alone first. Can my guard and I come to your study before the noon meal?"

King Ronan looked bewildered at the mention of a guard, but he asked no questions. "Yes, I'll be ready to receive you in half an hour," he said. "In the meantime, please, enjoy your victory." His eyes lingered on his daughter as he said it, their gaze softer. "All of your victories."

The king was mistaken if he thought Theo would be given the chance to celebrate with Elowen. He was engulfed by members of the court eager to congratulate him, but the princess was whisked back to the castle by her mother within minutes of the tournament ending. When half an hour had elapsed, Theo made his way with heavy steps toward the king's study, Paulson trailing him.

They were obviously expected, because one of the guards on duty opened the door to let them in. King Ronan was sitting behind a broad desk with his back to the window, and he waved Theo into a chair across from him. Paulson stood at position behind and to the side of Theo's chair.

"What's troubling you, Your Highness?"

"The investigation," Theo said promptly. "As you know, I accompanied His Grace to the site of the landslide."

"Yes," the king confirmed.

"Your Majesty, did you receive a report regarding a young man wearing a scarf, who was seen at the top of the slope prior to the landslide?"

The king looked perplexed. "A scarf?"

"A purple scarf," Theo said, nodding.

"The duke mentioned that there was one eyewitness who thought he saw someone suspicious at the time of the landslide, but he expressed the view that the witness wasn't very reliable, given no one else saw anyone. And he didn't mention anything to me about a scarf, purple or otherwise."

Theo's heart sank. He'd hoped to be wrong, for his warning not to be needed.

"Your Majesty, at the time you graciously consented for me to take part in that particular investigative trip, you said that the duke had a promising line of inquiry. Has that eventuated?"

The king leaned back in his chair, looking weary. "Unfortunately not. The latest report is that the trail he was following has dried up. We currently are no closer to understanding the cause of either the disasters or the magical imbalance, or even to confirming if they're linked."

"I think they must be," Theo said. "Even without magical

training, I felt a disruption while undertaking the maze run. It was close in time to the landslide."

"Yes, many people felt that," the king said heavily. "Proof or not, I have strongly suspected a connection for some time."

"It's struck me, Your Majesty, that all of the disasters are of a type that would generate a significant amount of Dust. For example, the dam bursting. But my guard, Paulson, felt only a fraction of the magic he would have expected on that occasion. He's currently undergoing extensive training in the craft."

"Is that so?" The king considered Paulson, who bent into a swift military bow.

"I have a suspicion, Your Majesty," Theo pressed on, "that the purpose of these disasters was specifically to release a huge quantity of Dust, with the intention of attempting to store it."

"Store it?" King Ronan repeated, startled. "That's not possible."

"As far as current magical understanding says, no it isn't," Theo agreed. "I've availed myself of your excellent library to refresh my knowledge of the matter. But it has been explored in the past, with just such experiments as these. Although in those cases, they were more organized and less destructive."

"And all unsuccessful," the king pointed out.

"Yes." Theo paused. "But that doesn't necessarily mean it's impossible. It may simply mean that the key to succeeding hadn't yet been found."

"And you think someone has found it?"

Theo shrugged. "I don't know that, Your Majesty. But I think someone is trying, at the very least. And the fact that enough magic appears to be missing from the environment after these experiments, with the impact of that sudden disappearance of magic potentially spreading far afield from the site of the incident...well, it does make me wonder if someone is succeeding in capturing released Dust."

"That would be alarming if true," the king said. He thought for a moment. "It's an interesting train of thought, but I don't think there's much reason to explore it. The investigation suggests that the incidents are not connected by one player."

"With respect, Your Majesty, I don't think that's true," Theo said. "I apologize if I overstepped, but I asked Paulson to make his own inquiries at the site of each incident. His own assessment of each area, and the accounts he received from witnesses who were very willing to speak with him, support the idea that magic disappeared on release at the time of each disaster. And that a young man with his features covered was seen at more than one location, usually holding a strange object of some kind."

The king frowned, his eyes flicking to Paulson then back to Theo. "That's not what has been reported to me."

Theo let out a long breath. "I mentioned the scarf earlier, Your Majesty, because I disagree with the duke. I considered the witness at the landslide to be clear and convincing. And he specifically described the young man he saw running from the landslide as having his face concealed by a purple scarf. Shortly after our return to the capital, I observed a servant of the duke's with just such a scarf. I understand that it's not conclusive, but there were other interactions I'd observed with regards to this servant that didn't seem right to me. I became concerned that if the evidence implicated a servant in the duke's own household, he may be placed in a difficult position as regards giving you a full report on the information gathered."

"Delicately put," the king said grimly. "I trust the duke's loyalty and honesty, Your Highness."

"Forgive me if I offend, Your Majesty," Theo said. "I have no reason to think poorly of His Grace. But given the possibility that he may be in a compromising position, I wished for a different source of information, to compare what the duke was reporting. That's why I asked Paulson to make inquiries on my behalf."

And what he found contradicts what your duke reported to you.

Theo didn't say the words, but they still hung silently in the air between the two royals.

"It may be that the matter has been investigated, and my doubts are unfounded," Theo went on. "But it should be noted that the young man in question has skill with magic, and on each occasion, he was either present at the disaster, or missing from his duties."

"I see." It was hard to read King Ronan's true thoughts, but at least he wasn't angry with Theo for making his own quiet inquiries, as he easily could have been. "Thank you for sharing your reflections with me, Your Highness." He stood, and Theo mirrored him. "I will think on the matter. And I look forward to celebrating the tournament's completion at tonight's celebration."

"Thank you, Your Majesty," Theo said, inclining his head.

"You fought well this morning," the king added, his manner becoming less formal. "It was a clean victory." His smile turned rueful. "Not a good day for the household of the Duke of Nirocha, it seems. Not that I mean any criticism. You bested your opponent in all honor."

Theo hesitated, wondering if the king had been perceptive enough to observe that the fight had become personal. Perhaps it would be better if he did know, at least to some extent. But after a moment's consideration, Theo banished the idea of telling the king what had happened between Bertrand and Elowen the night before. He didn't feel right to do it without first speaking to Elowen about it.

The castle was quiet throughout the afternoon, many people attending the commoner's events going on at the tournament field. Theo had no doubt the kitchen was bustling in preparation for the second celebration feast in as many days, but that activity was out of sight. He walked the corridors thoughtfully for a while before retreating to his rooms. He'd expected to feel a sense of release in sharing his suspicions with the king, but instead a vague unease hovered over him. Part of it was the fear that if the servant Elowen had a friendship with was exposed as a traitor, Elowen's inevitable distress and sense of betrayal would attach to Theo, as the bearer of that unwelcome news.

But the information that the investigation had brought to light had to be reported to the king. And if the duke wasn't going to fulfill that duty, what course could Theo take but to step in and do so himself?

The whole matter dimmed the satisfaction of having won the event against Bertrand, and the hours until the feast passed restlessly for Theo. He was in no humor to join any of the informal celebrations he could hear from his rooms. All he wanted was an answer about the investigation, and a chance to speak with Elowen.

Dinner, at which he would certainly be seated by the princess, promised the second one of these desires. But Theo's expectations were exceeded when his first wish was granted as he approached the dining hall.

"Prince Theodore." King Ronan hailed him, and Theo moved to his side, surprised when the king invited him to step into an antechamber across from the dining hall.

"A quick word before the feast begins," the king said. "I pursued the matter you raised with me, and I must thank you for your perceptiveness. When another investigator made inquiries, the situation unraveled quickly. The servant in question, a young man named Simeon, confessed to involvement in the incidents."

"He confessed?" Theo repeated, startled.

The king nodded. "He's being held securely, and will be further questioned by more independent investigators." The king's voice was grim, and discomfort flitted across his face. "The incompetence you were so quick to see doesn't reflect well on my governance, but I thank you for pointing it out nonetheless."

"You are not at fault, Your Majesty," Theo said quickly.

"You're gracious to say so." King Ronan was being restrained, but it was clear he wasn't happy. "The duke has recused himself from the evening's celebration. He is...embarrassed that he failed to see the truth in his own household."

Theo dipped his head in acknowledgment, politely pretending to believe the lie. The duke's embarrassment was presumably true enough. But Theo had no doubt that in reality, the duke was absent because he was being investigated under suspicion of having hidden evidence from his king as a result of that embarrassment.

"I wish I understood why the servant did it," the king said, probably deeming the topic safer. "He's been with the family for a long time, and from all I hear was highly trusted."

"Did he give no reason?" Theo asked carefully.

"He claimed he was angry with his employer, and wanted more power for the purpose of getting revenge," King Ronan said. "But my investigator didn't seem to find the reasoning convincing."

Theo raised his eyebrows. Had the investigator met the employer in question?

"To speak frankly, Your Majesty," he said, "I believe that the servant has truly been mistreated. Not by the duke, perhaps, but by the viscount. I've witnessed it myself on more than one occasion. And I've also seen evidence that the servant may have a grudge."

The king ran a hand through his hair. "Lord Bertrand has

always lacked his father's polish, but that's no justification for the servant to mount attacks on innocent towns across the kingdom."

"Certainly not," Theo agreed.

"It was a poorly thought through plan. He claims to have been trying to harness the magic, but that in each case it was more than he could manipulate." The king shook his head. "So much destruction and risk to life for no benefit."

"Unless he was trying to find a way to store the magic," Theo reminded the king.

"Perhaps." The king didn't look convinced. "There's nothing to suggest that yet, but he'll certainly be questioned on the matter."

"What will happen to him once the questioning is complete?" Theo asked.

King Ronan sighed. "I haven't figured that out yet. But the whole affair is bound to be painful and distressing."

Theo kept quiet, suspecting the king had no idea how close to home that distress would be.

"In any event," the king attempted a smile, "let us think of more cheerful matters. A feast awaits us."

"Yes." Not feeling very festive, Theo followed the older man from the room.

SEVENTEEN

Elowen

The celebration feast couldn't come fast enough for Elowen. All afternoon she chafed in her rooms as her maids prepared her, her mind full of Theo. She'd been impressed by his performance throughout the morning's fights. And what he'd said to Bertrand when he bested him...he'd won that fight for her. He didn't care about the tournament, he never had. But he'd cared about her situation.

Elowen's mind went back over their encounter that morning, when she'd told him her side of the story regarding the previous night. She'd been braced for him not to believe her or maybe not even to care whether it was true or not. But she'd wronged him when she imagined him acting with anything less than total honor.

Her maids commented on her flushed cheeks while they did her hair, and she let them believe it was the excitement of the tournament's completion and the upcoming feast. Never would she have admitted that her senses were tingling with the memory of the anger and protectiveness Theo hadn't been able to hide when she told him what had happened. She'd seen his hand flex as he walked away, and had wondered if he was going to beat Bertrand with his fists. In fact, she'd been shocked to realize that a part of her wanted him to.

She hardly knew what to feel. She'd dreamed of someone with a romantic manner, and Theo simply didn't have it, not even in that moment. Even then, he'd been doing all he could to hide his emotions. It was his actions that had spoken.

The readiness with which he acknowledged he'd been wrong in his assumptions and asked her to forgive him. The way his first thought was whether she was all right. His single-minded focus as he'd made it his mission to punish Bertrand on her behalf, and to warn him off attempting to impose on her again.

Those actions convinced her that Theo had emotions, strong ones. She hadn't expected the reaction from him, and she didn't deny that it had thrilled her all the way down to her toes. If anything, his actions were more meaningful to her without the gallant manner, because she knew they were genuine, and not designed to elicit a reaction from her.

Then he'd won, and she'd presented him with his choice. She'd been alarmed at the prospect of having to bestow a victor's kiss in front of all those people, but that didn't stop her traitorous heart from feeling a contradictory trickle of disappointment when he chose the handkerchief. She no longer knew what she wanted him to do, or how she wanted him to act. If he was acting according to the direction of her imagination, many things would have gone differently. But then he wouldn't be him. And, she realized in a moment of honesty, he wouldn't have awoken such fascination in her. There was still so much she didn't know of him, and she could think of nothing else but learning it.

At the feast, they would formalize their betrothal. The only thing standing between them and marriage would be Elowen herself.

She had taken her place at the banquet table long before Theo finally appeared. When he entered, he walked just behind her father, and his expression was too somber for a tournament victor. Their eyes met across the room, a silent question in Elowen's gaze.

Theo's face softened in a subtle way she might once have missed but had now come to recognize. She felt warmth spreading up her neck as he strode to her side, taking his rightful place as champion next to the princess for whom the tournament had been called.

"Your popularity appears to have grown," she told him, as several admiring cheers greeted his arrival from some of the more excitable of the young courtiers.

"Very gratifying." Theo's answering smile had a touch of humor in it, and Elowen chuckled.

"You fought very well today," Elowen told him. "I was proud to have you as my champion."

Theo said nothing, his eyes burning into hers with silent intensity. She'd tried to speak lightly, but somehow a hint of her feelings had crept in, and they suddenly seemed to be speaking about more than the tournament.

"Is everything well with you?" Theo asked, the words mild but a deeper sentiment behind them that made Elowen's heart thud pleasantly.

"Yes, of course," she assured him. She gave a weak smile. "I think I'll stay inside the banquet hall this evening, however."

A tightness appeared behind Theo's eyes, but after a quick scan of the room, his face relaxed again.

"Have you told your father what happened?"

"I haven't," Elowen admitted, fiddling with her spoon to avoid meeting his eyes.

Theo seemed to sense her embarrassment, and the next moment, his hand had slid over hers, stilling its movement. In fact, Elowen's whole body went still, unable to pull her gaze from their linked hands. His skin was rougher than hers, his fingers warm and strong. She felt enclosed but not trapped. Safe.

"Elowen."

She forced her eyes up to meet his.

"You've done nothing wrong, and you have nothing to be ashamed of." His voice turned rueful. "I, on the other hand…"

"No, Theo." Elowen's voice was a murmur as she spoke over him. "I don't blame you for the misunderstanding. I'm just glad you forgive me now that you know how it was."

"There's nothing to forgive," Theo said, his voice harsh. Collecting himself, he softened it immediately. "I don't wish to interfere, but I think you should tell your father."

Elowen's eyes drifted to the man in question, to see that the king was at that moment rising to his feet. The rest of the room followed, her and Theo among them.

"Welcome," King Ronan said, his voice carrying over the gathered assembly with calm authority. "I am delighted to celebrate the tournament's completion with you all. But first, I have news to share. I know many have been concerned by the recent disasters that have struck various regions of our kingdom."

The mood of his listeners shifted, the silence suddenly thick.

"These matters have been under investigation," King Ronan continued, "and I regret to say that the incidents appear to have been malicious in intent."

Murmurs spread quickly around the room, everyone assuring their neighbor that they suspected as much all along.

"However." The king's voice carried over the hubbub, bringing instant order again. "I'm pleased to report that we have a perpetrator in custody who has confessed to having caused these disasters with the intent of creating significant

Dust. Justice will be done for the damage caused, and there is every reason to hope there will be no more incidents."

Applause greeted these words, everyone beginning to speak at once. Elowen saw relief on many faces, all eyes bright with excited speculation.

"This is big news," she said aloud. "I knew nothing of this development."

"I believe it's just happened," Theo said. Something in his low, gentle voice sent unease over Elowen. His eyes searched her face. "Do you know who the perpetrator is?"

She shook her head, skimming the crowd anxiously. She hadn't noticed before, but the duke and his family were all conspicuously absent.

"On to the purpose for our celebration," King Ronan continued, smiling on his subjects' good cheer. "Patrick?"

"Yes." Patrick stood, his posture rigid as always as he cast his eyes over the gathered court. "Last night, we toasted our victors among the nobility in all events but one. It is my honor to officially close the tournament tonight, as we celebrate the victor of the weapons fighting." He turned to Theo, inclining his head. "His Highness Prince Theodore, second-born son of King Madoc of Siqual."

Everyone began to applaud, although Elowen noticed that not every face showed equal excitement. She gave Theo a warm smile.

"And, of course," King Ronan resumed, "in so celebrating, we formally mark the betrothal of His Highness to our own Princess Elowen."

At her father's gesture, Elowen and Theo moved to join him. Internally, Elowen reflected that her father had worded the declaration very neatly, as though the betrothal really did flow from the tournament victory. What would he have said if Theo had lost? The whole thing was as much of a farce as ever, but the betrothal itself was about to become very real. Nerves jittered over her as two servants moved toward the table, each holding a silver tray with a jewel-encrusted goblet.

One was carried to her father, who lifted it in both hands while Patrick received the other. When both goblets were ready, the king spoke again.

"With this cup, Princess Elowen and Prince Theodore formally accept the proposed alliance between the mighty kingdoms of Torrens and Siqual. And as they drink to seal their betrothal, we all anticipate the wedding to come, and the new era of shared prosperity that will follow."

Applause once again rang through the space, but again it was muted from certain sections of the tables that lined the walls of the banquet hall. There were still a significant number among her father's court who weren't enthusiastic about the marriage alliance. Elowen found she didn't care much. She would be living in Siqual, far away from any need to deal with their disapproval.

As she'd been told to expect, her father handed her the goblet he held, and Patrick gave his to Theo. The vessel was heavy, wrought from gold mined from Torrens' northern region. But the pattern engraved on it depicted the trees of Siqual's western region as they melted into the dunes of its desert, and the sapphires studding it had been refined and worked by a metalsmith from that kingdom. Likewise the other goblet showed the flowing rivers and temperate farmland of Torrens and was embellished with emeralds from the mines on the Duke of Nirocha's land.

She drank from the cup of Siqual, Theo from the cup of Torrens. So they marked their commitment to the kingdom of the other.

Feeling the weight of so many eyes on her, Elowen interlinked her arm with Theo's, taking care not to lose her grip on the goblet. Her eyes snuck to his, to find them steadily fixed on her face. For a heartbeat that seemed to last forever, she couldn't pull her gaze away. Then her father gave them the cue, and both tilted their cups to their lips and drank deeply of the wine.

Her father made another short speech, but Elowen scarcely heard it. She drained the goblet as she'd been instructed to do, grateful that it was less than half full. Whoever was in charge of organizing the goblets likely knew that she wasn't used to large quantities of wine. The two servants reappeared, and Elowen was surprised to see Theo's goblet still half full as he placed it back on the tray. He must have caught her expression, because as soon as they were released to return to their seats, he leaned toward her.

"Is something amiss?"

She shook her head. "I was surprised you didn't finish the wine, that's all. It's no matter."

"It was a large goblet," he commented. "And very full. If you finished yours, I'm amazed you were able to drink it all so swiftly."

"They were kinder to me and mine didn't have much in it," she laughed. "I only mention it because it's part of the cere- mony, we're supposed to drain the cups to show our full commitment, but it doesn't matter."

"I missed that aspect of the instructions," said Theo, his consternation clear. "My apologies. I hope I haven't offended.'

"Not me, certainly," Elowen said quickly. "And I doubt anyone else was close enough to notice. Truly, it doesn't matter."

He took a moment to answer, something in his face that made her breath feel thicker than usual.

"I assure you that while my etiquette may have failed, my commitment is absolute. Our betrothal is now sealed."

"Yes." Elowen lowered her eyes, wondering why she could hear her pulse thrumming in her ears. Surely that wasn't normal. "We are sealed."

She felt Theo's eyes on her, but she couldn't meet them, instead starting on her food. Theo copied her, and there was silence between them for several minutes.

Someone poured wine into their goblets—normal ones absent any fabulous jewels—but Elowen left hers untouched. Her nerves were wreaking enough havoc with her mind, she didn't want to addle it further. Theo, she noticed, barely touched his as well. He took a sip when the servants carried out the soup course, but he didn't seem to enjoy it. Blinking rapidly, he put the goblet down, and she didn't see him touch it again.

The previous night, he'd been relaxed and cheerful while chatting with the Carrackian royals. Tonight, they sat apart from their nearest neighbors, in the places of honor as the subjects of the betrothal feast, and Elowen had hoped for more personal conversation. But Theo didn't seem inclined to talk. She watched as he picked at his food, eating very little. About ten minutes into the meal, she saw him put a hand to his head, his gaze a little fuzzy.

"Are you all right?" she asked quietly.

He looked at her, seeming surprised by the question. "Of course," he said, his voice gruff. But he seemed confused in spite of his words.

Elowen wondered if he might be affected by the wine. She suddenly realized that there might be another reason he didn't finish the goblet, and barely touched the wine set in front of him. Perhaps they drank stronger wine in Torrens than in Siqual. Perhaps Theo found himself more affected by the small quantity than he expected, and was embarrassed to let it show.

But he only had half a goblet. How strong could it be? Elowen frowned to herself over little details as she watched him. Was it her imagination that his movements were less precise than usual? His conversation was certainly lacking.

She was being absurd, reaching foolishly for an explanation other than the obvious one that he had nothing much to say to her. If he had felt constrained by their betrothal, as she had herself, he would be wrestling with the implications of that now more than ever. He was allowed to prefer reflective silence over chatter.

After all, he hadn't claimed the kiss he'd been offered. He'd been her champion that day, in more ways than one. But hadn't she already realized that it wasn't out of an overflow of romance but was simply Theo acting consistent with the honor that characterized him? It was a good testament regarding the man she was to marry, but it didn't necessarily mean he was enthusiastic about the union.

Elowen felt deflated, but she tried not to dwell on it. She wasn't sure her emotions could sustain another round of chaos that day. She would be wisest to let Theo be, and speak of these matters later.

But when Theo excused himself early, rising as soon as the meal was complete, her resolution failed her. He'd barely left the room when Elowen announced her own intention to retire. Her mother looked surprised, but she didn't try to prevent her. Given the previous night's gala, the victory feast wasn't to be accompanied by a ball anymore, and if the victor had left, there wasn't any reason Elowen had to linger.

"Of course you must be tired, my dear," Elowen's mother said. "A solid sleep will do you good."

She nodded to the lady's maid waiting at the edge of the room. The woman stepped forward to accompany Elowen to her room and help her prepare for bed. Elowen walked out meekly beside the maid, but waited only until they'd left the noise and light of the banquet hall behind to stop.

"Foolish of me, but I need to return for something," she said lightly. "You go ahead without me, I'll meet you at my rooms."

"Are you sure, Your Highness?" the maid asked, uncertain.

"Of course," Elowen said, trying to mimic the authority her father always spoke with.

The maid nodded and carried on, and as soon as she was out of sight, Elowen ducked down a different corridor, one she knew led to the guest wing. Relieved to see no sign of servants, she disregarded dignity and ran, hoping she wasn't too late to catch him.

Fortunately, her quarry was moving slowly. After rounding two more corners, Elowen caught sight of Theo's tall figure and broad shoulders.

"Theo," she called softly, a little breathless from the run.

He turned, surprise then concern flicking across his face as he caught sight of her.

"Elowen. Is everything all right?"

"Yes."

She came to a stop, catching her breath as they looked at each other from several feet away. Theo's eyes scanned the corridor behind her, his expression hard to read as he comprehended that she was alone.

"I thought you were going to avoid leaving the banquet hall unaccompanied tonight," he pointed out, his voice low and far too appealing.

"Plans can change," Elowen said.

"Why...why did you follow me?"

His speech wasn't as crisp as usual, and for some reason his hesitance made Elowen feel bolder. She moved forward, narrowing the distance between them until she was only a foot away.

"I needed to know."

"Know what?" Theo asked cautiously.

"Why you changed your mind about choosing the kiss," Elowen said, her voice quiet but not hesitant. "When you won the event. You had the right as victor to claim a kiss, and you were obviously inclined at first to exert your right. So why didn't you?"

Theo's brow furrowed, and he studied her face as if looking for a hidden message. "You didn't want to kiss me in front of all those strangers," he said. "And I'm not interested in a kiss I win by force."

"Aren't you?" Elowen demanded. Wasn't their whole marriage won by force in a sense?

Theo looked more confused than ever, his blinks slow as his eyes roved over her face. He seemed even more affected by the wine now, but she knew he didn't drink more than half a goblet.

"Of course not," Theo said, his tone bewildered. "What kind of a man demands an artificial display of affection? What kind of a man would consider that a victory?"

Elowen swallowed, frightened by the sudden yearning rising in her. Was it so much talk of kissing that had her heart pounding, or was it the further evidence of his honor? Either way, what she was feeling was dangerous. It was too potent for an attachment that was unrequited. If she let herself grow to care too deeply for a husband who was trustworthy and respectful but emotionally indifferent to her, it would slowly rip her apart. But was he emotionally indifferent? She had to know.

She raised her eyes to his, and she could have sworn his gaze was on her lips before it darted up to meet hers.

"What if it wasn't artificial?" she whispered. "I need to know, Theo. Do you *want* to kiss me?"

His hand moved toward her in a jerky movement, then dropped.

"Don't ask me what I want," he said, his voice rougher now. "I can't afford to want you."

"What do you mean?" she demanded.

He gave a low groan, moving toward her without seeming to realize it. There were inches between them now. When he spoke, his voice was more ragged than she'd ever heard it.

"Your deal with your parents, Elowen, it's going to destroy me. You want me to earn our marriage by proving I want it enough, but that's exactly what I can't do. If I want you too much, something bad will happen."

Elowen's heart had increased to double time, the unexpected vulnerability drawing her to him like a doomed moth. She searched his face, speaking softly.

"I know opening your heart to someone means opening yourself to the possibility of being hurt, but are you really so afraid to risk pain that you—"

"Not me, you!" Theo cut her off, his words vibrating with intensity. "Something bad will happen to you."

Elowen frowned, confused. "I don't understand."

Theo seemed to be struggling as well, still looking dazed. "I don't know how to explain it. I just know that everyone, from the kingdom to you, will be safer if my emotions don't get tangled into it."

Hesitantly, he lifted a hand, running the tips of his fingers over her temple and down the line of her jaw. It was a sensation she'd craved since he touched her chin that morning, and she closed her eyes, leaning into his touch. His voice dropped to a whisper.

"I can't bear to see you hurt, Elowen. It's my job to protect you, or it will be soon."

She swallowed, struggling to marshal her thoughts. An intoxicating sensation still lingered on her skin where his touch had been. But she couldn't let his nearness distract her into wasting this rare moment of openness. Her voice was little above a whisper, too.

"But your coldness hurts me, Theo." He flinched at the simple words, but she pressed on. "I *want* to be wanted. I want to be appreciated for who I am, of course I do. But I also want to feel like I'm capable of inspiring emotion, of inspiring *passion*."

A ripple went over his features, one she could tell he tried to contain. He didn't succeed.

"Elowen." Theo shifted toward her, seizing her shoulders in a movement she didn't see coming, and rotating her so that she suddenly found her back against a pillar. He leaned close, lowering his face as he murmured into her ear. "You are."

Her pulse was racing, but she felt more daring than ever. This was nothing like the sensation of Bertrand looming over her. That had been cold fear—this was fire in her veins. She'd never wanted a man close like this before. The stiffness he showed on the surface hadn't driven her away. It had just made her yearn to get inside. She wanted to bring him out, wanted to know she and she alone had the love of this complex but endlessly honorable man, more than she'd ever wanted anything in her life.

"Then prove it," she murmured.

Theo's eyes burned with something that made it suddenly hard to breathe, and Elowen's heart tried to escape her chest as he laid an arm against the pillar above her head. His face inched toward hers, his inner defenses visibly weakening. But just as she was sure of victory, the sound of running footsteps reached her ears. Theo sprang backwards, his movements less than fluid.

Elowen turned, her breath coming too quickly, sure that she wouldn't be able to hide her flustered state from whatever servant was racing past on an errand.

But it wasn't a servant. Sophia came pounding around the

corner, her hair disheveled and her eyes wide. She skidded to a stop when she saw Elowen, but the tumult on her face clearly had nothing to do with the situation in which she'd found her friend.

"Elowen, I've been looking everywhere for you! You have to help me, we have to do something."

"Sophia!" Alarmed by her friend's babbling, Elowen moved forward, grasping Sophia's arm. "What's wrong? What's happened?"

"I know I told you I was worried he might do something," Sophia said, her voice choked with emotion. "But I don't believe he would do *this*. He wouldn't cause all those disasters. He couldn't!"

"Who? Sophia, what—?" Elowen's words cut off as she realized. She'd been so absorbed in the betrothal she'd forgotten about the announcement that came before it.

"Simeon," said Sophia, with a sob. "He's locked up in the dungeon, and they're saying he confessed to causing the fire, and the dam, and all the rest of it. But I don't believe it, Elowen! They say the king might rule for execution. We have to do something!"

Fear seeped over Elowen as she tried to make sense of it all. Her eyes moved to Theo, who'd been silent throughout Sophia's outburst. He looked grave, but not surprised. Had he known? His gaze was heavy as he looked between the two women, as if struggling to follow the rapid pace of the conversation.

Elowen opened her mouth to ask if he was all right, but Sophia cut her off.

"This is all my fault, Elowen," she said. "I have to fix it, I just don't know how."

"How could it possibly be your fault?" Elowen demanded. She frowned. "Sophia, it's time to tell me exactly what's going on with you. You said when the tournament started that you'd learned your mistakes hurt people other than yourself. What mistake did you mean?"

"Bertrand knows." Sophia's voice was a whisper, her eyes distraught. "He knows…" She glanced self-consciously at the still-silent Theo, then pushed on. "He knows my heart. He's been holding it over me, threatening to expose me to our parents. It's how he convinced me to tell him things about you that I never should have, like the foolish ideas of the perfect, romantic man we used to joke about. I'm so sorry, Elowen."

"Never mind that," said Elowen quickly, embarrassed to have that incident brought back to everyone's mind. She cast a look at Theo to see slow comprehension cutting through the fog that he still seemed to be struggling with. Was he really so affected by half a goblet of wine?

"I think it's made Bertrand harder on Simeon as well," Sophia said. "I know I said Simeon has been on the edge for a long time, but I can't believe he'd do this."

"Sometimes," Theo interjected gently, "if we really don't want to believe something, it's hard to see it clearly."

"It's not like that, Your Highness," Sophia insisted, more bold than Elowen had seen her in a long time.

"I agree with Sophia," she said quickly. "None of this adds up with what we know of Simeon. Can it really be true that he confessed?"

"It's true," Theo said. "Your father told me as much right before the feast." His eyes were sympathetic as they rested on Elowen's face. "You remember that we've spoken of this before. I believe there truly is evidence to suggest he was behind it."

"Then the evidence is wrong," Elowen said firmly. "I don't blame you for believing it," she added quickly. "Because you don't know him. But we do, and—"

She cut herself off as Theo swayed slightly.

"Theo," she said, gripping his elbow in alarm.

"I'm fine," he assured her. "I slept very poorly last night, and after this morning's event, my weariness has caught up with me. I developed a headache during dinner, it's why I retired early."

"You should sleep," Elowen told him. "I'm supposed to retire as well, and my maid will be wondering what's taking me so long." She put her arm through Sophia's and squeezed. "Walk with me, Sophia, we can speak more."

As they parted ways, Elowen looked back over her shoulder. Theo was doing the same, and their eyes met, silent acknowledgment of their interrupted moment passing between them. Her lips tingled with the memory of how close they'd come to knowing what his would feel like.

Along with the regret, and her fear for Simeon, something else was sprouting in her heart. Hope. She didn't understand Theo's hesitation, but she no longer feared that he was indifferent to her. If they could navigate through whatever had gone wrong with Simeon and the magic-induced disasters, she might find herself faced not with a prison sentence, but with a future she wanted to run toward.

EIGHTEEN

Theo

Theo lay on his side, confused by the pressure on his head. He raised a hand, wincing as he felt the heavy rock resting against his temple. No wonder his head felt like it was being slowly crushed. He tried to move the stone, but it wouldn't budge. Wind whipped around his face, and he shivered under its icy touch. He realized that his cheek lay against soft grass, and opened his eyes to see a moonlit scene, cliffs falling away right beside him, with an ocean crashing against their base.

It was a place he hadn't seen in a long time, but it was horribly familiar. From his vantage point, he could see the side of the cliff where it curved around not far away. It wasn't just a sheer drop. There were layers of stone, climbable by someone sure-footed. As Theo's eyes frantically scanned the cliffside, his eyes caught on a strange movement, and a moment later, moonlight glinted on the creature's forehead.

"I see it!" The clear voice reached Theo's ears as the turf beneath his head reverberated with hoofbeats.

Sluggishly, he turned his obstructed head to see Ochre riding at a breakneck speed toward the cliff's edge. The horse was galloping too fast, on the edge of losing control, just like when it had run alongside the flood from the dam. But this time its rider wasn't afraid.

Elowen sat astride the mare, her hair flowing freely behind her with the moonlight tangling in it and making it glow as strangely as a carbuncle's brow. She wore a golden gown to match her hair, and a thin scarf was around her neck. Skirts and scarf fanned out behind her as she rode, whipped by the wind.

"I see it, Theo!" she cried again, her eyes alight with excitement as she thundered toward the carbuncle.

"No!" Theo cried. "Elowen, stop!"

She didn't seem to hear him. He struggled to get up from the ground, his limbs shaky and weak as they tried to lift his body. Terror gripped him, his arms stretching uselessly out as the horse veered toward the cliff's edge and suddenly shied.

Elowen was thrown from the saddle, falling down, over the edge, into nothing, endlessly falling.

"NO!"

Theo woke with a ragged gasp, trapped energy still coursing through his veins.

A smaller gasp answered his own, and he opened his eyes to see a servant scurrying from the room, clutching flint. It took Theo's sluggish mind a moment to comprehend that he was looking at his suite in the Torrenese royal castle, and that the cliffside disaster had been a dream. It was no wonder it was hard to think straight, given how his head was pounding. The rock from the dream no longer sat on his temple, but the sensation of pressure on his head remained.

Theo sat slowly up, grimacing at the potency of his dream. The weakness in his limbs was lingering still. The servant he'd startled must have been lighting the fire, and it was a good thing. The room felt freezing, almost as cold as the wind-whipped cliffside his imagination had taken him back to in sleep.

He washed his face with the fresh water that had been left by his basin. It was harder than it should have been to shake off the stupor of the dream. His mind felt like it was underwater, the thickness and pressure in his head refusing to disappear.

Theo was surprised to learn how late he'd slept, and he made his way to breakfast as quickly as his unresponsive body would allow. When he entered the smaller dining hall the family used for non-tournament meals, he stopped short.

Elowen was there, as he'd expected, looking resplendent in a sky-blue gown, her hair partly pulled back at the top, with the rest flowing past her shoulders. The king, queen, and prince were also present. But it wasn't them who made Theo pause in the doorway, staring stupidly. Was he still asleep after all?

"Theo." The interloper rose, grinning. "Finally! Everyone's almost finished, when did you become such a sluggard?"

"Xavier?" Theo said the name cautiously, as if fearing some trick. The pounding in his head was a dull roar, and his mind was struggling to keep up. "But...you're not in Toledda."

There was a strange look in Xavier's eyes as he laughed in response to Theo's words. "I am, actually. But if you meant I'm not expected, you're right, of course." He bowed gallantly in the direction of the Torrenese royals. "I'm grateful for the generosity of Their Majesties in receiving me."

"We're delighted to host you, Your Highness," Queen Lisbeth assured him, although something about the line of her lips told Theo that she didn't fully appreciate the irregularity of Siqual's crown prince showing up unannounced.

Theo didn't blame her. It was absurd and inconsiderate and, frankly, just like Xavier. It must really be happening.

"When did you get here? *Why* are you here?" he demanded.

Dazed, he moved forward and took a seat beside Xavier. His

brother, he noticed, had taken the seat next to Elowen. Of course he had.

"I arrived late last night," Xavier said. "I thought I might have to find an inn, but the castle was still bustling with a gala, my good luck." He quirked one eyebrow in a way that gave his already appealing face a rakishly handsome air—as he was well aware, Theo knew from experience. "I was told that you'd retired hours before, however, which is why I didn't come bursting into your rooms at once. Theo, you've always been a dull dog, but retiring early from your own victory feast is a sad case even for you. What of Siqual's honor, little brother?"

A flash of anger went over Theo at these words, and he knew it showed in his face. Xavier's winning smile wavered, his brows puckering slightly in confusion as he searched Theo's face. Theo raised a hand to his throbbing head, trying to regain his equilibrium. He usually met Xavier's outrageousness with either long-suffering or laughter, depending on his mood. Anger wasn't a normal reaction, and Xavier knew it.

"You all right?" Xavier asked, more quietly.

"Of course," said Theo shortly, reaching for a still-steaming bun.

"It was a taxing day yesterday," Elowen chimed in, not seeming pleased with Xavier's chastising of his brother. "Theo had reason to be tired."

"Yes, I've heard of your victory," Xavier said, his eyes twinkling again. "I congratulate you, Theo! I have no trouble believing you fought valiantly with such a motivation." He inclined his head to Elowen, his voice lowering to the rumbling hum Theo had seen many a girl swoon over. "Truly, for any man of honor, it would be a privilege to fight for the favor of a woman of such grace and—to be bold, breathtaking beauty— as yourself, Your Highness."

Elowen blinked, taken aback and a little dazzled by the

change in tone. Theo restrained a groan that was only partly to do with his aching head. Xavier's compliments might be overblown, but his manner wasn't that of a flatterer. He made the words—which were, after all, perfectly true—sound so sincere. It was exactly the skill Theo had never learned, even when he *was* completely in earnest. He'd looked down on what he'd considered a frippery skill that Xavier wasted his time on. If anything, he'd gone out of his way to avoid adopting any hint of it.

Which probably meant he would never be acceptable enough to Elowen, and their wedding date would never be set.

Recognizing that he was being dramatic, Theo tried to drown his bitter thoughts in the sweet tea that had been placed in front of him.

"Theo fought not for my honor, but the honor of my kingdom." Elowen surprised him by responding head on to Xavier's words. "He was respecting our traditions, for which we're grateful. Even though some of them are a little meaningless."

"Yesterday's event wasn't meaningless," Theo interjected, putting his tea down too quickly so that it sloshed over the rim of the cup a little. His memory darkened as Bertrand's sneering face filled it. "It was a necessary win."

He looked up to find Elowen watching him, her look of surprise changing to one of concern. "Do you feel well this morning, Theo?"

"A little worn down," he acknowledged. "But nothing to cause concern." He wasn't about to admit that he was rattled and near incapacitated by a disturbing dream about her plunging off a cliff. He turned his attention to Xavier. "Are you staying long?"

Xavier shook his head. "I'll leave today. I actually came in hope of catching Prince Cassius. I've been very interested to hear that he made a diplomatic visit to Pulau. I don't believe any kingdoms of the Peninsula have done so in the last decade, and the place has always fascinated me. I happened to be in the north of Siqual when I heard about it, and my information was that he was likely to be returning via Torrens." He smiled disarmingly. "Which naturally I had a double interest in visiting given my favorite of brothers is here."

Theo just grunted.

"I crossed the border and traveled north, and heard along the way that they were making a last-minute stop in Toledda. So I hurried here myself."

"And what were you doing in the north of Siqual?" Theo asked dryly. "Official royal business?"

Xavier grinned. "Sure. If you like."

A sigh was the only response Theo gave. He was well used to his brother's disinterest in any royal responsibilities that didn't particularly catch his fancy.

"Well, you missed them," he said. "They left early yesterday morning."

"Yes, I've been told," Xavier replied. "I'm hoping I might catch up to them if I leave promptly. I'm only traveling with a couple of guards, so we can move quickly."

At least he was with official guards instead of running off alone without stopping to ask the king's leave. It wouldn't be the first time.

"I wouldn't count on it," Prince Patrick interjected. His brows were slightly raised, as if incredulous of the carefree attitude of his Siqualian counterpart. "They weren't in a large group themselves, and they made excellent time from the port city to the capital."

"Is that right?" Xavier mused. "Maybe it's not worth it. I don't want to chase them all the way to Crandell."

"Why not?" Theo asked politely. "You could stop at Dernanford on the way home, complete your circuit of uninvited visits to all the capitals on the Peninsula."

Xavier's mouth twitched in the hint of a smirk, apparently feeling himself on more familiar ground with Theo's dry responses.

"I think I'd be better off staying here for a little," Xavier said. He lowered his voice, sending the ghost of a wink at Elowen before adding, "The company is more bewitching than any in Carrack, I'm sure. Princess Elowen might be in need of some cheer provided by Siqual's interesting prince before shackling herself to its somber one."

"No doubt." The words, hard and bitter, slipped from Theo's lips. He stood abruptly. "Excuse me. I need to check in with my guard."

He saw the astonishment on Xavier's face at this reaction to his teasing, but worse was the hurt that crossed Elowen's features before she could smooth them. Theo winced as he bowed his head stiffly to the king and queen. What was wrong with him? Why couldn't he pull himself together? His head was throbbing so badly it was hard to marshal his thoughts at all. Never in his life had he felt so close to falling apart. He had to get away from witnesses.

He was out of the room and halfway down the corridor before he registered the footsteps behind him.

"Theo!" Xavier appeared at his side, his brow furrowed as he grabbed Theo's arm. "What's going on?"

"Nothing," said Theo curtly. "I'm sorry I lost my temper."

He tried to pull free of Xavier's arm to keep walking, but his brother hung on grimly.

"You're my brother, Theo. I know you better than my own reflection, don't try to tell me everything is fine with you when I can see plain as day you're in the middle of some crisis."

A servant rounded the corner ahead, eyes wide with

interest as she bobbed a quick curtsy before moving past them. Theo put a hand to his head, wishing it would settle for a moment so he could think.

"Come to my suite," he told his brother. "We can talk privately there."

Xavier fell into step beside him, saying nothing further until they reached the sitting room of Theo's guest suite.

"All right, out with it," the older prince said, as soon as the door was closed. "What in the Peninsula is happening to you, Theo?"

"I'm not well, I think," Theo acknowledged. He sank into an armchair. "Nothing serious, but my head feels like it's on an anvil this morning."

"All right," Xavier said slowly. "You have my sympathy, but are you really trying to tell me that an aching head has stripped you of the ability to recognize when I'm teasing you? You just about took my head off back there, Theo, surely you knew I was joking?"

"Yes, of course I knew," Theo said wearily, leaning his head back and closing his eyes.

"Well, I didn't think you usually cared about that kind of thing."

"I don't," said Theo shortly. "I'm just a bit short on patience this morning, that's all."

"Oh, that's all, is it?" Xavier said shrewdly. "Nothing to do with having a weak spot for a certain golden-haired goddess with eyes any man would gladly drown himself in and features more delicate than a woodland sprite's?"

Theo didn't lift his head as he grunted. "You've always had a talent for speaking pretty nonsense, Xavier."

"Only it's not nonsense this time, is it?" Xavier asked, his tone more earnest than Theo had anticipated. "All those things really are true of your princess."

"I suppose they are," Theo said softly. "But I would never have thought those words, or said them even if I did."

He looked his brother over, from the carelessly dashing way his hair swept over his forehead to the jaunty line of his jaw. Xavier was—always had been—the kind of man women lost their heads over. Theo had never imagined he would envy that. But then he'd never imagined any woman would have the effect Elowen had on him. Try as he might, he couldn't keep the edge of bitterness from his voice.

"I'm about as prettily spoken as a swamp troll. You were right, she is deserving of pity for being tied to the dull brother. I have no doubt she'd prefer you if she'd been given the choice. You'd know just how to give her what her heart craves."

"Whatever my reputation, I'll restrain myself from seducing your betrothed," Xavier said, with the self-deprecating humor that made him so popular among their set back home. "Theo, old boy, this isn't like you. Dare I say it, you're mooning! Are things really going so poorly with your princess?"

"She's not my princess," Theo said softly, his elbows on his knees now and his eyes on the rug beneath his feet. "I mean, I suppose she is my princess, or will be. But *she's* not mine. I can't win her, Xavier."

Xavier sat down in the chair next to him, searching his face in a way Theo could feel without looking up.

"What's going on, Theo? She seemed friendly enough toward you just now. Why are you convinced that you can't win her over?"

Theo closed his eyes for a moment, willing his head to settle down. A fire was burning strongly in the hearth of the sitting room, but it still felt so unseasonably cold.

"She wants me to want her," he said softly. The words felt dangerous, reckless, something he shouldn't say even to Xavier. But he seemed to have very little control of his words that morning, and they slipped out into the stillness of the private moment. "But I can't, Xavier."

"Whyever not?" Xavier demanded, his voice not hushed like Theo's had been. "Don't eat me for saying it, Theo, but she's just about the most delicious morsel I've ever seen."

Irritation flared in Theo, but after one look at Xavier's rakishly raised eyebrow, it was replaced by weary resignation. "You know I hate when you talk like that, Xavier," he said. "Don't waste your act on me, you don't fool me as much as you think you do."

He saw surprise flash across Xavier's face. For a moment his brother looked cornered, struggling for what to say. Apparently no roguish quip came to mind this time, because he quickly changed the topic.

"Enough riddles, Theo. What's amiss between you and your betrothed? Is her intellect dull under all that dazzling beauty? Or is she unprincipled? Do you worry she won't be faithful?"

"Don't talk about her like that," Theo snapped. "She's perfect. There's nothing wrong with her, it's me."

"So why don't you want her, then?" Xavier demanded.

"Not want her?" Theo groaned again. He buried his face in his hands, his voice coming out muffled. "It's ripping me apart how much I want her. She's all I can think about, it's going to consume me, and her, too."

"Why would that be a bad thing?" Xavier protested, incredulous at this display from his stoic brother.

"You know why!" Theo burst out.

If only his head would stop pounding. His thoughts were fuzzy and disordered, but his emotions weren't dulled to match. They were burning more fiercely with every passing minute. The combination made it impossible to find his usual control, words pouring from his mouth that he never thought he'd say aloud.

"The last time I wanted anything half this much, the thing I wanted died before my eyes because of my own stupid decisions. And Miriam almost did, too."

He looked up to find Xavier staring at him in confusion.

"You're talking about the carbuncle? Why would you even think about that? It was so many years ago."

"It might be a distant memory for you," Theo said bitterly, "but for me, it was yesterday. I haven't let myself pursue something just because I wanted it since that night." His eyes felt dull as he stared at his brother. "I leave that to you. You do enough in that arena for both of us and then some."

Xavier flinched, the movement so slight Theo wasn't sure if he'd imagined it.

"It was hard when I was young," he went on, his voice a murmur. "To deny myself the things I wanted. I learned that the best way was not to ever want anything too much. For Siqual, yes, of course, but not for myself. I thought I'd outgrown selfish desires, but then I met Elowen…"

His face dropped back into his hands.

"If I let my heart take control, I'll fail my kingdom. If I protect the kingdom by keeping my emotions out of it, I'll fail my wife before our marriage even starts. I can't bear to do either. I'm trapped, Xavier."

"Theo, this is madness," Xavier protested. "You're not in your right mind to be saying these things. Of course you're allowed to want things. Being royal doesn't mean you can't—"

"Don't lecture me on what it means to be royal," Theo cut him off. "You think it doesn't matter what you do, but the only reason you can live that way is because I cover for you every day of your life."

"Theo," Xavier started, but he struggled for words before going on. "Whatever my failings as Father's heir, I don't see what it has to do with you and Elowen."

"That's because you don't understand," Theo said. "You've never understood. There is no me. There's only my crown. But Elowen doesn't want my crown. She wants me to give her *myself*. And I don't know how to give her what she wants."

"You're scaring me, Theo," Xavier said. "What you're saying...the fact that you're saying it at all. Did you take a blow to the head in that tournament of yours?"

Theo gave a humorless laugh, but it seemed Xavier was in earnest. He pressed his hand firmly to Theo's forehead.

"You're burning up, Theo," he said.

"I'm not," Theo contradicted. "It's freezing in here."

"That's because you have a raging fever," Xavier said grimly. "You're flushed, your movements are affected, you should see how wild your eyes look. You said yourself your head has been pounding all morning."

"I do feel worse than I did when I woke up," Theo acknowledged. "Maybe you're right. Maybe I should sleep it off. You need to get on the road anyway if you have a hope of catching the Carrackians."

"We're well past sleeping it off," Xavier said firmly. "And I'm not going anywhere. I assume this castle has an infirmary. I'm taking you there."

Theo protested, but he didn't have much energy to fight as Xavier strode for the door. Theo listened as if through a tunnel as his brother flagged down a servant, demanding to know where the infirmary was and asking the man to send a message to Princess Elowen.

Before Theo knew it, he was being bustled through a section of the castle he'd never before explored. Everything ached, but it wasn't as though he was on the point of collapse. Honestly, he thought the unplanned outburst to Xavier was as great a cause of his exhaustion as whatever illness was affecting him. He felt a flash of irritation toward his overly helpful brother. It wasn't like Xavier to make such a fuss.

The royal physician had just ushered him onto a bed in the infirmary when Elowen hurried into the room. She looked pale and anxious, and Theo found himself reaching a hand instinctively toward her. He hated to see her distressed.

"What happened?" she demanded, her eyes darting from him to Xavier to the physician.

"It's nothing," Theo assured her. "Don't be concerned."

"I'll be as concerned as I wish to be," she told him curtly. "Don't be a hero, Theo, you haven't been well since yesterday evening. Did you think I wouldn't notice?"

He blinked at her. "Yes." The honest answer fell from his lips without any particular emotion.

"You're wrong, Theo." Her voice was lower now, a musical murmur. "I notice everything about you." Her eyes shifted to the physician. "Please tell me what's wrong with him."

"I don't know, Your Highness," he said, checking Theo over with a practiced eye. "He has a fever, that much is evident. I would guess some kind of illness. So far I don't see anything that causes me great concern."

"What *do* you see?" Elowen pressed.

Theo was finding it hard to follow the conversation, so he let his mind wander as the physician spoke. It was much more pleasant to focus his attention on Elowen, on the little crease between her brows as she listened anxiously to the physician, on the way her hair flowed like molten gold over her shoulders, on her perfect features.

"Do you perhaps not drink wine in Siqual?"

He had no idea why Elowen was asking Xavier about cultural matters. When had the physician stopped speaking?

"We do, of course." Xavier sounded confused.

"Does Theo?" Elowen pressed.

"He's not a drunkard, if that's what you're getting at," Xavier said. Was he offended on Theo's behalf? It was apparently Xavier's day for showing loyalty to his little brother. "It's not unusual for him to drink a glass of wine with a meal, but he's too principled to do anything to compromise his reason. So if you're suggesting he's just nursing a heavy head from a night of too much—"

"No."

Elowen's hair swished around her shoulders as she gave her head a quick shake. Theo watched the motion, mesmerized. He could have sworn the trickle of magic issuing from the movement felt different from other Dust. Sweeter, more familiar, like he'd learned the rhythm of her movements. What bizarre thoughts was his addled mind entertaining?

"I wasn't suggesting drunkenness," she said, her words still directed to Xavier. "I think we need to consider poison. I noticed last night that he seemed very affected after drinking wine during our betrothal ceremony. But he only drank half the goblet, if that. I was surprised it was enough to have that impact."

"That definitely doesn't sound right," Xavier said, alarm in his voice. "We need his guards in here. If there's a possibility of poison, this is a different matter entirely."

"Indeed." The physician sounded uneasy. Theo's eyes had drifted closed, and he couldn't tell which royal the man was speaking to. "Forgive me, Your Highness, but I don't think we should take any such steps without first seeking instructions from the king."

Someone was arguing back, but Theo's interest in the conversation was waning. Letting his focus drift to the sensation of Dust created by Elowen's movements around the room, he felt the soothing embrace of sleep creeping over him.

NINETEEN

Elowen

Elowen paced her receiving room, her arms crossed over her stomach. Neither the pacing nor the posture helped lessen the clenched sensation in her midriff. She'd been kicked out of the infirmary about an hour before to allow a series of tests to be run on Theo. Once they realized he'd lost consciousness, she'd sent a servant immediately to alert both her father and Theo's guards. She hadn't anticipated that once her father arrived, he would insist on her vacating the room while a team of physicians made a full assessment of the visiting prince. Whether it was to avoid distressing her or because he considered it improper for her to be in what had become Theo's sleeping chamber, she wasn't sure.

At least Prince Xavier had insisted on staying. The physician had treated the royal family all Elowen's life, and she had no reason not to trust either his medical judgment or his integrity. But she still didn't like the idea of Theo being prostrate and vulnerable without someone watching over him who took the threat seriously. His brother wouldn't allow anyone to hurt Theo further if he was present.

Could it really be possible that Theo had been poisoned?

The thought was horrible, and she tried to reassure herself that she was being foolish. The physician hadn't seemed to think it likely. He'd clearly thought Theo had contracted a disease, likely due to a weakened body from the rigors of the tournament. But he'd seemed absolutely fine to Elowen the evening before, up until their betrothal was sealed. His deterioration after that point had been visible.

In fact, he hadn't been himself in more ways than one. Were the things he'd said to her in the corridor, even the fact that he'd almost kissed her, merely the result of a feverish mind?

It was a depressing thought, but Elowen refused to let it crush her. Maybe the onset of an illness had lowered his defenses, and maybe at full strength, he wouldn't have chosen to let her hear and see those things. But the vulnerability she'd seen wasn't artificial. Whether or not he wanted to show them, he did have emotions where she was concerned. She just wished she understood why he seemed so afraid of them.

A frantic knock on the door made Elowen stumble in her pacing, and she surged forward, hoping desperately it was an update about Theo. But when she flung the door open, it was Sophia standing pale-faced between the guards flanking the doorway.

"Sophia!" She pulled her friend inside, shutting the door with a snap on the curious guards. "Are you all right?"

"Of course I'm not," Sophia said tensely. "Elowen, what are we going to do? How are we going to get him out of this mess?"

It took Elowen far too long to comprehend Sophia's words, and when she did, she felt a stab of guilt at how completely Theo's illness had made her forget her friend's predicament.

"Simeon," she said, lowering herself onto a settee with a hand to her head. "Simeon is still locked in the dungeons."

"Yes." Sophia's voice was impatient, and the way she was wringing her hands told Elowen that she was on the edge of falling apart. "And no one will help me. You're the only one who'll even believe me that it can't have been him." She paused anxiously. "You do believe it, don't you Elowen?"

Elowen didn't answer right away. She thought about Theo's words of caution regarding Simeon, and the incident with the scarf, and the servant's own declaration that he was bolder than she thought. She'd seen something in his eyes when he looked at Bertrand, something that told her he was reaching his limit.

Then she thought about the houses crushed under the landslide, and the devastation of the town below the dam. Not to mention the sight of the tower collapsing right on top of her and Sophia.

"Yes," she said softly. "Yes, of course I do. There's no way Simeon caused the disasters to get some kind of revenge."

Relief crossed Sophia's face, and she sank onto the settee next to Elowen.

"They won't let me see him," she whispered. "Father is so angry...he's shut himself up in his study and will barely look at anyone. There's no way he'll intervene for me. And Bertrand..." She shook her head.

She had no need to finish the sentence. Elowen knew how unlikely Bertrand would be to help either his sister or his servant. Especially after what Sophia had said the night before, about him holding Sophia's forbidden affection over her to get his way.

"Why would Simeon confess to something he didn't do?" Elowen asked.

Sophia looked troubled, but gave no answer, leaving Elowen to her thoughts.

The only reason she could think of was to cover for someone, but it was extreme lengths to go to. Maybe he would do it to protect Sophia, she reflected uncomfortably. But Sophia was certainly not behind any of the disasters. Bertrand flew to mind, but she knew her resentment toward the viscount was coloring her thoughts. Bertrand had no great skill in magic to allow him to pull off these attacks. He also had no incentive to harm his own kingdom and flood his own family's lands. And loyal as Simeon was to the family, she didn't think he'd be willing to cover something this serious for Bertrand. If anything, she was convinced Simeon was becoming less and less willing to pander to Bertrand at all.

"I want to help Simeon," she told Sophia. "I really do. But I'm afraid I have another crisis on my hands as well."

"What do you mean?" Sophia demanded.

"It's Theo."

The clenched feeling was back in Elowen's chest, but before she could elaborate, there was another rap at the door. Elowen flew from her seat, her heart in her throat as she recognized an assistant from the infirmary.

"Do you have an update?" she asked breathlessly.

He nodded. "Yes, Your Highness. I was asked to give you this." He handed her a folded parchment and retreated, apparently not expecting her to send a response.

Elowen unfolded it quickly, scanning the short message in handwriting she'd never seen before.

Princess Elowen

Theo regained consciousness, but he's still very feverish. He comes and goes. The physician has completed an assessment and says it's an infectious fever and will pass with rest and the right medicine, but I'm not satisfied. I'm unwilling to leave Theo, so would be grateful if you would come to the infirmary to discuss. The king has left now.

X

. . .

ELOWEN CRUMPLED the note in her hand, anxiety coursing through her. She should probably disapprove of the Siqualian prince encouraging her to go behind her father's back in returning to the infirmary, but she didn't care about that. If Xavier didn't want to leave Theo's side, he must be seriously afraid for his safety. She turned to Sophia, her mouth dry with her reluctance to say out loud just how ill Theo was.

"I'm sorry, but I have to go. Theo is—"

"Go," said Sophia, saving her from having to find the words. Determination hardened the noblewoman's soft features. "This is my fight. I'll find a way."

Had there been time, Elowen would have asked what exactly she was going to find a way to do, but her mind was too full of Theo to delay. She reached the infirmary in minutes, glad to see Theo's own guard stationed at the doorway, his expression grim. He was joined by another man in the same uniform, likely one of the guards Prince Xavier had brought with him. At least someone was taking Theo's situation seriously, much as she wished it had been her own people showing appropriate care.

She swept straight into the room where Theo had been laid, her eyes flying at once to his still form on the bed. Not entirely still, actually. He seemed to be in a light sleep, grunting from time to time, and turning his head unseeingly.

"Is he worse?" Elowen asked anxiously, stopping at Prince Xavier's side.

The older Siqualian prince had taken a seat beside the bed. His straight jaw—a feature he shared with his brother—was clenched in a way that made him look very different from the dashing flirt who'd paid her extravagant compliments earlier.

"Yes, in my opinion, he is," he said. "According to the physician, no. His fever is apparently no higher, and the physician assures me I'm merely suffering from the natural anxiety of a fond brother." He met Elowen's gaze unflinchingly. "Apparently he doesn't know that I'm not exactly famous for family loyalty or affection, and I've never yet been accused of courting anxiety."

Elowen sank into a chair on the far side of the bed, taking Theo's over-warm hand in hers. His fingers twitched, their usual strength nowhere to be found.

"Yes," she said frankly. "Your reputation for being heedless to the point that you're unable to take anything seriously is pretty well established. If you're worried, I have no doubt there's good reason for it."

Prince Xavier blinked, unsure how to take her blunt words. Then a slow smile spread over his face, banishing the shadows for a moment.

"I can see why my brother is so smitten with you. You're very engaging, Your Highness. If circumstances were different, I might try to cut him out. Since you know my reputation so well, you may also have heard how much I favor golden-haired beauties such as yourself."

"I have heard it," Elowen said shortly. Her cheeks were pink, but not from the flirtatious words. Prince Xavier thought Theo was smitten with her? Lest the outrageous prince think she was discomposed by his banter, she made her voice extra flat. "And don't try to dupe me, please, I'm not in the mood. Whatever impression you might wish to give, your affection for your brother is extremely clear to me, so I don't for a moment believe you would try to sabotage his betrothal."

"You and Theo are apparently perfectly matched," Prince Xavier said dryly. "And you're perfectly right, I would never truly try to do my brother an injury."

His eyes were troubled as they rested on Theo's face, some

deeper, unexpressed thought behind the words. Then his tone became businesslike, and he lifted his gaze to Elowen again.

"The physician examined him carefully, and I can acknowledge that he seemed to be thorough and capable, and made no objection to me remaining at Theo's side throughout. He gave a report to your father and brother about ten minutes ago."

Elowen made a noise of annoyance. "Of course they would call Patrick in to receive the report but no one thinks that I, as the one betrothed to Theo, would like to hear it, too."

A fleeting smile crossed Prince Xavier's face. "You and Mim would get along. She's always complaining about things like that. And she's absolutely right, of course. Heaven knows I don't want to be involved in half the reports I'm forced to receive, why they're turning away a royal sibling who's actually interested is beyond me."

"Well, I appreciate you letting me know," Elowen said. "And I'm sure your sister does, too. My own brother would never think to do that."

"Yes, what ails him?" Xavier asked, momentarily distracted. "Theo's a dull dog, I know, but it's all show with him. He's perfectly rational underneath, if you can get past the martyrdom. But His Royal Highness Crown Prince Patrick appears to have been tragically born without a personality."

"You shouldn't speak of your host that way," Elowen pointed out. "He is a prince, you realize."

"And I'm sure he'll make a very dutiful king one day," Prince Xavier said, his eyes twinkling. "Don't think it escaped me that you didn't contradict what I said." His tone turned serious again. "But never mind that. The physician said they've tested Theo for every type of poison known in Torrens, and there's no indication of any."

Elowen searched Theo's face, watching as his eyes flickered open for a moment, then closed again.

"But you're not convinced?" she asked.

"I'm not," he confirmed. "Theo has no particular enemies that I know of, but is there anyone here in Toledda who might have a grudge against him?"

Elowen winced as she thought of the half-hearted applause during their betrothal ceremony. "Any number of people," she admitted. "There's still plenty of resentment about recent history with Siqual, and not everyone is excited about the marriage alliance. But it's hard to believe any of the grumblers would go as far as to poison a foreign prince under my father's nose."

"There's no limit to what people will do if they think they can get away with it," said Prince Xavier unemotionally. "So your people have been giving Theo a hard time, have they? No doubt he didn't complain, but he doesn't deserve that, and neither does our kingdom."

"Let's not argue about politics," Elowen said impatiently. "I'm sure we have different perspectives on the relationship between our two kingdoms, but that's really not my concern right now."

Prince Xavier raised his hands in a conciliatory gesture. "You're right. The point is, your description of Theo's demeanor last night is too suspicious to be a coincidence. And the things he said to me this morning...I've seen him sick and feverish before. But I've never seen him lose control of himself like that. Maybe we're wrong, maybe he hasn't been poisoned. But if it's a sickness, I'm convinced it's much more serious than what they're saying. I don't like it, Elowen."

She barely noticed that he'd dropped her title, and in any event she had no chance to respond.

"Your Highness." The physician bustled in, looking scandalized. "Forgive me, but you're not supposed to be in here. We have His Highness's care well in hand, there's no cause for you to be distressed."

"Can you really be confident in ruling out poison?" Elowen demanded, ignoring his words. "What makes you so sure?"

"First of all, Your Highness, I have no reason to suspect it," the physician said patiently. "We haven't had a poisoning case in all the time I've worked in the castle, and that's been forty years at least. There are many known substances that could cause illness, even death, in humans, of course," he acknowledged, seeing her about to protest. "And I don't mean to say it would be completely impossible. But the production of all of those substances is carefully regulated. I understand your concern, but it is more common than you think for people to fall ill from imbibing unusually strong wine." He raised his hands to again stop her interrupting. "Nevertheless, given your concerns, His Majesty ordered a full assessment, and I'm pleased to be able to assure you that His Highness's system shows no sign of any of the substances I mentioned."

His eyes were kind but with an edge of indulgence. "To speak frankly, Princess, if he'd drunk powerful enough poison last night to addle his mind and attack his body, then gone to bed without taking an antidote, I would expect him to have already succumbed."

Elowen's lips felt numb. These words did not reassure her as they were obviously intended to do.

"So given we're most likely dealing with an infectious fever, I must insist that you leave the patient to rest, Your Highness."

She knew the physician's real motivation was not getting in trouble with the king, but she didn't argue. She rose, waiting until he'd moved back into the main area before speaking quietly to Prince Xavier.

"I'm not convinced, either. I'm going to make inquiries of my own. You'll stay with him?"

Prince Xavier nodded grimly.

Elowen swept from the infirmary with purpose, but her steps slowed as she made her way down the corridor. She would need to be careful with her inquiries. Getting anyone official to tell her anything was already near impossible most of the time. Asking leading questions of the servants would likely get no better response.

After some thought, Elowen made her way to the kitchens, doing her best to feign a cheerful demeanor. She tried to enter unobtrusively, but that was too optimistic. All activity stopped at the appearance of a member of the royal family, and the head cook moved forward quickly to intercept her.

"Your Highness, may we be of assistance?"

"No, I just wanted to thank you all for the marvelous feast you prepared last night," Elowen said with her sunniest smile. "You did our kingdom proud, as I know you will again for the wedding feast."

"Is the date set, Your Highness?" the cook asked, eyes alight with professional interest.

"No." Elowen felt her face heating, the question sending her emotions into tumult. "Not yet."

"Of course, Your Highness." The cook bowed. "Perhaps we could interest you in something to eat now?"

Elowen was itching to be out of the conversation—the head cook wasn't someone she could casually question. But she forced her impatience down.

"I would be glad of one of those cheese pastries I've always been fond of."

"I will prepare it with my own hands, Your Highness," the cook said, bowing low. "Shall I bring it to your suite?"

"I'd rather wait here, if I may," Elowen said. "It's so interesting to watch you all work."

A few of the kitchen staff exchanged looks, and she had

sympathy for them. None of them would be able to relax or perform their tasks naturally with her in the room. But she wouldn't stay longer than necessary. Once the head cook had bustled away, Elowen smiled at the nearest scullery maid.

"Were you working last night?"

"We all were, Your Highness," the girl said, wiping her forehead with an arm and inadvertently leaving a big streak of flour behind. "It was a big event. It's kind of you to thank us in person, Your Highness."

"Oh, the food was wonderful," Elowen said blithely. Hopefully they wouldn't ask for more detail because she didn't think she could remember a single thing she'd eaten. She'd been too full of nerves about the betrothal, then concern at Theo's demeanor. "The wine also was especially fine, although I confess I didn't drink any after the ceremonial cup for the betrothal." She sent the girl a sheepish smile. "I don't have a very good head for it."

The maid bobbed a curtsy. "I'm sure I wouldn't either, Your Highness, if I were ever to imbibe."

She hurried to knead the dough she was working on, and Elowen concealed a sigh. She wouldn't get anywhere with this girl. She was too nervous.

"The wine in the ceremonial goblets was a special vintage, Your Highness," another voice chimed in.

Elowen turned eagerly to see an assistant cook stirring something in a large cauldron.

"Was it? That must be why I noted the flavor particularly," Elowen said.

The assistant cook nodded. "It was from the border region down south. To symbolize the alliance, of course."

"Of course," Elowen agreed politely. She hesitated. "Do you know who poured it?"

The assistant cook looked up, eyebrow raised at the strange question.

"I only ask because I wanted to thank the person," Elowen hurried on. She lowered her voice. "My goblet was less than half full, which was a relief to me because I wasn't sure I'd be able to finish it all in one go as required."

"I'm glad it was to your liking," the assistant cook said.

"We noticed that the prince didn't drink all of his," said a nearby scullery maid, sounding unimpressed.

"Hush." The assistant cook quelled the maid with a look. "Don't mind her, Your Highness."

"It's all right," Elowen said. "Prince Theo meant no offense. He didn't know that aspect of the ceremony." She frowned, trying to sound naively curious. "I wonder why he was given a full glass and me only half. Who did you say poured it?"

The assistant cook thought about it. "I'm not sure, Your Highness. The goblets were set aside in there all afternoon to ensure they weren't knocked over in the bustle." She pointed to a storage room that appeared mostly empty from the glimpse Elowen could see through the open door. "And it would have been poured maybe half an hour before the ceremony so as to let the wine breathe."

Elowen had wandered toward the indicated door as the assistant cook spoke, trying to make the movement seem casual. She peered inside, noting the shelves lined with huge bags of flour and empty crates. It wasn't the main pantry, but some kind of overflow storage, probably little used. She realized with a jolt that there was another door on the far side of it.

"Does that storage room lead out into the corridor?" she asked.

"That's right," the assistant cook said. "Sometimes we carry dishes from there straight to the dining hall. That's what would have happened with the ceremonial goblets last night, too."

A prickling sensation was passing down Elowen's arms. So the goblets had been unattended in the storage room for hours, accessible without even entering the kitchen. Anyone could have gotten to them. And it was clear from the specific designs which one was hers and which Theo's. It seemed unforgivably careless, but given the physician's words, she shouldn't be surprised. There had been no attack by poison in the castle for decades. The kitchen staff had become complacent.

"Here you are, Your Highness." The head cook had returned with a pastry which Elowen felt far too ill to eat.

"Thank you," she said, her voice wavering slightly. Forcing a smile, she left the kitchen, trying to think of a way to investigate what had happened without using her father's authority. It didn't seem hopeful.

CHAPTER

TWENTY

Elowen

Elowen had made no further progress when she was called to lunch a short time later. She had no appetite and could hardly bear to sit idle while the few courtiers present chatted about the tournament as though nothing was amiss. None of them knew about Theo's situation. And none of them cared about Simeon.

She watched without much interest as a servant brought wine to her father for his approval. But as his brow furrowed and his gaze slid to her, she straightened, wincing internally.

Sure enough, as soon as the servant was gone, the king called her to his side.

"Elowen," he said with a warning note in his voice. "Why did the kitchen send this wine specifically to oblige you? Why do the kitchen staff have the impression that you have a particular interest in the wine used in the betrothal ceremony last night?"

"I just asked some questions, Father," Elowen said. "Trying to figure out how someone might have put poi—"

"That's quite enough," the king cut her off, with a sterner

tone than she was used to from him. "Elowen, this is not a game. You absolutely cannot spread these unfounded rumors about foul play."

"They're not unfounded," Elowen insisted earnestly. "Father, I truly believe Theo was poisoned last night. We have to figure out how and with what!"

"Elowen." The sharp command pulled her up. "You've expressed your suspicion, and you've been taken seriously. A thorough assessment was undertaken by our most experienced physician. If there was any sign of poison, I would not hesitate to initiate a proper investigation. But there isn't. And you poking around asking questions will achieve nothing but gossip."

"But what if the physician is wrong?" Elowen said desperately. "What if it's a type we haven't encountered before, and he missed it?"

"The prince is ill, Elowen," the king said. "It's not a catastrophe. And incidentally, even that information should be kept private. You don't seem to understand how serious it is for you to throw around these accusations while Prince Xavier is here. Wars have been started on less provocation."

"Prince Xavier doesn't want war," Elowen said impatiently. "He wants his brother to be safe, which is the same thing I want."

"Prince Theodore is perfectly safe in the infirmary, and will continue to receive excellent medical care until he's fully recovered," the king said calmly. "In the meantime, I absolutely forbid you to question the servants or say anything to anyone that might lead to unhelpful suspicions."

Elowen wasn't finished, but her retort died on her lips as she saw who'd just arrived to join the luncheon.

Sophia!

The other girl looked pale, her brow still lined, but something had changed since they'd last spoken. Elowen could tell. Sophia was accompanied by a few others, one of them the last person Elowen wanted to see.

"I'm surprised to see Bertrand and Sophia here," she said, her eyes flicking to her father.

The king sent a dignified look toward the door. "The duke returned to his lands this morning to conduct his own investigations," he said. "I believe his children chose to stay in the capital."

Returned to his lands was a nice way to say that the duke had been exiled in disgrace, Elowen reflected. The mortification of their servant's supposed treason would be crushing for the family, and it was no surprise to her that the duke was absent. Sophia wouldn't leave while Simeon was in trouble, she knew. But Bertrand…the identity of the servant in the dungeons had inevitably spread, and Bertrand was holding his head surprisingly high for how closely Simeon was connected with him.

Elowen's eyes were narrowed as she watched him take a seat beside his sister, far too close to her own chair for her liking. It hadn't been lost on her that no one had a bigger grudge against Theo than Bertrand. Would he really dare to attack a foreign prince? She knew he hated Theo, but would he risk war? Elowen returned to her seat, her thoughts swirling. If she told her father about Bertrand's behavior toward her, and the conflict between him and Theo before their fight in the tournament, would he take her fears more seriously? She knew the answer. Any hunch or suspicion of hers would never weigh against the medical evidence of the physician.

"What's happened?" she asked Sophia in an undertone.

Her friend just shook her head.

Frustration rose in Elowen, but she didn't have the chance

to press. Bertrand was speaking to the man next to him, his strained voice carrying.

"Yes, of course I'm shocked, can't you think of a more intelligent question than the one ten others have asked before you?"

"You kept him so close, My Lord," the other nobleman said, not succeeding in hiding his glee at Bertrand's embarrassment. "It's incredible that he was able to cause such mischief without you knowing of it."

"I understand now why he had become increasingly unreliable," Bertrand said, his gruff voice full of resentment. "But I confess I never imagined him capable of this."

Elowen searched his face, her eyes narrowed. Was his outrage manufactured? The anger seemed real enough. He was discomposed in a way she'd rarely seen before, his usual smooth manner gone.

"Just as I never thought he'd steal from me. Apparently loyalty means nothing anymore." The last words were uttered in a lower voice, something dark behind Bertrand's eyes.

"Let it rest, Bertrand," Sophia said wearily. "He's in the dungeons, what more do you want?"

"Steal from you?" Elowen repeated, her eyes flying between the siblings.

Sophia gave her head another small shake, but Bertrand transferred his attention to Elowen.

"Yes, Your Highness, the servant I foolishly trusted with a position far beyond his merits wasn't satisfied with harming both my affairs and my reputation. Since he was taken by the royal guard, I've discovered that he ransacked my belongings without me noticing. I can only assume he intended to find enough of value to run away before his misdeeds came to light. Fortunately, he didn't manage that."

He glanced up the table, his face twisting into a look of polite derision that made his manner much more familiar.

"I don't see any sign of our noble victor."

"He's resting after the exertions of the tournament," Elowen said shortly, watching him for his reaction.

One eyebrow curved artfully upward. "He has a delicate constitution, it seems. Was he really overpowered by his efforts in the tournament? Or is it that, having secured what he needed and formalized the betrothal, he no longer feels any need to court our favor and pander to our ways by continuing his public duties?"

"Of course that's not the case," Elowen snapped, annoyed to see that many of the courtiers within hearing range were murmuring disapprovingly to one another. Of course they were glad of any reason to think poorly of the Siqualian.

"I hope not, my dear Princess." Bertrand leaned forward. "I would hate to see you with the kind of man who loses interest once he's gotten what he wants from you. Women as beautiful as you do sometimes have that problem, I'm told."

Elowen felt her cheeks heat, as much from anger as from his insinuations. She longed to hurl accusations at him, but she knew she had to hold her tongue. She had no proof that he'd done anything untoward. Even his brazen appearance at lunch seemed to mock her suspicions. And she didn't know if she could trust her suspicions in the first place. She had no impartial argument against him, only her own scathing dislike.

She contented herself with glaring at the few others who were still muttering about Theo's absence. None of them seemed to even notice.

Prince Xavier had been right. Theo didn't deserve the suspicion and poor treatment he'd received.

Theo. She was itching to get back to him. She cast another look over the assembled members of the court, searching for hidden enemies. She hated to suspect her own people, but if someone had attacked Theo, it must have been someone Torrenese. There was no other explanation. If he had even been attacked, she amended, her certainty wavering. The physician had said that exposure to poison would likely have killed him by now. Would Theo be dead already if he'd drained the whole goblet as he was supposed to do?

She'd hoped to wait Bertrand out, but he showed every sign of settling in for a long meal. Unwilling to delay, Elowen lowered her voice as soon as he was distracted with his food.

"Sophia, tell me. You found something out."

Sophia moved a thin sliver of ham around her plate with her fork. She didn't seem to have much appetite.

"I spoke to Simeon," she said, her words barely above a whisper.

"They let you see him?"

Sophia shook her head. "They refused. But I...found a way."

Elowen frowned in confusion but stayed on the main point. "And?"

"I...he didn't say much. I mean, there's not much to tell," Sophia said lamely.

"What are you talking about?" Elowen hissed. "He must have said something."

Sophia shrugged, the fact that she was hiding something written as clearly across her face as if she'd used ink.

"He did. He said that I should stay out of it."

Bertrand claimed their attention again, and Elowen let the matter drop. She wasn't done, but she couldn't focus much on Simeon's plight with Theo's situation still so uncertain. As soon as politeness allowed, she rose from the table and made her way toward the infirmary. She swept past the guards on the door, stopping in the doorway of Theo's room.

"What's amiss?" she asked, alarmed to see Prince Xavier on his feet, with an air of departure.

"He's worse," the prince said shortly, the set of his brow

telling Elowen that she'd missed some kind of conflict. "We're leaving."

Elowen had been studying Theo's flushed face. He was still unconscious, and the way his eyelids kept twitching suggested his dreams weren't restful. But the other prince's words made her eyes snap to him.

"Leaving?" she repeated stupidly. "*We*? You want to move him?"

"The physician still insists that it's only a fever, and it's been made clear to me that no investigation is underway regarding who might have poisoned him." Prince Xavier's dark, rather thin brows were drawn all the way together as he shot a look at her. "Except for whatever inquiries you made. Did they convince you to rule out poison?"

"No," Elowen admitted miserably. "I learned that the ceremonial goblets, with Theo's clearly recognizable, sat for hours in a place where almost anyone could have gotten to them. And my father is unconvinced by my theory, and unwilling to start an investigation without medical evidence of poison."

Prince Xavier growled in his throat, but his pale face betrayed the fear hiding under the anger.

"That means whoever did this to him is still at large," he said. "He's not safe here. My people have already organized a carriage. Theo and I will leave within the hour."

"But surely he's too unwell to be moved," Elowen protested.

"That's the physician's argument," Prince Xavier replied. "But to be frank, Princess, I don't trust anyone here. You've admitted yourself there's widespread resentment against Siqual in general and Theo in particular."

"I didn't say that," Elowen cried. Theo moved his head restlessly, but his eyes didn't open. She lowered her voice. "Plenty of people like him and support the alliance."

"But it only takes one effective malcontent to take action," Prince Xavier said. "I don't wish to offend you, and I believe you do care about Theo. But that's not enough, not when by your own account you're kept out of important matters just the same as my sister is. I was present in some of the negotiations for this alliance, I know how hard Torrens was hit a few years back when Siqual withdrew from some of our trade agreements due to our suspicions that Torrens was plotting against us."

"I don't know anything about that," Elowen said, more frustrated than ever by her exclusion from such matters. "Like you said, I'm kept out of those things. I don't understand what you're getting at."

"I'm saying that for all I know, this whole proposal was a clever attack planned by the crown, as retaliation for those losses," Prince Xavier said grimly.

Recognizing how close their alliance was to disaster, Elowen swallowed her initial outrage. "Not a well-orchestrated attack if so," she said firmly. "You and I both saw at once something didn't seem right."

"No one was expecting me to be here," Prince Xavier said. "If they'd sent news of an illness to Siqual, it would have raised no suspicion of foul play without your observations from last night, and the things I've witnessed myself."

"Prince Xavier, please," Elowen said desperately. "Don't endanger him further by subjecting him to days and days on the road. Surely you can see it's not practical. Sindon is so far!"

"I'm not taking him to Sindon," the prince said. "Crandell is much closer. Carrack is our ally, Prince Cassius will see that Theo's symptoms are properly investigated."

"We're allies as well!" Elowen protested. She hadn't even noticed, but at some point her hand had closed over Theo's where it lay on the covers. It was warm. Too warm. It felt so wrong to be debating his care without being able to consult him.

"Not yet," Prince Xavier contradicted. "Whatever reputation I have for being heedless, I'm awake, Princess. And I'm good at finding out what I want to know. I've made my own inquiries, and I know that in spite of the tournament being complete and the betrothal sealed, there's been no talk whatsoever of setting a wedding date." His voice darkened. "It's almost as though there was never any intention of holding a wedding."

"No, you're wrong!" Shame washed over Elowen. "That's my fault. I was the one who delayed setting the wedding date. Father has been eager to move forward the whole time, it was me who wanted...who wanted..."

She trailed off, unable to put words to what now felt like an absurdly childish campaign. She'd been so determined not to be rushed into tying herself to Theo, and now she could barely breathe for the fear that she didn't have any time left with him.

"Elowen." The quiet voice made both of them freeze, their attention snapping to Theo.

His eyes were open, and his expression was peaceful as he looked up at Elowen. "You're back. You went away somewhere."

"I'm here, Theo," she said, her throat tight. "We're trying to figure out what's wrong with you so we can make you well again."

Theo coughed, the sound pained. "The physician said it's an infectious fever," he said. "I just need to rest. It's not even...a very high...fever." He closed his eyes for a moment, squeezing them shut as if fighting a wave of pain.

"No, Theo," Elowen said desperately. "Whatever it is, it's serious."

"I'm afraid you may be right, Your Highness." The physician's somber voice cut into their conversation. "Prince

Theodore, I must tell you that your fever has now become higher than I like to see."

"Can't you treat it using magic craft?" Elowen demanded. "I know that was part of your training."

He bowed in acknowledgment. "You're right, Princess. Magic has its own boundaries, however. It is not a simple cure for all illnesses. But it's true that I generally have success with alleviating symptoms, if nothing else. I confess I expected Prince Theodore's symptoms to respond better to magical treatment than they have. I'm afraid there's little more we can do at present than wait out the fever."

Theo didn't answer, his eyes drifting closed again. It was difficult to tell if he was following what was being said. The physician's eyes were serious as they returned to Elowen.

"But the severity of the illness does appear to have increased. I must urge you, Princess, not to subject him to travel at this moment."

"It's not up to me," Elowen said, frustrated. "I don't want him to go." She laid a hand on Theo's head, her fingers finding their way through the dark hair which wasn't in its usual orderly state. "I don't want you to go, Theo."

His eyes slowly opened again, concern mingling with confusion in his gaze. He didn't seem able to find words, however.

"You say he's worse now?" Prince Xavier said, agitated. "I've been saying it for hours, and you wouldn't acknowledge it until I announced my intention to leave." He turned to Elowen. "Is that what you call impartial medical care?"

She ran a hand over her face, feeling helpless and afraid. She didn't believe the physician was trying to harm Theo, but she didn't know how to convince Prince Xavier that both their poisoning suspicion and the crown's good intentions could be true.

"Maybe my father will order an investigation if you formally request it," Elowen tried. "I know he wouldn't at my request, but he might at yours. Especially if he understands that the alternative is you removing Theo from Toledda like this."

"I'm sorry Elowen," Prince Xavier said, his voice low. "But there's no way it would happen quickly enough. And at this stage, I don't think I could trust any investigation. This is my brother's life at stake. I can't afford to take chances."

Elowen's anxiety threatened to overwhelm her, but she knew she didn't have the power to stop Prince Xavier from doing as he saw best. She wasn't even sure she knew what was best. If someone had attacked Theo right in front of the king and gotten away with it, how could she be sure Theo would be safe in the castle? But he didn't seem in any state to endure the rigors of the road, either.

If only he was able to decide for himself! Unlike her and Prince Xavier, he would be able to think clearly, undistracted by emotion. She hadn't sufficiently valued his calm good sense until it wasn't available to her anymore.

True to his word, the older Siqualian prince had his brother ready for departure before another hour had passed. The king had sent a messenger to Sindon, and in the meantime had tried to dissuade Prince Xavier from doing anything hastily, but he'd had no more success than Elowen. It was a difficult situation. Theo was a grown man, not a child under their care. However unwise they thought it, how could they refuse his brother the right to oversee his treatment? Elowen could see that her parents were offended by the older prince's suspicion, but she could also see their unease at the possible implications for the alliance. Trying to prevent the Siqualians from leaving would only increase Prince Xavier's mistrust.

In one thing the king and the visiting prince were united.

Theo's passage through the castle was swift and observed by few people. He roused enough to walk with his brother's support, and the carriage waited as close as possible to the side door through which he was led. The king was undoubtedly concerned about the rumors that might spread, but Elowen was more aligned with Prince Xavier's motivation. She knew that he hoped to delay news of their departure to prevent whoever might have attacked Theo from trying again while he was in transit.

Before she knew it, Elowen found herself standing by the carriage, watching as Prince Xavier settled his barely conscious brother as comfortably as possible.

"Theo." Elowen's throat was tight, fear overwhelming her. She shouldn't entertain the premonition that was rising, that she'd never see him again. "I...I'm sorry you have to go."

"I'm going." Theo's voice was deep and steady in spite of the confusion in his eyes as he made his observation. "I'm not supposed to return home until after we're married."

"Yes, I know," Elowen said miserably. "That was the plan. But your brother thinks...he wants to..."

"I understand."

The timbre of the words was so low it was a rumble in Elowen's ears. She was sure that whatever he said, Theo didn't remotely understand what was going on. He'd barely seemed to follow any of the arguments about his care.

"I'm sorry, Elowen." There was a raw pain in his eyes that twisted at her insides. "I'm sorry I couldn't please you enough to make you want to set a date. I wanted to, but...I don't know how."

"Theo, no." Elowen's protest came out choked. "That's not —you're not—"

The carriage was moving, she had no time to find the words. Theo leaned back against the seat, his lids heavy but his eyes still fixed on her face. Slowly, he raised a fist, resting it over his heart in a gesture she knew well.

Elowen's breath caught, and she had to curb the impulse to run after the carriage and call him back. He was gone, and the future she'd finally begun to embrace felt like it was slipping through her fingers.

TWENTY-ONE

Elowen

Elowen spent the next hour wandering the castle gardens in a haze, unable to bear doing nothing but unsure what to do. She didn't blame Prince Xavier for wanting to remove his brother from what he saw as danger, but she was terrified as to the outcome. If they were right, and there was something sinister at work in Theo's condition, taking him further from where it happened would surely take him further from any answers they might find.

Except that no one but Elowen seemed interested in finding answers. Her fear was enough to make her willing to defy her father's orders and make further inquiries, but she didn't think it would get her anywhere. They needed a proper investigation. Elowen stilled her aimless steps around the garden. She needed to change her father's mind.

She hurried back into the castle, demanding of a passing servant where the king could be found. He scurried off to find out, and Elowen twisted her hands impatiently as she waited. Finally he returned, with the news that the king and prince were together in the king's study.

Elowen felt her brow lower. No doubt they were discussing

Theo's abrupt departure. Did they intentionally leave her out of the conversation, or did it not even occur to either of them to include her?

She strode with purpose down the halls now, ignoring every servant she passed. Thankfully she encountered no courtiers, in spite of needing to traverse a significant stretch of the castle. Her movements were fierce, and she could feel the Dust they stirred up clamoring for her attention, begging to be harnessed and used. Maybe it was because of her determination to stop accepting her powerless position, but she'd never felt the magic of her movements more strongly. If only she had something useful to do with it. If only she could heal Theo. But that was advanced magic, well beyond her simple skill level. Even the physician hadn't been able to do much against his rising fever.

When she reached the door to her father's study, one of the guards hailed her. She ignored him, pushing the door open with unnecessary force. Or at least, that's what she hoped her flourishing movement would make them think. She hadn't meant to use magic to make the door fly faster, and she didn't want Father and Patrick to get distracted from the main point by realizing she'd done it by accident.

"Are you talking about Theo?" she demanded.

Her father and brother both stared at her, the first bewildered and the second irritated.

"Elowen, you can't just come charging in here like—"

"I've had enough of being told what I can't do for the moment, actually, Patrick," she said crisply. "I want to know if you're talking about Theo."

"Yes, Elowen," said the king wearily. "Of course we're discussing the situation. It's a disastrous turn of events."

"For which you share a significant part of the blame," Patrick said. "So you might wish to consider your tone."

"Me?" Elowen said, outraged. "How am I to blame for someone poisoning Theo?"

Patrick made an impatient noise, and the king frowned at the still-open door.

"Elowen, you must stop with these wild accusations."

Responsive to his gesture, Elowen closed the door, and Patrick immediately took the opening.

"You've created enough trouble already," he accused, his voice tight. "I'm astonished, Elowen, to have learned just now that the reason there's been such confusion about wedding plans is that Father gave you license to delay the wedding according to whatever whim might take you. I don't understand it at all."

"Well, you wouldn't," Elowen said, pushing down her own regrets in favor of annoyance at her brother. "You don't understand anything about it, but that doesn't mean it was foolish."

"The outcome proves that it was," Patrick said. "The alliance is at serious risk. The Siqualian heir has lost faith in our intentions, and Prince Theodore has left Toledda not only without marrying you but without even any definite commitment to do so."

"That's not true," Elowen protested. "The ceremony last night was a commitment. The betrothal is sealed."

"You're both right," their father said, cutting off the rising argument. "The betrothal ceremony certainly helps make it more official, and according to the treaty we signed with Siqual, it binds us. However," his voice was heavy, "according to Torrenese law, an actual marriage is necessary to bind our kingdom to the alliance."

"Hopefully the Siqualians don't realize that," Patrick said grimly. "I don't want them to use it to find a way to go back on our agreement."

"The Siqualians?" Elowen protested, her face pale at this

information. "They're not the ones set against the alliance. Look in your own house, Father!"

"What does that mean?" Patrick asked sharply. "I don't know if you're accusing me or making a confession of your own, Elowen, but unlike you, I'm fully committed to this alliance."

"I wasn't doing either," Elowen snapped. "And how dare you claim that you're *more* committed than I am, Patrick? Last I checked, you weren't being expected to tie yourself body and soul to a stranger and leave your home and family forever in support of this alliance. I am completely committed."

"Elowen makes a fair point, Patrick," the king said softly. "It's she, not you, who has been expected to pay the cost of this alliance, and she didn't try to fight it."

Patrick didn't look convinced, but Elowen didn't care about his opinion.

"I didn't mean our family when I said the trouble is within our own house. I meant Torrens. There's been plenty of opposition to the alliance, and plenty of animosity toward Theo. It's just been subtle. Until now." She turned to her father. "It's not a wild accusation, Father. You weren't sitting beside him at dinner last night. After he drank from the ceremonial goblet, he began to deteriorate noticeably."

"Elowen." The king was trying to speak patiently. "The physician checked him carefully. There was no sign of poison."

"No sign of any kind of poison we've seen before," Elowen said stubbornly.

"Elowen, I'm not as oblivious as you think," Patrick said, his tone calmer now. "I'm aware that not everyone is happy about the alliance. But it was my impression that much of the court was coming around to Prince Theodore. His performance in the tournament won him a lot of favor. And even if some don't like Siqual, it's an absurd leap to imagine they would try to kill foreign royalty without specific provocation."

"Bertrand had provocation." Elowen said the words quietly. She knew she would be censured for making her accusation more specific, but she couldn't help herself. "He hates Theo, and has been doing everything he can to drive a wedge between us since the moment Theo arrived. Sophia told me plainly that he has been expecting—and is expected—to elevate his family by marriage to me for years now."

There was an uncomfortable silence then, to her surprise, Patrick inclined his head.

"I'm aware of his aspirations. There was even a time when... well, I won't say anyone explicitly encouraged those expectations, but they weren't unreasonable given Lord Bertrand's standing. I'm not surprised he took a dislike to Prince Theodore. But the family has everything to gain from our kingdom's prosperity, and they would not sabotage an advantageous alliance."

"Listen to me!" Elowen said in frustration. "He *has* been sabotaging the alliance, since the moment Theo arrived. And it's more personal than you know. Right before the final event of the tournament, they had a...dispute." She flushed at the memory of Theo's face as he'd declared his intention to *have a conversation* with Bertrand about what he'd done at the ball. "And then Theo humiliated Bertrand by besting him in front of everyone."

"You forget that there's no evidence of poison." The king's firm words cut across his children's argument. "Lord Bertrand might dislike Prince Theodore. He might even wish the alliance wasn't happening. I'm displeased to hear it, but I can certainly believe that he's been causing discomfort for you regarding your upcoming marriage. But it's absurd to think that he would take such a drastic step as attempting to kill the prince. The consequences—the risk to himself—is simply too great for a personal grudge." His expression became wearier. "I think perhaps you've let the treachery of his servant color your perception. The duke's family has always been loyal to Torrens and there's no reason for that to change."

"I'm not judging Bertrand more harshly because of his servant. If anything, it's the other way around," Elowen insisted. "I'm confident Simeon didn't do what he's accused of. If he confessed, he must be covering for someone else, and try as I might I can't think of anyone it could be but Bertrand."

She could tell immediately that it was the wrong thing to say. Both her listeners looked exasperated, her credibility visibly dropping in their eyes.

"And please tell me how Bertrand's personal vendetta against Prince Theodore would lead him to cause disasters across our kingdom. One of which devastated his own lands!" Patrick said impatiently.

"I can't," Elowen said. "I can't explain it. But Bertrand is better at putting on a front than you realize. I've seen a side of him that I'm sure neither of you have."

A knock at the door made them all look up, and the next moment, the king's steward entered, looking somber.

"Your Majesty," he said, holding out a missive.

The king didn't immediately open it, frowning down at the seal. "This is the seal of my Council of Lords," he said.

"Yes, Your Majesty," the steward confirmed. "A messenger just delivered this. He said he'd come directly from the Duke of Nirocha's manor here in the capital."

"Very good."

Elowen's father dismissed the steward with the words, waiting until the door was closed before ripping open the letter. His expression darkened before Elowen and Patrick's eyes.

"What is it, Father?" Patrick demanded.

"The Council of Lords has just met."

"Without the sovereign or a representative?" Patrick looked outraged.

"It's not unheard of. In certain circumstances, the council will meet to reach unanimity before presenting an appeal to the crown. But for a meeting to be called so urgently in peacetime is irregular, to say the least."

"Urgently?" Elowen repeated, her eyes narrowing. "What was the topic of the meeting, Father?"

The king let out a heavy breath before meeting her eyes. "Your betrothal, Elowen. It seems news of the Siqualian princes' departure spread quickly in spite of our efforts. Several members of the council appear to have taken great offense. They're bringing a formal motion to dissolve the betrothal as allowed under Torrenese law."

Patrick let out a soft noise of annoyance. "Well, they'll be disappointed."

The king didn't answer at once, causing anxiety to trickle over Elowen.

"You surely aren't considering agreeing, Father?" she said.

"I am not," he confirmed heavily. "But it's more complicated than you realize, Elowen. There are certain aspects of the alliance that I can't effectively enforce, with regards to trade and communication, and..." He trailed off, giving his head a shake. "To put it simply, for the alliance to succeed, it has to have a certain amount of support from my lords."

"So convince them that it's for everyone's good!" said Elowen. "Tell them that he only left because he's ill!"

"That is obviously what I intend to do." The king rose, and his children both mirrored the motion. "Patrick, you'll accompany me."

"Of course, Father," Patrick said, his stern features more set than ever.

"Who brought the motion?" Elowen asked quickly, realizing her window for gaining information was closing.

"The duke," the king said, with a grim glance at the missive.

"The duke is still on his lands," Elowen protested. "It was Bertrand, it must have been! Is it inconceivable that in his father's absence, he would take charge and use his father's name and seal to call the lords together and plant his seeds in their minds?"

"If Bertrand acted on his father's behalf, we must assume it's with his father's approval," Patrick said.

Elowen didn't assume anything of the kind, but the two men were already leaving the room. Her brother sent her a look that made it clear he felt he was cleaning up her mess, and she could have screamed with frustration. They were so determined to miss what was right in front of them. It was almost unbelievable that his status and position could protect Bertrand so completely and yet, at the same time, it was barely even a surprise. Hadn't Bertrand been indulged and covered for all his life? Even sweet Sophia had always been ready to smooth over his misdemeanors. Elowen herself had made excuses for him, she realized with discomfort, not out of any desire to think well of him, but to try to justify his behavior to Theo to avoid embarrassment for everyone.

No more.

She swept from the room, following the direction she knew her father and brother would have gone. She didn't enter the audience hall in which her father usually conducted such meetings, however. She paused outside the door, directing her question to one of the guards on duty.

"Is the viscount, Lord Bertrand, in this meeting?"

His expression was hard to read, but she was beyond caring what conclusions he might draw.

"No, Your Highness. He did not attend."

Of course not. He wasn't about to start doing his own dirty work now.

"I require two members of the royal guard to accompany me," Elowen said imperiously.

"Your Highness?" He was startled.

"I'm merely going to visit Lady Sophia, but I am concerned for my safety on the road," Elowen said in a tone that didn't invite argument.

The guard bowed, nodding toward his fellow. The other man moved promptly away, and in a short time, returned with two other guards.

"Thank you." Elowen held her head high as she strode toward the entryway of the castle. "You will stay with me at all times, do you understand?"

"Of course, Your Highness."

Her new companions seemed bemused, but they were too well trained to ask questions. She was glad, because she had a feeling that if she voiced her determination to be protected from Bertrand, it would lead to exasperation from her family. But the viscount had shown his true colors the night of the ball, and deciding to confront him didn't mean she had to be careless. There was no Theo here to come to her aid this time.

The thought brought a lump to her throat, but she refused to dwell on her emotions. The short trip to the duke's manor took no time at all, and when she'd been ushered into a large parlor, it wasn't Sophia she asked for.

"Lord Bertrand?" the confused housekeeper asked. "Yes, Your Highness, he's here. But..."

"Please tell him I wish to speak with him," she said.

She looked uneasily around the space, wondering what felt

off. Something was different. It was too silent, she decided. Like the whole house was tensed, waiting for some blow to fall. Elowen's thoughts flew back to the castle. How was the meeting with the lords going? Would her father convince them not to be offended with Theo? Would he tell them it was Prince Xavier who'd insisted on removing his brother? Unlikely, since that wouldn't help change the mind of anyone inclined to be offended with Siqual. She was sure her father wouldn't disclose her fears about poison, which meant that it would be difficult to explain Prince Xavier's actions.

"Princess." Bertrand had appeared in the doorway, his eyebrows raised in an infuriatingly smug expression. "You've sought me out. What an honor."

"Bertrand, I need to speak with you," Elowen said, her voice hard.

He bowed. "By all means." He glanced at the guards. "Perhaps we can walk in the gardens."

Elowen hesitated. She felt more secure in the room with her guards right there, but it might be best for all if they couldn't hear everything said.

"All right," she said, not very graciously. "My guards will naturally wish to accompany me."

"Naturally." Bertrand looked amused.

Her shoulders stiff with tension, Elowen followed him out of the manor and into a manicured garden.

"You may stay here," she told the guards, as they paused just outside the building. "But if I leave your sight at any time, come and retrieve me immediately."

"Yes, Your Highness." They exchanged a look as she turned away, which she pretended not to see.

Bertrand offered Elowen his arm, but she ignored it, walking forward with purpose until they were just out of the guards' hearing range.

"Very wise to set safeguards for yourself," Bertrand commented. He plucked a bloom from a nearby bush, offering it to her with a gallant sweep of his arm. "I'm flattered that you feel you can't trust yourself to be alone with me."

Elowen crossed her arms, ignoring the flower and fixing him with a hard stare.

"Enough games, Bertrand," she said. "You're the one who called the meeting of the lords, aren't you?"

He raised one thin eyebrow. "I didn't know you were interested in matters of state."

"There are a lot of things you don't know," Elowen said in a clipped voice.

A steady wind was blowing, and although their corner of garden was well sheltered, a nearby tree at the edge of the space was bending a little from the onslaught. The movement of the leaves called to Elowen, their magic leaking out for anyone to take hold of. It wasn't a lot of Dust, but it would be enough to give Bertrand a zap if he tried anything. She was determined not to be caught off guard by him again.

Heartened by the thought, she pressed on. "Give me a straight answer, Bertrand. Are you the one who proposed the motion to dissolve my betrothal?"

He raised his arms, gesturing at their surroundings. "Do you see me in a meeting at the castle?"

"Of course not," Elowen said darkly. "This is what you do. You set things in motion, and you hide behind others while they give voice to your demands. How many times have I seen you use Sophia that way?" Her eyes narrowed further. "How many times have you hidden behind Simeon?"

Displeasure flickered over his face, and he folded his arms.

"If you think I'm unwilling to stand by my actions, you're mistaken, Princess," he said smoothly. "Of course I oppose your betrothal to a Siqualian prince."

Elowen drew in a sharp breath. "Why?"

"Because you're mine," he said, the words flippant. "You've always been intended for me. I'm the one who loves you and I'm the one who will marry you."

Elowen recoiled, the plain speaking rattling her more than she wanted him to see. One word in particular sounded unnatural and harsh on Bertrand's lips. He didn't know what love meant.

"But I'm not concerned," Bertrand went on. "The betrothal tournament was helpful for us all in showing us the kind of disrespect we can expect if we were to ally ourselves with Siqual. I think our kingdom is wise enough to know how to respond."

The calm words didn't fool Elowen. Bertrand might want to seem as though he'd always been willing to wait things out and trust the outcome, but every instance of his infuriating meddling contradicted that suggestion.

"You poisoned him." The accusation fell from Elowen's lips, her anger getting the better of her. "You attacked him out of jealousy."

Both of Bertrand's eyebrows were up now. "Poisoned? What are you talking about, Princess?"

Elowen ground her teeth. "You know what I'm talking about."

"I wish I did," he said, his placid demeanor unconvincing thanks to how well she knew his temper. "You accuse me of being jealous?" He gave an incredulous laugh, and his next words dripped with disdain. "Of Prince Theodore? What would I have to be jealous of?"

"Everything," Elowen said disbelievingly. "You have no hope of matching him in any way."

Bertrand's eyes narrowed a little. "If you're thinking of our fight in the tournament," he said, "naturally I allowed him to win to save everyone embarrassment. The tournament was never real, Elowen." His expression turned pitying. "Did you think your stiff prince really was some kind of noble champion?"

"I know his sickness isn't natural," Elowen said angrily. "And Father knows it, too. Inquiries have been made."

She hoped to rattle him with this information, but she was disappointed. His expression was politely curious, and he made a show of thinking over her words.

"Do you really believe he's been intentionally harmed?" he mused. "If you're right, I must advise the king to interrogate Simeon further. It would be too coincidental for the prince to be attacked just as he was ready to point a finger at the perpetrator of the disasters." He gave her an innocent look. "You did know, didn't you, that your prince was the one who informed on Simeon?"

Elowen wanted to believe he was lying, but remembering the things Theo had said, it was perfectly plausible. Her heart sank, but she refused to let Bertrand drive a wedge between her and Theo, as she'd allowed him to do too many times. She wished Theo had trusted her enough to talk it all out with her, to let her convince him it couldn't be Simeon. But given every-thing, she couldn't be surprised he'd been unsure of his reception.

"Simeon must have put the plan into motion before his arrest, not realizing he was already out of time," Bertrand said sorrowfully. There was malice in his eyes as he continued. "If he used magic to attack the prince, he can probably use magic to reverse it."

Elowen stilled. Was he making a veiled offer? Some kind of bargain?

"I can get Simeon to talk," Bertrand said. "I guarantee that if there's something to tell, he'll tell me with the right handling."

Elowen waited, sure there was more. She wasn't wrong.

"I'll do it in a heartbeat, Princess. Simply declare to your father your desire to marry me instead of the Siqualian prince. The matter can be settled neatly if we act now, while the lords are still debating our kingdom's future."

TWENTY-TWO

Elowen

Elowen stepped back, disgusted by the thought. But there was fear under her revulsion. Bertrand hadn't said it in as many words, but she thought she understood. He was offering to save Theo, but only at a cost she never wanted to pay.

She couldn't let Theo die. But she also couldn't trust Bertrand. Who was to say he had a way to help Theo? She wouldn't be surprised to learn he was making it up to manipulate her.

"You'll get nothing from me," she said, her lips numb with the fear that she was making the wrong choice.

She turned abruptly, not waiting to see his reaction to her rejection. She hurried back to her guards, and the tension in her shoulders eased only once they were flanking her. What did she do next? Her anxiety for Theo was stronger than ever. But she couldn't let Bertrand get what he wanted. Everything in her told her that would be disastrous.

Had there been any truth to Bertrand's words about Simeon? Had he somehow manipulated Simeon into using magic against Theo? He'd offered to speak to Simeon on her behalf about using magic to help Theo, likely believing she'd have no way to speak to Simeon without him. But Sophia had somehow managed to talk to Simeon. Maybe she could help Elowen do the same.

She'd reached the manor's courtyard and was just mounting the horse a stable boy had been holding for her, when her friend rode into the yard. Sophia was pale and on edge, too distracted by her thoughts to notice her guest until she was hailed.

"Sophia!"

The other girl started, dismounting and hurrying to meet Elowen, who also strode forward so they met in the middle of the courtyard.

"Elowen! Have you been looking for me? I'm not staying, I just stopped by to change my clothes for something more appropriate for riding."

"Where are you going?" Elowen asked.

"Just riding," Sophia said in a voice that wasn't natural.

"You mean avoiding Bertrand," Elowen said bluntly, her voice lowered so as not to be overheard. "You're right, he's here. I've just seen him."

"I need to be quick, then," Sophia said, barely seeming aware of her agitated words. "I can't let him corner me right now. I don't want to face his anger or his questions."

"And this is the same brother you thought I should marry?" Elowen said grimly.

Sophia lowered her eyes, her expression tortured. "I'm sorry, Elowen," she murmured. "I don't think that anymore. I...I wish I knew how to explain. I wish I understood it myself. For as long as I can remember, I've been taught to make excuses for him. I really did convince myself that it would be good for everyone if..."

She trailed off, taking a deep breath before looking back into Elowen's eyes. There was steel in the round, gentle face.

"I'm not making excuses anymore. I don't want to fight Bertrand, I know I'm not a match for him. But that doesn't mean I have to help him."

Elowen frowned. "Help him do what?"

A cheerful whistling announced the approach of a groom, and Sophia ushered Elowen toward the house. Elowen curtly told her guards to wait for her outside this time, then neither of the girls spoke again until they were in Sophia's rooms with the door closed.

"Never mind my problems with Bertrand, they're nothing to do with you," Sophia said. "What did you want to speak to me about?"

"I need to see Simeon," Elowen said at once. "I think he might know something about what's going on with Theo."

Her friend looked confused. "About the prince leaving? How would he know anything about that? He's been locked in the dungeons since yesterday."

Elowen searched her friend's eyes. "Do you really not know why Theo left? Did we hide it better than I think, or have you just been distracted by Simeon's situation?"

Sophia's brows were drawn together in an alarmed question. "What do you mean? What don't I know? I thought he left because the betrothal was sealed and he didn't want to kick his heels here until a wedding date was set. I understand a lot of people have taken offense at that."

"That's not what happened at all," Elowen said fiercely. "Theo's brother spirited him away because Theo is gravely ill. It came on suddenly, after we drank the ceremonial betrothal toast, and both Prince Xavier and I suspect he was poisoned. There's no medical evidence of it, though, so no one else will believe me, and that made Prince Xavier suspicious enough to remove Theo from a community he believes might be trying to kill him."

Sophia's face had frozen in shock as she listened, and for a long moment after this account, she stared at Elowen in silent horror.

"What is it?" Elowen demanded.

"You...you really think he was poisoned?" her friend whispered.

"Yes, I really do," Elowen said. "And I'm sorry to grieve you, Sophia, but I can't think of anyone more likely to do it than Bertrand. Maybe acting through Simeon, although I would hate to believe it of him."

Sophia shook her head violently. "Simeon would never do it. But Bertrand..." She glanced nervously toward the closed door, then steeled herself. "Do you remember how Bertrand said that he discovered Simeon stole from him?"

Elowen nodded. "He was furious about it. More about that than the humiliation of Simeon's treason, it seemed to me."

Sophia swallowed. "Simeon didn't steal from him," she said. "I did."

"What do you mean?" Elowen demanded.

"Bertrand only discovered the theft just before lunch, and he assumes Simeon took it before he got arrested. But I took it, not Simeon. And I did it today. I only just got clear before Bertrand returned, and that's when he noticed."

"You took what?" Elowen asked impatiently. "Sophia, what's going on?"

Sophia drew a breath. "When I saw Simeon in the dungeons, it's true that he told me to stay out of it, like I said. At least, he told me not to try to advocate on his behalf. But he did ask me to do one thing. I could tell he hated to ask me to involve myself, but it was clearly important enough that he needed me. He said that he'd seen Bertrand with a small, black, leather bag, and that it was imperative that I get it and hide it somewhere Bertrand wouldn't be able to find it. There was no time to tell me why, the guards were coming around, and I had to get out of there."

"Coming around?" Elowen repeated, her eyebrows raised. "What exactly did you do to get into the dungeons, Sophia?"

"Never mind that," Sophia said briskly. "The point is, I returned home immediately. I don't know where Bertrand was, but he wasn't at the manor. I searched his rooms and I found the leather bag."

"What was in it?" Elowen demanded. "Or were you too circumspect to look?"

"Of course I looked," Sophia said, exasperated. "I'm not completely spineless, Elowen."

Elowen felt a smile flicker across her face, before memory of their circumstances banished it. It was nice to see her friend coming back. She hadn't put it together before now how the timing of her betrothal had linked with Sophia's increased timidity. What kind of pressure had Bertrand been putting on her all that time?

"It had two small vials," Sophia said. "One was empty, and one was full of liquid. They were both marked, but I didn't recognize the words. Plus there was a folded-up parchment with them. It looked like complex magical instructions, but I couldn't make much sense of them. I wrote the words from the labels down, and I hid the rest. I didn't know anything of sickness or accusations of poisoning. I was worried about what he'd used the empty vial for, but I didn't imagine something as bad as this."

Elowen's heart was pounding by the end of this explanation. "That must be the poison he used," she said. "Simeon didn't know Bertrand had already used it. He must have seen it and realized what it was, or at least that it was dangerous. But he hadn't done anything about it yet, and then he was arrested and it was too late." She frowned, trying to piece together the timeline. "If Bertrand believes Simeon stole it, though, he must have used the contents of the vial before Simeon was arrested. He must have put it in Theo's goblet hours before the feast, which I know for a fact was possible. But Simeon didn't know that, because it wasn't really him who stole it, it was you, much later. Unless you've told him, Simeon still has no way to know one vial was used."

"I haven't spoken to him since I stole it," Sophia said. "I've been lying low as much as possible, trying to avoid attention that might make Bertrand suspicious of me."

Elowen held her friend's gaze earnestly. "We should take the vials to my father at once!"

"Do you think so?" Sophia bit her lip. "We have no evidence of what they are. I've been to the library, and checked books on every language known on the Peninsula. I can't make sense of the words."

"We have to try," Elowen insisted. "You'll have to be bold, Sophia, and testify to my father that you found them in Bertrand's room."

"What this will mean for my family..." Sophia's voice was barely a whisper.

"I know." Elowen put a hand on her shoulder. "I know, Sophia, and I'm so sorry. But if he really did something to Theo...I can't let Theo die, Sophia. I just can't."

Her friend searched Elowen's face, her anguished expression softening slightly. Then she rose, moving with determined steps into her sleeping chamber. There was a shuffling, grinding sound, and a minute later she returned with a small leather bag gripped in her hand.

"Let's go."

Elowen stood as well, eager to be gone before Bertrand

could learn of their intention. She watched as Sophia stashed the bag in a pocket of her dress, then the two of them hurried from the manor. Mercifully, they didn't encounter Bertrand, and in a matter of minutes, they were riding for the castle, once again flanked by the princess's guards.

Elowen made straight for the audience hall, Sophia hurrying by her side.

"I'm sorry, Your Highness, but it's a closed meeting," one of the guards told Elowen gruffly.

She drew herself up. "I need to speak to my father. It's urgent."

"The king is not to be disturbed," the guard told her, not unkindly.

"It's urgent," Elowen repeated. "I need to speak to him now!"

The guards looked at each other, hesitating for a moment. Then one of them said, "I'll inquire, Your Highness, but it's not our orders."

Elowen waited impatiently as the man slipped into the room. A minute passed, then he returned, taking his position without speaking.

She was about to demand an answer when another form followed him through the door. Not the one she'd wanted to see.

"Elowen, what is this ruckus?" Patrick hissed sternly. "Father can't be spared right now because he's trying to resolve the crisis your actions brought on."

Elowen ignored the accusation, grabbing hold of his arm earnestly. "Patrick, I *have* to speak to him. It really is urgent! We have information—not just information but evidence—about Theo's condition."

Her brother's brows drew together, and he shot a quick look between the several guards standing nearby. He shook off her hand, instead ushering her several paces away and lowering his voice.

"Elowen, enough with this! If you say the word *poison* one more time—"

"We have proof, Patrick!" Elowen insisted. "Sophia found these vials in Bertrand's—"

"Enough." Patrick's voice was so forbidding, she fell silent. "When will you learn the responsibility that comes with your position, Elowen? You can't throw around accusations in a public corridor."

"Well then where can I throw them around?" Elowen said with spirit. "You wouldn't listen to me when I tried to speak to you in Father's study."

"If you want to argue more with Father about the situation, you can do so after this meeting. The Siqualians made a choice to leave Toledda and seek medical care elsewhere. We must all abide by that decision, which means there's no urgency to further discuss the cause of his illness. Any information you have will have to wait until we've dealt with our own crisis." He jerked his head toward the audience hall, his voice grim. "After all, if there's no alliance, there's not much need for us to intervene in Prince Theodore's recovery, is there?"

Elowen tried to protest, but he didn't stay to hear her. He strode straight back into the meeting without a backward glance, leaving her fuming and more desperate than ever.

"Elowen." Sophia's voice was hesitant. "Am I right in thinking that the alliance has nothing to do with your need to intervene in Prince Theodore's recovery?"

A hiccup that would have liked to be a sob escaped Elowen. "I love him, Sophia," she murmured. "I didn't realize it until I thought I might lose him. I've been a fool, creating barriers that ended up hurting us both. I *want* to marry him. More than anything else."

"Maybe your father will listen to you, once the meeting is done," Sophia said.

"Maybe." Elowen didn't feel hopeful. "But it might be too late." Her face set. "We need to take the matter into our own hands in the meantime." She glanced around. "Come on."

Sophia followed her down several corridors, rapidly approaching the castle's library. Elowen had dismissed her guards. She was safe enough in her own castle.

But Theo hadn't been, she reminded herself miserably. Her eyes flicked to the place near the library entrance where Theo had seen her speaking with Simeon and disapproved. She wished she hadn't let him get away with saying nothing and pretending he wasn't bothered by it. There were a lot of times where she wished she'd been more assertive and pushed him harder to open up to her. But she hadn't known him well enough then to be sure she'd like what she found if she got inside his head. Now that she had no fear of seeing who he really was, it was easier to see that she'd been too passive.

"Elowen, I told you," Sophia said in a murmur as they entered the library. "I checked in here, I couldn't find any translation of those words."

"You said you checked all the languages of the Peninsula," Elowen said. Her mind went back over what Prince Cassius had said. The serious Carrackian prince had seemed very certain that someone on the continent wished harm on their Peninsula region.

Elowen swept through the sanctuary with steps too loud for the hushed space, ignoring the startled looks from the group of trainee scribes settled next to a large, arched window. She didn't have time to linger. She would have to be direct. Scanning the large room, she saw a young man in the robes of a record-keeper replacing tomes on a shelf near the center of the space. She marched up to him.

"Good afternoon," she said. "Do we have anyone in the castle trained in the languages of the continent?"

The man blinked at her, so taken aback that he almost forgot to bow.

"Your Highness." He took a moment to collect himself, hugging his books to his torso as he thought. "Not as far as I'm aware. We have literature on the continent, but most of it is outdated, given we haven't had diplomatic relations with any of those kingdoms since the war."

"So if I wanted to translate something, there would be nothing here to help me?" Elowen asked, crestfallen.

"I don't know about that." He scratched his nose absently. "There's always *something* in here that can help. This is the finest library in Torrens."

Elowen smiled faintly at the pride in his voice. "Can you help me, then?"

"Yes, Your Highness." He lovingly placed his books on a table, taking a moment to neaten the little stack before leading her down a few rows of shelves. "We have a few books on the culture and ways of the continent kingdoms," he said, pulling out the volumes in question. "This is generally considered the best, as it was written by someone who'd actually spent time there."

"Usually helpful," Sophia commented dryly.

The young record-keeper nodded sagely, apparently missing her tone. He flicked through the book in question, stopping at a certain chapter.

"He talks about language here. He says there are different dialects in different kingdoms, but a common tongue is used for all matters of trade and diplomacy."

"Does this common tongue use the same script as our language?" Elowen asked, glancing at the note Sophia held, where she'd copied what was on the labels of the vials.

"It does," the man confirmed. "It comes from the same root tongue as ours, actually, but I suppose they've evolved quite differently over time. Ah look. There's a glossary at the back, with translation of quite a number of common words. You could try there."

"Thank you."

Elowen practically snatched the book from him, turning her shoulder on his scandalized expression. She carried the book to a nearby table and bent over it, Sophia's face close to hers.

The other girl laid the note flat against the table, and the two of them started scanning the glossary for any that matched.

"Here!" Sophia pointed excitedly. "This is almost the same as one of the words from the empty vial, isn't it? It says it means *unhurried* or *at leisure*."

"That doesn't sound too sinister," Elowen said optimistically. "There's another word with it, though, maybe if we find that it will..." Her words trailed off as she caught sight of the word she was searching for.

"Death," she read. "It means death."

She looked at Sophia, her voice hollow.

"A slow death."

TWENTY-THREE

Elowen

Elowen's mind whirled, thinking of what the physician had said about Theo's symptoms not being severe enough for poison, and how it had been too long since ingestion for Theo to still be alive. Whatever had been in that vial, it wasn't any kind of poison they knew. It was something else entirely, something that shouldn't exist.

"I found a word from the other vial's label," Sophia said. "Magic."

"And this one." Elowen's eyes moved quickly through the glossary. "It says it can mean *use* or *requirement*, depending on context." She passed a hand over her eyes. "This is hopeless. Those are two words out of," she counted, "twelve on that label. We can't translate it with the tools we have."

Sophia took a moment to answer, her gaze thoughtful as it passed between her note and the glossary. "We can't make out every word," she acknowledged. "But I think it's enough to give a sense. The empty vial must have been some kind of poison, how else can you describe a substance that brings slow death? So the logical answer is that the full one is an antidote."

Elowen nodded slowly, remembering what Bertrand had

said. She'd suspected him of trying to twist her into some kind of bargain. And that made more sense if he had something to bargain with. He'd just needed to interrogate Simeon, who he thought knew where the vials were.

"And it seems the antidote either uses magic, or requires magic," Sophia said. "At least, that's my best guess based on the words we can find."

"So just drinking it might not be enough," Elowen said, aghast. "I suppose that answers my question."

Her friend looked up at her bitter tone. "What question?"

"Whether I should just abandon caution and ride after Theo on the fastest horse I can find, and make him drink the contents of the second vial."

Sophia said nothing as she closed the book and returned it to its place. With a word of thanks to the record-keeper, the two of them walked from the library, stopping at the nearest alcove big enough for them both to step into.

"That's exactly what you should do," Sophia said, speaking as if there'd been no interruption to their conversation. "But you need to take more than just the vial. You need to take someone skilled in magic. Someone you trust."

Understanding passed between them.

"But he won't know what to do," said Elowen in a murmur. "He can't read this any more than we can."

"But it came with instructions, remember? They weren't in a different language. Just technical magical terms. Maybe they'll make sense to him."

Elowen thought it over.

"How did you say you got into the dungeons, Sophia?"

Her friend grimaced. "I used magic. To knock out the guard on duty."

Elowen's eyes widened. "That's a serious offense."

"I know it is," Sophia acknowledged. "But as I think you

understand, when the life of the man you love is in danger, there's a lot you suddenly find courage to do that might have seemed impossible before."

Elowen searched her face, startled by the frank words. Her heart ached for her friend, because knowing the duke's family well, she didn't see much hope in that direction, even if Simeon's name was cleared. But this wasn't the time.

"It's also difficult magic," she said. "Especially since you seem to have done it in such a way that the guard didn't realize he'd been hit. At least I assume so, since no alarm was raised."

Sophia nodded. "He would have woken and thought he'd dozed for a moment. As for how I got away with it, it helps that no one would imagine I was capable of anything like it."

"*I* didn't imagine it," Elowen confessed. "How exactly did you do it?"

"I used a repetitive, swinging motion," Sophia said matter-of-factly. "A large pendulum, that I took from the grandfather clock at the manor."

"That's why the parlor felt so silent!" Elowen exclaimed. "Never mind," she added quickly, in response to Sophia's perplexed look. "Go on."

"Well, the type of motion matters, doesn't it? The swinging of a pendulum is steady and rhythmic, and it lulls people, makes us think of sleep. It was the perfect type of movement to use to fuel a sleeping enchantment. I first asked to see Simeon, knowing I'd be refused, but needing a legitimate reason for my presence there if it raised questions later. Then, when I was leaving, I stood on the stairs leading down to the dungeons, out of sight of both the corridor above and the guard's position below, and swung the pendulum back and forth until I'd gathered enough Dust to give me a few minutes of unconsciousness from the guard."

Elowen hardly knew what to say. "That's...impressive," she said. "And a little scary."

Sophia lowered her gaze. "There's so much I haven't told you, Elowen. The lessons you and I did with Simeon were only the start. There were many other times, just him and me..." She drew a shuddering breath. "At least, until your betrothal was announced, and Bertrand became much more controlling of everyone, including me, and impossibly demanding of Simeon. And I was too scared of him finding out what I'd been doing." Her expression was determined. "I swear Simeon never overstepped, Elowen. He's always been so honorable. We studied alone together, but never once did he..." She gave a laugh that was more sad than humorous. "I used to hope he would kiss me. But he never even came close."

"I don't doubt either one of you," Elowen assured her.

"Anyway, I've advanced a lot more in magic craft than you know," Sophia said. "Simeon says I have a real aptitude, although of course I know it's nothing to his." Her eyes were troubled as they met Elowen's. "He's incredible, Elowen. I wouldn't be surprised if he was capable of the things he's been accused of, in terms of magical power. But he would simply never do it."

"I know he wouldn't," Elowen said firmly. "We both know he doesn't belong in the dungeon. The question is, can you get him out?"

"Maybe." Sophia sounded nervous. "I assume you already know that the cells are reinforced with enchantments that prevent occupants from harnessing magic while inside. And the walls of the cells have extra layers of protection to stop them being broken open with magic. But the guard had keys. If I could buy a few minutes again, get hold of the keys, and just let Simeon out through the door..." She shrugged. "If Simeon got clear of the reinforced cell, I doubt he'd have any trouble getting us out of the dungeons."

"We won't delay," Elowen said, jittery nerves filling her as she made up her mind. "You go and get Simeon, I'll get three horses. Theo's carriage was moving slowly. We'll be able to catch him before dark if we ride hard."

She half expected her friend to protest, but Sophia hadn't been exaggerating about finding her courage. The prospect of freeing Simeon had clearly galvanized her.

"You'd better take the vials just in case," she said practically, handing the bag over. "If I get caught in the dungeons, they might be confiscated."

Elowen took them, feeling like she was sending her friend to the gallows. "Be careful," she said anxiously.

After a moment's debate, they set their meeting point, just outside the castle wall on a road that acted as a thoroughfare to the eastern region of Torrens. It was sure to be crowded enough that they wouldn't stand out.

"We need to be clear of the capital before Simeon's absence is discovered," she said. "Or we won't have a hope of getting out."

They parted ways, and Elowen wasted no time in going to the stables. Having Ochre and two other horses saddled for her was no trouble. It wasn't unusual for her to ride through the city with friends. Finding a way to leave with all three horses and no human companions was harder. But she managed it by playing two grooms off each other so that each thought the other was accompanying her to assist with the horses. She could have used the help, she thought wryly. The castle horses were very well trained, but even so it was no easy feat to lead three at once.

Nevertheless, she made it to the meeting point by the arranged time. She stood beside Ochre, the hood of the traveling cloak she'd donned pulled low as she tried to shield herself from view with the mare's flank. The capital wasn't in a state of alert, and she didn't expect all travelers leaving the city to be closely inspected. But there was still a significant risk of the guards on duty noticing her, and if she was recognized as the princess, it would be the end of her adventure.

She had no warning of Simeon and Sophia's approach. One moment she was waiting nervously, the next they were at her side.

"How did you do that?" Elowen demanded.

"Simeon's been cloaking our movements," Sophia said matter-of-factly. "It's very clever. He uses the movement of each step to deaden the sound of the next one. It's fiddly and difficult, and only a few—"

"All right, you can sing his praises later," Elowen said, her nerves raw from the tension. She looked at the servant. "Are you all right, Simeon?"

His brow was heavy, and Sophia interjected quickly.

"There was no time to explain anything to him, I just told him we were going to save Prince Theodore's life and he had to trust me."

"Your Highness, you should never have taken this risk for me." Simeon's voice was low and urgent, and his gaze encompassed Sophia, too. "Neither of you should have. I can't in good conscience agree to such a reckless plan, not for my sake."

"Then you have no need to worry, because it's not for your sake," Elowen said briskly. "Sophia was telling you the truth, we broke you out to save Prince Theodore's life, and I won't take no for an answer. We can explain once we're out of the city."

His eyes widened slightly, and he said nothing more. But his muscles were still taut with tension as he helped Sophia to mount one of the spare horses, then vaulted lightly onto the other himself. Every second seemed an eternity to Elowen, who knew that their only hope was to get out of the city before the guards had any idea they were looking for an escaped prisoner. To her immense relief, the gate they'd chosen was busy, a thick stream of people moving through it. They joined the crowd, heads lowered as they walked their horses past the gate.

As soon as they could move freely enough, they urged their mounts to a canter, joining the eastward road that led to Carrack. There was no conversation as they pushed to a gallop, thundering over the ground at a speed that still wasn't fast enough to satisfy Elowen.

Once the capital was far behind them, some of the invisible tension lifted from their group, and they slowed to rest their horses with a brief walk. Elowen listened as Sophia told Simeon why they'd taken such a drastic step.

"So it was poison in the vial?" he murmured, aghast. "I knew he was meddling in some dark things, but I didn't think he'd go to those lengths." His face darkened. "He manipulated me skillfully."

"Manipulated you how?" Elowen demanded. "You have some questions to answer, Simeon. "Why in the Peninsula would you confess to crimes we know you didn't do?"

His shoulders slumped in weariness. "I shouldn't have," he said. "That's clear to me now. But he told me to." His lips twisted in a bitter smile. "And I've gotten into the habit of doing what I'm told."

Elowen saw the way his eyes flicked to Sophia, and her frown deepened.

"Explain what you mean."

Simeon returned his eyes to the road. "It's always been my job to look out for the viscount and assist him in whatever way he wishes. But it's only more recently that he started to give me very specific instructions that he would never explain. He would send me away, or order me to stay in a certain place. And often he would then berate me for doing exactly what he'd told me to do, as if I'd done it in disobedience to his instructions."

"Always in front of witnesses," Elowen added darkly.

"Yes, of course, I could tell it was for show, although I didn't yet understand the reason. But naturally I didn't expose him." He spoke simply. "I was used to that type of treatment."

Sophia's expression was so distressed, Elowen regretted sneaking a look at her friend. They increased their pace again, the horses' strides making short work of the road that Theo and his brother would certainly have taken. Would they reach them before dark? Before pursuers caught up with them? And if they did, would it be in time for Theo?

There was plenty of time to think about what Simeon had said, and the next time their horses needed to walk, Elowen was ready with more questions.

"The scarf was Bertrand's?" she guessed. "The purple scarf. He made a show of having it presented to you, knowing you would follow his prompting and accept it. It occurs to me now that many of the duke's servants were at the forest. There was time enough while we ate dinner for Bertrand to demand a report from one of them and to realize he was at risk of exposure. So he passed the risk to you, as usual. Did you realize that accepting the scarf was implicating you in the landslide?"

"I didn't," Simeon said. "Not exactly that, anyway."

Frustration flared in Elowen. It was galling how well Bertrand's tactics had worked. That conversation was what had made Theo suspect Simeon, when the report about the scarf should actually have implicated Bertrand himself. He must have been the young man who ran away from the landslide. Theo had even gone as far as to do Bertrand's dirty work for him by reporting Simeon to the king.

"I think it will fall to me to say what Sophia is too gentle to," she said tartly.

"No, it won't." Sophia cut across her words. "Of course I'll say it. Simeon, what were you thinking? I know you're smarter than that. After so many instances, you must have figured out that he was up to something bad, and was setting you up to take the fall for him. Why didn't you tell me?"

"I wanted to protect you, Sophia," Simeon said softly.

It was the first time Elowen had heard him drop the title, and the way his voice caressed Sophia's name told her that a lot more had happened since last she'd observed their doomed romance.

"I wanted to shield you from grief and from the shame your brother would bring on your family if he was discovered in still more misdeeds. Better me than him, is what I told myself at first. But that was before I understood the severity of what he was doing, that he was involved somehow in the disasters."

Still more misdeeds? There was no opening for Elowen to question him.

"And after you understood that?" Sophia demanded. "Why did you cover for him still?"

He met her eye. "Because he told me plainly that he knew how you felt about me, and he would expose you to your parents and the court if I defied him. He had quite a detailed plan for your future from that point on, right down to the specifics of the arguments he would use to convince your parents to marry you to an older nobleman whose reputation for cruelty, among other things, is well known among the men of the court, if not the women. The plan was very plausible."

Sophia was silent and pale, but Elowen let out a cry of disgust.

"She's his sister!"

"He has no family affection," Simeon said simply. "Only

family pride, which is not the same thing at all. I knew his threats weren't empty, and I couldn't be the one who gave him reason to do it. But when I came across the vials, and was confronted for the first time by concrete proof that he was working for someone far more powerful and dangerous, my resolve was tested."

"What do you mean?" Elowen asked quickly.

"The vials had notations in some other language, for one thing," Simeon said. "They didn't come from anyone inside Torrens."

"It's a language from the continent," Elowen told him.

A shadow passed over his face. "That's…alarming. Whoever gave him those vials has far superior magical understanding than we've attained in Torrens. I only caught a brief glimpse of the instruction sheet that was in the same bag, but it described a type of magic I've never even heard of before. If you asked about it at our guild, they would tell you it was impossible."

"So why didn't you expose him then?" Sophia demanded. "Loyalty to the kingdom should have overcome a desire to shield our family's reputation, Simeon."

"I know it should have," he said. "And I was trying to figure out how to go about it. But in the meantime, I needed the viscount to believe I was obedient, so he wouldn't use the contents of the vial on you."

"On me?" Sophia said, startled.

"That's what he threatened when I confronted him about the vials," Simeon said. "But he didn't call it poison. He said it could compel you to do whatever he told you. I wanted to get the vials away from him before telling anyone what I suspected, so I'd have evidence and so he couldn't retaliate against you. And I would have managed it, too. He was so sure of my obedience by then, I don't think it occurred to him that I might defy him and steal the vials. Except next thing I knew, the royal guards were at my door, and the viscount was telling me that I knew what would happen if I didn't confess to whatever they accused me of."

A strong part of Elowen wanted to tell Simeon that he'd been foolish, letting Bertrand use his love for Sophia to tug him around like a puppet on a string. But after a moment's reflection on the impact Bertrand had managed to have on her own betrothal without even resorting to open threats, she decided to hold her peace.

"So when you sent me to retrieve the bag, you were sending me to heroically rescue myself?" Sophia said, seeming entertained by the concept.

Elowen pulled the bag out of her pocket, extracting the paper and handing it silently to Simeon. "What's the unknown type of magic? Does it explain how he poisoned Theo without leaving a trace?"

Simeon scanned the page eagerly, his brow creasing as he tried to make sense of it.

"I see," he said softly. "It's not a compulsion enchantment like he claimed. But it's also not a poison exactly. It's an enchantment wrapped around the liquid. Consumption of the liquid triggers the enchantment, which then acts on its own impetus. It's a magical malady, though, not like the effects of any traditional poisons. I think it must have been designed to look like a natural illness."

"Well, then it worked," Elowen said flatly. Unease gripped her, for a moment taking her beyond her own and Theo's problems. "I don't like the thought that the continent has such superior magical skill over the Peninsula," she said uneasily.

No one replied, the three of them pushing their horses forward in unison, troubled thoughts circling each mind.

By the time they rested their horses again, hours had passed since they'd left the capital. Elowen was weary and sore, but as determined as ever. It would be dark soon, and they still hadn't caught sight of their quarry. At least no pursuers had yet caught them, either, although she had no doubt there'd be quite a mess waiting for her when she returned to the capital.

"So Bertrand really was behind all the disasters?" It was Sophia who broke the silence this time. "I'm finding it hard to accept."

"I don't know for certain," Simeon said. "It's not as though he's admitted it to me. Something was definitely off in his actions the day the tower collapsed. And I have reason to think he had opportunity to damage the foundations of the dam before he left the estate for the capital. But he can't have been acting alone in that instance, because I don't think he intended to be there in person when it actually burst. He made sure I was, of course," he added bitterly.

"He also made sure to make a fuss publicly about how he had no idea where you were because you'd left without leave," Elowen said, resentment bubbling again. "Even then, he was already setting you up to take the fall if he got caught."

"Well, whatever he's involved in, I doubt he's the architect," Simeon said. "He has his talents, but this is outside them. Whoever gave him these vials has a bigger plan, and the viscount either doesn't understand or doesn't care that he's a pawn in their game."

"Do you think the antidote will work?" Elowen asked, less interested for the moment in the bigger picture than Theo's life.

"Not by itself," Simeon said. "You were wise to investigate the meaning of that label. If you'd just gotten him to drink it, I doubt it would have any effect. The instructions make no sense according to our magical knowledge, but the mechanics of it are clear enough." He saw they were both watching him expectantly and added, "When the antidote is drunk, it will release magic, which I'll need to harness to attack the sickness enchantment still clinging to Prince Theodore."

"Release magic that you need to harness?" Elowen repeated. "Hold on. An enchantment released by drinking the poison is impossible enough. But at least that's a formed enchantment, like we sometimes use. You're telling me the other vial contains stored magic, not molded to any particular use? That's...not possible."

"Not according to our magical knowledge," Simeon agreed. "It's not completely unformed magic, I don't think. It's sourced from the right kind of movement and given some hint of shape already."

The conversation was becoming harder to follow, and Elowen decided to worry about the broader magical implications later. They were passing the turnoff to a tiny town, and she glanced to the side as the road branched.

"Look!" She pulled up her horse. "Is that them?"

CHAPTER
TWENTY-FOUR

Elowen

Urging Ochre forward, Elowen navigated down the small street and pulled alongside the carriage trundling down the side road. The uniformed guards flanking it gave away the identity of the occupants.

"Halt there," one of them called, as a pair of them swung to face the new arrivals.

"It's all right!" Prince Xavier's face had appeared in the carriage window, and he called to the driver to stop. As soon as the vehicle wasn't moving, he flung open the door and descended to the road. "Princess! What are you doing here?"

Elowen ignored him, clambering into the carriage and falling to her knees. Theo was halfway to lying down, propped against the far side of the carriage. His pulse thundered under her fingers, and his face was more flushed than ever.

"He's getting steadily worse," Prince Xavier said through the open door. His own face was haggard. "I didn't want to stop for the night before we reached the border, but I didn't think he could take much more of the road. The driver said there won't be another town for a long way after this."

"We can save him," Elowen said. She turned around. "Simeon, can you do it in here, or do we need to carry him out?"

"The shelter of the carriage is good," Simeon said, appearing at the entrance to the vehicle, shadowed by a wary-looking guard. "In fact, it would be even better if we were moving, because this is a large object. I may want the extra magical boost from its movement."

"What's going on?" Prince Xavier demanded.

"Theo *was* poisoned, sort of," Elowen said.

"Sort of?"

"And we have the—sort of—antidote," Elowen hurried on. "But Simeon has to administer it using magic craft." She raised her voice. "Drive on."

"But—" Prince Xavier's sputtering protest gave way to a sigh. "Yes, all right," he said, apparently to the driver.

"Your Highness!" one of the guards protested.

"Ride alongside them if it makes you feel better," Prince Xavier said. "But the princess is betrothed to Theo. He trusts her, and she has as much right as anyone to help him."

Warmth crept over Elowen as the carriage started moving, and Prince Xavier and Sophia fell out of sight. Waiting only for Simeon's nod of approval, Elowen unstopped the second vial and tipped its contents into Theo's slightly open mouth.

At once, she felt something, faint but insistent, tugging on her senses. She tried hard to focus on it, but it was like a scaly fish, slipping through her fingers. Simeon was clearly having more success. He was leaning forward, sweat beading on his forehead as he gave his full focus to the task. Elowen thought she felt him draw on the movement of the carriage at one point, but she couldn't be sure. After a tense minute that seemed to last an hour, Simeon sat back, his concentration dissipating before her eyes.

"What's wrong?" Elowen asked, alarmed.

"Nothing," said Simeon. "It's done."

"It is?" Elowen searched Theo's face eagerly. "Are you sure?"

"Oh yes." Simeon's voice was weary, his energy depleted from whatever massive effort he'd just expended. "I felt the other enchantment let go. It's gone now. He should recover rapidly."

As if in response to these words, Theo's eyelids flickered. When he winced as they went over a bump, Elowen rapped on the carriage roof. The vehicle came to a ponderous stop.

"Elowen?" Theo was blinking at her, still seeming confused, but his eyes sharp now. It was such a relief to see that vacant look gone from his gaze, Elowen let out a tiny sob. He sat up properly, looking around him. "Did I leave Toledda, or was that a dream?"

"Theo!" Elowen threw herself forward so her torso was draped over his lap. Amazingly, he no longer felt hot to the touch.

He started in surprise, then, slowly, laid a hand on her hair.

"It's all right," he said softly. "Everything will be all right."

Elowen knew there was so much he still didn't know, but his words comforted her nevertheless. She realized that Simeon had discreetly withdrawn from the vehicle, and she raised her eyes, which were suddenly feeling wet, to Theo's.

"Don't leave, Theo," she begged, a choke in her voice. "Please, please stay with me. I don't want you to go. I'll set the date for our wedding as soon as we get back to the city. I'll—"

"No." Theo's response was startlingly strong after the weakness of his earlier words.

Elowen recoiled at the stern tone, and Theo softened his voice at once.

"What I mean is, no, I don't want you to be bullied or pressured into setting a date. Not by me, not by anyone. I want to win you first, just like you wanted. I'm determined to."

Elowen's eyes were fixed on his face, her heart too full to find words. She'd better try, though, because he needed to know what he meant to her. Her thoughts were still a muddled mess when a shout from outside made them both look up.

"Elowen!" It was Sophia, her voice reaching them from a closer distance than where they'd left her. She must have run after the carriage when they stopped, and she sounded frightened as well as breathless. "He's coming! He's here!"

"No," Elowen whispered, knowing at once who Sophia must mean. Only one person had such a hold on her friend.

"Is that Lady Sophia?" Theo asked, trying valiantly to catch up. "Where are we, Elowen?" He lifted a hand to his head. "Everything is a haze of chaos since..." His eyes found hers, his gaze dark and still more tumultuous than usual. "Since you followed me from the victory feast."

Elowen's cheeks warmed, unable to look away from the beam of those dark eyes. She still knelt on the floor of the carriage, and Theo leaned forward, one hand brushing her chin where it angled up to face him. The memory of their almost-kiss made the air in the confined space of the carriage deliciously thick, but there was no time to dwell on that.

"A lot has happened since then, Theo," she said, speaking quickly. "No one believes me, but I'm certain Bertrand put something in your wine at the betrothal ceremony. You've been deteriorating steadily since then, and he barely waited until your brother whisked you away from Toledda to initiate a motion with the Council of Lords to dissolve our betrothal."

Theo's eyes narrowed, his hand dropping to her shoulder and tightening in a possessive gesture that made her want to throw herself into his arms.

"He tried to trick me into agreeing to marry him in exchange for helping you." Elowen stumbled over the words, her ears now able to pick up distant hoofbeats. "But Sophia and

I figured it out without him. We broke Simeon out of the dungeons and came after you, and Simeon just used his skill in magic to administer the antidote and save your life."

Theo blinked under the onslaught of dramatic information, seeming unsure which part to respond to.

"Simeon never did any of it, Theo," Elowen told him earnestly. "It was all Bertrand, he just used Simeon as a shield, and he did it by threatening Sophia, because Simeon's in love with her. And now Bertrand is here. He must have chased after us all the way from the capital."

That sharpened Theo's expression. He shifted forward, as if to get out of the carriage, taking hold of both her shoulders now.

"Stay here," he told Elowen. "I won't let him touch you."

"No, Theo, I'm not the one in danger from him," Elowen said impatiently. "He said to my face that he's determined to marry me, so he's not going to kill me." She paused. "Although I'd almost rather he did kill me, because now I know what it is to have the loyalty of a good man, I think I'd prefer to die than be married to a man like Bertrand." What was she babbling about? The ferocious intensity of Theo's gaze brought her thoughts back in line. "The point is, it's you he's determined to eliminate."

"I'm not afraid of Bertrand," Theo said. "I told him once before to stay away from my promised wife, and I told him what would happen if he ignored me."

He felt at his side, frustration crossing his face when he found no sword strapped there. It didn't slow him down, however. He stepped from the carriage, his movements still less steady than usual.

Her heart in her throat, Elowen followed. Darkness was falling in earnest now, and she could barely make out the place some distance away where Bertrand had pulled up his horse in front of Sophia, Simeon, and Prince Xavier. Simeon's form sagged visibly from his magical efforts, but he stood boldly by Sophia's side.

The Siqualian guards clustered near their crown prince, with the exception of Theo's personal guard, Paulson, who'd been waiting by the carriage. As he stepped into position beside his charge, Elowen let out a cry of relief. Bertrand wasn't alone.

"Elowen!" Patrick was more furious than she'd ever seen him, but Elowen still felt her tension drop away. Bertrand couldn't attack anyone in front of Patrick and the pair of Torrenese royal guards who flanked him.

"Patrick, I'm so glad you came!" Elowen hurried forward to meet her brother as he and Bertrand dismounted.

"I can imagine," he said angrily. "How you were going to extricate yourself from this mess without my intervention, I can't guess." His eyes slid to Theo behind her, and he stilled, surprise crossing his face. "Prince Theodore! I'm delighted to see you so much improved." He gave his sister a meaningful look. "It seems fears regarding your illness were overblown."

"No, Patrick." Elowen shook her head. "He didn't just recover by himself. Simeon used magic to save him. That's why we—"

"We can discuss the matter later," Patrick rapped out through clenched teeth. He glanced around, clearly not wishing to lay out the situation in front of the various witnesses.

Bertrand didn't share this hesitation. "Don't be angry with her, Your Highness," he said to Patrick. "It's my fault. She can't be expected to know better, but I should have. When I heard that the prisoner had escaped, I knew at once that I was to blame. When Elowen came to me with her frenzied accusations that I'd somehow attacked Prince Theodore and caused his illness, I spoke my mind without thinking."

"What are you talking about?" Elowen demanded. "Patrick, he's lying to you."

"On the contrary, what he told me has turned out to be exactly true," Patrick said curtly. "I was called once again from the council to learn that our prisoner had escaped from the dungeons. You can imagine my agitation. When Lord Bertrand came to me and asked if your whereabouts were known, I was mortified to be unable to find you. He told me that he'd confided his concern to you, that if someone *had* attacked Prince Theodore, it was most likely that the servant in the dungeons had orchestrated the attack before his arrest."

"When I speculated to the princess that the servant might also know how to reverse it," Bertrand interjected, "I never imagined she would do something so dangerous as break him out of the dungeons in a desperate attempt to force him to help." His voice was full of self-reproach.

"No one would imagine it," Patrick said crisply. "Elowen, what were you thinking?"

Elowen ignored him, anger toward Bertrand burning through her. "A clever lie," she said. "Just enough truth to make it particularly dangerous, but the heart of it still completely false. That's your area of special skill, isn't it, Bertrand?"

"I don't know or care who you are," Prince Xavier said to Bertrand in a cold voice. He looked at Patrick. "But I assure you that my brother was not recovering naturally. I was more afraid for his life than ever until the princess and her companions arrived. I didn't personally see what this servant did, but the improvement in Theo is miraculous."

"Convenient that no one saw what you did, Simeon," Bertrand said sternly.

"*I* saw," Elowen contradicted, moving to stand by Simeon's side in a silent show of solidarity. As if connected by a string,

Theo moved with her, his presence bolstering her as she added, "And I know what you did, Bertrand."

"You haven't shown your judgment to be worth consideration by anyone of sense, Elowen," Patrick said harshly.

"Don't speak to her that way." Theo put a supportive hand on Elowen's shoulder, his eyes fixed on the Torrenese prince. "I won't tolerate disrespect toward my wife, not even from you, Patrick."

The words sent heat flaring through her, and with it came the heightened awareness of Dust that emotions seemed to unlock for her. Ochre was nearby, her reins held by one of the guards, and Elowen could feel the magic released by her movements as she stamped uneasily and flicked her tail. The horse was a familiar, comforting presence, and the magic shared that same flavor in her mind. Without a clear plan for why, Elowen found herself reaching out to harness the Dust. She caught the glance from Simeon that said he'd noticed it, but no one else appeared to.

Meanwhile Patrick was silent, looking taken aback at Theo's rebuke, even a little offended. But it was Bertrand's reaction Elowen was interested in. She hadn't missed the angry spark in his eyes at Theo's words.

"She's not your wife yet, Your Highness," the viscount said smoothly, the emotion carefully hidden now. "And you might be wise not to speak of that event with such certainty. You're not quite up to date with the state of affairs in Toledda."

His words ignited Elowen's anger, but also her fear. If her father bowed to the council and dissolved her betrothal, would she be powerless to stop Theo from leaving again? The Dust she'd been gathering from Ochre's movements clamored at her, and without thinking much, she sent it toward Theo, giving shape to her desire not to be parted from him. She could feel an invisible strand stretch between them, thin and weak in line with her limited abilities, but still comforting in her mind. It wasn't a difficult enchantment for the magic, given its essence of attachment and affection that came from her bond with Ochre.

"You speak out of turn, Bertrand," Patrick was saying curtly. "More than enough discussion has happened here on the open road."

"You're right, Your Highness." Bertrand bent in a half-bow. "We should all return to the capital to unravel this—"

He cut himself off, his eyes suddenly widening, although Elowen couldn't see in the growing darkness what had caught his attention.

"Simeon, stop!"

Bertrand's words had Elowen looking around in bemusement. She barely caught a glimpse of the servant's confused face before another shout from Bertrand was drowned out by a sudden, rushing wind.

"Simeon, I command you to STOP!" Bertrand lunged forward as he yelled, and Elowen realized with a thrill of fear that his eyes weren't on Simeon, but on her.

She heard Sophia's scream and Patrick's shout. There was a flash of movement in the corner of her eye, then she felt Theo's arm snake around her, pushing her back behind his body as dust and gravel rose from the road in a blinding wall.

TWENTY-FIVE

Theo

Theo raised a hand to shield his eyes from the flying dirt. He'd thought it was coming toward them in a wave, but he realized now that they were in the center of a whirlwind. He could feel Elowen warm at his back, huddling against him to protect her own face. He had no idea how he'd stayed at her side. He'd felt the gust force him backward away from her, and for a split second, he'd fully expected to be lifted from his feet and flung backward. But then he'd felt a sharp tug, and the next thing he knew, he was yanked back toward Elowen, able to pull her behind him and shield her.

It took all his willpower now not to turn and enfold her in his arms, to try to keep her safe from all sides. But his instinct told him it was more important to keep his body between her and the enemy.

Because Bertrand was inside the whirlwind as well.

"Princess!" Bertrand's arms were over his face as he struggled through the plunging chaos. "Where are you? Come here, I won't let Simeon hurt you!"

"No, Bertrand." The other voice, strong and defiant, was Theo's first clue that a fourth person was inside the dust maelstrom. Simeon struggled forward, fighting to stay upright. "Not this time. I won't let you hide your crimes behind me."

Anger twisted Bertrand's features. "Bad things happen when a servant forgets his place, Simeon."

"I won't let you hurt Sophia, either," Simeon said fiercely. "I'm stronger than you, Bertrand, and I'm done being your puppet."

"You've lost, Bertrand," Theo shouted over the melee. "You didn't manage to kill me, and you'll never be able to win Elowen. Don't make things worse for yourself by persisting. Every one of us knows this storm is your creation, not Simeon's."

"Don't be absurd." Bertrand gave a nasty laugh. "I have no skill in magic, as everyone knows. Simeon, on the other hand, is celebrated for his prowess."

"I didn't do this," Simeon protested. "I don't know how you did, either. There was no source of movement big enough to turn into this." He gestured around him at the swirling tunnel of dust they were still trapped inside. In spite of his visible exhaustion, his expression was determined. "But now that the storm is providing so much movement..." He trailed off, a look of concentration then alarm crossing his face.

"What's wrong?" Elowen cried.

"All the Dust is still locked into an active enchantment," he shouted. "I can't access it. I don't know how that's possible."

Bertrand was so quick, none of them realized he was in motion until his fist came crashing down on the back of Simeon's head. The servant, too focused on his magic to defend against such a physical attack, crumpled to the ground.

"Simeon!" Elowen screamed, leaping forward, but Theo stopped her with an arm around her middle.

"Stay back!"

Theo kept his eyes fixed on Bertrand, realizing that he was

sliding some kind of metal object back into his pocket. He'd hit the servant with more than just his fist, it seemed.

"Keep away from us." Elowen's voice was fierce, and she'd positioned herself right against Theo's side.

"I was protecting you," Bertrand insisted. "He said it himself, he was trying to get the magic back from his wind to make another attack."

"Who are you performing for?" Theo snarled. "We know what you are, Bertrand."

A very ugly look settled onto the viscount's face. "Then you know you'd be unwise to cross me." His gaze fixed on Elowen. "Come, Elowen. I've had enough of your games."

"You're the only one playing a game, Bertrand," Elowen told him. "And you've lost even that. I never belonged to you, and I never will." She turned her eyes up to Theo's. "I belong to you."

"Elowen." He hardly knew how to put words to the tangle of emotions rising in him as he drank in her upturned face. His thumb brushed gently along her chin. "You don't *belong* to anyone."

"I know," she assured him, her voice soft and something in her eyes that made his heart beat at double speed. "I was just speaking in language Bertrand understands. I'm trusting you to know me better, to understand what I'm really saying."

"Enough of this." Bertrand's voice was no longer as raised, and Theo realized the wind was slowly losing force. Whatever enchantment Bertrand had managed, it wasn't limitless. "We could have made Torrens the strongest it's ever been, but I should have known you were too childish and misty-eyed to play any useful part." He loomed out of the swirling dust. "I was never going to allow the alliance to go ahead, and if I have to eliminate both of you to ensure it, instead of just your prince, so be it. I'll see you dead before I see you a Siqualian's wife." His mouth curled in a sneer. "You're not indispensable to Torrens, and you're certainly not necessary to me. I'll replace you in a heartbeat with someone more malleable."

Anger bubbled within Theo, but Elowen just gave a disbelieving laugh. "Is that supposed to distress me? I pity any girl who catches your eye, Bertrand. You're mad to make these threats so openly. You can't think you'll get away with violence against us."

Bertrand's answering laugh made the hair on the back of Theo's neck prickle. "Of course I will. When the Dust dissipates, and it's clear you were all felled by magic, do you think I'll have any trouble convincing them Simeon did it, and his own enchantment ricocheted on him, too?" He pulled the metal object from his pocket again. "Tragically, I'll be the only survivor."

His movement was so quick, Theo barely had time to throw Elowen behind him again. His arm was raised in front of him, and he let out a grunt as something invisible slashed across it. Blood dripped down from the wound as his mind tried to catch up with what it was seeing.

"Theo!" Elowen cried.

"I'm all right," he said quickly.

The cut was shallow, a fact that seemed to frustrate Bertrand. He raised the object again, his eyes full of malice.

"I don't know how you got inside the storm," Bertrand growled. "But don't get in my way. I'm doing her first on purpose, because I want you to see what happens when you try to take from me something that's mine."

Something fierce and determined flamed to life within Theo. It went beyond anger, beyond even fear. It was a bone-deep certainty that he would do anything to protect Elowen, because he loved her. He wanted her to be safe, to be his, to be by his side forever. He wanted it with his whole being, and that desire wasn't something to fear or deny. It was something to treasure. And it was his fuel as he threw himself toward Bertrand.

"Theo!"

The name turned to a scream on Elowen's lips as Bertrand again brought his strange weapon slashing through thin air, and another slice appeared on Theo's other arm. Pain lanced through him, but he pushed it aside. He'd been asleep since the evening before, moving through the world in a haze. Everything was sharp now, and clearer than it had ever been. He wasn't about to hesitate.

He collided with Bertrand, but the force of his impact didn't dislodge the weapon from Bertrand's hand as he'd hoped.

"Elowen!" Theo shouted, as he wrestled with the viscount in an attempt to stop him wielding it again. "It's a magic weapon. Use magic to defend yourself!"

"If Simeon couldn't harness this wind, there's no way I can," Elowen cried.

"Bertrand doesn't control everything," Theo reminded her. "Just the small patch he wants you to see. Reach beyond the storm for movement!"

Bertrand landed a punch in Theo's distraction, and he barely got his lacerated arms back up in time to stop the other man from breaking free. The viscount's sneering laugh reached his ears.

"She won't be able to reach past the storm. We're sealed in."

Movement drew Theo's eye, and he risked a glance at Elowen. She'd dived for Simeon's prostrate form, and seemed to be tugging at the other man's pocket. Theo couldn't afford to keep watching. His mind was sharp, but his body was still affected both by his recent illness and his injuries. Bertrand managed to wrench an arm free, slashing the weapon through the air with his eyes on Elowen.

Theo shouted in rage, but no cry of pain came from the

princess. He twisted frantically around to see her still standing, her expression determined as she wielded a large, fanlike object. She was swirling it in a figure eight pattern through the air, stirring up a steady trickle of Dust which she had obviously used to good effect.

Bertrand's incredulous growl brought a grim smile to Elowen's lips.

"You forgot one other thing you don't control, Bertrand," the princess said. "Me."

Taking his opening, Theo shifted his grip to Bertrand's wrist, bringing his hand down with all his force against his own leg. The strange object at last clattered to the ground, and Theo kicked it away. Bertrand lunged after it with an angry shout, exposing his back. Theo tackled him, pinning him to the ground just as the swirling wall of gravel and dust finally faltered, then, with unnatural abruptness, dropped away.

Instantly a cacophony of shouts and screams reached their ears, and their small space was flooded with people.

"What's going on?" Prince Patrick demanded. "What was that? We couldn't see or hear anyth—" His eyes widened as they found Bertrand, still being crushed under Theo's weight.

"Paulson," Theo said, ignoring the Torrenese prince. "This man just tried to kill both me and the princess. He needs to be securely detained."

"And searched for any more strange objects," Elowen interjected, as the Siqualian guards all hastened to obey their prince.

Theo gave a quick nod of agreement, relinquishing a sputtering Bertrand to the guards. He saw that Lady Sophia had run straight to Simeon's prone form, lifting his head gingerly onto her lap. Meanwhile Xavier materialized at Theo's side, his eyes quickly finding the injuries to his brother's arms.

"These wounds need binding," he rapped out, causing another flurry of activity from the Siqualian guards.

"Prince Theodore." Prince Patrick's voice was deep and strained. "I don't understand what's happened here, but I would caution you to get all the information before placing too much weight on my sister's theories regarding Lord Bertrand."

"I'm not interested in your caution," Theo said brutally. "And it's not caution, it's blindness. If you had more sense, you would have been genuinely cautious by properly investigating your sister's suspicions before the viscount had the chance to cover his tracks. There's nothing whatsoever wrong with her judgment. If you don't believe her, then believe the testimony of my own eyes and ears." He glanced at Bertrand, who was protesting in outrage as two armed guards hauled him to his feet and a third searched him thoroughly. "The son of your most influential duke just told us to our faces he was going to kill us both and make it look like his servant Simeon was behind it."

Prince Patrick's face was ashen by the end of this speech, and Lady Sophia let out a squeak of distress. Theo looked toward her to see Simeon stirring at last, a soft groan escaping him. He blinked several times, then his features relaxed at the face he saw hovering above him.

"Sophy?"

Theo saw Prince Patrick's eyebrow go up at the soft greeting, and Elowen apparently did too. She jumped in quickly, distracting her brother.

"Everything he said about Bertrand is true, Patrick. He tried to convince us the storm came from Simeon, and when we wouldn't believe him, he knocked Simeon out and turned on us. He said he was never going to let the alliance proceed."

Theo shook off the guard currently trying to bandage his arm, moving quickly to Elowen's side.

"You were amazing at the end there," he said.

She smiled, lifting the large fan-like instrument and

showing him how it folded back into an object no longer than a quill, and not much thicker.

"Simeon always carries one of these," she informed Theo matter-of-factly. "And fortunately, I've been taught how to use it. I harnessed the Dust it stirred up to make a magical shield in front of myself." She winced as she raised a hand to her neck. "Not a very good shield, but good enough, thankfully."

Following the movement with his eyes, Theo was horrified to see a diagonal red mark along her neck. He sucked his breath in through his teeth, his fingers hovering over the spot but not touching for fear of hurting her.

"I could feel it slashing me," Elowen said. "But it was dulled, and not enough to make me bleed."

Black fury coursed through Theo at the thought that Bertrand had aimed for Elowen's neck. He turned, his gaze murderous as it fell on the disgraced viscount.

"Don't worry about him," Elowen said. "He'll lose everything because of his actions, you shouldn't waste your energy on him."

"I don't understand it, Bertrand." The words burst from Prince Patrick. "How could you do it? Why would you risk everything for such petty, personal reasons? I know we once spoke of the possibility of you marrying Elowen, but it was never promised to you."

Irritation flared in Elowen's eyes at this information, but it was Simeon who spoke.

"Your Highness." He struggled to his feet, assisted by Sophia. "I know I have no standing, but may I speak?"

"Of course you can," Elowen said. "Patrick needs to hear what you have to say."

The prince didn't look as convinced, but he inclined his head stiffly.

"First, Your Highness, I acknowledge my crime in breaking

out of the dungeons," Simeon said. "I swear I wouldn't have done it had I not been convinced that Prince Theodore's life hung in the balance."

"Which it did," Elowen cut in earnestly.

"Do you wish to make excuses for yourself, or do you have information to share?" Prince Patrick asked coolly.

Dust and motion, he was obnoxious. How had Elowen lived with him all these years? Surely she'd prefer the company of Xavier and Miriam when she came to live in Sindon.

"I believe, Your Highness," Simeon hurried on, "that the viscount had another motivation beyond his personal resentment. I've suspected for some time now that he was communicating with someone clandestinely, and more than once I've overheard a comment that made me wonder if he was being prompted by some other party to prevent the alliance."

Bertrand yanked his arm defiantly in a half-hearted attempt to get free of his captor, his eyes full of hatred as they rested on the servant.

"If you mean my father, Simeon, you're wrong," Lady Sophia said earnestly. "I know he doesn't like the marriage. It's no secret that he'd hoped Bertrand would marry Elowen and that he resents us forming an alliance with Siqual."

Prince Patrick looked startled by this information, but Sophia wasn't finished.

"But he would never condone Bertrand attacking a foreign prince. They've been arguing constantly because of Bertrand's behavior toward Prince Theodore, you know they have."

"I didn't mean him," Simeon assured her. "I meant that I think someone has been paying the viscount to do their dirty work, someone who instructed him to stop the alliance at all costs. I think it's the same party that's been using the viscount to set up these disasters across the country, and I don't for a moment believe the duke had a hand in those."

"You mean the crimes you already confessed to?" Prince Patrick asked dryly.

"I did, Your Highness," Simeon said calmly. "I did it to protect someone the viscount was threatening, but it was the wrong decision. I swear I won't resist the guards when they return me to the dungeons, and if I can be given a hearing before His Majesty, I will plead my case and hope to convince him of the truth with the evidence available."

"Of course you're not going back to the dungeons," Elowen said, exasperated. "Patrick, you're becoming distracted from the point. What do you care about Simeon's reasons for covering for Bertrand? What I want to know is who was in Bertrand's ear to intentionally cause harm to his own kingdom?"

"It's not a plausible tale," Prince Patrick said. "Even leaving Bertrand out of it, why wouldn't an enemy of Torrens choose more strategic targets than abandoned buildings and out of the way villages?"

"The purpose of stopping the alliance was to weaken Torrens," Theo said. As an afterthought, he added, "And Siqual, most likely. The purpose of the disasters was quite different, I suspect."

Prince Patrick frowned. "I've heard your theory that the purpose of these disasters was to elicit a large volume of magic for the purposes of trying to store it. But I agree with my father—no experiments have ever succeeded in achieving that goal, and there's no evidence that situation has changed."

Theo leaned down, carefully picking up the object he'd wrestled from Bertrand. He held it up, twisting it around so everyone could see. Then, striding away from the group, he lifted it just as Bertrand had done, and brought it slashing down in the direction of a tree several feet away.

Gasps went around the group as a sharp gash appeared in the bark.

"I didn't know you were skilled in magic craft," Prince Patrick said uneasily.

"I'm not," Theo replied. "Wielding whatever this is required no magic craft at all from me. But clearly it was created with much more advanced magic craft than we know. I suspect the whirlwind was created using another such item."

"We did find this in the viscount's pocket, Your Highness," one of the guards said gruffly, handing Prince Patrick a curiously carved wooden object.

"Wood for a force of nature, steel for a weapon," Simeon murmured. "That shows consistency with the laws of magic that we *do* know."

No one replied, although Theo noticed Paulson nodding thoughtfully.

"If someone has found a way to store magic…" Prince Patrick said. "The magnitude of that development…"

"We know," Elowen said quietly, when he trailed off. "It would change everything." Her voice turned grim. "We have a general idea who's behind it, Patrick, and it's not good news. But I'd rather explain it all once, when Father and Mother are present as well."

"Every word is nonsense," Bertrand spat, apparently finally master of himself enough to get the words out with a semblance of calm. "I'm not a hand for hire. I'm the son of a proud house, with no reason to do anyone's bidding for any price. And so I'll tell His Majesty."

"And I'll be telling him the truth," Lady Sophia said, her voice calm but carrying.

"Sophia, hold your tongue," Bertrand hissed.

Her face was incredibly sad as she looked at him. "I think I'm done holding my tongue, Bertrand." She turned to the royals. "Our family's wealth is gone. We're not yet penniless, but we're close to it. We've been doing all we can to conceal it, because we've lost none of our wealth of family pride. But the truth is we're on the point of ruin. Our estate has always relied heavily on exports, and when Siqual and Carrack both halted trade agreements with Torrens a few years back, we were hit very hard. My father and brother have both been unable to forgive the other kingdoms, and the idea of the alliance was not received well in our household." She drew a breath. "We might have weathered it had Bertrand not continued to incur such very high gaming debts in spite of our reduced circumstances."

"Sophia, learn your place!" Bertrand's hiss was furious.

Sophia continued as if he hadn't spoken. "I've been anxious many times recently that Bertrand seemed to be spending money he didn't have. If someone offered him a substantial amount of gold, I think it would be a motivator he would find hard to refuse."

"Curse your disloyalty, Sophia," Bertrand growled at her.

"You accuse her of disloyalty?" Elowen cut in, outraged. "When you've been trying to sabotage an important alliance since the beginning?"

"There was no disloyalty in trying to prevent Torrens humiliating itself with an alliance with a kingdom so far beneath us," Bertrand scoffed.

"You fool," Theo said, hardly able to believe the man's shamelessness. "Do you really not understand that if an outside player wants to prevent the alliance, it's because they don't want our kingdoms to be strengthened by the connection?"

"Not to mention whatever you helped do to capture and remove the Dust released by those accidents was disruptive enough to throw magic off balance all across our kingdom," Elowen added. "Many people have suffered from it, and who knows what the ongoing effects will be?"

"I'm ashamed of you, Bertrand," Sophia said, the words quiet and personal.

"How dare you?" he breathed. "How dare you talk about shame when you've been carrying on like a tavern wench with some servant?" He spat at Simeon's feet.

The sandy-haired young man had reached his limit. He loomed forward threateningly, his pleasant face set like steel.

"You will not speak of her that way."

"Enough." Prince Patrick's voice brought instant silence. "I'm shocked at the display before me. We will return to the capital immediately, and try to untangle this whole deplorable mess."

"Yes, let's," Elowen agreed, letting out a long breath.

"Load the viscount into the carriage," Prince Patrick started, but Xavier jumped in.

"Surely he can make the journey thrown across a guard's horse," he said cheerfully. "Theo and Elowen are both injured, they should ride in the carriage. I can borrow the princess's mare."

Elowen looked faintly bewildered by this declaration, her hand rubbing at her neck as she tried to protest. "But I'm not really inju—"

"Trust me, Princess." Xavier had stepped close, his voice low enough that most of the group wouldn't hear. "When it comes to my little brother, you have to take what openings you can get."

"We don't need your meddling, Xavier," Theo said, unimpressed. But for all that, he didn't rescind his brother's instructions. In fact, he was perfectly pleased with his situation when he found himself alone in the carriage with his intended.

They rumbled into motion, and for a long moment, there was silence between them.

"How are your arms?" Elowen was the one to break it.

"They're fine," Theo said dismissively. "The wounds are shallow. They'll heal."

"And the rest of you?" She searched his face anxiously, her voice a whisper. "You were so ill, Theo. I thought you were going to die."

He grimaced. "I think I was close to it. I've never experienced an illness like it. I still don't understand it."

"I do, a little," Elowen said.

Theo listened soberly as she explained about the vials, the investigation she and Lady Sophia had undertaken, and what Simeon had told them on the road.

"The duke's family will be crushed by this," he observed once she was done.

"Yes," Elowen agreed, her voice sad.

"Do you think Sophia's right that her father wasn't involved in the disasters?" Theo asked. "I had my guard make inquiries after we visited the landslide site, and I have reason to think that he was no longer sharing all the evidence with the king. Before that trip, he said he had a promising line of inquiry, but after it, that apparently dried up, which seemed suspicious to me. I had assumed he was trying to hide the embarrassing truth about his servant, but now..."

"Now it seems he was covering for Bertrand," Elowen finished, her voice heavy. "That I can believe."

"If it was after the landslide visit he changed his approach, then he must have recognized Bertrand's scarf in the description from the witness. It must have been torture to begin suspecting his own son. Unless he was involved all along, in which case it would only be the fear of exposure plaguing him."

"I don't think he was involved," Elowen said. "I can't believe it of him."

"Well, either way, his standing will suffer," Theo observed. "And perhaps it deserves to, frankly. I've never met someone as dangerously indulged as Bertrand, and we've seen the consequences with our own eyes."

"Yes." Elowen's exquisite face wrinkled in a frown. "He should never have been given half the license he was, by any of us."

"Bertrand is the least of my concerns now," Theo said. "It seems Cassius was right about the threat from the continent, and it's terrifying to think their magic craft is advanced so far beyond ours."

"It is," Elowen agreed. "If there's another war, it won't bode well."

Theo leaned forward, taking one of her slim hands in both of his. "But we'll be so much stronger together. And..." He hesitated. "And I hope our kingdoms will stand together, although I don't mean to pressure you."

"Theo." She laid her other hand over his, her touch light but determined. "Surely you know by now."

She swallowed, seeming nervous, and he searched her eyes seriously.

"Theo, you said before that you wanted to win me before we set our wedding date."

"I meant win your heart," he said quickly. "I didn't mean to make you into a competition, or—"

"I understand." She cut him off with a laugh. "What I'm trying to say is that you've already won me. If it was up to me, we'd get married tomorrow."

Theo's breath caught, fire surging up through his veins at the look in her eyes. For a long moment, they just stared at each other. Then he looked to the side, observing with approval the presence of curtains on the carriage windows. He pulled them both closed with purposeful movements before shifting onto the opposite seat, beside Elowen. She was blushing adorably, her eyes shy as they looked up into his.

He lowered his face so that his mouth hovered over her ear. "In case you think I'm only capable of passion when my mind is addled by mysterious magical ailments," he murmured, his lips brushing the shape of her ear and eliciting a pleasant shiver, "I'm going to kiss you now."

Elowen raised her face to his in a silent invitation, and Theo at last pressed his lips against the soft, irresistible ones that had been haunting his dreams. Elowen returned his kiss with an eagerness he would never have expected from the demure face she'd shown him when they first met, and a low growl of approval escaped him. The movement of their lips was perfectly in sync, and the sensation was bliss. One of her hands was splayed against his chest, and her hair had come loose enough to flow freely over the fingers he'd slipped under it so he could cradle her head.

Without breaking the kiss, Theo snaked an arm around Elowen's waist, tucking her against him where she fit like they were made for each other.

Maybe they were. Not long ago, he'd thought sentiment like that ridiculous, but he'd been wrong about so many things, why not this, too?

"Elowen." He pulled back, his breathing uneven. "I'm so sorry."

"What for?" she asked, sounding dazed. "If you're apologizing for your kissing abilities, trust me, you don't need to."

Theo's chuckle rumbled in his chest. "I'm glad you feel that way, my love, since my kisses will be reserved for you alone until the day I die."

She laid a contented head against his chest. "They'd better be."

"I'm sorry for the pain I caused you by keeping you at a distance," Theo tried again, his bandaged arms wrapping around her. "I was afraid of what would happen if I let myself want you too much."

Elowen looked up, searching his face. "You said something like that, the night of the victory feast," she said. "But I don't understand why."

"I didn't fully understand, either," Theo acknowledged. "Until Xavier came, and I started to unravel, and some things came to the surface that I'd been trying to keep down for a long time." He squeezed her shoulder. "There'll be time enough to tell you all about it later. But suffice it to say, I made a vow a long time ago that I would never pursue what I wanted. I didn't realize I was making a vow, but that's what happened inside me. Somewhere along the way, that turned into a determination never to even want anything, at least not for myself. I thought it was selfish to have desires, and you terrified me because from the moment I saw you, I desperately wanted you to be mine."

"You never gave a hint of that," Elowen said, accusation in her voice. "I thought you were notably unimpressed when we met."

Theo gave a pained laugh. "That's unforgivable of me. I should have told you immediately that you were, and are, and I'm convinced always will be, the most heart-stoppingly beautiful woman I've ever met."

Elowen's already perfect features broke into a smile that took his breath away, and she snuggled closer against him.

"Go on," she said invitingly.

"I swear that what I feel for you isn't shallow," Theo assured her. "I fell in love with the person I got to know, your quiet strength, your kind heart, your humor. But I couldn't let myself admit how captivated I was. Until you were pulled into it, and my choices hurt you as well as me, I never realized how deeply I'd come to believe that I wasn't allowed to want anything, and how much that belief had driven my life. I let resentment grow toward my brother, and," he shook his head regretfully, "I almost sabotaged my marriage before it even began."

"Well, fortunately you came to your senses in time," Elowen said sunnily. "And I think I can overlook the whole thing if you promise to pay me extravagant compliments at least twice a day for the rest of our lives."

Theo didn't know whether to laugh or grimace. "I don't think I know how to do that, I'm afraid. I suppose I could take lessons from Xavier."

Elowen scrunched up her straight little nose. "No, don't do that. I don't care for his style of gallantry. Forget the extravagant compliments. I'd prefer humbler ones if it means I can always be sure they're sincere."

"Excellent," Theo said with a hint of humor. "Because I don't know how to be anything but sincere."

"No," Elowen agreed. "You're the truest man I've ever met, Theo. And I've come to love you for it."

His heart soared, more full than he could ever have imagined. He knew that he would always be his stiff self on some level, and he had a feeling he would at times disappoint his vibrant wife with his lack of emotional expression. But he was determined to be a good learner. And something told him that learning from Elowen would be an intoxicating experience.

"I'm glad I caught myself a valiant prince after all," Elowen added in a teasing tone, slipping her hand beneath his arm.

"You didn't catch me," Theo said with dignity. "I caught you, through my prowess in a rigorous tournament."

Elowen's laughter was musical. "I don't count that, because I didn't get to choose the nature of the events. I don't especially care about your skills in jousting or archery."

"What would you have chosen?" Theo asked with a smile, very ready to join in.

"Kissing, of course." Elowen checked it off on her fingers. "Eloquence of compliments. Ability to melt my heart with a single soulful glance."

"I don't like the sound of that," Theo growled.

"Oh dear." Elowen's face fell comically. "It's not a promising omen for our marriage if you don't like the sound of any of that. Not even kissing?"

"I meant," Theo protested, "that I don't like the sound of a tournament featuring all those things. I know I'm considered steady to a fault, but I think even I would crack if I had to watch a series of men demonstrate their ability to melt your heart with a single glance."

"Good point," she conceded. "To be fair, no one's yet achieved that, anyway."

"I will work on it," Theo promised solemnly.

"And we've already agreed to trade eloquence of compliments for sincerity," Elowen reminded him.

"Yes."

A dimple appeared on Elowen's cheek. "As for the other one…"

"Yes?" Theo asked, his lips curving up expectantly at the corners.

"Well, I don't think a single round is enough. Most tournament events would require you to demonstrate your skill on at least two separate occasions. Otherwise how can we be sure it wasn't a lucky accident that you rendered me incapable of coherent thought on your first attempt?"

Theo reached for her, a rumble of agreement in his chest. "As always, Princess," he murmured, his lips already brushing hers as he formed the words, "I wish only to please you."

"And I wish only to be yours."

Elowen's whisper filled the space, and Theo's heart ached with a joy so fierce it was almost painful as their lips met once again. Whatever challenges lay ahead, together they were strong in a way that went beyond any borders or alliances. For the first time since childhood, he was excited for the future, eager to embrace the joy it would bring. With Elowen by his side, nothing was out of reach.

And he would protect not only her, but her heart, until his dying breath.

EPILOGUE

Elowen

Nerves fluttered over Elowen as she viewed herself in the looking glass, her familiar form swathed in layers of finery. The white silk dress had a high neck and long sleeves that hugged her upper arms before billowing so wide that they flowed out from her elbows like water. The fabric was smooth and unadorned, but the purple brocade overdress was embroidered with intricate patterns and adorned with jewels.

Her wedding gown was perfection. And the nerves that filled her were the pleasant kind. It was really happening. In one week, she was really going to marry Theo.

"Is Princess Elowen here?"

Elowen started at the well-known voice sounding in the next room as if her thoughts had summoned him.

"Your Highness." The head seamstress sounded scandalized. "The princess is in the middle of a fitting for her wedding gown. You mustn't see the garment before the wedding day."

"She is?" Theo sounded surprised. "My apologies. I asked where she could be found and was directed here. I didn't know it was the seamstresses' workplace."

"They're just finishing up, Theo," Elowen called. "Wait in the receiving room, I'll be free in a minute."

As soon as the gown was off, she hurried back into her regular dress, aided by a tutting assistant seamstress. Elowen ignored the girl. She was glad Theo had sought her out. He'd told her at breakfast that morning that there was a matter he wanted to discuss with her, but it was astonishingly difficult to find a moment alone together. Elowen had thought the tournament a big deal. The bustle the castle was in over the impending wedding put it to shame.

She emerged from the dressing room, smiling sunnily at her almost-husband. Theo's answering smile didn't hide how his eyes darted to the doorway behind her.

"No peeking!" she scolded him. "You'll have to wait until the wedding to see the gown. Another of our traditions that's important to us, however silly it might seem."

He took her hand, raising it to his lips in a comfortable gesture that Elowen would never have believed him capable of when they first met.

"It's not silly at all. Even my stiff self is looking forward to all the fuss of the big day."

Elowen laughed, not sure whether to believe him. "You came looking for me?" she prompted.

"Yes." He was still holding her hand in his, and he drew it through his arm. "Walk in the gardens with me?"

"I'd love to," Elowen said delightedly. "My wardens are expecting me to be in this fitting for another half an hour, so your timing couldn't be better."

The head seamstress shook her head at the princess's joking words, but her smile was indulgent. Theo led her out of the room, making to turn left.

"There's a closer garden if we go this way," Elowen informed him, pointing right. "It's smaller, but still nice."

"Let's go to the one with the willow pond," Theo said. He tugged her gently along, and she surrendered readily.

The garden he'd chosen was a little further away, but they were fortunate to encounter no one but servants between the seamstresses' workspace and the garden's entrance.

"If you wanted to talk to me about Father's decision regarding Bertrand, he's already told me," Elowen started, before Theo had a chance to speak. "I know Bertrand probably deserves execution, but I'm glad Father decided on imprisonment instead. It's already so awful for Sophia and her family." She snuck a look up at him. "Father said you told him that your family won't push for execution in spite of the attempt on your life?"

"Yes," said Theo. "I made a very compelling argument in my letter, and they accepted it, although reluctantly. I confess I was less motivated by any feeling of mercy for Bertrand or his family than I was by the mood of the court here. I'm grateful your family believes our account, but there's still insufficient evidence to prove to the skeptical that Bertrand really made an attempt on my life. Your Father doesn't need the court's approval to order an execution, of course, but we would never get true support for the alliance if people felt that I'd had a highly influential nobleman executed on a flimsy accusation in order to remove him as a romantic rival."

Elowen wrinkled her nose, hating that interpretation of events, but knowing Theo was wise.

"I just wish I could be sure the conditions of his imprisonment won't become comfortable over time," Theo added.

"I don't think they will," Elowen said earnestly. "You know how seriously Father and the Council of Lords took our testimony. Whatever they think about the poisoning enchantment, they know he threatened our lives out on the road, even if many of them likely don't believe he was actually going to go through with it. It helps his case that miraculously no one actually died in any of the disasters he caused. But he's still guilty of crimes against Torrens."

"I'm just glad your father accepted that he was behind the disasters," Theo said. "Last I heard, Bertrand is still denying it."

"Well, then he shouldn't have slipped up and failed to burn one of the letters from the ones who were paying him," Elowen said scornfully. "Not to mention the gold they found in his rooms that wasn't Peninsula standard. Once they accepted Sophia's testimony that she found the vials in his room, I knew it was over."

"It would have been hard for them to find any other way to explain the evidence from Sophia, Simeon, and the witnesses from multiple disaster sites regarding the scarf," Theo added by way of agreement. "Especially when combined with the testimony of the servant Bertrand forced a report out of as soon as we got back from the landslide and the servant who was ordered by Bertrand to present the scarf to Simeon as publicly as possible." He frowned. "It troubles me that there's still skepticism about our report regarding the objects with stored magic."

"Yes, it was unlucky that both objects were dry of magic by the time they were examined by the Craftsmen's Guild," Elowen said with a sigh. "For what it's worth, you convinced me, Theo, when you pointed out that the young man witnessed at several disaster sites always seemed to carry an object, and how the balance of magic across the land was affected as if a large volume had been removed from its natural cycle in the environment. I think you're right that Bertrand was capturing the magic from the disasters and storing it in the objects. Although I don't think the objects he used when he attacked us can be from those incidents, because they weren't large items, like all the witnesses described."

"Which leaves the question of what happened to the large objects that captured the magic from the disasters," Theo said grimly. "We can only assume they went back to whoever hired him. The real disappointment to me is how little information Bertrand has so far given about his employers. If his evidence is to be believed, he knows almost nothing about them, and was willing to do their bidding for money without any idea of their true purposes. I'm not sure I can believe that." He sighed. "That was another reason I argued against execution. If he's still alive, there's always hope that he may be compelled to provide more information at a later time."

"True," said Elowen, ready to change the direction of the conversation. All the talk of execution made her feel queasy. "And even if the lords didn't all agree, Father believes us that it must be someone from the continent, you know. He was actually quite impressed by Sophia's and my investigative work with the writing on the vials." She could hear the dry note in her voice as she added, "Not so much impressed as unflatteringly surprised. Still," she brightened again, "he was gracious enough to tell me he regrets not taking my concerns more seriously and coming out of the meeting when I tried to call him."

"He wasn't the only one to underestimate you that day," Theo said, squeezing her hand where it rested comfortably on his arm. "It was their loss, and it could have cost more than my life."

He stopped walking, turning to face her and taking both of her hands in his.

"I'll never be tired of thanking you, Elowen. You didn't stop fighting for me when I couldn't speak for myself, and I'm alive because of it."

She lifted one of her hands, bringing his with it and rubbing her cheek against the back of his hand.

"There's no need to thank me, because I didn't do it for

you," she said. "I did it selfishly, because I couldn't bear to lose you."

Theo gave a low chuckle, casting a swift look around before lowering his forehead to rest against hers.

"Now I'm wishing this was just a moment stolen for the two of us."

Elowen raised her head, confused. "Isn't it?"

"Actually, we're meeting someone," Theo said, reclaiming her hand and walking forward. "By the willow."

Intrigued, Elowen followed, content to wait for her answers. She was feeling content about most things lately, in fact. The last time she'd felt really anxious was the morning after their return, when the Council of Lords resumed their long-winded debate about her betrothal. But the anxiety didn't last long. The news of their late-night return, with Theo recovered and calmly incredulous of all questions as to his level of commitment to the betrothal, helped lower the tension. It hadn't taken much probing to reveal that the council had in fact been called by Bertrand, and that he'd received no authorization from his father to use the duke's name in doing so. With Bertrand locked up for suspected treasonous activities, no one was eager to keep arguing for his motion.

The willow came into sight, its branches drooping over a small pond that sat in the middle of the garden. Elowen recognized the figure under it with surprise.

"Sophia!"

The other girl looked around at her call, her expression telling Elowen she didn't know what Theo was up to either.

"Just one more coming," Theo said.

"Who—?" Elowen's question fell away as a lithe figure with sandy hair strode into view, his steps more confident than they used to be, but his posture bent slightly as if carrying a heavy weight.

"Why is Simeon here?" Sophia asked, her voice faint.

"Because I asked him to come," said Theo. He looked down at Elowen. "My letter to my parents included more than a plea for leniency. I didn't want to tell you about it until I knew the outcome."

Elowen had no idea what he was talking about, but there wasn't time to ask. Simeon had reached them, his eyes darting to Sophia then quickly away, and Theo took charge of the conversation.

"Thank you Lady Sophia and Simeon for coming," he said. "I wanted to talk to you both about your future. Will everyone allow me to speak plainly?"

"Of course, Your Highness." Simeon bent in a bow. Sophia just waved a helpless hand as if to say, *why not at this point?*

"Thanks to Elowen's insights and my own observations, I'm aware of your situation," he said. "And I would like to help you. Forgive the question, but am I correct that you both wish to wed?"

Sophia let out a small, strangled noise, and Simeon's eyes widened.

"That is speaking plainly, Your Highness," he said blandly.

"You didn't answer the question," Theo said. He looked first at Sophia. "Lady Sophia?"

"I..." Sophia's face colored. "Simeon knows how I feel, but it doesn't matter what I want. My family will never let me marry someone of his station."

"Simeon wouldn't have remained at his current station if your brother hadn't intentionally prevented him from advancing," Theo commented. "But that's not the point. Please answer my question."

"Yes." Sophia's eyes were on her slippers.

"I would be mad not to want a future with the kindest, most intelligent and most beautiful woman in the kingdom," said Simeon softly, his gaze on Sophia's averted face. "But I have no expectations. Sophia is right. Our union would never be sanctioned."

"That's why I think you'd do best to run away together," Theo said flippantly.

Elowen started, her eyes flying to Theo's. "Those are words I never imagined you would say," she told him frankly. "I thought Simeon's position as a servant would offend you. It seemed to bother you that I was even friendly with him."

Theo smiled at her, shifting a loose strand of hair that had fallen to her shoulder. "No, love, I was jealous," he admitted. "Not that I ever believed there was anything untoward. But you were so comfortable with him, so natural. I wished I knew how to be that way with you."

"Truly?" Elowen didn't know whether to laugh at this confession. Meanwhile Sophia and Simeon were both goggling at the somber prince's unashamed declaration.

"Well, I agree," Elowen went on. "I don't think difference in class should keep you two apart."

"I'm gratified by your support, Princess Elowen," Simeon said seriously. "But I would never ask Sophia to run away with me."

"I was afraid you'd be too honorable," Elowen said, unimpressed.

"Yes, a deplorable trait," said Theo politely.

She gave him a look. "You know that's not what I meant."

"I do." He spoke briskly. "I have more than just vague encouragements to offer you both. It's not just for Elowen's sake I wish to help you. Simeon, you saved my life, and you did it even though I'm the one who falsely accused you of treason. I'm ashamed I fell for Lord Bertrand's manipulations and furthered his deceptions." He glanced at Elowen. "I'm ashamed I let jealousy color my thinking. And I intend to make it right."

"How?" Elowen asked eagerly.

"My father agrees with me that for the service of saving my life, Simeon should be awarded a title." His gaze was serious as it rested on the other man. "It's only a barony. The estate isn't large, and you won't hold a great deal of influence in the Siqualian court. But you would enter the ranks of the nobility."

"You want to make me a...a baron?" Simeon looked dazed.

Sophia on the other hand, was watching Theo as if mesmerized, her expression hopeful.

"Of course a baron would do very well for himself to marry the daughter of a duke," Theo acknowledged. "But, since you've all given me leave to speak freely, the daughter of a disgraced duke won't make a brilliant match anyway."

"I don't want a brilliant match," Sophia breathed. "I want Simeon."

The servant's head whipped toward her, something blazing in his eyes at her words.

"If you're willing to embrace a new kingdom, you can have a fresh start away from all the people who knew you in your former positions and may never be able to get past your differ-ence in status."

"I would like nothing better than to leave the Torrenese court behind me forever," Sophia said fervently. She checked, her face turning a little pink as she twisted toward the man beside her. "Well, there's one thing I might like better."

"Sophia." Simeon's voice was a low murmur, the change in his tone making Elowen feel like she was eavesdropping.

"We'll leave you to talk it over," Theo said firmly. "But please be assured the offer is genuine, and comes with the goodwill of the Siqualian crown. If you accept, we would be delighted if you would share your magical knowledge with us once settled in Siqual. There's a great deal I would like my kingdom to learn from some of what I've seen in Torrens."

"I would be honored, Your Highness," Simeon said, his eyes straying back to Sophia's face.

"We'll leave you in peace," Theo said, sending Elowen a meaningful look.

She followed him readily, waiting until the pair by the willow were out of sight before speaking.

"Theo, you're incredible!" she said, tears in her eyes. "This is the perfect solution for them. And I'll have my dearest friend with me in my new kingdom!"

"Call it an early wedding present." Theo snaked his arms around her waist, pulling her neatly against him. "Why does one more week feel like an eternity?"

Elowen laughed. "I don't know, but it does. I can hardly believe I was trying to *delay* our wedding through the whole tournament. I could give my former self a slap!"

"Absolutely not," said Theo, his voice low and delicious. "No one is allowed to lay a finger on my bride, not even herself."

Elowen gave a gurgling laugh at the ridiculousness of the conversation. The sound was cut off as Theo lowered his lips to hers, his arms warm and possessive around her back.

The sensation of him drove everything else away. They would always have enemies, close to home and further away. No one knew exactly what was coming from the kingdoms of the continent, but Torrens and Siqual had withstood the attack against them, and together they would stand strong.

Elowen's heart soared as she kissed her serious, not-so-stiff, surprisingly passionate prince in the peace of the garden, nothing but joy in her heart for the future ahead.

NOTE FROM THE AUTHOR

Thank you for reading *A Treacherous Motion*. I hope you enjoyed visiting the world of Ryki. I would be so grateful if you would consider leaving a review on Amazon—it would really make a difference!

Interested to see Xavier lose his heart, and also to find out more about what's threatening the peace on the Peninsula? Check out Book Two—*A Wayward Movement*.

And if you're curious about Cassius and Flora's story, you can read all about it in *Ties of Dust*. This standalone full-length novel acts as a prequel to the *Magic of Dust and Movement* series.

Join up to my mailing list at deborahgracewhite.com to be kept up to date on new releases, specials, and giveaways, such as bonus chapters. You'll receive some great freebies, too, including *An Expectation of Magic*, a novella which is a prequel to my completed YA fantasy series *The Vazula Chronicles*.

Plus, you'll receive *Dragon's Sight*, an 8,000 word prequel to my completed YA fantasy trilogy *The Kyona Chronicles*.

Again, thanks for entering the world of Ryki! I hope to see you back again.

ALSO BY DEBORAH GRACE WHITE

Find a complete list of my published books
and reading order here on my website
deborahgracewhite.com

Acknowledgments

I'm so grateful to the people around me who support me to pursue writing. First and foremost, my husband Ray, who's always cheering me on.

To my beta readers, Dad, Alora, Constance, Mum, and Mel W, a huge thanks for dropping everything and getting through this book for me on such a tight timeframe! To Shae for the thorough and professional proofread. As always, any remaining errors are mine.

Thanks to Moorbooks for the cover that perfectly captures Theo and Elowen and the movement of the series. And to Becca for a gorgeous map that really pops.

To you, the reader, thank you for giving me the privilege of being an author. Especially to all those of you who patiently waited a whole year for this one!

And most importantly, to God, who knows our hearts better than we know them ourselves.

About the Author

I've been a reader since I can remember, growing up on a wide range of books, from classic literature to light-hearted romps. The love of reading has traveled with me unchanged across multiple  continents, and carried me from my own childhood all the way to having children of my own.

But if reading is like looking through a window into a magical and beautiful world, beginning to write my own stories was like discovering that I could open that window and climb right out into fantasyland.

I cannot believe how privileged I am to actually be living that childhood dream and publishing my own novels amidst the fun and chaos of life with my husband and our four little ones.

I've never outgrown my love of young adult stories, so the genre of young adult fantasy was always going to be my niche. Feel free to email me at deborah@deborahgracewhite.com and introduce yourself! Or subscribe to my mailing list at deborah gracewhite.com for free giveaways, sales, and updates.